PRAISE FOR
FOREFATHERS
& FOUNDING FATHERS

This book will challenge everything that history books have taught us about the "founding years" in the American colonies. Michael Gorton is authentic and believable in this historical fiction tale of four radical individuals who were ahead of their time and planted the seeds that enabled our founding fathers to nurture and grow our great democracy. Young adult readers will make text-to-text and text-to-world connections as they journey four hundred years in history where horrific truths are revealed. *Forefathers & Founding Fathers* is an amazing historical account that defies everything we know about the beginning of America, including our Thanksgiving feast with the pilgrims. It leaves the reader wondering what else we are in the dark about. Students are given many opportunities to argue and evaluate Gorton's claims, evidence, and differing points of view on the events in the book as they question, problem solve, and research.

—Marla Conn
founder, Readability, Inc.

History is exciting, especially in the greatest country in the world, and now brought to life by a thinker par excellence, Michael Gorton. This story vibrates with wisdom and insights. I look forward to the movie!

—Mark Victor Hansen
author of *Chicken Soup for the Soul*

Brilliant! Intoxicating! I found myself absorbed in the relationships, the politics, and the struggles. Much more than a history lesson—it is a collection of leadership portraits that shaped our nation's destiny.

—General Rebecca Halstead (ret.)
author and inspirational speaker

All great people, achievements, and nations are established in the wake of pioneers who have gone before. In this book, you will discover that our founding fathers were standing on the shoulders of true giants. Michael shows us that we owe a debt of gratitude to many people we had not known before.

—Jim Stovall
best-selling author of *The Ultimate Gift*

We should make this required reading in every American History class—and, while we're at it, hand it out to all members of Congress!

—Clay Loney
Fox News anchor, Tulsa

Gorton's novel is fast paced, informative, and brings historical figures back to life. He provides accuracy to historical events and sheds light on their significance even into the present day.

—Tyler Thompson
PhD candidate in history at Texas A&M

Historically real firebrands, savages, and shrews as the main characters who weave history with love, friendship, adventure, and standing up for what's right—what's not to like? Get yourself a copy of the book, m'girls and m'boys, today!

—Aimee Brown
editor, author, and martial artist

This book is a page turner! When history becomes provocative, educational, and downright entertaining, you know you're enjoying a great novel. Gorton is a master storyteller who makes history incredibly relevant to the challenges we face today.

—Laura Carabello
president of CPR Online

Gorton's tale provides real insight into what early colonial life was like through the eyes of our enlightened forefathers who joyfully embraced the adventure of the New World while bravely challenging the status quo on behalf of religious and individual freedom.

—Suzanne Barger
senior marketing executive

Wow! We are standing on the shoulders of giants. Gorton amazingly captures the essence of the essential moments in the early years of our nation. This is a must-read for history buffs! Bravo, Gorton, well done and truly entertaining!

—Michael McIntyre
CEO, Benefits America

By seamlessly interlacing documented facts with down-to-earth dialogue, Michael Gorton has penned a user-friendly depiction of American history and an engaging picture of pioneers who were truly ahead of their time.

—Pam Gerber
philanthropist and entrepreneur

Delightfully written, historically precise, *Forefathers & Founding Fathers* provides an insightful and fascinating snapshot of the people who helped shape this country's future. Gorton has produced a timely reminder that America was founded on radical inclusion—a lesson more recent leaders should heed.

—Frank Andorka
writer and historian

Forefathers & Founding Fathers is a fascinating book. Although it's billed as historical fiction, it's so well written that it's difficult to tell where history ends and fiction begins. A great story—well told!

—James F. Young
consultant and executive coach

Michael Gorton beautifully unveils what it means to be an American. What a fascinating read and what an incredible legacy.

—Benjamin Gorton
from a distant branch of the Gorton clan

Awards ***Forefathers & Founding Fathers*** has received:

FOREFATHERS & FOUNDING FATHERS

FOREFATHERS & FOUNDING FATHERS

HISTORICAL FICTION
MICHAEL GORTON
SECOND EDITION

BROWN BOOKS
PUBLISHING GROUP

© 2016, 2018 by Michael Gorton

All rights reserved. No part of this book may be used or reproduced in any manner without written permission except in the case of brief quotations embodied in critical articles or reviews.

First edition 2016. Second edition 2018.

This book is a work of fiction based on a true story and real events. It was drawn from a variety of historical sources. For dramatic and narrative purposes, it contains fictionalized scenes and dialogue. This was always done with respect and honor to the people and events depicted, and the author has tried to be true, to the best of his ability, to the spirit of these historical individuals and the trials they endured.

Forefathers & Founding Fathers

Brown Books Publishing Group
16250 Knoll Trail Drive, Suite 205
Dallas, Texas 75248
www.BrownBooks.com
(972) 381-0009

A New Era in Publishing®

Names: Gorton, Michael.
Title: Forefathers & founding fathers / Michael Gorton.
    Other Titles: Forefathers and founding fathers
Description: Second edition. | Dallas, Texas : Brown Books Publishing Group, 2018. | "Historical fiction."
Identifiers: ISBN 9781612542720
Subjects: LCSH: Pilgrims and pilgrimages--United States--History--17th century--Fiction. | United States--History--Colonial period, ca. 1600-1775--Fiction. | Man-woman relationships--United States--Fiction. | Democracy--United States--Fiction. | LCGFT: Historical fiction. | Action and adventure fiction.
Classification: LCC PS3607.O783 F67 2018 | DDC 813/.6--dc23

ISBN 978-1-61254-272-0 (PB)
ISBN 978-1-61254-302-4 (HC)
LCCN 2018939969

Printed in the United States
10 9 8 7 6 5 4 3 2 1

For more information or to contact the author,
please go to www.ForefathersAndFoundingFathers.com.

To Jerry White, who taught me the trait "polite persistence," and to all my entrepreneurial friends who constantly change the world by exhibiting that trait.

TABLE OF CONTENTS

A Note on History and Historical Fiction. xiii

Cast of Characters xv

PART 1
FOUNDING FATHERS 1

Chapter 1:   George Washington and the Continental Congress 3

Chapter 2:   Command of the South. 9

Chapter 3:   Founding Fathers. 17

PART 2
FOREFATHERS 23

Chapter 1:   The Maplett Haberdashery: London, 1628 25

Chapter 2:   The Globe Theatre. 29

Chapter 3:   The Maplett Residence: The Following Day 33

Chapter 4:   News from Manchester 45

Chapter 5:   Saint Mary Magdalene Church 51

Chapter 6:   Anne Marbury. 55

Chapter 7:   Transition 63

Chapter 8:   Per Aspera ad Astra (Through Hardships to the Stars) 77

Chapter 9:   Plymouth 89

Chapter 10:   The Pequot War. 99

Chapter 11:   Plymouth Collaborations 111

Chapter 12:   Plymouth Inquisition 123

Chapter 13:   Abitio Plymouth 131

Chapter 14:   Anne and the Antinomians 147

Chapter 15:   Aquidneck. 155

Chapter 16:   The Ousting of Coddington 159

Chapter 17:   Abitio Portsmouth. 169

Chapter 18:   Roger Williams 175

Chapter 19:   Shawomet 179

Chapter 20:   Miantonomo. 187

Chapter 21: The Raid on Shawomet 195

Chapter 22: Abitio Hutchinson 205

Chapter 23: Boston Trial of Samuel Gorton 211

Chapter 24: Return to London 225

Chapter 25: Winslow in London 237

Chapter 26: Return to Shawomet 245

Chapter 27: Fire Flower 251

Chapter 28: Warwick Colony Years 261

Chapter 29: Mary Dyer and Quaker Persecutions 267

Chapter 30: Samuel Gorton—Later Years .275

Chapter 31: Forefathers and Founding Fathers 283

Afterword 285

Lineage 289

Time Period Notes: Historical Context 292

Historical Notes 295

Acknowledgments 299

Bibliography 301

About the Author 303

Index 305

A NOTE ON HISTORY AND HISTORICAL FICTION

When I first started researching this novel, my goal was simply to write an historical account for a few friends and family to read, but as the research progressed, I came to see it as an important part of our early years that has been largely ignored or buried! I discovered a lost part of history that needed to be told. In light of the potential impact, I spent significantly more time researching the details and crafting them into the tale. The project and the story itself were intoxicating. I think perhaps anyone who has worked on an adventure like this understands how it becomes part of your existence.

A piece of history that has waited nearly four hundred years to be written, *Forefathers & Founding Fathers* tells the tale of the founding years in the American colonies. It was a time of extreme turbulence during a period known as the Great Migration. The Puritans that came to this New World in the name of religious freedom actually created the opposite. Boston was a theocracy that oppressed any but a staunch Puritan viewpoint. It was an intolerant environment that created an atmosphere ripe for the killing of Quakers and the Salem "witches." As you will learn in this book, there were banishments, hangings, and other atrocities committed against those who did not conform.

When we think about the founding fathers of the United States, we envisage Thomas Jefferson, John Adams, Washington, and many others in the late 1700s. In Boston or the Plymouth Colony of 1640, any one of those founding fathers would have been banished, whipped, or killed for their beliefs. It is a difficult image to reconcile: those sweet Pilgrims who celebrated the first Thanksgiving with the Indians banishing Thomas Jefferson for the *radical* idea of freedom of religion, separation of church and state, or civil government!

This is the exciting tale of four individuals, all of whom are considered founders of the Rhode Island colony. From that smallest of colonies, they opposed slavery and fought for freedom of religion, democracy, and equal rights in the mid-1600s. For those beliefs, they were ostracized, banished, whipped, and killed, but in the process, they planted the seeds that would sprout and be used by our founding fathers to grow this great democracy. This book tells the story of a few of the significant *forefathers* to our *founding* fathers.

A NOTE ON CALENDARS AND DATES

Often, when reading historical materials, one will see the year written as 1592/93. This is not because we do not know the exact year. The Julian calendar assumed a year of 365 days and six hours. It is the six hours that create leap year every fourth year. In 1582, Pope Gregory reformed the Julian calendar, recognizing the fact that a year is really 365 days, five hours, and forty-eight minutes. Eleven minutes (and change) a year does not seem like much, but after hundreds of years, it makes a big difference. With the implementation of the Gregorian calendar, the true date was off by ten days. The solution was that people went to bed on October 4, 1582, and woke on October 15, 1582. One could joke that it was a nice, long night's sleep! Of course, many were very angry the pope had stolen ten days of their lives. Most of Europe switched, but England held out until 1752. In addition, during that same time period, the first day of the New Year was moved from March 25 to January 1.

These facts represent an important historical note for this book because precision of some dates requires understanding both the real date and the beginning of the year. As an example, February 27, 1632, in most of Europe was February 17, 1631, in England.

A NOTE ON THE STYLE AND HISTORICAL ACCURACY

All of the main characters in this book come right out of the history books. Every scene is based on real historical events or extrapolation based on historical events. Still, the book and character development have been written to entertain while spotlighting an important part of American history. I think we all know that modern English was not spoken in the 1600s, but I wrote in modern English because I want people to be comfortable reading this story.

Forefathers & Founding Fathers

CAST OF CHARACTERS

Canonicus (1565–1647) Grand sachem (chief) of the Narragansett in power when the Pilgrims arrived at the Plymouth Colony. Became friendly with the English, ultimately joining them in the war against the Pequot. Passed power to Miantonomo during his lifetime.

Miantonomo (1600–1643) Narragansett grand sachem and nephew to Canonicus. He was friendly with the English colonists but was accused of treachery by Winthrop and the Boston authorities.

Samuel Gorton (1592–1677) Early American settler, cofounder of the Rhode Island Colony. Founder of the Warwick settlement. Married Mary Maplett in England and had nine children, three born in England and six in the colonies.

Mary Elizabeth Maplett Gorton (1609–1678) Wife of Samuel Gorton, Mary was the daughter of a well-educated and prominent English family. Mary's father took great care to educate Mary in a time when women were not educated. Much of Samuel's success and ideas can be attributed to influence from and love for Mary. Unfortunately, no picture of Mary exists.

Anne Marbury Hutchinson (1591–1643) Born in Lincolnshire, England, and immigrated to Boston during the 1630s. Hutchinson was the focal point of the Antinomian Controversy in Boston and was subsequently banished from Massachusetts Bay Colony.

xv

Roger Williams (1603–1683) Born in England and came to the colonies in 1631. Massachusetts Bay Colony banished Williams in 1635 for spreading "dangerous" ideas. He left Boston and founded Providence Plantations, which ultimately joined with Warwick to become Rhode Island.

Mary Dyer (1611–1660) An English-born Puritan who came to Boston in 1635, she supported Anne Hutchinson during the Antinomian Controversy. Later, Dyer became a Quaker. She and her husband, William, were cofounders of the Portsmouth Rhode Island settlement.

John Winthrop (1588–1649) An English-born lawyer who immigrated to Massachusetts and founded the Massachusetts Bay Colony. Winthrop served nineteen terms as governor of the colony. Winthrop ruled the colony from an authoritarian perspective and, during his terms, oversaw the banishment of Roger Williams, Anne Hutchinson, Samuel Gorton, Mary Dyer, and many more.

Robert Rich, the Earl of Warwick (1587–1658) The second Earl of Warwick (England), he held significant interests in the New World. Ultimately, Rich would chair the Committee for Foreign Plantations and become the lord high admiral of the English fleet. Lord Warwick oversaw and presided over many legal decisions with regard to settlements in the colonies during his term as chair of the committee.

Forefathers & Founding Fathers

Edward Winslow (1595–1655) An Englishman born in Worcestershire, Winslow traveled to Plymouth on the *Mayflower* and was one of the signers of the Mayflower Compact. He was a highly respected leader and governor of Plymouth.

William Coddington (1601–1678) Born in Lincolnshire, England, to a wealthy family and sailed to Massachusetts in the Winthrop Fleet of 1631. He was a friend of Henry Vane and supported Anne Hutchinson during the Antinomian Controversy. When Hutchinson was banished from Massachusetts, Coddington chose to leave and join the Portsmouth Compact. However, in Portsmouth, Rhode Island, Coddington opposed Anne Hutchinson and ultimately drove her out of the colony.

Nathanael Greene (1742–1786) Greene was the great-great-grandson of Samuel and Mary Gorton. He rose from the rank of private in the beginning of the Revolutionary War to become the number-two general next to George Washington. Greene took over the campaign in the southern colonies during a time of dismal defeat at the hand of British general Cornwallis. Under Greene's direction, Cornwallis was ultimately defeated, which earned him the title of *Savior of the South*.

*The novel you are about to read is based on historical events.
The characters are all real, and the story follows historical accounts
as closely as possible based on the author's research.*

PART I
FOUNDING FATHERS

1

George Washington and the Continental Congress

> Those who expect to reap the blessings of freedom, must, like men, undergo the fatigues of supporting it.
> —Thomas Paine

In the summer of 1775, a full year before the Declaration of Independence, George Washington reported to the Continental Congress in full uniform. He informed them that it would be his honor to serve but not his intention to take control of the army. Because of his continuing work with Congress and their knowledge of his military experience, there was not a serious alternative. From that day forward until the war's end, he served as commander of the Continental Army.

In his term as commander, he won very few battles. He and his troops were almost always outmanned, outgunned, and, at least in the beginning, undertrained. The traits that Washington possessed were resilience and the ability to select the right men to serve under his command.

George Washington

During the years of war leading up to the autumn of 1780, along with his numerous defeats, Washington dealt with the death of his troops from starvation, exposure, and disease; lack of funding; and soldiers deserting or changing sides. At one point, Congress even considered a motion to remove him as commander, but that never gained traction.

In those same years, he oversaw the treason of Benedict Arnold and the mutiny of Pennsylvania troops. Washington was horrified by the actions of Arnold and never reconciled that treason. With diligence, he worked with the soldiers and found a way to bring the Penn troops back into the fray.

With all the challenges that Washington faced, perhaps no man in the history of the United States was better suited for the job of commander, considering the resources he was given. Washington turned impossible odds and a no-win situation into victory in the Revolutionary War. Washington was always the first to explain that it was the quality of his generals that ultimately led to victory, and Washington's favorite general was Nathanael Greene.

October 1780

The windows were open, and a light autumn breeze flowed through the hall as George Washington sat perfectly upright in his chair and focused on Thomas Jefferson, who was flipping through his notes.

"General, I can understand your interest in this man, but I fail to see the rationale of giving General Greene this post. With the exception of Trenton, a victory that we attribute to you, he has not orchestrated a single victory. Furthermore, I see a man who has no formal military training or experience, has complained about how this Congress is funding the war effort, and has only achieved his rank through field promotions that you have bestowed. What we really want is an experienced officer who can prevail in the south, a front that has been dismal."

Washington thought carefully about Jefferson's comments as he studied the faces of the scant membership in the hall that fall day. He had

Leaders of the first Continental Congress–Adams, Morris, Hamilton, and Jefferson

been before Congress on several occasions and appreciated the nature of their discussions. While he had not always agreed with their mandates, they almost always granted his requests—the one glaring exception being more resources to fight the war that was the country's greatest challenge.

"Mr. Jefferson, my confidence in Nathanael Greene is based not on his ability to deliver victories to this Congress or to me. During the years we have fought this war, Greene has become an expert student of military strategy and tactics. He has never been in a fight where he was not outnumbered at least two to one and where he had but a fraction of the munitions of his opponent. While you have clearly and correctly articulated that this man has won no battles, in my estimation, he has won nearly all by inflicting casualties and knowing when to strategically retreat. General Greene's skill is that of staying alive while constantly wearing down and chiseling away at the enemy. I hope you are aware that it is not always the formal military training that makes a good general but, sometimes, the spirit of the man who lives under the skin. I would point out to this entire Congress that we have had several formally educated generals who have failed miserably against the British and Lord General Cornwallis in the southern campaign."

General Washington stood and, in doing so, became a presence that filled the room. Washington and Jefferson were both six foot two, a height that easily towered over most of the other members of the Congress. "Mr. Jefferson, the *complaint* that you have mentioned regarding how this war has been funded is one that you know I hold as well. Our army has been severely underfunded, and that has been a problem. What you should also be aware of is that while General Greene has not received pay, he has utilized his personal resources to pay his officers and troops and to make certain they have at least a semblance of proper armaments. I believe you will share my sentiment that this predilection is one that brings great value to our cause."

Jefferson smiled and nodded his head in agreement. "I know a fair amount about Greene's Rhode Island family. I also understand the fact that his financial commitment to the war will likely put him in debt, so I do appreciate the value of his contribution."

"Well, then," Washington placed his right hand on his chin for effect before closing with Jefferson, "I submit to you that this is indeed the kind of man we want directing our efforts in the south. General Greene has a significant commitment to the effort that goes well beyond his command of the troops."

"General," John Hancock interrupted, "from our perspective, the south is lost. Is it your belief that somehow General Greene can magically transform this situation?"

"Yes, sir, Mr. Hancock," Washington replied. "That is exactly what I am saying. I daresay that Nathanael Greene is the best general in the Continental Army, present company included."

This comment drew guffaws from the Congress, particularly from Jefferson, who stood up and argued, "General Washington, without your leadership, this war would have been lost in short order. You cannot expect this Congress to accept that supposition."

"Greene is my best general," Washington responded in his most convincing tone. "I expect under his guidance we will develop a successful strategy to regain the southern states. This will remove the pressure from me while we complete the war effort in the north."

The members of the Continental Congress looked from face to face. Most were nodding agreement—if General Washington believed in Greene, they would give him their faith as well. Most importantly, they were all aware that General Washington had far more important things to do than stand before this Congress.

John Hancock banged his gavel. "I have heard enough. Shall we call for a motion and vote?"

"I hereby move that General George Washington may appoint Nathanael Greene to serve as commander of all troops from Delaware to Georgia," John Adams announced. "Through this appointment, Nathanael Greene will become second in command of the Continental Army."

"I will second that motion." Thomas Jefferson looked up at Washington and reflected his smile.

"All in favor?"

"Aye!"

George Washington smiled and waited for the Congress to dismiss him. In his mind, he now had the important tool to deal with Lord Cornwallis and turn the tide of this war.

2

Command of the South

> The battle, sir, is not to the strong alone;
> it is to the vigilant, the active, the brave.
> —Patrick Henry

Nathanael Greene took command of the southern Continental Army from the small fort at Hillsborough, North Carolina, in December 1780. Over the past few years, British general Lord Cornwallis had routed every Continental officer he had faced. The war had seen the rise and fall of Generals Robert Howe, Benjamin Lincoln, and, most recently, Horatio Gates. Cornwallis had crushed them all.

Nathanael Greene

As Greene took command, Cornwallis owned the south. From his ownership position, he could bring supplies in from England and deploy resources to the weaker British position in the north. At the same time, Cornwallis set out to identify colonists still loyal to the British throne (Loyalists) in the south who could help to reinforce the British position of strength.

Greene's analysis was that his southern Continental Army was poorly equipped, weak, and lacking inspiration. He knew they could not win battles, so he taught his new command how to use their weakness as a strength and how to turn the British strength into a weakness. Within weeks, his new strategy began to show success.

His initial meeting with his staff took place in a ragged and tattered tent that had been used by his predecessor, General Gates. Greene studied Brigadier General Isaac Huger, who had been appointed second in command. He was an articulate, well-educated son of a wealthy merchant who had significant military training and experience. Most importantly, he was a general who respected George Washington and the chain of command.

"Our strategy will be to divide our troops and force Cornwallis to do the same," began Greene as the two studied a map depicting prior battles fought against the British. He tucked his right index finger behind his ear while the other three fingers rubbed his cheek, clearly using this gesture to help him finish his thoughts. "We, the men of the Continental Army, *know* this country, and we will use that to our advantage. We will only engage when forced to do so or when the odds are in our favor. Otherwise, we will divide and conquer. We will hit and run, and we will run faster because we carry less."

"I like this strategy." General Huger looked over the maps while supporting his weight on his left hand. "I am sure you know we have not had a victory in some time, and any kind of win will improve morale."

"I do understand. We will dispatch messengers to let everyone know of Colonel Campbell's victory at Kings Mountain. We will use that as our first victory, and because of the number of British troops captured, it will also spark Cornwallis to engage in a chase, which we will not let him win. You see, we know he has us outmanned and outgunned, which means victory on the battlefield is difficult, but where we *can* win is in quick engagements and constant movement. We will become the bumblebee that stings a bear. We can irritate him, and through that irritation, he will begin to make mistakes. When we observe his mistakes, we shall capitalize."

Greene studied the room and noted that all of the staff was nodding in agreement. "What are our current numbers?"

Continental Army

"On paper, sir, we are just over two thousand three hundred," Huger answered, "but that is only on paper. I believe we have less than a thousand Continental regulars along with assorted militia and volunteers."

"Even that will change soon enough. We will send a detachment up the Catawba River with two goals: first, to distract Cornwallis, and second, to improve our position by increasing our numbers, collecting supplies, and demonstrating that we can sting and run. We will consequently improve the morale of our officers and troops."

"Understood, sir." They all nodded in agreement.

"Tell everyone along the way that Morgan will attack the fort at Ninety Six," Greene added. Brigadier General Daniel Morgan, a cousin to Daniel Boone, had become a critical partner to Greene's strategy and, like Greene, had outperformed the British on several occasions, winning improbable battles.

"But, sir, we cannot win," Huger protested.

"You are correct," Greene interrupted, "and we shall never go there. It is simply a ruse that only you and I will know." Greene stopped and watched Huger smile in understanding. "Lord Cornwallis knows he has us on our heels and expects us to be in retreat. Gentlemen, retreat is exactly what we shall give him, but we shall call it a strategic retreat. We should also remember that he expects us to ultimately engage under my new command, and that is where we shall keep him guessing."

Over the next forty-five days, Greene orchestrated a series of small victories and fleet-footed retreats. Cornwallis and his men went from clearly owning the south to chasing the elusive Greene. During the month of January and into mid-February, the chase-and-ruse game continued, with Greene's forces winning almost every skirmish on the field or in the mind. By February 13, 1781, Cornwallis, now exasperated, finally determined the true location of Greene's full force. Studying the maps, he realized that he could push Greene to the banks of the Dan River and use the river as a wall to prevent Greene's escape. With this, he and the British army could deliver the fatal blow to the Continental Army of the south.

The sprint for the Dan River had begun!

Greene's men used all the intelligence available and moved as quickly as his small army could in the cat-and-mouse, bumblebee-and-bear contest. He clearly knew that a direct engagement with Cornwallis with their backs to the Dan would mean the end of his army. Not only did he need to arrive at the Dan before Cornwallis caught him but he needed to get just over two thousand troops across the swollen river.

With his objective now singularly focused, Cornwallis was intent on quickly closing the gap. Even though his men were feeling the effects of the chase, they correctly concluded that Greene's men must be exhausted. The British had food and supplies, while Greene's had little to none. The calculus on both sides now seemed certain. Cornwallis would overcome Greene on the banks of the Dan.

That conclusion is precisely what Greene had hoped for. Tired and exhausted, Greene's men made one final, impossible push, marching most of the night on February 13 and into the fourteenth. What Greene knew, but Cornwallis did not, was that Greene had arranged for dozens of boats and ferries to carry his men and meager supplies across the Dan.

Cornwallis arrived at the Dan as the last of Greene's troops were arriving on the opposite bank. The river was too swollen to cross without bridge or boat, and thanks to the strategic planning of Greene, no bridges were intact, and all boats were on the opposite bank—along with the Continental Army of the south. Greene had not only achieved a victory in a decisive race but had accomplished one of the most masterful military achievements of all time.

The race to the Dan had been won, and with that victory, Cornwallis had his first insight into the caliber of general he now faced.

Cornwallis was left with only one path, and that was a march all the way back to the coast. In spite of the fact that not a single shot had been fired at the Dan, word spread quickly amongst patriots and loyalists in the south that General Nathanael Greene and the southern Continental Army had outsmarted the British and won a decisive victory.

On the northeast banks of the Dan, after only a short rest, Greene called his senior officers together and once again did what no one would have expected. "I think that we should now cross the Dan and engage Cornwallis," Greene announced.

"But General, we are outnumbered three-to-one. They have more cannons and dry powder than we. We could not possibly win such an engagement," Huger countered.

"These things are true, but I remind you that we are not here fighting this war for our personal safety. We fight for the liberty and freedom of our children and generations to come," Greene responded in a thoughtful tone.

"And how would our demise accomplish this?" Huger argued, noticing that the other officers were supporting his position.

"It is simple, General Huger: we shall not die. No one expects us to cross the Dan and engage. We shall begin with the element of surprise, and we shall fight like we outnumber them. In their confusion, we will strike a blow from which they cannot recover." Greene paused for a moment and stood so the next part of his argument would have impact.

"As it now stands, Cornwallis will march to the sea, where he will reprovision. During that march, he will develop a new and deadly strategy. We have seen his tactical and strategic abilities during this war, and I for one do not wish to give him time to prepare." Greene looked from one man to the next.

"Gentlemen, now is the time to strike the blow that no one expects and change the course of the war," Greene continued. "Our alternative of resting and building resources will always see us outmatched by the British war machine. If we rest, they also rest. If we take time to find dry powder, they have time to receive five times the amount we collect."

Greene slammed his fist down on the table. "This must be our strategy, but it cannot prevail unless everyone agrees that now is the time to strike!" Greene could see all of the men were shocked at the proposal, but the sheer force of Greene's delivery was an infection that quickly consumed the room. "Each and every one of you must realize what is about to happen will be not just another battle in a long war but instead a decisive blow that will change the course of the war."

General Huger could feel the energy in the room explode into agreement with the strategy presented by Greene. "Yes, General Greene, I for one see that you are right. With surprise and passion for our cause, we can win a battle with Cornwallis at this time! I shall have my men ready at your command."

Greene's army did what no one expected: he crossed back over the Dan River and, in a surprise attack, engaged the British on March 15, 1781, at Guilford Court House in North Carolina. This became an extremely bloody battle with both sides taking heavy casualties. At one point, in desperation, Cornwallis ordered the cannons be filled with shot rather than cannon balls, even aware that more British soldiers would be killed in this deadly move than Continental soldiers.

Between the race to the Dan and the Battle at Guilford Court House, for the second time in a matter of just a month, the British were forced to recognize the brilliance of Nathanael Greene and how he had now changed the tide on the southern front.

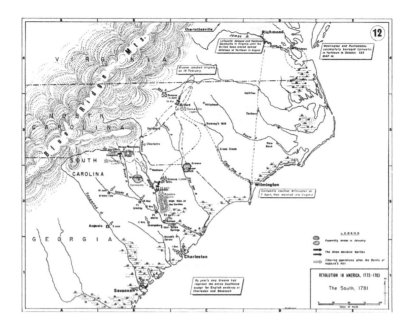

Cornwallis's march to the sea had started as a strategic move to regroup and develop a strategy that would deliver a fatal blow to Greene. After the battle at Guilford Court House, the British had no alternative but to flee to the coast. For the first time, British regulars came to realize that this ragtag group of patriots could win the war.

Over the next three months, as the spring of 1781 led into the summer, the southern Continental Army would retake the Carolinas and force Cornwallis to the banks of the Atlantic Ocean. General Greene's strategy had proven effective against the overwhelming odds and resources of the British. Cornwallis went from being oversupplied and confident of victory to frayed, in a constant defensive posture. At the same time, Greene's army transformed itself from a tattered militia hanging by a thread and awaiting inevitable defeat to a confident and strong force that would not be defeated.

The southern forces pushed Cornwallis into the vice grip that Greene and Washington had begun to form in Yorktown, Virginia. General

Washington, for the first time in the war, held a strategic and numerical advantage. Washington brought seventeen thousand troops to the siege while Cornwallis's numbers had diminished to nine thousand.

With Cornwallis holding the town of Yorktown, the siege began on September 28. By October 17, Cornwallis was asking for terms, which culminated with his surrender on October 19. With that surrender, the unlikely patriots had won the war against the most powerful army on earth, securing independence from Britain.

3

Founding Fathers

We hold these truths to be self-evident, that all men are created equal, that they are endowed by their Creator with certain unalienable Rights, that amongst these are Life, Liberty and the pursuit of Happiness.

—Thomas Jefferson

The decisive battle of the American Revolution was won on October 19 in Yorktown, Virginia. With George Washington's victory and General Cornwallis's surrender, the war would come to a close, leading to the Treaty of Paris, signed by King George III of Britain and the newly born United States.

Healing, rebuilding, and celebrations were the order of the day as 1781 came to an end. The nation now had full power to plot her course and finalize construction of the new government.

The American people could consider themselves fortunate that two of the greatest political geniuses who ever lived—Jefferson and Adams, along with the help of many others—were able to author and piece together what would ultimately become the founding documents of the United States. Behind those two were hundreds of others supporting the formation of this new democracy.

Still, Congress had its work cut out for it as the bold words from the Declaration of Independence and the hopeful words of the Constitution began to shape the nation.

War had definitely taken a financial and physical toll on Nathanael Greene, but during the conflict, he had refused to allow anything to slow the progress of his southern army. Greene was a northerner whose family had been in Rhode Island since its founding in the 1630s, but it was the south that most celebrated his victories and the south that offered him status and land grants.

During the celebrations after the war, Nathanael Greene would be invited to many events, but the one he most looked forward to was a private dinner with Thomas Jefferson at Monticello. He had a sense of the impact of Jefferson on the forging of his new country and held a great appreciation for the bold and eloquent words of the founding documents. Jefferson and Greene had traded letters during the course of the war, but the two had not met in person.

While waiting for Jefferson to arrive, Nathanael sat staring into the fireplace of this private yet magnificent dining hall with his wife, Catharine. "We have lived a great life, Catharine," he observed. "I have had the privilege of accomplishing many important tasks."

Catharine put down her glass of wine and nodded. "Your leadership as a general was valuable to George Washington. You are the reason he was able to lead our forces into victory."

Nathanael rubbed his cheek thoughtfully. "Catharine, you give me far too much credit. As we came to the final year of the war effort, Daniel Morgan and General Huger played decisive roles in our victory."

Catharine looked gently at her husband and replied, "If I am exaggerating, then why did Washington ask you to be a member of his trusted cabinet in our new government? Why has Thomas Jefferson invited us to this private dinner, and why have the southern states issued enormous land grants to our family?"

Nathanael sighed. "Providence has walked with us, my dear, but alas, I am now tired. A long rest would do me good."

With that, Jefferson came into the private dining room. "General Greene, it is with great pleasure that I take this dinner with you."

Forefathers & Founding Fathers

Surrender of Cornwallis at Yorktown

"The pleasure is ours, sir," Greene answered as he shook Thomas Jefferson's hand. "May I introduce my wife, Catharine?"

Jefferson towered more than a foot over Catharine, a fact that was exaggerated by her curtsy and offer of her hand. "My pleasure, Mrs. Greene." He took her hand and kissed it.

"You may know that during the course of the war, I have opposed you and your methods, but at this time, I must admit that our victory would not have been possible or at least as expeditious without your genius. For that, our nation must thank you."

Nathanael smiled. "Thank you, Mr. Jefferson."

"My home state of Virginia owes you a debt of gratitude, General Greene," Jefferson responded. "There are many things I would like to discuss, but mostly, I want to hear more about the man who wore General Greene's uniform. The tides of history will describe your victories, and perhaps this experiment that Adams, the Congress, and I have concocted will become something great, but mostly, we are the sum of those who came before us."

"We are indeed," Greene answered. "My family has been in this country since the beginning days of the first colonies."

"Yes, I know a bit about your forefather, Samuel Gorton. It seems he had similar *radical* roots to mine in a time when it was even less safe than our current epoch."

"I am impressed, Mr. Jefferson," Catharine interjected. "You must truly know your history of the early colonies to be aware of the Greene and Gorton families during the founding years of Rhode Island."

"I have a passion for history," Jefferson responded, "among other things. Still, I know only a little and would love to hear more."

"My great-great-grandfathers were John Greene and Samuel Gorton. The two men were close friends and founders of the Warwick Colony. While they together were instrumental in the formation of Warwick, it was really Samuel who was the firebrand. Samuel was the one who stood on the front line and withstood the slings and arrows of that time. Samuel was the one who believed in civil government and freedom of religion long before it became a mainstream belief."

"Yes, I am vaguely aware of Samuel Gorton's role and controversial position in the early colonies," Jefferson noted. "I suspect my friend John Adams and his fellow Bostonians would rather bury that part of history."

Samuel Gorton

Roger Williams

"While I am quite proud my name is Greene, I think it is the Gorton side of my roots that is the most interesting," Nathanael responded thoughtfully. "Not so long ago, the name Gorton was simply not spoken in the colonies without fear of reprisal. My great-great-grandparents, Samuel and Mary Gorton, sacrificed much and risked everything to plant the seeds of freedom that we enjoy today. In many ways, I am saddened that he gave so much during his lifetime yet did not live to see the fruits of his labor. The country has begun to recognize Roger Williams and his efforts. I believe that is right and appropriate, but we seem to have forgotten the freedom fighters who really opposed the Puritans with the ideals that you have written into our Declaration of Independence. Of course, it was not Samuel alone who fought those battles, but he and three others of whom I am aware."

"THAT story, General Greene, is the one I want to hear!" Thomas Jefferson lifted his wineglass. "Let us settle in to a great dinner coupled with a bit of our important history. Please begin! Tell me the tales that have been passed down in your family."

Catharine's eyes lit up as Nathanael settled in his chair and gazed into the distance as if he were able to see a scene from the past. "Please, Nathanael, tell us the story of Mary and Samuel!"

Nathanael laughed. Catharine never tired of hearing the love story between Mary and Samuel. "Well then, I hope we have plenty of wine!" Nathanael's eyes sparkled as he lifted his glass, took a sip, and began, "My great-great-grandfather, Samuel Gorton, was a haberdasher in London, but alas, Samuel was no haberdasher . . ."

PART 2
FOREFATHERS

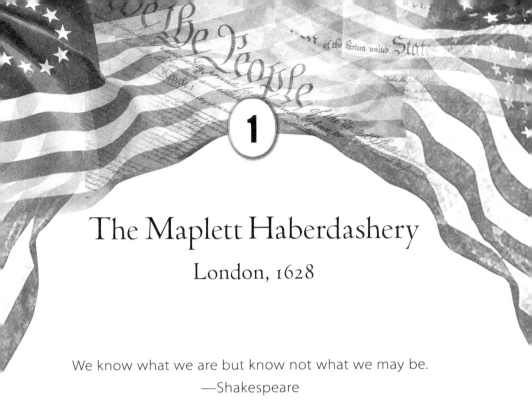

1

The Maplett Haberdashery

London, 1628

> We know what we are but know not what we may be.
> —Shakespeare

April 21, 1628
It had been quite an ordinary day for Samuel Gorton, and he did not like ordinary. At the beginning of the day, he had reported to work at Maplett's Haberdashery at the first light of dawn and had set out the summer's display of cloths and fabrics. This year, point lace, silk jackets, ribbon, and all things French would be very fashionable. There were many things Samuel had come to appreciate during his time working here, but each day, he cringed at the imminent visit of the pompous noble lords and ladies. They would fawn over frivolous things like "this pomegranate color" and "that soft material" and say, "Oh, won't we look just like the Queen of France!" On this day, their reactions had been no different.

Samuel heaved a hefty sigh as he recounted the day's events, overwhelmed by the musty scent of wool on the inhale. Samuel wore a clock-watch around his neck, but it was not a good one and served more as a status symbol than an actual timepiece. Clocks small enough to fit in one's pocket had been around for nearly one hundred years, but even the most expensive ones were little more than crude time instruments. Today was one of those days where his watch was definitely not correct. Still, from the shadows outside the window, he could tell his day of work was almost done.

As he was wrapping up and preparing to close the shop, he heard the familiar creak of the front door swinging open.

"SAMUEL, MY BOY!" a croaky old voice greeted. Samuel jumped, startled by the unusual entry of old Mr. Maplett, his business partner, who made a point to never show up near the end of the day. Samuel took in the impressive figure of Maplett and sensed an upbeat mood based on his gait and great, crooked smile. Chuckling, he made his way over to Samuel and slapped his shoulder three times.

"I'm curious. How is your adjustment to life in London?" Maplett asked.

Samuel had moved to London from his small home village of Gorton outside Manchester less than a year ago. While educated in divinity and law, his apprenticeship had been with an old clothing merchant in Manchester, and he had come to London just as soon as he had finished, specifically to find work at a high-end haberdashery. Yet he found himself dissatisfied and bored. Samuel hesitated, searching for words.

"Honesty is encouraged here, m'boy." Mr. Maplett's fat old fingers still rested heavily on Samuel's shoulder, and he shook and squeezed it warmly.

"Well, honestly," Samuel answered, "the city is a bit overwhelming... and I miss the smells of my home in Manchester. There was a seemingly endless forest just on the edge of our pasture where my brother, Thomas, and I used to play and explore. London seems to be endless cobblestone and people everywhere."

Samuel stared into Maplett's silence, took that as a cue, and continued, "And I even miss my mum a bit, and her cooking... especially her cherry tarts and shepherd's pie. Ah, and I can't stand the nobility. They are puffed up and vain, all of them. Well, all except the adventurous and well-traveled

Robert Rich, the Earl of Warwick

Robert Rich, Earl of Warwick. I look forward to his visits, clever comments, and tales of travel to the New World. Truly, more than anything, it just isn't what I thought it would be, Maplett. I am bored. I find myself wanting more."

"How long was your journey from Manchester to London, lad?"

"Well, sir, I suppose you could make the journey on a good horse in under a week, but I took ten days."

Old Mr. Maplett let out another one of his hearty guffaws and said, "Welcome to London, Gorton. You may never get used to the patrician aristocracy of our nobility, but you will learn to tolerate 'em. Perhaps ye'd benefit from a break. You work too hard, m'boy!"

"I suppose I do, sir," Samuel responded. "I am not sure if I ever told you, but when I traveled here from Manchester, it was to take a position at a haberdashery on the other side of London. On that day, when I was to meet with the proprietor, I stood outside a broken-down shop with little hope or opportunity."

"Remind me, which place was it, Samuel, m'boy?"

"Smithy's, over on the other side of the river."

"Oh yes, I know the shop. It's been around for a while, but you did well by not taking that position. It's not a high-class shop like our Maplett's. I believe it was providence that you came here instead."

"Perhaps," Samuel reflected. "I remember that I wandered around London for a day and had just about resolved to return home to Manchester when I came upon your business, sir. Something about that moment compelled me to come in and just look around."

"Walking in this door was a notable and consequential decision, lad. I asked you what brought you to London, immediately liked you, and thus began our partnership. Your timing was perfect."

"I feel so lucky for this opportunity, sir. It's just that I suppose I miss my home and need a bit more time to establish roots here in London."

"I can understand that, and it is part of the reason I am here today. I've come to invite you to join Mrs. Maplett, my daughter Mary, and meself for the weekend. We have plans to attend a play at the Globe and have a wholesome spring feast topped with some fine lagers and ales. It may not be the same as your mum's, but my Mrs. makes a fine shepherd's pie."

"I would be delighted, Mr. Maplett," Samuel replied.

"Very good! You will meet us at the Globe Theatre at half past seven," Mr. Maplett said as he took his coat from the iron stand and shrugged into it. He grabbed his cane from its usual corner and began to make his way to the door before speaking again. "Please do not use that miserable clock-watch of yours to arrive on time, as its accuracy eludes its purpose."

Samuel pushed the cover back on his watch and studied it. "It is true, Mr. Maplett, but I love the complexity, in spite of its shortfall."

Maplett nodded as a glimmer of understanding sparked in his eye. "I do see the value and attraction to the complexity. Listen, m'boy, you should plan on spending the weekend at the Maplett home with my family, and make sure to snuff the candles on your way out!" He waved his cane in farewell as he opened the heavy oak door, once again revealed his crooked grin, laughed, and slammed the door behind him.

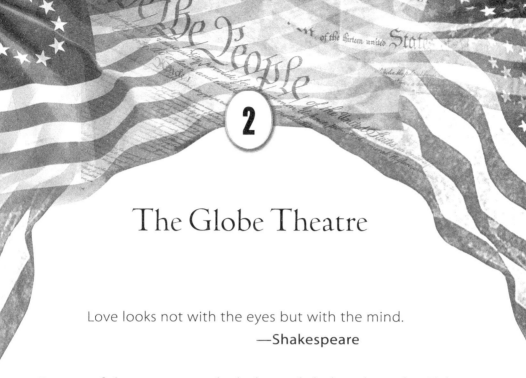

2

The Globe Theatre

Love looks not with the eyes but with the mind.
—Shakespeare

In spite of the many times she had attended plays there, the Globe Theatre remained a place of wonder for young Mary Maplett. The smell, the legends, the drama, and even the tragic fire that all but brought it to the ground in 1613—it was all so enchanting! Since she had learned to read as a girl, she had been devouring every Shakespeare play she could get her hands on. She was quite certain that there wasn't one play or sonnet or even a single published word by the man that she had not read. And whenever her papa brought her and her sisters to the Globe, she was in heaven.

"John, dear, where is Mr. Gorton? The play will start any minute!" Mary's namesake and mother asked.

Just as they were craning their necks in an effort to spot him, Samuel came up behind them and said, "Here I am, Maplett family!"

"M'boy!" John Maplett exclaimed, and Samuel braced himself for Maplett's usual shoulder slap.

"Samuel, I'd like you to meet my darling wife, Mary."

Mary curtsied, offered her hand, and said, "It's a pleasure, Mr. Gorton. John has told me that you are the best partner he has had in the shop."

"Thank you, milady." Samuel took and kissed her hand and then bowed in response.

29

Maplett continued, "And this lovely pearl is my daughter, named after her mother for her equally astounding beauty."

At that moment, Samuel's eyes met with the bluest pair of eyes he had ever beheld. In the following seconds, Samuel's ability to utter words escaped him as he gazed at her alabaster skin with perfectly rosy cheeks. A few stray, golden ringlets framed her face, the rest being swept back in a half-up fashion.

"How do you do, Mr. Gorton?" Mary said, curtsying.

"It is the utmost pleasure to meet you, Miss Maplett," Samuel finally spoke, taking her hand and bowing.

Mr. Maplett interrupted the moment with a boisterous laugh. "Let's be seated, shall we? The play will be starting soon! Mary, sit by Samuel, won't you?"

"Yes, Papa," Mary agreed politely as she daintily took her seat between the two men.

Samuel nervously surveyed the room, acutely aware of the beautiful woman seated to his left. He racked his brain for something to say to her.

Ask her about the weather, he thought. *No, don't do that . . . too obvious. Perhaps ask her how she got her hair to be that curly. What am I thinking? That would be ridiculous. Ask her about the play? Yes! That's it!*

"What play is it we are seeing, miss?" Samuel finally mustered the courage to say.

Mary turned her pretty head to face him, her curls falling over her shoulder as she did.

"*The Taming of the Shrew*, Mr. Gorton," she replied curtly.

Samuel swallowed hard, feeling more nervous than before. "Who wrote it?"

"Why, the great William Shakespeare, of course!" Mary's voice lifted joyfully to speak the name of her favorite playwright.

Samuel had read a few of Shakespeare's works but was not familiar with this particular one. "I am not familiar with this one, Miss Mary."

Mary laughed euphoniously, tipping her head back slightly and then catching her breath to say, "You *are* funny, Mr. Gorton."

Samuel sat quietly, not understanding what he had said that was so humorous. Mary's gaze fell upon the confused look on his face, and the smile faded from hers.

"You can't be serious. You *do* know who William Shakespeare is, don't you?"

"Well, yes, of course. Any educated person in England knows of Shakespeare." Samuel tucked his right index finger behind his ear while the other three fingers rubbed his cheek, thinking about the situation in which he now found himself. "Why, even some uneducated from my town of Manchester know Shakespeare. I simply regret to say that I do not know this particular play."

Mary gasped, and a few heads turned in curiosity.

"Might I guess that you have familiarity with *Hamlet, Twelfth Night,* or *Romeo and Juliet*?"

Gorton was a bit surprised by her level of knowledge on Shakespeare but assumed it was because she had been raised in London, where many of his plays were first seen in this very theater. "Actually, *Julius Caesar* and *Hamlet* were required reading in my education," he responded, trying to rebut and sound educated.

"Only those two?" she inquired but did not await a response. "How can you not know this particular work? I suspect you will perhaps learn something special tonight."

Gorton wanted to respond but was still transfixed by her and mesmerized by her beauty. He felt certain that silence would be the better part of education this particular evening.

"Mr. Gorton, I have seen virtually every one of his plays multiple times, and I have been reading his work since I was very young."

"*You read*?" Samuel asked, surprised.

For a long moment, Mary was silent. When she finally regained her composure, she laughed lightly. "Yes. I read. I also write stories. It is my belief that women must learn for themselves. We must form our own opinions—and have the right to exercise the same civil liberties as your gender. Is that a problem for you, Mr. Gorton?"

Samuel rushed to make himself clearer. "No, no, please do not misunderstand me, Miss Mary. I find myself pleasantly surprised to find your opinions so similar to my own. I would love to talk to you more about your opinions on women's education and gender roles in church and state. With our beloved Queen Elizabeth barely a score and five in the grave, we are already realizing that she was and may be our best sovereign ever. It's just that I have never had the pleasure of meeting a woman who could read, much less one with education."

"Do *you* have an education, Mr. Gorton?"

Samuel noted Mary's asperity. "Why, yes, Miss Mary," "While I have apprenticed and work as a partner in your father's shop as a haberdasher, I do have formal education in divinity and law."

Mary's expression softened, and the corners of her mouth nearly turned up into a rueful smile. She was well aware that her education and ability to read were truly rare. In fact, they were the primary reason she had not yet been betrothed. For the most part, educated men were intimidated by her education, while uneducated men seemed oblivious. Mary firmly held the belief that her love of education must be appreciated by any man she might marry. Such a trait was beginning to seem like a near-impossible anomaly.

Samuel forced himself to refocus on the stage as the curtain opened and the play began. Even though this was his first visit to the Globe, a near-impossible dream during his youth, something inside told him that he would always remember Mary on this night, not the private Maplett seats on the upper level of the Globe Theatre.

After the play, as they rode back to the Maplett home, the very complex story of Petruchio and Katherina swirled around in his head, but it was little more than a temporary distraction compared to the lovely and witty Mary Maplett.

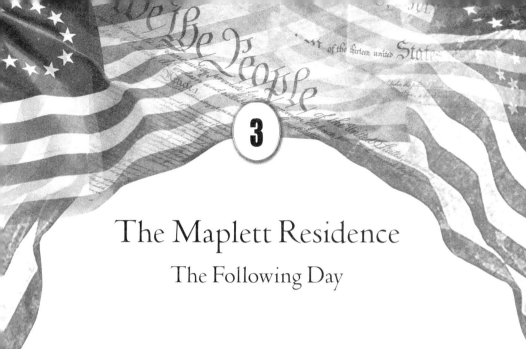

The Maplett Residence
The Following Day

> For where is any author in the world
> Teaches such beauty as a woman's eye?
> Learning is but an adjunct to ourself.
> —Shakespeare

April 22, 1628

Samuel awoke at the home of the Mapletts early enough to watch the sunrise. He made his way down to the first floor and out the back door to the family's small garden. There, he sat for a few moments, silently thinking about the previous evening. The play had been compelling, but his mind was stuck on Mary. He had been initially captivated by her lovely appearance, but now he was even more curious about her unusual education and strong will. He wanted to hear her tell some of the stories that she had written. He wondered about her progressive views toward women. He wished for the opportunity to ask for her thoughts on the exciting yet perilous migration of people to the New World. He felt compelled to share his thoughts with her even though he scarcely knew her.

Samuel's train of thought was cut off by the creaking of the door and the unusually silent footfalls of Mr. Maplett.

"Good morning, Mr. Maplett. I'm surprised! I barely heard you coming!" Samuel jested.

Mr. Maplett laughed one of his signature laughs, a pipe between his teeth muffling his words as he said, "Yes, m'boy. Morning is one time that I love to keep sacred with quiet."

A few moments of silence followed as both men listened to the sounds of the mourning doves cooing. They breathed in the fresh and dewy smell of a new day interlaced with the rich aroma of Mr. Maplett's tobacco-filled pipe.

"Did you sleep well?" Mr. Maplett questioned after a long drag, smoke billowing from his nose and mouth as he spoke.

"Indeed. Thank you for inviting me to the play and for inviting me into your home," Samuel responded.

"Well, boy . . . I should be honest with you. I didn't just invite you over for the fun of it. I . . . eh . . . have ulterior motives, you could say."

Chuckling lightly, Samuel asked, "What are you up to now, Mr. Maplett?"

John Maplett's face remained serious as he took another long drag from his pipe, preparing himself for what he was about to say. "You know our Mary is the eldest of her five surviving siblings. All are doing quite well in their upbringing, but I must say that Mary is, and always will be, my favorite. We couldn't be more satisfied with the state of our children's educations and lives, but of course, there comes a time when we must decide to send them off into the world. Mary and I think it is now time for young Mary to do so."

Samuel swallowed hard, a nervous expectation building in him as to what was coming next.

"Samuel, m'boy . . . I think you'd be a fine match for my favorite headstrong daughter. You are from a small town, but your family and mine are of similar classes. Both you and Mary would bring education and wealth to the marriage that you could pass on to your children. I have even been thinking of what might happen to the haberdashery when I pass on. Neither of my sons, John or Thomas, holds any interest in the clothing business, so I suspect none will care to take it over. I already regard you as a son, and I believe it would be prudent to plan on you taking ownership of Maplett's Haberdashery when old age or disease finally takes my life." Maplett took a break from speaking to puff on his pipe.

"Not to mention that I want the best for my little girl, and I think you'd come pretty close," Maplett said with a glimmer in his eye and a smile on his mouth. He continued, "What do you say, m'boy?"

For a few short moments, Samuel thought. It wasn't like he had a choice. Mr. Maplett was his business partner and the best friend he had made since his move to London. And, of course, Mary Maplett was radiant in mind and body. Although the proposition of marrying Maplett's favorite daughter coupled with the responsibility of taking over the family business made him quite nervous, Samuel knew that it was just the kind of opportunity for which he had come to London in the first place. He knew well he could not decline this opportunity, which John had clearly thought through.

"Mr. Maplett, I would be delighted to consider marriage with your daughter and to run the haberdashery for the man who is the closest thing to a father that I have this far from home. I should say, it would be an honor," Samuel added nervously, reaching out to shake Maplett's hand.

Maplett stood up with a great chuckle, opened his arms, and pulled Samuel in for a near-chest-breaking hug. "I will dispatch a messenger to seek approval from your father. Let us speak not of this to Mary until we have word back from your family in Manchester."

"Yes, sir, Mr. Maplett."

"Ah, and Samuel, m'boy?" John said, finally releasing Samuel from his warm bear hug.

"Yes?"

"Perhaps you should call me John," he suggested, eyes twinkling, adding one of his signature, firm shoulder smacks like the period at the end of the sentence.

"Yes, of course, John. I would be delighted to take your daughter's hand in marriage," Samuel said, smiling brightly. "I must ask whether she is part of your scheme."

"That's the spirit!" John exclaimed. "Trust me, m'boy, young Mary will be pleased that someone finally appreciates her education and headstrong opinions."

"John, dear!" Mrs. Maplett called, poking her nose out the door. "I hate to interrupt such important business matters, but breakfast is ready, and it is time to be seated!"

"Coming, love!" John answered, and the two gentlemen made their way inside and seated themselves at the table.

Samuel sat across from Mary, who looked as radiant in the morning as she had the previous night with her blue eyes aglow with the excitement of her favorite playwright's work. Her fair blonde hair was long, loose, and wavy, reaching past the middle of her back. Her eyes met his, and with a smile, she bade him good morning.

"A good morning, indeed," he agreed, adding, "I look forward to more political discussions this morning."

A lovely, lilting laugh escaped Mary's mouth, and she said, "I don't know, Mr. Gorton. Perhaps you'll find my politics too progressive. I think I should be quite disappointed if you disagree with me and you never wish to speak to me again."

"I doubt that is possible, Miss Mary," Samuel said, looking directly into Mary's sky-blue eyes.

Mary blushed scarlet. At that moment, Mrs. Maplett and the servants came out of the kitchen bearing a variety of plates full of delectable foods. Eggs, ham, fresh fruits, pastries, salmon, and hearty breads were presented ornately on the platters. Samuel's mouth watered at the sight. The elder Mary, with the help of her lady servants, arranged the platters in the middle of the dining-room table so they might eat family-style, passing the plates around and serving themselves.

"Sarah and Ellen, do join us for breakfast! You worked so hard you deserve to join in the feast, and we have plenty to go round," Mrs. Maplett said to the servants.

Samuel had never seen such a thing: Mrs. Maplett—a woman of class and wealth—first helping the servants cook the meal with her own two hands and then inviting them to eat at the same table. It was unheard of, but Samuel, not at all displeased, found himself wondering why. Servants lived their lives with the families for whom they worked. Why shouldn't they be considered almost part of the family?

The servants, flattered and always grateful, sat themselves at the table with the rest of the family. "Will you bless the meal, Mr. Maplett?" the Mrs. requested.

Samuel watched as each person seated at the table reached out and joined hands with the person sitting next to them and copied their actions. His family came from Catholic roots prior to King Henry, and of course they were currently members of the Church of England, but they had never joined hands like this before meals. Then everyone bowed and closed their eyes, and Mr. Maplett's jovial and jesting tone became reverent and serious as he spoke to God.

"Father in heaven," he said. "We thank you for this meal and for the hands who prepared it. I thank you for King Charles, the family joined at this table, and for the abundance of blessings you have poured out over us. Father, we are thankful for your son, his life, and his death; we are ever in your debt. You are a good and gracious God and Father; I pray that we would be instruments in Your plan. We love you and praise you. In Jesus's Holy Name, we pray. Amen."

Of all the things that had surprised Samuel from the moment he sat down at the dining-room table, this was the one that surprised him most. He had never heard someone pray like that before, and he found that in his heart of hearts, he longed to understand the wisdom and the knowledge of God that would lead someone to speak that way. As an Anglican, Samuel had been raised to believe that all people were born as sinners and that in order to achieve salvation a person had to spend their life doing good deeds, following religious laws, and never questioning religious leaders. However, Mr. Maplett's prayer had not focused on any of these things but instead had emphasized a one-on-one relationship with God. Samuel's mind continued to ponder on this absurd and foreign notion.

"Samuel, dear . . . Are you well? You may eat now!" Mrs. Maplett said, forcing Samuel's train of thought to a screeching halt as the servant girls and young Mary giggled at him staring off into the distance while everyone else had begun to eat.

"Sorry, Mrs. Maplett, I-I suppose I was daydreaming," Samuel apologized. "That prayer was quite different from what I have been accustomed to."

"You will find that we Mapletts do many things different," Mary responded.

Again, Mary and Samuel's eyes met, but this time, it was Samuel blushing and Mary smiling coyly.

The meal was impeccable. Samuel tried each food on the table, and by the time he was finished, he could barely breathe. John had implied that the Maplett and Gorton families were from similar standing, but that was simply not the case. The Mapletts were wealthier and better educated than any Gorton of whom Samuel was aware.

When the meal ended, Mary invited Samuel to see her small but treasured collection of books and plays in the family's home library.

"Look here," she said, pointing. "This shelf is mine. This section holds the plays, next are the works of fiction, and this parchment contains a list of books I'd like to read." Mary turned to see a startled look on Samuel's face. "What is it, Mr. Gorton?"

"We had only one book in the home. All of the reading I did growing up and in my studies was in the library. The thought of a family library is astounding!"

Mary blushed and looked up into Samuel's eyes. "I sometimes forget how fortunate my family is to possess treasures such as these. I spend most of my time here by the fire in the winter, reading, of course. In the summer, I spend as much time as possible outside, but I find it difficult to tear myself away from books. My friends Olivia and Isabel say I'm antisocial, but that isn't true . . . I guess sometimes I would rather just socialize with the imaginary characters on these pages. Does that make sense?"

"Perfect sense. Of the many manuscripts you have read, what is your favorite?"

Without hesitation, Mary responded, "*Don Quixote* by Cervantes. I have read it probably seven times, and each time I pick out something different and fall in love with it all over again. Your turn. What is your favorite work of literature?"

Samuel paused, folded his arms, and rubbed the stubble growing on his cheek. With a great sigh, he finally answered, "To be quite honest, I don't have a favorite. I was raised with the belief that the Bible was the only book of importance. I . . . I've never really read for fun." Samuel hung his head, embarrassed. For a moment, they were both silent, and Samuel contemplated the broad gap between Mary's life and his own.

"Well, you have to start somewhere, and there's no time like the present! First things first, you had better read this one. It's called *The Tempest* by Shakespeare, and it's in my top ten favorite plays. Then read *Beowulf.* No one knows who wrote it, but it's the earliest known secular piece of literature. It's an epic poem and a thrilling adventure! Then, of course, you *must* read *Don Quixote.* Simply because it's my favorite and because I know you'll love it too." As she named each book, Mary handed it to Samuel.

"Thank you! I am excited to get started. I shall read these and report back as soon as possible!" Samuel said, running his free hand over the book covers.

"You are most welcome," Mary said, making her way over to a pair of ornate, high-backed chairs by the fireplace on the other side of the room, inviting him over once she had sat down. "Come, sit!"

Samuel did as she requested.

"So you want to know more about my political beliefs, now, do you?" Mary inquired, looking at him with those stunning blue eyes.

Samuel nodded vigorously.

"Well, I cannot promise that you won't hate me or question my docility once I've told you." She raised an eyebrow and studied Samuel briefly.

"I can affirm that I will not hate you, Miss Mary! I was raised in a family where no one ever questioned the things we were told or doubted a thing. I left my small town because I can't live like that. I have to ask questions, I have to deliberate and learn more and hear the opinions and viewpoints of others." Samuel paused, fidgeting with the pages of the three books in his lap. "Now enough with the suspense! Let us please get on with this."

"All right, all right!" Mary dropped her eyes, clenched her hands, then, lifting her chin, continued with courage. "Well . . . to start, I believe that women should no longer be silenced in the church, or in any setting, for that matter. I mean, where did this notion come from that men are to be the only leaders in the church? Paul wrote that the older women *should teach and admonish the younger women*, and the way it is now, you would think that was a sin! I agree with your opinion on Queen Elizabeth. She was clearly one of the great leaders in history. Further, there is evidence of a female apostle named Junia. I have heard that Coptic and Ethiopic translations of Paul's letter to the Romans mention her."

Mary's eyes sparkled with vision. "Imagine a world where there are women working the same jobs as men," she continued. "And imagine female members of Parliament! I believe someday a woman's opinion will be considered just as valid as a man's . . . the way you seem to be treating my opinion now. We are just as capable, in many respects, as your gender. Why not provide us with similar opportunities to contribute? There are whispers, you know, of women in eastern England, educated by John Cotton and John Wheelwright, who are beginning

John Cotton

John Wheelwright

to expand the position of women in the church. I have heard of one in particular named Anne Hutchinson who has been educating women in her own home. I know that Archbishop George Abbot, along with London Bishop Laud, has been reminding people that these practices do not conform to the established practices of the Anglican Church, but I hope, one day, I can meet her." Mary trailed off, lost in thought.

When she had returned from her daydream, she asked Samuel, "Have I upset you yet?"

Samuel smiled as he studied Mary, perfectly posed in her Elizabethan chair. "I must admit it is foreign to me, but no! I am intrigued by your enlightened views, and I would also like to meet Anne Hutchinson. But I cannot help but be concerned for you. I think of Joan of Arc, who had only the best of intentions yet ended up being burned at the stake."

"Well, yes, but Joan was a soldier, not a teacher. I can see women in many roles, but soldier seems less likely."

Samuel rubbed his right finger behind his ear. "Perhaps you are right, but should the truly enlightened perspective have any limitations?"

Mary smiled as she watched him. "It is a peculiar thing you do with your finger behind your ear and those others rubbing your cheek."

"Yes, yes, it is. Now back to the topic, please."

"Of course, I should remind you, Mr. Gorton, that Joan is now a registered and respected symbol of the Catholic League. Perhaps, one day, she will even reach sainthood!"

"Yes, perhaps—"

"And just now I used the term 'peculiar,' but I do love the way you rub your index finger behind your ear when you are thinking," she interrupted.

"I suppose it's a nervous habit. I think I've always done it," he responded.

"It's charming."

"Thanks, Miss Mary. 'Charming' seems an inappropriate term for a man, but I thank you nevertheless." Samuel grinned. "I must say, I'm learning new things from you, and my desire to know more is growing." He paused for a second and intentionally stopped himself from tucking his index finger behind his ear again. "Returning to your original question, you are doing the very opposite of upsetting me. Now, be the strong lady that you are, stop worrying about what I think, and do tell me more!"

Mary gave him a divine smile and continued, "I suspect you know that some Anglicans have become so distressed with how the Church of England is being run that they have left our country and traveled across the Atlantic to the New World so that they can worship in complete freedom?"

"Well . . . I believe so. You are referencing those Pilgrims who founded Plymouth Colony about eight years ago," Samuel began but was cut off by a zealous Mary.

"But the question is: Will they find the freedom they seek? From what I have been hearing, the Plymouth Colony is essentially becoming the Anglican Church all over again. Yes, they claim to be Separatists from our doctrine, but I am told this is not the case. I wouldn't be surprised if nobles are sent over to establish a New World royal family. Lords, ladies, dukes, duchesses, princes, princesses, queens, and kings. The colonists need someone brave and outspoken to combat the pattern that's ingrained in our minds from centuries of being ruled by the divine right of kings. Sometimes I wonder if it is not now the time for the people's turn to rule," Mary said, impassioned.

"Why not you?" Samuel asked.

"You jest, Mr. Gorton!"

"I do not! You know more than any governing official, nobleman, or esteemed and scholarly man I have ever heard talk. Why not you?"

"Because I may believe in a day when women and men will be equals, but I am not a fool. I'd be hanging from the gallows or consumed in a fire like Joan! Besides, who would listen? I am but a woman," Mary said, her voice revealing her disappointment.

Again, silence fell between the two of them. Eventually, Samuel broke the silence. "What would you say if I asked for the best single piece of advice you could give someone?"

"Well, that's an interesting question. I suppose I would say you should ignore the confusion that surrounds us, enjoy the moment, and learn from everything."

"Interesting," he responded.

"What about you, Mr. Gorton?"

"We don't fail until we quit, and we should never quit anything important," Samuel answered without hesitation.

"I like that. I like it a lot," she responded with a reflective grin.

The fact that Samuel and Mary were inseparable that weekend did not escape John Maplett. In this time of informal courtship, he observed their continued and relentless interactions. It seemed providence had brought Samuel into his haberdashery and into their lives. That evening, Mrs. Maplett made her shepherd's pie and cherry tarts, which were just good enough to make Samuel feel more at home.

That weekend at the Maplett's house, Samuel felt welcomed as a part of the family, which was very nice considering how far away he was from his own Gorton clan. Sunday came, and Samuel joined the family for church and Bible study at home for the sum of the day. Mr. Maplett continued to speak of the saving grace of Jesus by his death on the cross, and Samuel grew more curious of this point of view, of not having to *do* anything good to be made right with God but simply trust that Christ alone could bridge the gap between God and humanity.

Samuel was also taken by surprise at the way it wasn't Mr. Maplett preaching to his family, but Mr. Maplett initiating a conversation to which his wife, daughter, and Samuel were freely able to contribute. This family was an anomaly, but Samuel was quickly deciding to adopt their way of things and integrate it with those things he had learned during his own upbringing in Manchester.

4

News from Manchester

> Let me not to the marriage of true
> minds Admit impediments.
> —Shakespeare

May 16, 1628

It was just past the middle of the day on Tuesday when John Maplett's first footman, whom he had dispatched as a courier to Manchester, walked in the door of the haberdashery and asked for his boss.

It took Samuel a second to realize the impact as his business partner unfolded the note. "Your father approves and sends his congratulations, m'boy, though he sends regrets that he cannot attend." Maplett hugged Samuel Gorton and then slapped him heartily three times on the shoulder.

"This—this is great news," Samuel responded. "May I take the day, sir, to get things in order and begin preparations for the wedding?"

"No, son, you may not. We are going to do this the proper way." He paused for a minute to study Samuel. "I will leave early and have Mrs. Maplett prepare a feast. You will join us for dinner, and I will make the announcement to the family, as is customary."

"As you wish, John." Samuel looked up as the familiar creak of the wooden door and bells rang, announcing the entrance of a customer.

"You take care of the customers and close up. I will handle the rest for you this evening." Maplett centered his hat, grabbed his walking stick from the corner, and briskly left the shop with his first footman.

It was an unusually busy day at the shop, and then, with just a little over an hour before closing, Robert Rich, the second Earl of Warwick, strode through the door. "Where is my favorite haberdasher?" he roared as he stood with his usual commanding presence in the doorway.

"Lord Warwick!" Samuel always brightened when this particular visitor dropped in. He had a sense that the earl was a bit of an iconoclast amongst the lords of London, with his adventures and investments in the New World.

"I have news, Gorton! I have news that you, the most unique haberdasher in all of England, shall be the first to hear. I am preparing to dispatch once again to the wilderness, where I shall take control of the Somers Isles Company on the Mosquito Coast."

Robert Rich, the Earl of Warwick

"I am afraid I do not quite know where that is, my lord."

"Of course you don't, mate! The Mosquito Coast is just north of the equator in the wilderness of the New World. No one knows where it is, except Amerigo Vespucci himself! The weather is perpetually warm, and the ocean is blue as the sky and clearer than rainwater. It would be paradise were it not for the damned infernal mosquitoes that travel in clouds so thick you cannot see through them."

"It sounds like Paradise Hell," Samuel added and then laughed.

"Though the journey is a long one, it is a place you must visit, my friend."

"I cannot imagine that I shall ever make such a journey, my lord. The dangers of the road between Manchester and London seem extreme enough, much less the endless waters of the Atlantic."

"I think that you shall, and I predict that you will, my haberdasher friend. There is so much more to you than the shopkeeper I have come to enjoy."

"I do attest to enjoying the tales you bring into this haberdashery. What news regarding John Winthrop's request for colony land?"

"It is imminent that John Winthrop will be granted a colonial land patent by King Charles. I have been working with Winthrop and the king to make certain this guarantee occurs. Plans and provisions are being secured this moment. This colony is quite distant from the Mosquito Coast, which is far to the south."

John Winthrop

And so it went for the remainder of the workday. Robert Rich regaled Samuel with stories of adventure in the New World as Samuel minded the shop and took care of customers that wandered in.

As he prepared to shut down for the day, the earl changed his tone.

"I spoke with the good John Maplett before coming into the shop today, mate," he said seriously. "I do not know your customs in Manchester, but here in London we post an announcement, which we call banns of marriage."

"Yes, we post banns in Manchester as well. I expect to be doing so tomorrow," Samuel responded.

"It is an event worthy of celebration, but I must tell you: I have known this Maplett family for many years. I have watched young Mary grow up, and while she is more captivating than a spring flower, you must know she is educated and opinionated."

"I know this, my friend, and it is one of the things I find most fascinating about her."

"Alas, of course you do, my proprietor friend. A sprite like this one will push you to places I believe you belong. I see great things in you, Samuel Gorton, and a woman like Mary Maplett will make certain you achieve those great things."

"Thank you, my lord. I assume I have your blessing, then?"

"You do, mate. You do indeed, though I regret I'll not be here for the ceremony, as I will be sailing within the week."

"And when will you return to England?"

"If the winds cooperate, I shall return before the freezing winds of winter. By then, your ship to the *new world* of marriage shall have already sailed as well."

"Indeed," Samuel responded.

"Well then, may you enjoy fair winds and following seas to match your fair bride, mate."

The two men said their goodbyes, hugged, and went their separate ways. Samuel completed the closing of the haberdashery and began the short walk to the Maplett's house, where his new life was about to begin.

It was Mary who greeted Samuel at the door. He wondered if she already knew but certainly could not tell.

"You look beautiful," Samuel said, the words escaping his lips impulsively.

Both he and Mary blushed.

"Thank you," she said, bowing in a curtsy so as to hide her rosy face.

When she had composed herself, she cleared her throat and said, "Father came home early and instructed us to prepare a feast of celebration. The house has been a frenzy all afternoon as preparations have commenced on a celebration for a purpose we know not." She paused briefly. "I have actually come from the kitchen, where mother and I have prepared fresh bread, cheese, cured ham, and other delicacies. Samuel, do you know father's secret? Do you know the nature of the celebration?"

"I do, but your father has sworn me to secrecy, so please do not ask."

"Well then, if this is the ongoing nature of our friendship, then I shall accept it as is." She pretended to pout and then smiled broadly. "Perhaps, as I finish dinner preparations, you can tell me how far you've gotten in the first books I assigned you to read?"

Their eyes were locked on each other, each of them beaming, communicating silently the things they were too shy to say out loud.

The moment was only broken by the entrance of John Maplett into the room.

"Mary, run along and help your mum and the staff finish up. Samuel and I have some business matters to discuss." He watched as she left the room and then led Samuel into his study. "It appears that there will be more to this than just an arranged marriage, m'boy."

"Yes," he stuttered. "I have never met anyone with whom I have connected better than Mary."

"That is grand, lad. It is good for you and good for me. We look forward to many years of business partnership and grandchildren here in London."

"Yes, and I promise that I shall never fail to recognize the significance you have brought to my humble life, John."

"Take care of my daughter and my shop. That will be more than a man in my position could ask."

"I will, sir."

"Then let us go and begin this celebrated eve." John led Samuel into the dining room, where others were beginning to gather.

When everyone was seated at the dinner table, John Maplett began with a prayer. Once complete, he raised his hand in the air.

"And now for the announcement. I have spoken with my young business partner and communicated with his father in Manchester. It seems we have reached a final understanding on an important business arrangement. Samuel will begin the process of running the haberdashery."

John paused while he observed the facial expressions of his adult children, who seemed perplexed by the announcement. With that, his eyes sparkled, and his biggest crooked smile spread across his face and then, contagiously, to everyone in the room. He paused for a moment to add impact. "By itself, this seems a bit unusual, so I shall add the important tidbit. You see, tonight I can announce a new son in the family with the marriage of Mary and Samuel."

John Maplett stared at his daughter, who stood, quickly erased the shock, smiled, and began to cry happily. "Thank you, Father!" She ran around the table and hugged her father and then her mother.

Samuel pushed out his chair and stood up. He walked over to the other side of the table, took Mary's soft, dainty hands in his, and looked into her blue eyes. He admired her fair golden locks and her skin the color of alabaster pearl. But when he looked upon her, he now saw more than that. He saw her intelligence, her passion, and her joy for life. He briefly had an image of her flipping the pages of a manuscript that was just inches away from her face, engrossed in another world, a world they would now share.

"Mary, you are radiant," he said, "but over the past weeks, I learned that you are much more than a beauty. You have a beautiful mind and a heart full of passion. You see the world as it should be, and you make me want to work to build that world that you imagine. You are funny, you are fascinating, and I want to spend the rest of my life memorizing the way your face glows when you read a book or watch a play. Tomorrow, I hope that you help me post the banns."

Through a giddy giggle, Mary said, "Yes. Yes, I will!"

In one fell swoop, Samuel picked Mary up by her waist and spun in a circle, her skirt billowing and both of them laughing. When he stopped and put her down, she was still in his arms, and he took the opportunity to kiss her forehead.

Mr. Maplett interrupted, chortling loudly, his arms open wide for a hug. He pulled them both in and squeezed them tightly enough that they struggled for air.

"I hope ye don't mind. The rest of us are still here with a feast prepared, and you aren't married yet, so I instruct you to conduct yerselves accordingly! Shall we plan for a wedding this weekend?" John Maplett asked. "You can marry in our church if you wish, and Mrs. Maplett and I can throw a dance in your honor at our home. I daresay God has brought the two of you, you most unusual and improbable spirits, together. I am so happy to have the both of you together and in our lives. This is fantastic! Fantastic, I say!"

Mr. Maplett sat and instructed everyone else to do so. "As Aristippus has said, let us now eat, drink, and be merry!"

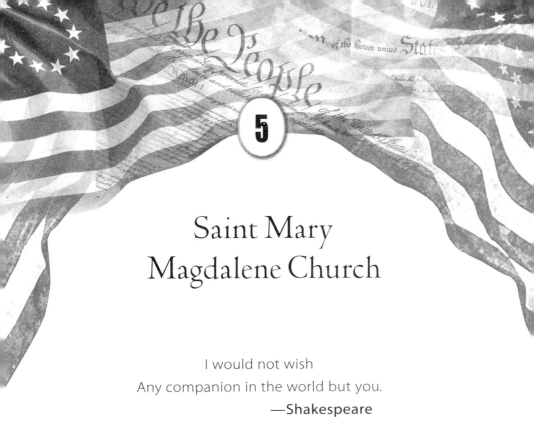

5

Saint Mary Magdalene Church

> I would not wish
> Any companion in the world but you.
> —Shakespeare

May 20, 1628

Samuel and Mary were wed in the afternoon on the twentieth of May at the Church of Saint Mary Magdalene in a service performed by John Maplett's personal friend and former bishop of London George Montaigne. In her hair, Mary wore traditional wildflowers and wheat sheaves, which had been brought in from the country that morning.

Saint Mary Magdalene Church

The couple displayed an extraordinary and unusual connection, joining their hands continuously from the recitation of their vows to the cake celebration. Theirs was a wedding of romance and happiness, not a typical display for this church and in this time. It seemed the world was at their feet, with a successful haberdashery business, friends of power and education, and a true romantic connection. Their entire future lay before them, and they felt they could take on anything that came.

Mary looked around and studied the church she had attended since her earliest memories. Just two months earlier, she would not have guessed she could be here today in this ceremony. Deep inside, she was content and happy in a way that she had not thought possible.

The ceremony was followed by eating, drinking ales, and baroque music. The culmination of the celebration centered on the ritual of the cake, which was really a large collection of buns. Samuel and Mary stood on opposite sides of the buns, with the stated task of kissing. According to ritual, if they were able to kiss, they would be blessed with many children. And so they did.

". . . We'll have five children," Mary said.

"Seven, if I believe *this* wedding cake," Samuel jokingly corrected her.

"Ugh! I shall be with child for the next twenty years if I am to believe this cake!" Mary shot back. They both laughed.

"Anyway, if I have my way, and I think I shall, there'll be four little boys and two little girls . . . and they'll be named George, Thomas, John, Charles, Elizabeth, and Anne. They will be the most well-mannered and best-educated children in all of London," Mary said.

"What if they don't grow up in London?" Samuel said, suddenly serious.

Not catching on to his change in tone, Mary asked, "Quit your joking. What a preposterous suggestion! Where on earth else would they grow up?"

"What about the New World?" Samuel suggested, thinking about his conversation with Robert Rich.

"The colonies?" Mary asked, totally shocked by the suggestion.

"What an adventure if, in a few years, we sailed across the sea to the colonies so that we might live and worship as we truly believe? Why not give our children the hope of a better future and perhaps even freedom from the oppression of King Charles and the Church of England one day?" As he spoke, Samuel played with his new bride's curls. He always wondered how she could look lovelier each day than she had the day before, but she always seemed to manage it. Today, she was more beautiful than he could have imagined in her white lace gown with mocha underlay. For the wedding ceremony, she had worn a long, lace veil that reached nearly down the aisle from the altar. John Maplett had his seamstress make up the finest ruffle dress shirt, silk jacket, matching dress pants, and stockings for Samuel. They both looked as fancy and dapper as possible in their wedding clothes.

"Samuel Gorton . . . Can you possibly be serious in this comment, or are you simply speaking from the intoxication of ales and our marriage?" Mary asked, astonished.

"I assure you, Mary Gorton, I am quite serious indeed." Samuel did not smile. "I had a visit from the Earl of Warwick in the haberdashery last week. He has significant investments in the New World and has filled my imagination with adventure, freedom, and a new way of life."

"I've always believed I would live a life of adventure," Mary mused. "Still, we have a comfortable existence here in London, with friends, family, and a business to sustain us. Life in the colonies is so treacherous and dreadful."

"We are blessed indeed, dear wife, and now we have been granted the will to commence the adventure together. It can be any adventure we choose, be it on the cobblestone streets of London, the sparse ruts of Manchester, or the wilderness of the Americas."

"I think with father's wish that we run his haberdashery, we shall be relegated to the streets of London, enhanced by the manuscripts of the great writers. Wherever we roam, dear husband, I expect life with you shall be a great adventure."

"It will indeed, Mary Gorton. It will indeed," Samuel exclaimed, standing up and picking up his new bride. Her laughter echoed and filled the celebration hall from the tile floor all the way up to the high ceilings as Samuel carried her back inside and up the stairs to spend their first night together as husband and wife.

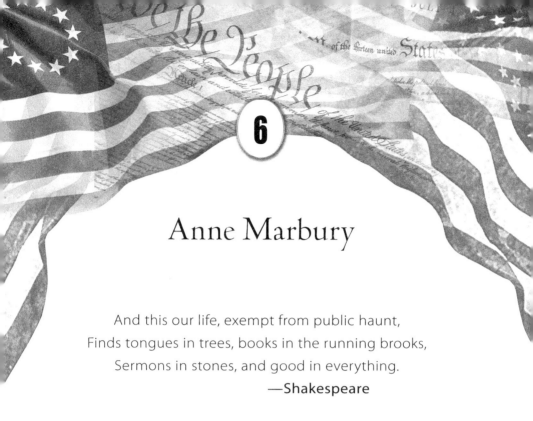

6

Anne Marbury

> And this our life, exempt from public haunt,
> Finds tongues in trees, books in the running brooks,
> Sermons in stones, and good in everything.
> —Shakespeare

1634

Anne Marbury Hutchinson watched as cattle and provisions were loaded on the *Griffin*, a three-mast ship that had made the trip from England to the New World several times. Unlike many of the ships that would carry people and supplies to the New World, the *Griffin* was a veritable luxury liner.

Anne Marbury Hutchinson

Just a year earlier, Anne's eldest son, Edward, had made the journey across the Atlantic to New Boston along with his uncle. As she observed the flurry of activities this day, it occurred to her that within an hour, she would be boarding the *Griffin* and leaving her home country for the last time. A flood of emotions engulfed her as she turned and studied the hills and town and country connected to the dock. Tears ran down her face with the realization and the memories of her childhood that ran through her mind.

55

1606

Fifteen-year-old Anne Marbury watched her father as he retold the tale she had been hearing her entire life. It was her favorite story, one she never tired of hearing, and one that would guide the course of her life.

"The banging on the door was enough to wake all of our neighbors. Bishop Alymer, Sir Owen Hopton, Archdeacon Lewis, and a host of justices of the peace all arriving with a ruckus to arrest me. I, Francis Marbury, was to be tried for heresy!

"What is heresy, ye ask, darling Anne? I'll tell you! Today a heretic is no more than a man who breaks the supreme law of the church and seeks to undermine Queen Elizabeth. Bishop Alymer claims that I am a heretic because I have rattled the bishop of Peterborough because he and much of the clergy lack any formal education. It is a fact that Peterborough is a buffoon, and Alymer is nothing more than an idiot and a fool.

"Oh, we had our trial, but it was not one that could be conducted with fairness, because the Anglicans see only their perspective. Like the Catholic Church before them, they have become so powerful that they only see their doctrine, not their weaknesses."

"But, Father, don't they burn heretics for their crimes? Why were you not burned at the stake like Joan of Arc?" Anne asked.

"I believe, sweet daughter, that God guided the bishop's hand in this matter. I believe he wanted to have me delivered to the pyre. Instead, I was sentenced to Marshalsea Prison, a dark place filled with smugglers, pirates, thieves, and men accused of sedition. While my two years there were dark and scary, I learned to better control my temper. I think the bishop wanted me to reform, but in retrospect, I only became stronger in my beliefs. It is those beliefs that have ultimately created the fame that delivered us to this esteemed church as vicar, and it was those beliefs that provided the opportunity for me to deliver the sermon during the ascension of King James."

"My daddy, who never gave up his values and beliefs and became preacher to our king!" It was Anne's favorite part of the story. Her daddy,

Anne Marbury Hutchinson's father, Francis Marbury, was sentenced to Marshalsea Prison in London for two years for "heresy"

friend to Sir Francis Bacon, teacher of Captain John Smith, but most importantly, preacher to the King of England!

"You are an unusual and strong-willed young lady, and by virtue of your father and mother, you can read, write, and have been taught to think. This is something that almost no girl in England can say. From my story, the most important lessons for you, Anne, are that you must control your temper, but you must stick to your beliefs."

November 1610

At nineteen, Anne began to focus her studies on medicine and midwifery. For the most part, she spent her days working with her father, helping to write sermons and research scripture. She did maintain one childhood friendship with William Hutchinson, who had recently moved to London from Alford, ostensibly to grow his thriving cloth trade but really to be closer to Anne. Of course, the move to London had transformed Hutchinson from a local merchant to a wealthy proprietor. Had business been a bit slower, Hutchinson would likely have asked Francis Marbury for his daughter's hand, but trade and travel were such that the opportunity was delayed.

Francis Marbury was not oblivious to William's feelings for his daughter, though Anne was. "Anne, that young man William Hutchinson and you have been friends since childhood. I think if you gave him the opportunity, he would surely ask for your hand."

"Father, I fear I would not be a good wife or mother. My passion is working with you, doing research and writing sermons, and I have delivered babies as a midwife and care not for the pain those mothers endure."

"Yes, daughter, you are fond of saying such, but your mother and I both see how you light up when William visits. No one else has that impact on you."

"For now, it is not a question but instead a theory—your theory, Father. I have not been presented with its reality, and I refuse to consume time in speculation. Besides, Father, I am not interested in the business of the cloth but instead in the cloth of the clergy. My friend William is not a member of that cloth."

"A clever lass you are, young Anne!" Francis Marbury smiled. "Clearly your literary wit comes from the Dryden branch of the family."

1612

The death of Anne's father, Francis, in February 1611 hit her very hard. For nearly a year after his death, Anne grieved. William Hutchinson called on her periodically but knew well that she was ready for nothing more than friendship. William's business continued to grow as he began purchasing and selling in many of the major ports across Europe. With travel, he was often gone for weeks at a time. Still, persistence and a warm friendship ultimately prevailed. The couple posted banns and were married in August of 1612.

The Hutchinsons left London and moved to Alford, where they had first met years before. Anne continued her work as a midwife and, in a huge reversal, had fourteen children between 1613 and 1634.

She used her role as a midwife to teach the gospel, thus continuing the passion her father had instilled in her during her upbringing.

While living in Alford, Anne became familiar with a minister named John Cotton, who was preaching in the nearby town of Boston (England, not Massachusetts). The couple attended services as often as they were able to make the twenty-one-mile trek. Around the same time, Anne's brother-in-law, John Wheelwright, began preaching a similar message to that of Cotton. Ultimately, William Laud began to crack down on the preaching of ministers like Cotton and Wheelwright. Cotton was branded a criminal and, in order to avoid prison, embarked for the New World, coincidentally to the town named after his English hometown: Boston.

Anne Hutchinson was already forty-two and pregnant when she and husband William decided to travel to the New World so they might follow their friend, mentor, and exiled preacher John Cotton. She agreed to allow her eldest son, Edward, to go before them but decided to wait until after her fourteenth child was born before making the voyage with William and their remaining children.

Cotton had left because of persecution and possible imprisonment, issues that the Hutchinsons did not face. William Hutchinson had become a successful merchant and had amassed a reasonable amount of wealth. Because of this, the decision the couple and children had made was more complex, but not difficult. For Anne, religious freedom was more important than the successful business.

1634

Anne watched as her children cantered up the gangplank from the dock to the *Griffin*. She took one last look, turned, and boarded, carrying her infant child, Susanna.

The voyage was a relatively simple and comfortable crossing. Once in Boston, the Hutchinsons built what would be one of the largest homes in the colony. Along with that home, they also purchased several tracts of land in the surrounding areas. The family fit well into the growing community. Anne often utilized her midwifing skills, and William began agricultural and livestock businesses along with civil duties for the general court.

In England, Anne Hutchinson had also preached and given conventicles, or private sermons on religious topics, in her home, mostly to women. Anne's popularity amongst the women of Boston soon grew, and before too long, she was hosting several dozen people per week, some of them men. While she had studied under John Cotton, now the most popular minister in Boston, many in the colony did not think women should preach or teach any but the young. As her popularity grew, soon the colorful young nobleman Henry Vane began to attend. Vane was soon elected governor of the colony.

Hutchinson taught that the soul was not directly tied to one's outward behavior. She believed that God spoke directly to believers. Thus, one did not require the guidance of formal ministers. Instead, individuals could build a one-on-one relationship with God. This challenged the established social order and alarmed the mainstream Puritans but was attractive to individuals who maintained primary focus on their occupations and trades.

Reverend Symmes had waited several months to report his beliefs to former Governor Winthrop, but when he did, they were acerbic and detailed. "You should know that this woman has been teaching and now has fifty or sixty people per week coming to her home for religious instruction."

"Reverend, I think you perhaps exaggerate these numbers. I have heard of Mistress Hutchinson teaching women in our community, but how can this be an offense?"

"It is an offense, Governor, because men, not women, are allowed to teach the word of the Bible. It is an offense because men are now attending, and *a woman* is teaching them! Mostly, it is an offense because what she teaches is not consistent with our beliefs. I daresay it is blasphemy. The woman is a heretic and should be charged accordingly."

"Reverend Symmes, the Hutchinsons have been model citizens here in Boston. William has brought great trade and commerce, they own one of the larger homes in our town, and Mistress Hutchinson has midwifed the birth of many children with great skill."

"This must be stopped!" Symmes insisted.

"Let us watch and see what happens. I promise to investigate further and determine if this is a problem we need to address."

When Symmes left his office, John Winthrop sat back in his chair. He agreed wholeheartedly with Symmes that this type of activity needed to be quelled, but he needed to handle this in his own way. He was well aware the Hutchinsons followed the Antinomian view: that believers were saved by their faith alone, so they were not bound to follow religious laws or religious authorities. This was a direct challenge to the Puritan worldview that salvation was not necessarily tied to following religious laws but, instead, through having faith and divine grace. Winthrop considered himself to be a modern-day Moses, leading the first exodus of the Puritan faithful to the New World. He knew well that his mission would not be successful if Hutchinson were allowed to continue. Still, he first needed to find a way to return to the governor's seat. Young Governor Vane was very popular, but he lacked the skills Winthrop had as a lifetime politician.

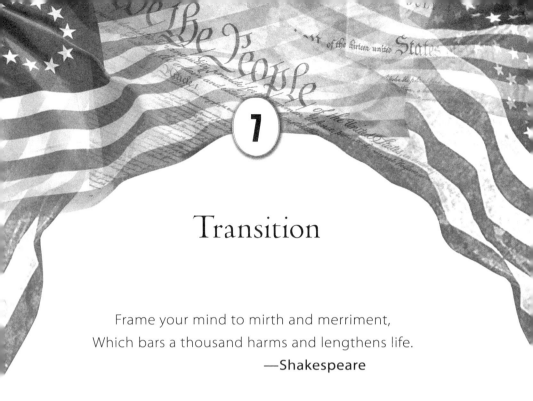

Transition

Frame your mind to mirth and merriment,
Which bars a thousand harms and lengthens life.
—Shakespeare

In the weeks following the wedding, the familiar smell and daily activities at the haberdashery took on a new meaning. Mary came every day during the middle of the day to bring lunch to Samuel. During that period, they would talk nonstop, much to the entertainment of patrons and Mary's father.

"Children, your conversation reminds me of my youth. Our household was always filled with intellectual conversation, debate, and discussions," John told them.

"I have heard a bit about your father, Reverend John Maplett," Samuel offered. "I'd love to learn more."

"Well, m'boy," John began, "Mary's grandfather, John Maplett Senior, was a well-known member of the clergy. Like young Mary here, he had an insatiable appetite for knowledge. When he was not preaching the word of our Lord, he was studying history, astrology, alchemy, and the other sciences. Father was a mentor and teacher to the late Francis Bacon."

"Lord Chancellor Francis Bacon?" Samuel interrupted with incredulity. "Your father knew Sir Francis Bacon?"

"Of course, m'boy. Indeed, he was often in our household when Mary was a younger lass. I am sure she remembers."

"Of course I do, Father," Mary chimed. "Sir Francis was always preaching three things: first, that we should uncover the truth; second, that we should serve our country; and finally, that we should participate in our church."

"Mary's brother John remained close to him up until the time of Lord Bacon's death three years ago," John continued. "I daresay Lord Bacon played a role in young John's education and decision to enter into medical school. He certainly always favored young John."

Samuel's head and mind would swirl as he listened to conversations such as these. It was true that his family was somewhat prominent in the bucolic town of Manchester. Mary's family, on the other hand, lived in a world where they could, if they chose, get an audience with the king himself. For his part, Samuel would have been lucky to earn an audience and speak with the mayor of Manchester.

Over the next year, Mary continued to come to the haberdashery every day. She developed the habit of bringing books on science, education, and literature, which they would read during their lunch visits and continue in the evening hours by the candlelight in their own home.

While he continued to handle all accounting, John Maplett began the process of transferring the daily management of the haberdashery to Samuel. In early November of 1629, Maplett came into the shop after a three-week hiatus. His absence had become the norm and seemed part of the natural course to Samuel.

"Samuel, m'boy, I believe the transition is now complete. The shop is doing well under your stewardship, and it seems you can now handle all activities unrelated to accounting without my oversight."

Samuel grimaced as he tried to understand whether there was a hidden message in his father-in-law's comment. "John, I am quite comfortable in the daily operations but recognize, in spite of the partnership, that this is your business, and I am your employee. I believe, out of respect for what you have built, I need to keep it that way."

John slapped Samuel three times on the back, an act that Samuel had come to expect in all meetings with his beloved father-in-law.

"M'boy, I have come to love you as a son. Unfortunately, it is likely clear to her siblings that Mary has been my favorite. Still, you must know my health is beginning to fail, and I do not know how much longer I will be in London before meeting our Lord above."

"John, you are rambling," Samuel started to say, and then he stopped to study the serious look on his father-in-law's face, which had suddenly transitioned from familial to serious business partner. "I am sure you have many years remaining on this earth," he added.

"That may be true, but I still do not know the best way to complete this transition. In my will, I have ceded forty shillings to Mary. It is this shop that I worry about. My good friend William King, who understands these legal matters, has advised that I bequeath the haberdashery to Mary. While in principle I agree, that would be an affront to my other children, and this I cannot do."

The impact of what John was saying became clear to Samuel. In the event of John's death, the haberdashery would become an asset to be divided in the estate. "I understand."

"I do have a suggestion, m'boy. None of the other children want to run or own the haberdashery. I started this shop with a fifty-pound inheritance from my father. Clearly, this business is worth more now, but I believe Mary's siblings would be amenable to an appropriate dispensation. I think we should arrange for a loan so that you can purchase Maplett's Haberdashery from my wife and Mary's siblings."

"I do not know if I could do that, sir. My mother and father have raised me strictly to never borrow or make loans. The concept is simply against most everything I believe and, if I must say so, abhorrent."

"M'boy, I have come to admire your candor and purity, but while I am in agreement with your perspective, my enduring goal is the care of young Mary and my grandchildren to come," John stated flatly. "I have an acquaintance by the name of John Duckingfield. He seems a good and decent sort, and he has been known to make such arrangements."

"I just don't know if I can do this, John."

"I understand, son. Just promise me that you will consider it so that your wife and future children do not lose their position in London's society."

Samuel studied his father-in-law. In his eyes, he could see a deep love for his daughter Mary and her pathway to the future. While he and his young bride had, on many occasions, discussed moving to the wilderness, those discussions were little more than wild aspirations and had always ended with a resolve to stay in London, where their future was more secure. Furthermore, the question of doing so had always been clearly negated by discussions with John. He always had excellent and convincing arguments that dispelled all thoughts of leaving the safety and stability of London.

"OK, John, I promise to consider it," Samuel acquiesced.

"Excellent!" John hugged and then slapped Samuel three times on the back. "Besides, you are correct that I plan to live a long time whilst you generate income in this shop!" He wrote Duckingfield's name and address on a small sheet of parchment, handed it to Samuel, placed his hat on his head, grabbed the walking cane from the corner, and departed with a guffaw.

It was the last time John Maplett would visit the place of business that had maintained his family's livelihood for a generation. Under his stewardship, Maplett's had become the favorite haberdashery of the noble and royal class and a recognized fixture on Milk Street in London.

January 18, 1630

Mary's brother, John Maplett, had come to look up to Samuel and see him as an older brother—this in spite of the promising career he was developing as a medical doctor and the favor he had earned in King Charles's court. Young John and Samuel had spent many the hour discussing literature, politics, and theology.

On a cold January morning, young John burst into the haberdashery. He did not have to speak. Because his work and responsibilities were such that he never came to the haberdashery, Samuel immediately knew why he was there.

"Samuel, we must close the shop and rush to the parish of St. Lawrence. Father is on his deathbed."

The funeral of John Maplett was a significant event in London. In the late 1500s, his father had become a renowned member of the London educated class, touching the lives of many from London's elite. As such, Maplett's Haberdashery had become the clothing store of choice for most of London's wealthy and powerful.

Amongst Maplett's children, young John had begun to distinguish himself as a medical student who would ultimately become personal physician to King Charles and his French wife, Queen Henrietta Maria.

The haberdashery itself was often frequented by the educated, the elites, and the royalty, most of whom viewed Maplett as an equal. Samuel thought he had come to understand the link between his father-in-law and many of the patrons of the shop, but he was caught off guard by the number of lords who insisted on speaking at the funeral. Maplett had been a truly influential member of the London community who was appreciated and would be genuinely missed.

⟫•◦•⟪

Over the next two years, the disposition of John Maplett's estate would slowly be relegated by John's wife, Mary, who had been named the executrix, along with the help of John's friend and legal advisor, William King. Recognizing that the haberdashery was the sole source of income for Samuel and Mary Gorton, the executors took every measure to buy time for the young couple. While they lived a very comfortable life, Samuel and Mary had saved what they could to pay her siblings, but the shop was simply not producing enough to fully dispense with the amounts required to be distributed. Samuel considered asking his friend Robert Rich, Earl of Warwick, to become an investor and part owner in the shop, but Rich was struggling with his own issues both in Parliament and with his investments in the New World. Ultimately, in 1633, Samuel was forced to comply with the promise made three years earlier to the late John Maplett and meet with John Duckingfield for the purpose of securing a hundred-pound loan to pay Mary's siblings and mother for the haberdashery. The arrangement called for monthly payments followed by full payment on the one-year anniversary of the loan. It was an atrocious instrument, scheduled to cost the Gortons 135 pounds but ending up costing nearly 190. This was a huge amount of money and particularly for a man of Gorton's stature.

By the middle of 1634, it was clear that the shop had not been generating enough revenue to pay Duckingfield in full. Samuel and Mary were desperately working to find solutions. Both had been raised with the belief that borrowing and lending were aberrations, but both also recognized it had been necessity to secure the loan. It had been a risk both agreed to, but one that had caused much consternation.

This was also an important period that would train the couple for the challenges of life ahead. Mary Gorton was a strong woman in her own right and was proving an educational force in Samuel's life. Like Samuel, she had the ability to think through problems and derive solutions. Where she had an advantage was her knowledge of London culture and the associated business dynamics. Samuel came to rely on Mary as his confidant and prime advisor.

One month before the principal on the loan was due, Duckingfield showed up at the haberdashery. "You will pay your debt, Gorton, or I will have you publicly charged with corruption and thievery."

Gorton had studied law and knew that, although perhaps unjustified just yet, there was merit in what Duckingfield had said. "Sir, I have paid thirty pounds of this debt and will work to continue such payments until you are paid in full. You can count me as an honest man."

"I count you as a scoundrel who does not have the capacity to pay his debts!" Duckingfield threatened in a sour tone. "What you have paid does not even amount to the interest on the amount you owe. The full principal of one hundred pounds is still due in full and should be paid before the end of next month."

Samuel felt a knot in the pit of his stomach. All that he had sacrificed to give Duckingfield had amounted to less than a net zero. He had worked diligently to repay the debt, but clearly this man would accept nothing short of admonishing Samuel and Mary for their efforts.

Later that evening, Mary and Samuel discussed the situation. "I think, perhaps," Mary suggested, "that if we sell many of our personal belongings, we can secure a stay in his demand. Do you think Duckingfield would give us six months?"

"To what end, my dear?" Samuel asked. "This is a desperate and angry man who does not listen to the voice of reason or hear the peaceful whisper of God's word."

"This I know, but it is a problem of our own making, my dear," Mary answered. "We took the loan so as to keep the haberdashery, but perhaps that was folly. Have you considered that the perfect comfortable life we believed London would afford us is not so perfect?"

Samuel considered what Mary was saying. Since John's death, life in the haberdashery had been a constant struggle. Income generated had been divided amongst her mother and the siblings. Now that Mary's mother and siblings were paid off, most of the income went to Duckingfield.

In addition to the financial woes, after assuming the role of Bishop of London in 1628, William Laud had begun asserting oppressive doctrines unfavorable to many. Many of Laud's changes seemed a return to the ways of the Roman Catholic Church. The Protestant revolution still burned strong in many who viewed the Catholic Church as corrupt. Indeed, the many Puritans that had fled England during the last few years suggested that Laud was responsible for an acceleration of movement to the relative wilderness of the New World. To make matters worse, Laud had just been promoted to the highest religious post in England. As the Archbishop of Canterbury, his tyranny would know no boundaries in England.

Given their debt to Duckingfield and Laud's escalating religious tyranny, Samuel began again seriously considering a notion he and Mary had discussed with frivolity in the past. "Mary, we have two children and a third on the way. Dare we consider our long-held dream of moving to the Americas?"

Mary did not dismiss the notion. "I think perhaps God is sending us an ardent message, my husband. I know many of our kindred spirits who have fled to the colonies to escape Archbishop Laud's travesty of justice. John Cotton has now departed for Boston, along with Anne Hutchinson and John Wheelwright. Over the years, we have come to admire them and their teachings, and now they have departed our beloved country. Is it reasonable that we be far behind them?"

"You always wanted to travel to eastern England to hear Cotton and meet Anne Hutchinson," Samuel responded. "Alas, is it now the case that I shall have to take you across the ocean so that might finally happen?"

"Let us observe the hand of God, as he clearly moves us in that direction: west to the colonies."

Samuel thought for a moment, then responded. "I have always believed we don't fail until we quit, and we should never quit anything important . . ."

"This is not quitting, Samuel," Mary encouraged him. "Instead, it is finally embarking on the adventure we always dreamed of. I daresay the move to the colonies will hold far more significant challenges than these petty problems in London."

"I think you are correct, my pearl. Coming from your wise lips, I shall consider it to be a mandate. Much as I hate to leave our comfortable and familiar surroundings in London, I believe you are correct that it is now time. I should first like to consult with Robert Rich so we can make appropriate plans before we finalize a move west." Samuel knew that saying they would move to the colonies was one thing, but implementation of that plan was yet another.

Samuel met with Duckingfield and convinced him to provide an extension. The Gortons sold belongings and made arrangements for a large payment of forty pounds, which would grant the Gortons six months to secure capital that would retire the loan. It was now in Samuel's control to execute the ultimate solution.

As luck and destiny would have it, and because of the much-revered Maplett family name, Samuel was able to secure a buyer and sell the haberdashery for three hundred pounds to a young apprentice who had family money.

With the sale, Gorton had a family friend draw up a simple document showing the loan was paid in full and arranged a meeting with Duckingfield.

"One hundred pounds will not be sufficient to pay this note, Gorton," Duckingfield protested after reviewing the document.

"This was the agreement, Mr. Duckingfield. I have already paid you seventy pounds, and with this payment of one hundred pounds, you will have earned more than a healthy profit," Gorton answered.

"As I have said, you are a scoundrel who does not pay his debts." Duckingfield frowned.

"I say you are the scoundrel, Mr. Duckingfield, intent on extracting unearned money from an honest man!" Samuel was angry that he was in this position. He had never felt comfortable with the idea of taking a loan, and now that concern had become justified. He also knew that Duckingfield could make his life miserable if he did not meet his demands.

Duckingfield stood, red faced. "I have given you a loan because of my respect for Mary's father. Because of this, you have been able to retain possession of his haberdashery and sell it for a handsome profit."

"What amount would satisfy you?"

"I will take no less than 125 pounds today. Tomorrow, it will be more," Duckingfield demanded, feeling he had the upper hand.

"That is an absurd request and a profane amount!" Samuel fought to control his temper. "I will give you 110 pounds today if you sign this agreement and release," Samuel negotiated.

"No," Duckingfield countered adamantly. "I will not take less than 120 pounds." He started to walk to the door.

"Agreed, then. One hundred twenty pounds, and you sign the agreement absolving me and my family from all debt," Gorton acquiesced as he worked to control his temper.

Duckingfield turned, grabbed the quill and parchment, signed, took his money, and, without another word, left the room.

Samuel smiled as Duckingfield left the shop. It had been a mistake to take the loan, but it was a valuable lesson learned. He hoped that he would not hear from or see Duckingfield again in this lifetime.

All in all, things had gone better than he expected. Not only had he found a buyer for the shop but he had the opportunity to continue working as a paid employee of the haberdashery for up to a year as he and Mary awaited the birth of their third child. Most importantly, this opportunity gave them time to prepare for the move to the New World.

⫸•⫷

1636–37

"You should have come to me, Gorton," Robert Rich said. "I would have happily invested in your haberdashery, but I will say I am happier you have chosen the path to the New World."

"What can you tell me about where we should settle?"

"I could use you in my southern endeavors. We have many a man, but not many good men," the Earl of Warwick offered.

"The Mosquito Coast sounds intriguing. Would it be a good place for my family?"

Rich frowned, considering this. "I think not. Knowing you as I do, I would suggest Boston. The population there has grown to perhaps a couple thousand. While I have not yet been, I did play a role in securing the patent for the colony." Rich studied his friend, who was nodding, then continued his description. "A few years ago, they established a park, which they now call Boston Common. They have the beginnings of a school where the children could study Latin, mathematics, and theology. I understand that John Harvard of the Charleston Colony has provided resources to start a college in Boston."

"These are good things, my friend. Perhaps Boston is not the wilderness I had anticipated."

Forefathers & Founding Fathers

"There is, of course, the added benefit of a tavern, operated by an experienced proprietor named Samuel Cole. There are two inns that house newcomers and even a small hospital to treat the sick."

"This all sounds promising. Yes, I think we shall endeavor to Boston."

"Indeed, Samuel. I think Boston is the place for you, but perhaps not as a haberdasher."

Over the next couple of months, Samuel reported to the haberdashery every day as employee and master trainer to the new owner. While his employment would continue until the fall of 1636, he would take a break after a few months to celebrate the birth of his third child.

Samuel sat in his favorite Elizabethan chair with young Sam, now five years old, perched on one leg and his daughter, Mary, now three, on the other.

"Samuel, I know we have discussed names for this baby, but I have a new thought as we look forward."

"I thought we agreed to name the baby John if it were a boy or Anne if it were a girl," Samuel reminded her.

"I am quite certain this baby will be a girl," Mary said. "I want this daughter to be named Mahershallalhashbaz Gorton."

"Named what?" Samuel asked, thinking Mary was playing an intellectual joke that he failed to understand. "What kind of joke or riddle is this?"

"This is not a joke but, instead, a real name with historical significance. It is a name from the ancient Hebrew text Isaiah."

"I do not recall a name such as that in my readings, dear wife. Can you explain to me this significance?" Samuel persisted. "This is an unusual name and will certainly bear impact on our daughter's future."

"I consider this to have a double meaning. The name has a meaning: *hurry to the spoils*. By extorting us so cruelly as we carried this baby, Duckingfield has changed the course of our lives. With this change, we now finalize our plans to leave England and head to the New World for a true adventure."

"I understand, my wife. Can I assume the second meaning is a variation on the word 'spoils' as we move our fortune to the New World?"

"Your intuition is correct on this matter. With the birth of Mahershallalhashbaz Gorton, we shall hurry to the opportunities of the New World."

"Alas, this will test my abilities at spelling," Samuel added.

And so it was that during this time of struggle, with the young Gorton family being forced into the reality of uprooting from their home in London, the third child of Samuel and Mary Gorton took the name of Mahershallalhashbaz Gorton, called Marsha or Maher.

<hr />

It was a quiet, gloomy, typical winter day early in March of 1637 when Samuel Gorton walked through the doors at Maplett's Haberdashery for the last time. A full seven months had passed since his last day of working there, but he felt compelled to visit one more time before beginning his journey across the expansive ocean.

As he walked in the door, his senses were flooded with the familiar smell, dank mood, and sights. A new apprentice named William Littlefield was working the front while the new owner was at the fair buying product.

"Ah, Mr. Gorton, welcome!" Littlefield greeted him. "Is there something I can get for you today?"

"Greetings, William," Samuel responded. "I just felt compelled to drop in one more time before our departure to the New World."

"Of course, sir. When do you embark on that treacherous voyage?"

"Tomorrow, actually, but I would not call it treacherous. I think adventurous is the better term." Samuel looked around the shop. The new owner had not changed much, though Samuel was annoyed to see a stack of papers in the corner where old Mr. Maplett always set his walking cane.

"Well, sir, if I may say so, I do not understand why you would go to that godforsaken place when you had so much opportunity here in London."

Samuel studied the young man for a moment. "Well, m'boy, I suppose I have a lesson for you. You should never allow the opportunities of the past to eclipse the adventures in your future." Samuel smiled to himself as he thought about the wise words that he had just spoken. Perhaps John Maplett was touching him one last time, here in the shop where it had all begun.

"Do you mind if I write that down, sir?" William grabbed his quill. "I think you said I should never allow the opportunities of my past to eclipse the adventures of my future. Is that correct, sir? Is that your own saying?"

"It is correct, and I have just made it up." Gorton once again smiled at his own cleverness.

"Thank you, sir. It is a good saying, and I shall cherish it." William Littlefield turned to focus on a customer who had just walked in the door, but he turned back briefly to Gorton. "I wish you a safe journey, sir."

"Thank you, William Littlefield, and a good life to you." As he walked out the door, a tear came to Samuel Gorton's eye. This place that had meant so much to him, and that had been such a pivotal point in his life, would now become part of the past. Samuel knew that when he exited these doors today, he would not likely enter them again.

Nine years earlier, Samuel Gorton had walked into Maplett's Haberdashery for the first time. When he did, Samuel had no idea how significant that decision would be. Maplett's Haberdashery had been the place he had built a relationship with John Maplett, which in turn had led to his marriage to Mary. Now, with Mary at his side, Samuel was ready to face the new challenges of the New World, whatever they might be.

8

Per Aspera ad Astra

(Through Hardships to the Stars)

> What pleasure, sir, find we in life,
> to lock it From action and adventure?
> —Shakespeare

Samuel, his wife Mary, and their three children, along with their housekeeper, Ellen Aldridge, and Samuel's older brother, Thomas, all gathered in the dining room at the Maplett house. Thomas had lost his wife a few years earlier and had become enthralled in the idea of traveling to the New World. Samuel welcomed his older brother's interest and support in the endeavor. Ellen Aldridge had been with Mary since her early childhood. She had, in fact, become the nursemaid for the Gorton children, and while not excited about the journey, she simply insisted on joining the family to their new home.

Mary Maplett had prepared a feast for their departure, but the mood was somber, held by the belief this would be their last time together. Even the normally energetic children were nervous about the weeks they would spend on the ocean.

The Gorton family boarded the ship on the Thames just east of London. They departed with high hopes of a five-week voyage across the Atlantic to a promising new home in America. It was a typical day in the early spring of 1637. The sun had been hiding behind the

Winthrop Fleet

English clouds for the better part of the last three months, yet spirits and expectations were high. Within days, the weather changed for the worse, the prevailing winds turned against them, and their small ship experienced one of the more difficult transatlantic crossings to date. During the several weeks of the voyage, they were subjected to endless, raging storms, some of which pushed the ship off course and others of which seemed determined to push her all the way back to London. All in all, the end result was an extended journey and a delayed arrival at Massachusetts Bay.

There were numerous reasons why the passengers prayed for favorable winds to deliver them to their destinations. The passenger compartment had been originally designed as a munitions and cargo hold. It was an overcrowded single room where everyone spent most of the days and slept wherever they could find space to do so. Often, the hold leaked, and sleeping was done in wet bedding. There was little light, and the air was always dank and putrid. There were no bathrooms on the ship. While the ship carried barrels of "clean" water, by the end of the second week at sea, most was not potable, so everything was mixed with ale to kill bacteria. Bathing, if done at all, was in salt water, and most of the passengers wore the same clothing during the entire journey. Because the ship relied on winds, there were days when virtually no progress was made on the voyage and even days when winds forced the ship in the opposite direction.

Mary and Samuel quite often found themselves escorting their little ones up to the main deck to hurl their most recent meal over the edge due to the rotten smells or the violent rocking of the ship. Many passengers beneath the deck began showing signs of scurvy, and Mary worried about her little family. She spent much of her time trying her best to keep them healthy and steer them clear of those who had contracted the various maladies common at sea. Two passengers died before they reached the halfway point, and this added greatly to the weight on Samuel and Mary's shoulders. The transatlantic voyage would, once again, test the strength of their relationship and the resolve of Mary Elizabeth Maplett Gorton. Samuel, while a strong and persistent force, was made even stronger by Mary, who managed to stay strong and optimistic.

Each day on the ship was a torture for the passengers, while the crew seemed to find joy in their misery. The journey seemed as if it would never end. Everyone longed for land and prayed for it daily, sometimes hourly. Even the novice passengers learned the value of winds at their back or of crosswinds that would provide tack and motility to shorten their prison sentence on the ship. The common feeling amongst the passengers was that if they had known how grueling the journey would be, perhaps they would have stayed home. Each day, someone would ask the captain his expectations on the remaining length of the voyage, and each day, he would make patient projections and calculations.

The Gortons arrived in Boston on May 10, 1637. The family sat upon the dock, not knowing how to transition back to walking on solid ground. The children giggled at their unstable "sea legs," but Mary grumbled and groaned, feeling dizzy and sick from the change.

Samuel stood with Mary and his brother Thomas, surveying their new American home while the children played at walking again under Ellen's watchful eye. Behind them was the clear, crisp ocean air, intermingled with the smells of the growing colony. With dirt roads and wooden structures for homes, businesses, and church, all surrounded and fenced in with roughshod pickets, the Bay Colony was a stark contrast to London's cobblestone streets and ornate rock buildings protected with a rock-wall fortification around the city center. Still, even with its rustic wilderness look and population of a few thousand, Boston was a welcome sight after three months at sea. This was the New World, and now that the difficult

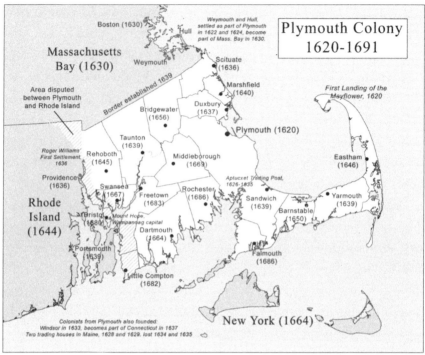

Plymouth Bay Colony

journey had ended, the Gortons could begin to build and plan a new life of religious freedom safely distant from the archbishops and royalty of England.

For the new Massachusetts Bay Colony, it was a time of growth and transition. There were constant squabbles as the church controlled both religious and government decisions. Unfortunately, the Gortons soon found that Boston was, in many ways, more oppressive than the Anglican Church in London. It seemed that the leadership of the Bay Colony favored strict rules and harsh punishments, but these viewpoints were not unanimously supported. Author Samuel Groom chastised the Boston intellectuals, stating that they had moved to the New World to escape religious bigotry only to create an environment even more harsh than that found in the Old World. The authoritarian church and harsh punishments here mirrored those going on in the Spanish Inquisition.

A longtime admirer of Anne Hutchinson and some of the other enlightened thinkers who had relocated to the Boston colony, Mary

Gorton had looked forward to the possibility of meeting with Hutchinson and participating in the growth of her teachings.

"I think we should seek counsel from Cotton, Coddington, Hutchinson, or Wheelwright," Thomas Gorton suggested.

"Yes, brother, that is what we should do," Samuel responded. While Thomas was the older brother, Samuel had become significantly more accomplished and educated. As such, Thomas generally deferred to Samuel's perspective, treating him as if he were the older sibling.

Finding Hutchinson, who now owned a prestigious home near the center of town, was an easy task. Two days after arriving in Boston, Samuel attended a private service in the Hutchinsons' home. He was surprised that Anne, a woman, was openly conducting the service and that nearly thirty men and women were in attendance, including her husband and her brother-in-law, John Wheelwright. It did not take long for him to understand the significance of Hutchinson's delivery. She was a knowledgeable and passionate speaker who managed to keep her audience focused and enthralled with her religious and educational teachings.

As Hutchinson spoke, she portrayed perspectives similar to those held by Samuel and Mary. After the service, he introduced himself to John Wheelwright. Samuel could tell that these were people who had come to the New World for reasons similar to his own, seeking freedom for all individuals, not just specific groups.

"Mr. Gorton, if you and your wife have time, perhaps we should stay around and continue our discussions," John Wheelwright suggested. "I would also like to introduce you to another couple with whom I believe you will find affinity." He motioned to a man and woman on the other side of the large room in the Hutchinson house.

"This is William and Mary Dyer. They have been in the colony for three years now and hold similar perspectives to your own. Perhaps more importantly, Mary Dyer is well educated, like your Mary Gorton."

Samuel exchanged greetings with the Dyers, and they compared notes on the parts of England in which they had all been raised.

As the great room in the Hutchinson house cleared, Wheelwright joined the conversation with the Dyers and Gorton. "I would very much enjoy it if perhaps we could all sit and continue our discussions."

"I do have time." Samuel sat down at a hewn wooden bench in the Hutchinson home alongside his brother Thomas. He glanced over and noted that Mary Gorton had begun to engage in what appeared to be an enlightened conversation with Anne. Samuel smiled as he watched the two women talk. Mary had been nervous about meeting Hutchinson, but Samuel had been confident that the two would find significant commonalities, and it seemed that he had been correct.

"Have you begun to develop a plan for your new life yet?" Wheelwright inquired, continuing his conversation with Samuel.

"Mary and I have followed the teachings of Reverend Cotton. Like you, we left England to escape the mandates being established by Bishop Laud."

"Can I assume I am correct in my initial observation that Mrs. Gorton is educated?" John asked while studying Mary and Anne from across the room.

"Very much so. I am educated myself, but I would daresay she is more so than me," Samuel answered. "Not only that, but Mary has an uncanny ability to see through most problems. I have come to rely on her in a very significant way."

"I as well," Thomas added.

"So it would seem," Wheelwright observed. "Mrs. Gorton and Mrs. Hutchinson are not conventional women. Their influence will be like that of a magnet here."

"That is good," Samuel smiled. "Mary has long heard about your movement in eastern England and wanted to attend sermons. I have joked that rather than traveling a day across solid ground, I have instead embarked on a lifetime voyage to this distant colony."

"Better here than there. Laud has done much to suppress our beliefs in England. But back to my original question: What is your plan?" John asked again.

"We were hoping to establish a home here in Boston," Samuel answered.

Forefathers & Founding Fathers

"Tell me a bit more about yourself, Mr. Gorton."

"I was born just outside of Manchester in Lancashire. Father cultivated the land and had sufficient resources and willingness to support my goal of a modest education, where I focused on theology and law. After that, I chose to apprentice as a haberdasher. I moved to London and took a partnership with John Maplett's haberdashery in central London."

"Yes," Wheelwright broke in. "I know the shop and am very familiar with the Mapletts, a family worthy of distinction whom I hold in great regard."

"It was during my apprenticeship that John Maplett decided I would be a good husband for his daughter, Mary," Samuel added.

"Ah, and now I understand a bit more about Mary *Maplett* Gorton."

"It wasn't until after we were married that I began to fully grasp the position of her family in the London hierarchy, but it was Mary's education and enlightened thinking that attracted me to her. Perhaps I would have been comfortable living in London, but she has inspired me to do more."

"You have mentioned that you were followers of Cotton. Can you tell me a bit more about your fundamental beliefs?"

Samuel was beginning to understand why Wheelwright was probing, and because of his awareness of the current problems brewing in Boston, he decided to be open in his response.

"We left London because we were concerned about the corruptions and teachings of Archbishop Laud and the direction he was taking the Anglican Church. We came here with the belief that this New World should support religious freedom. I am perhaps even more radical in that I also believe women should be given more rights in the New World. Further, I have grave concerns about government playing too big a role in the church and the church overseeing the government."

Wheelwright closed his eyes and nodded as he digested what Gorton had just said. "Let me say two things. It is important that you make note of the fact that this colony is ruled and governed by the Puritans."

"I am a man of deep faith, but I do not think people can properly practice their personal beliefs in a theocracy," Gorton clarified.

"It is an interesting thought, but perhaps one that you should be very careful about articulating in this colony."

"And I thank you for your advice on that matter," Samuel answered without committing one way or another. "What is the second thing?"

"Yes, of course." John smiled. "It is true that many have left England for the very reasons you have expressed—that is, with the exception of a woman's role in the church and decisions of state." He glanced over at Anne Hutchinson. "You should be aware that Anne Hutchinson is an exception, and one not appreciated by the local government."

"I will remind you that the greatest period in English history was during the reign of Queen Elizabeth," Samuel interjected.

"Indeed, Mr. Gorton, and you have just heard my sister-in-law speak, which should give credence to your thinking on this matter. Still, I suspect it will be a long time before women have the rights and responsibilities of which you speak." Again, he glanced at Anne, who now was actively engaged in conversation with Mary.

<hr />

Over on the other side of the room, Anne Hutchinson and Mary Gorton had been getting acquainted with great pleasure. Mary Gorton expressed how she had long wanted to meet Anne Hutchinson, Reverend Cotton, or Reverend Wheelwright and explained how she had been educated by her father. "I wanted to debate," Mary said, "but I could not express my views on the streets of London without fear of lashings or worse, though my grandfather was a well-known educator and a reverend."

The two women discovered Anne's father and Mary's grandfather had had a mutual friend in Sir Francis Bacon and that Anne's husband, William, had used to frequent Maplett's Haberdashery. Anne was always pleased when new women attended her conventicles, but she felt a special interest in young Mrs. Gorton.

"Tell me about your husband, Mrs. Gorton," she asked.

Mary smiled. "Samuel is a brilliant, God-fearing, and hardworking man, but we try not to mention that around him!" Both women laughed. "I am certain he would want to meet you, Mrs. Hutchinson," Mary added.

"Well, shall we go make that happen?"

The two women walked over to where Samuel had been talking to John Wheelwright.

"Samuel, may I present Anne Hutchinson?"

"I have enjoyed discussion with your wife, Mr. Gorton. She will be a valuable asset to our Boston community."

"Thank you, Mrs. Hutchinson. I am quite proud of her education, wit, and forward thinking," Samuel responded while smiling at Mary. It seemed this was a good start to their life in Boston.

"Mr. Gorton was telling me about some of his goals and beliefs," said John. He stopped and turned to Samuel. "Please finish what you were saying."

"My goal is to contribute to building this new colony, and I plan to commit myself and my resources to that successful end." Samuel explained.

"And welcome those resources might be. For now, though, we must attend to pressing matters," said Anne. She stopped momentarily and then continued, "I trust we will see you again tomorrow?"

"Indeed. We shall look forward to the opportunity," Samuel answered.

<hr />

In his first three days, Gorton had learned much about the governance and current unrest in the colony. Clearly, there were struggles between Hutchinson, who had become known as an *Antinomian*, and the mainstream Puritans. But he felt confident that, because of support from recently elected Governor Vane, the Antinomians would ultimately prevail.

Governor Henry Vane was the son of one of the most powerful men in England, and even though he openly maintained both Puritan values and support of the Antinomians, he retained the support of Archbishop Laud. The whole thing seemed a great contradiction, but with Vane in the governor's seat, Boston was clearly a town where Gorton could live.

The following day, the Gortons returned to the Hutchinson home to once again hear Anne teach and to continue discussions with Wheelwright. Again, she delivered a compelling sermon.

"Another great sermon, Mrs. Hutchinson," Samuel commented.

"Thank you, Mr. Gorton. As you might have guessed, it is a great passion of mine, and the ability to speak the Lord's word, I believe, is a gift."

"Indeed. It is a true blessing that in this colony we are able to express ourselves freely, as we were unable to do in England," Samuel observed.

"Unfortunately, Mr. Gorton, I believe the question of our ability to freely express ourselves is currently under debate," Wheelwright responded. "You may be aware that Mr. Winthrop would love to quash our activities and return to a Boston colony that strictly adheres to a Puritan-only code. Just four days ago, the general court convened in an attempt to find me guilty of contempt and sedition. They failed, but you should recognize the winds of change in this colony are much like those winds that carried you across the ocean to Boston. On some days, they seem to be firmly at your back, and then, without warning, they turn and push you into a passing storm."

"Indeed, I am aware, but Winthrop is no longer governor, and Mr. Vane seems a man of great presence," Samuel said. "It is my observation that he supports our cause and, therefore, the tide of change is against the fundamental Puritanism."

Anne Hutchinson spoke up. "I fear you may be wrong, Mr. Gorton. In the constantly shifting winds, John Winthrop has managed to convene a session that will be held in Newton two days hence on May 17. Winthrop is a clever man with far more political experience than Governor Vane, and he would dearly like to regain his title as governor."

"This is not good. What will become of these daily services if Winthrop returns to power?" Samuel asked Anne Hutchinson.

"The services will most assuredly end," Wheelwright responded for Hutchinson. "Worse, the penalty might even be death."

John Wheelwright's statement put a pall on the conversation. The people standing around and listening mumbled dissent, but they knew there was little they could do besides pray that Vane would prevail in any conflict with Winthrop.

"Is there anything we can do?" Mary Gorton asked.

"In your case, you are not yet accused," Anne answered. "While we would welcome your support, I would guess the prudent path would be to leave for Plymouth or follow Roger Williams to Providence."

"Who is this Roger Williams?" Samuel asked. "I have heard his name mentioned before."

"He holds similar views of religious freedom but has chosen to move rather than fight to change the orthodoxy. Last year, he founded a colony that he has named Providence Plantations, and he is welcoming any religious minority," Anne responded.

"Have you met him?" Samuel asked.

"I have not, though I hope to someday," Hutchinson responded. "Williams has done a good job of befriending the Narragansett and the Pequot tribes. I have heard that he even speaks their language."

Narragansett Indians receiving Roger Williams

"I will make a point to meet Williams," Samuel decided. "His decision to not fight this Puritan theocracy seems a smart one, though I do not know if that is a pathway I personally could take."

"I am certain his methods are very much unlike your own, my Samuel," Mary chided. "You are much more of a firebrand than pacifist statesman."

"Alas, my wife knows me well and reveals my secrets." Samuel laughed.

For the next two days, the Gortons came each day to the Hutchinson home to hear services. On each day, they spent time afterward talking and discussing how best to turn the Massachusetts Bay Colony into a place of religious freedom. On May 17, word spread quickly that Henry Vane had been ousted, with Winthrop regaining power as governor of the colony.

After their daily service on the eighteenth, Anne strongly advised the Gortons to move on before they became a target. She was familiar with Nathaniel Morton and Edward Winslow of the Plymouth settlement and felt confident the Gortons could find more contentment there and perhaps continue the mission of liberty and religious freedom.

And so, Samuel, along with his family, brother, and housemaid, made arrangements to leave Boston just eight days after their arrival in the New World.

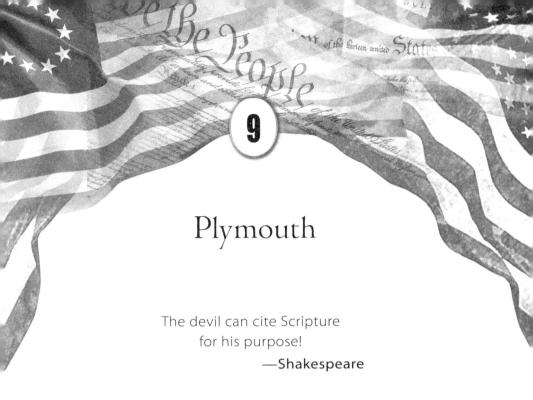

9

Plymouth

> The devil can cite Scripture
> for his purpose!
> —Shakespeare

May 19, 1637

Samuel and Mary had not sailed the treacherous Atlantic in the hold of a cargo vessel to become victims of the Puritan ethic. Fortunately, the next leg of the journey did not require embarking on a ship. For this leg, they purchased a "carriage," a sturdy vehicle, if little more than four wheels and a wooden flatbed.

"Papa, why do we have to leave Boston so soon?" little Samuel asked.

"There is conflict brewing in Boston, children," Gorton told young Samuel and his sister Mary. "We left London so we could find a place to live without conflict. Your mother and I believe that place may be Plymouth."

"And how long will it take to travel from Boston to Plymouth?" little Samuel asked.

"I am told the distance is just over forty miles, but roads here are not like those in England, so we will average only about three to four miles per hour," Gorton answered.

"But don't worry, little Samuel," Thomas added. "The days are long enough so that we can make the journey in a day. We will not need to spend the night out in the wilderness."

"Yes, but how long will it take?" little Samuel persisted.

"All day, son. We will start before the sun rises and hope to reach the Plymouth Colony before dark," Samuel answered.

Before sunrise the following morning, several travelers collected by the gate on the edge of town, all departing at the same time.

"We travel in large groups to discourage the Indians from attacking," Samuel explained to the kids as several families and other merchants all rolled out of town together. "There is currently a war between the colonies and a local tribe known as the Pequot, but those Indians have not commonly engaged in open hostilities with merchants and families. Still, we should maintain a state of readiness and mind ourselves to stay alert."

Traveling from Boston to Plymouth

During the day, the adults walked while the children mostly rode on the wagon and kept an intent and fearful eye on the trees lining each side of the heavily wooded pathway between Boston and Plymouth. The men all carried muskets at the ready, while the women kept reloading materials within close reach.

"Papa, I saw someone move in the woods," young Mary proclaimed in an excited tone about two hours into the trek.

Everything stopped as the settlers prepared for an imminent attack. Within moments, another sighting was made, and after a few minutes, the men collectively decided the prudent course would be to continue on to Plymouth. Tensions remained high as everyone kept a keen eye on the treeline, and many observers confirmed young Mary's observation. This high stress level remained until midday, when the group met with several merchants traveling north to bring wares to the Boston colony.

"Don't worry, we make this trip several times per week," one merchant assured Samuel and his group. "The savages constantly lurk in the woods and watch us. We think they are friendly Narragansett, and it is curiosity on their part more than anything else."

Samuel wondered about use of the term "savages" for the local peoples. He found it objectionable but readily admitted he knew little about the Indians and their customs. Still, he remained alert, and the balance of the day's trek was uneventful. The party arrived in Plymouth right after sunset. It had been a fourteen-hour day. All of the adults ached from the forty-mile walk, but at last, they had arrived at their final destination. They flowed through town to a small inn, where the Gortons would stay until they found a home to rent.

Even though Plymouth had been founded nearly a decade before the Massachusetts Bay Colony, it remained a smaller settlement with a population well under a thousand inhabitants. Plymouth had been founded by radical English Puritans who wished to separate entirely from the Anglican Church so they could worship in a way they felt brought them closer to God, while Boston, on the other hand, had been founded by wealthier, better-educated, mainstream Puritan reformists who wished to remain part of the Anglican Church. Because of this, Boston remained closer to the crown of England and consequently was provided more resources.

Samuel and his family could immediately tell the difference between the town of Boston, which seemed more like London, and the agrarian air of Plymouth. The smaller colony reminded Samuel of his old home near Manchester. Samuel was feeling confident in his ability to integrate as he followed up on a few contacts he had made in Boston to find a home for his family. He settled on a gentleman named Ralph Smith, the landlord of a good-sized homestead outside of town. The home had originally been given to Smith when he served as religious leader for the town, a job from which he had recently been terminated. Because the new minister was not in need of a home, Smith had been allowed to stay. The house was significantly larger than his needs, and because of this, he was happy at the prospect of having the Gorton family living there and paying rent.

"I am happy to rent the larger portion of my home to you, Gorton, but I want a four-year lease and would prefer a renter who can pay and won't create trouble around town. It has been my experience in the colonies that the townsfolk are quite intolerant of anything that fails to meet their standards."

"I understand, Mr. Smith. We have the resources to pay and can make a significant payment in advance."

"What skills have ye?" Smith inquired.

"My formal training was in law and theology, though I did an apprenticeship and became a partner as a haberdasher," Samuel responded.

"Well, you won't find much use for haberdashery skills here in Plymouth," Smith scoffed.

"I grew up the son of a man who was the leading husbandry producer in our part of Manchester. My brother Thomas and I know well how to cultivate the land and tend to livestock. I assume we can provide a livelihood with that skill."

"Indeed, you probably can. I might add that unless your theology is in perfect alignment with the thinking of Reverend Reynor, you'd best keep it to yerself."

"Understood," Gorton replied, with a fair amount of consternation. Was there anywhere religious authorities would not attempt to dictate the worship practices of his family?

"That isn't good enough, Gorton," Smith persisted. "I need to hear ye tell me that you can stay within the local doctrine and abide by Plymouth custom."

Wearily, Gorton agreed. He signed the lease agreement and paid the rent, plus a substantial deposit.

Returning to the inn, Samuel announced to the family that their new home had been secured. Excited, they all packed and began the move into the large home they would share with Ralph Smith and his family. By the time the family was finally spending their first night in the new home, they were all exhausted. Still, they were thrilled to finally be slumbering in their own *real* beds. It had been a long four months leading to this new home in Plymouth.

The morning following that first night in their new home, Samuel awoke as he always did, just before sunrise. He wandered out the back door with a chair and sat watching the light of the sun begin to kiss the horizon and everything beneath it. Then he began to pray. He prayed that his family would be safe in this unfamiliar place, that they would remain healthy, and that his children would grow up stronger and smarter than their parents. He prayed that his perspective on religion, freedom, and government wouldn't endanger his beloved wife or his precious little ones. More importantly, he prayed that his children would grow up to be passionate and to always stand up for their beliefs and their civil liberties. He prayed that his grandchildren would grow up in a New World where they could share their beliefs with their neighbors and where, though they might be different, none would be persecuted.

Silently, Mary came out and sat to his right. She had been so quiet that he didn't even notice she was there until she slipped her hand into his. Briefly, he opened his eyes and looked upon the face of the woman he had fallen for so quickly nine years earlier. He leaned over and kissed her, and then the two of them continued, turning their chairs to face each other, joining hands and praying for their home and their future in this new Plymouth Colony.

It wasn't long before the little ones came out, asking for breakfast. The family christened their new home together by throwing the only ingredients they had—eggs and the fatback of a pig—together in a frying pan. Simple though it was, the unanimous opinion was that it was the best thing they had eaten since their departure from London, and it should be made more frequently. After breakfast was consumed and bellies were full, Mary and Samuel left the children with Ellen—or

Miss Ellen, as the children were required to call her—and went out to explore the town. It was still very much new frontier. Bumpy dirt paths would take a person nearly anywhere they wished, but there weren't many places to go. In town, there was a church, a general store, a town hall, and a small fabric store with a very limited selection. Little homes speckled the edges and outskirts of the town, but the population was still miniscule. Few people were brave enough to live in such harsh conditions, and many of the people who were brave enough died of illness brought on by the chilling New England winters. Luckily, the Gortons had arrived at the start of a mild summer, with enough time to adjust and prepare before the worst of the fall and winter hit.

Once they had reached the center of town, Mary and Samuel decided to go into the church, where they would attempt to meet the pastor. The inside of the church was a simple wooden-frame structure, in stark contrast to some of the ornate cathedrals the Gortons had been inside of in England, but this was no surprise considering the majority of Plymouth settlers were stoic, God-fearing individuals, committed to a simple life that frowned on any activities—such as card games or plays—that they believed did not honor God. They imprisoned themselves to a lifestyle free of any "unnecessary" pleasures or fineries.

Poor little Mary: when the Gorton family had just arrived in Boston, the nearly four-year-old had seen the masses of people dressed in humble grays and blacks, with dark circles under their eyes and frowns upon their pallid faces, and she had been terrified. "Mama," she had asked, a tremor in her sweet voice, "are they ghosts?" While Plymouth was said to be a more progressive town than Boston, thus far, the Gortons had not been able to discern a distinction between them.

Samuel's and Mary's footfalls echoed in the bleak chapel, which was empty aside from the pews, the pulpit, and the cross at the altar. The couple looked at each other, communicating silently how grim they thought this little Puritan church was. Then a man came out of a door in the front corner of the church.

"Hello?" he said, the pitch of his voice turning up in question. *They must not get visitors often,* thought Samuel.

"Hello there. My name is Samuel Gorton, and this is my wife, Mary. We just arrived here from London via Boston, and we were just becoming acquainted with the town. We wanted to meet the pastor of the church we will be attending," Samuel said in introduction.

"Yes, I am he. Reverend Reynor. John Reynor," he said, sounding slightly irritated.

"It's good to meet you," Mary said with a smile and a polite curtsy.

Reynor's eyes widened and blazed, his mouth shrunk, and the color drained from his face.

"Mr. Gorton, was it?" he asked in a voice like a guttural growl.

"Yes, Reverend, Samuel Gorton—" Samuel answered.

"You. Must keep a tighter rein. On your wife." He was trembling and speaking through his teeth, barely intelligible.

Samuel looked at his wife and back to the reverend, appalled. He sidestepped in front of her defensively.

"I beg your pardon, Reverend?" Samuel questioned, his brow furrowing into a frown.

Still trembling, Reverend Reynor erupted, his face now turning fiery red with each word. *"Wives are not to speak out in public! Do you understand, Mr. Gorton?"*

Samuel was stunned by the spontaneous outburst of this man he had only just met. He immediately considered the dichotomy between the enlightened conventicles and conversation in the home of Anne Hutchinson and his first introduction to Reverend Reynor. As calmly as possible, he took his wife's shaking hand, pulled her more completely behind him for protection, and took a step toward the livid reverend. Then, in a firm and defiant tone, he said, "You have made yourself quite clear, Reverend. But, with all due respect, you have no right to demand that my wife remain silent in public."

Samuel could see, seconds after the words had left his mouth, that the reverend was astonished that someone had disobeyed him and then defended it. With a furious holler, the reverend yanked Mary from behind Samuel and drew back his arm. Samuel wasn't sure what was happening until he heard the chilling, sharp sound of skin hitting skin. *Whap!* But Samuel felt nothing until the crippling sound of his wife's scream resounded in the church. Her knees buckled, and she collapsed to the wood floor.

"*Mary!*" Samuel screamed, keeling to the ground beside her, his fists curled tight as he resisted the urge to strike this man of God in his own sanctuary.

Mary's hand was on her cheek, which was hot and pulsing after the impact of Reverend Reynor's hand.

"Are you OK, my love?" Samuel asked, cradling his wife's head in his hands, stroking her hair as he watched a red streak begin to darken her face. He took a deep breath and told himself to remain calm.

She nodded in response, not speaking for fear of being struck again. Samuel turned his head to face the reverend, fighting the tears welling up in his own eyes, containing his anger.

"That ought to teach you both a lesson. Women are not to speak out or show any emotion in public. Men are not to defy their superiors." He stopped for a second to glare first at Mary and then at Samuel. "Welcome to Plymouth. I trust you now understand your position in this community?" Reverend Reynor seemed remarkably calm. A sly smile curled upon his face—almost as if nothing out of the ordinary had happened. "I expect to see you both on Sunday."

Samuel held eye contact with the man, noticing the uncanny green color of his eyes, which at this moment seemed to slightly resemble those of a serpent. When Samuel was unable to muster the words to respond to the detestable man, Reverend Reynor turned on his heels and walked back to his office, clearly quite proud of himself. Once he had left, Samuel gently took Mary's hands and assisted her off the ground, and the couple walked out of the church hand in hand.

It wasn't until after the large oak doors closed behind them that Samuel could clear his head enough to suggest they leave the town of Plymouth immediately.

But Mary disagreed. She said, "This is exactly why we are here, my firebrand husband. I don't even want to think about how many times this has happened before or even how much worse it has been. We came here to give people hope and teach them how to use their voices even when they are told not to speak. I can take it, and so can you."

Samuel shook his head in astonishment at Mary's comment. The anger he felt on her behalf roiled inside him, and he stayed silent as he struggled to rein it in. When they arrived at home, Samuel asked Ellen to mix up some kind of cooling salve that Mary could apply to her cheek to hopefully reduce the bruising and to brew some hot tea with honey. He then demanded that his wife lie down and let him take care of her.

"Samuel, I am fine!" Mary assured him. "You don't need to nurse me back to health. It was a slap, nothing more. We both need to toughen up and prepare ourselves for things like this. I am sure we will see and experience many more situations that will wound our spirits and make us uncomfortable, but we have to learn how to recover quickly and immediately move forward."

"You are an amazing woman, but these things I have prescribed are part of your express recovery plan. Hot tea with honey, just as you like it, and lavender salve," Samuel insisted as Ellen entered the bedroom holding a tray with a teapot, two cups, and a small dish containing the gooey but aromatic salve.

"Thank you, Ellen," Mary said gratefully as Samuel took the tray from her.

"Mr. Gorton, would you also like me to get lunch started?" Ellen asked.

"Yes, please, Ellen," Samuel answered.

Samuel set the tray on the bedside table and poured the two cups of tea, handing one to his wife, and then he dipped his fingers in the lavender salve and gently applied it to the red mark upon Mary's face. She bit her lip to keep from wincing.

"I think we should tell people," Samuel said, dipping his fingers to apply a second coat.

"What will that help?" Mary questioned softly, her eyes closed.

"We can't be the only ones, and I would be willing to bet that the people he has wronged before have been too scared to tell anyone. If we speak up, others will be encouraged to speak up, too. They will realize what happened to them was not an isolated incident. They will start to see how corrupt and controlling the Church of England is and how behaviors like his have been accepted and shrugged off for far too long."

"I should remind you, dear husband, that we are in Plymouth, not Boston. I believe in Boston they choose to stay Anglican, but these Pilgrims here in Plymouth have separated."

"Yes, of course, you are correct. Still, it's time for people, especially these Separatists, to see that it isn't Christianity that is oppressive, but instead the people in authoritative positions who are abusing their power. The people must receive the freedom of religion they had expected upon coming here," Samuel said, his voice raising passionately.

"Sounds like a fine idea, but I figure we should make some friends first." Mary laughed her lovely, melodic laugh.

Samuel planted a soft kiss on her forehead, smiling at the sound.

"My incredible bride. Optimistic even in the most challenging situations. Smiling even when she's battered and bruised. *Though she be but little, she is fierce,*" Samuel said, quoting his wife's favorite playwright.

The Pequot War

> Cry "Havoc!" and let slip the dogs of war,
> That this foul deed shall smell above the earth
> With carrion men groaning for burial.
> —Shakespeare

June–September 1637

The Gortons wasted no time making friends. Samuel spent the next few weeks planting crops, returning to the farm life that he and brother Thomas knew well. While exploring the Plymouth settlement, he began introducing himself to locals he happened to meet while carrying on their normal course of business. He had the good fortune to meet Edward Winslow,

Mayflower in Plymouth Harbor

whom he immediately befriended. Winslow had arrived on the *Mayflower* and was one of the senior leaders of the Plymouth settlement. Winslow immediately introduced Gorton to Nathaniel Morton, who, according to Winslow, was in need of a friend and mentor. Morton, Winslow suggested, could provide necessary introductions and help the Gorton family become established.

Morton interviewed Samuel and, of course, made light of the similarity of their names. "I suspect you and I are actually cousins,

Samuel. My side of the family was intelligent enough to spell our name right, whilst yours failed."

"It may be worse than that, cousin. My family comes from a stock of simple farmers who could not spell at all," Gorton joked. "I would consider adopting your spelling if it means I am assured friends in this new wilderness outpost."

"Since we have attended services today, let us both go to the pub, where we can share an ale and become better acquainted," Morton offered.

For the next several hours, Samuel and Nathaniel discussed life in the colonies. Morton was the nephew of Plymouth governor William Bradford and had come over just two years after the colony was established. Because his father had died when he was only eight, he moved in with and was raised by his uncle. That relationship with William Bradford, governor of the Plymouth Colony, had given Morton both power and access in the colony.

As their pub meeting was winding down, Captain Thomas Prence came in and chatted briefly with Morton concerning fortifications on the outside fence.

"Captain Prence," Morton said, "I should like to introduce you to my new friend, who has just recently joined our colony. Samuel Gorton has come to us from London and is a useful sort, courteous in his carriage to all."

"It is my pleasure, sir," Prence responded.

"Thank you, Captain. My family and I look forward to becoming established in this community and participating in any way possible in its growth."

"Mr. Gorton, you may be aware that tensions with the Pequot Indians have escalated, and with the help of Roger Williams, we have enlisted the Narragansett tribe as allies. I have been tasked with drafting able-bodied men into our militia to participate in the fight."

"You can count on me, Captain. My brother, Thomas, will also likely be willing to join your force."

"Very well, and an excellent addition you will be," Prence responded.

Forefathers & Founding Fathers

"As I have stated, we look forward to contributing in a positive way to our new home. I am not a soldier, but brother Thomas and I are excellent hunters and quite comfortable in the woods," Samuel said. "Any special instructions at this point in time?"

"We will depart in two days, first thing in the morn, with thirty able-bodied Plymouth men to join the fight at Fort Mystic. Because you have no military experience and little knowledge of the local savages, we will brief you tomorrow as we depart on this expedition," Captain Prence answered.

"What can you tell me of the expedition?" Samuel asked.

"Mystic is on the water, and in the past, we have found that boats are the fastest and best passage. This time, however, we have been instructed to march so we can make observations and reconnaissance, which we will deliver to Captain Mason at the fort." Captain Prence then described the necessary provisions Thomas and Samuel would need, thanked Samuel for his willingness to volunteer, and planned a meeting time and location for the following morning.

⟐

Thomas and Samuel joined Captain Prence, his lieutenant, William Holmes, and twenty-seven other men in the early morning before dawn. At first glance, it was easy to tell which men had served as professional soldiers, as they had metal helmets, whereas the militia tended to be wearing cloth or straw hats.

Prence immediately summoned Samuel to walk with him. "Our orders are to march to Providence," he explained. "That will take approximately two days. Once there, we will spend two days training and developing a joint strategy with Roger Williams and his militia. Williams has secured the support of the Narragansett tribe, so I suspect we will have some Narragansett in our group as we go forward from Providence."

"Garnering the support of Roger Williams is welcome news, Captain. I look forward to the opportunity to meet with him," Samuel told Prence.

Prence inclined his head. "I daresay that Williams is a valuable asset because of his friendship with the Indians, but a welcome guest in the Plymouth settlement he would not be. Many, including myself, consider his political and religious beliefs to be radical and unwelcome in a Separatist Puritan protectorate."

Samuel considered Prence's comment and carefully constructed his response. A part of him wanted to clearly articulate his admiration for Williams, but Prence had just avowed his animus, and Gorton had made a decision to work and live within the confines of accepted Plymouth norms.

"Like Williams, I see the value in learning the ways and language of the local tribes. Such knowledge would bring great value to our settlement," Gorton finally answered.

"Samuel, I have conversed with our governor, Edward Winslow, who has spoken that he believes you are man of skills and knowledge that would be precious assets to our colony. This is a good thing, but I also know you have been admonished by Reverend Reynor," Prence said gravely. "The reverend holds little power in comparison to the governor, but he is a clever man and capable of converting and contriving the beliefs and perspectives of those around him. You would be best served staying within the axioms of our colony and befriending the reverend."

"I must admit that I was angered by the reverend striking my wife. This is not something that would have happened in London," Samuel argued. "Mary comes from a family well known and respected amongst the aristocracy."

"Indeed, the governor knows this to be the case, and I think it is part of the reason that you will be a welcomed and valued member of our community. There is something that I know, and I would not be surprised to learn that the governor also knows or will soon learn." He paused so he could focus on negotiating his way over a dead tree that had fallen in the path. "I have been told that you attended private services in the house of Anne Hutchinson. This is not something that would be considered acceptable in the Plymouth Colony. Many believe Hutchinson to be a witch, sent to test the Boston colony. I feel certain her sins will be summarily dealt with now that Vane has lost the governorship of that colony."

"Captain Prence, I believe we all made the treacherous journey to the New World seeking religious freedom. It seems to me that Mrs. Hutchinson is exercising only that."

"Indeed, Samuel, but the tides are against Hutchinson and the Antinomians of Boston. She would not be welcome here in Plymouth. Any affiliation to her or her followers would be detrimental to you and your family. If you do not wish the tides to flow similarly against you, I would advise you to consider caution before embarking on a similar pathway."

"I wholeheartedly agree with you, Captain, and I shall endeavor adherence to your counsel," Samuel responded, holding back what he truly wanted to say.

⟹•○•⟸

The following morning, Prence's militia was up and marching in the early dawn light. About an hour after sunrise, Gorton was startled by several almost simultaneous *thwack* sounds. These were immediately followed by one of the militia screaming out in pain and Lieutenant Holmes barking out commands.

Samuel observed three soldiers who had found a tree, dropped to a knee, and were searching for a target with their muskets. Another volley of arrows was loosed at the militia, but this time, none hit their marks. An explosion of muskets fired in response to the flight of arrows. Some of those muskets were fired in fear, but others had found targets. Samuel searched the woods but found nothing. Their adversary, it seemed, knew well how to stay invisible amongst the trees.

Samuel scanned the men, looking for his brother Thomas, and found him reloading. Thomas had always been comfortable with a musket and had proven a good shot on the hunting expeditions they had often taken. For a few seconds, all was quiet as Samuel and several others searched the tree line while several others amongst the militia reloaded.

The next few moments, which seemed like an infinite amount of time to the militia, were shattered by synchronized, bloodcurdling screams. It seemed to Samuel that the tree line was instantly filled with painted, shirtless natives who screamed as they loosed arrow after arrow and ran directly into the midst of the militia. Explosions rang out as muskets fired, searching for targets. Within seconds, the chaos ended.

Samuel's ears were ringing as he stood and scanned the surrounding woods. Several bodies of shirtless Indians lay scattered on the ground. There were four dead Indians and two seriously injured ones. Two of the militia had been struck by arrows. One was a graze that could easily be bandaged, but the other was in the leg and would require medical attention.

Samuel turned his attention to one of the Indians. He had had been hit by two musket balls but was still alive. Samuel expected to look down on a godless savage but instead found an injured human being crying out in pain. Without proper medical knowledge, he tried to evaluate the injuries and provide comfort to the Pequot warrior. For just a second, a connection was made between Samuel and the young Native American.

"What are you doing, Samuel?"

Gorton looked up and recognized Jonathan, a member of the militia, wearing a metal soldier's helmet. Unlike most of the others in Prence's militia, this was not Jonathan's first battle. He had been trained as a soldier in the king's army and had fought in several skirmishes in the New World.

"This man is injured," Samuel responded. "I think we can save him."

"Let me have a look," Jonathan stated as he knelt beside the young injured Indian. He drew his knife and, with great precision, slit the Indian's throat.

"What have you done?" Gorton fell backward, horrified. "He would have lived! We should have saved that man!"

"And allowed him to go on to slaughter more of our women and children?" Jonathan replied with a dark laugh. "You farmers add to our numbers, and sometimes you are handy with a musket, but trained soldiers you are not. We are not here to take prisoners and coddle the savages. They are here to kill us, unless we do our job first." With that, Jonathan stood and walked away, not waiting for Samuel to respond.

Samuel stared at the young man, now lifeless in a pool of blood. His brief connection with the Pequot would begin to shape Gorton's perspective on the local tribes, often called *savages* by his fellow militia and settlers. Samuel did not see it that way. For him, what he had just observed was a senseless killing, perhaps murder. Jonathan's merciless taking of that life had burned a negative impression on Samuel's soul, and he knew he could never look at war or the Native Americans in the region the same way again.

As Prence's militia arrived at Providence, they observed a very small settlement with twenty or thirty wooden homes, a rough building used for church assembly, and a trading post. The settlement was surrounded by a palisade of twelve-foot-high pickets sharpened to points at the top. Colony founder Roger Williams came out to greet the small band, and he assigned a woman with medical training to tend to the injured Plymouth soldier.

After brief introductions, Williams invited Prence, Holmes, and Gorton into a private meeting. "Three days ago, the Fort Mystic militia, led by Captain Mason, won a decisive victory," Williams began. He then told the remainder of the tale of how English soldiers and their Narragansett allies had wiped out an entire Pequot village.

Williams continued, "There are a few remaining Pequot tribes that, having heard of the Mystic battle, have chosen to desperately continue the fight, but it is my sense that this war has shifted the balance of power amongst the local Indian tribes. For decades, the Pequot have been the main power in this region. With this war, that power will shift to the Mohegan and Narragansett."

"So what of our militia?" Prence asked.

"All local town militias are now ordered back home to protect their settlements from what remains of the Pequot uprising," Roger Williams answered. "You are welcome to spend the night in our settlement before returning to Plymouth in the morning, but there is no longer need for further training or a march to Fort Mystic. We believe the war is now over. Our allies, the Mohegan and Narragansett, will now sort out the remainder of dealing with the Pequot."

"This is excellent news, and we wholeheartedly thank you for the hospitality. We shall accept your offer and rest for the night. In the morning, we shall endeavor to reach Plymouth with a rigorous day's march."

"We could arrange transportation via boat, which, although a greater distance, would be both faster and provide safer passage with a lower possibility of further attack," Williams offered.

"Thank you again," Prence said. "I am concerned that Plymouth is without the most able-bodied members of its militia." Prence stood up, shook William's hand, and departed with Holmes.

⟹•◉•⟸

Roger Williams looked squarely at Gorton, wondering why he had decided to stay after the other two had departed. "Is there something I can do for you, Mr. Gorton?"

"I spent several days with Anne Hutchinson and the Antinomians in Boston. I was hoping you may have some word on their fate?" Samuel asked.

"In what sense did you spend those days, Mr. Gorton?" Williams asked cautiously.

"My wife has long been an admirer of Hutchinson and Reverend Cotton," Gorton said, sensing William's concern. "We arrived just over a month ago in Boston from London and enjoyed services and significant conversation in Hutchinson's home. In that time, I came to admire their understanding and align myself with their vision and that of William and Mary Dyer. Upon the ousting of Governor Vane, Mary and I decided to leave Boston and find a home in Plymouth."

"I fear that in these difficult times, the long-standing relationship between Hutchinson and Cotton may be coming to an end. In any case, by my estimation, leaving Boston when you did was the right course, though I doubt anyone who follows the teachings of Anne Hutchinson would be welcome in Plymouth. Many in the colonies, such as myself, do not agree with the strict vision of the Boston Puritans. Having been in a similar situation, I fear the worst for Mrs. Hutchinson and her followers in Boston. The governor is a clever man and well appreciates the value of quelling opposition."

"Yes, Mr. Williams, so I have come to realize, but I also hold a personal belief that we don't fail until we quit, and we should never quit anything important."

"Those are fine words, Samuel, but I hope you understand that sometimes it is more prudent to just walk away."

"I suppose that may be the case, but I have always stood my ground to a fault," Samuel answered.

"Well, perhaps both pathways lead to the same endpoint, eh? Anyway, it is unfortunate that Vane lost his control. He is a good and fair man, but a young man who lacked the experience and treachery of his adversaries."

"I guess that chapter has been written now that Winthrop is back in the governor's seat in the Massachusetts Bay Colony. What will become of Vane now?" Samuel asked.

"I heard he will return to London, where his family holds great power and respect," Williams answered. He was quiet for a moment, looking out the window at the small colony. "These are difficult times. I find it disturbing that our brothers in Boston have tried me for sedition and heresy, expelled me from their colony, and yet have prevailed upon me to assist in this abominable war with the Pequot. I have complied, bringing the Narragansett in as allies in this conflict, but it is a terrible thing, terrible."

"I have a sense that you are in opposition to this war?" Gorton questioned.

"Indeed, I am, but I also understand the importance of protecting our new home," Williams answered. "I simply believe there would have been better ways to accomplish this end. The most recent battle, I fear, history shall view more as a massacre of innocents than a battle between our militia and Indian braves."

Samuel could sympathize. "Yesterday, during our short skirmish, I discovered a young Pequot suffering from two musket balls. In his eyes, I saw a fellow man in pain and set out to help. A certain member of our militia had a different intent and slit that young boy's throat."

"Indeed, my friend, there has been much senseless killing in this war. Perhaps in every war this is the case. Have a look at this and tell me your thoughts." Williams handed Gorton a parchment with the simple words:

> Boast not proud English, of thy birth and blood
> Thy brother Indian is by birth as good
> Of one blood God made Him, and Thee and All,
> As wise, as fair, as strong, as personal.

Gorton studied the words. In an instant, he realized he was sitting in the presence of a man who understood something much deeper than a simple conflict or the Pequot War.

"I hear you have come to learn the tongue and the ways of the Indians," Gorton suggested.

"I have," Williams responded. "I have made friends among them and have begun to absorb an understanding of their cultures."

"I think I should like to do the same, Mr. Williams."

"Where many of our English brothers have taken lands from the Indians, I negotiated and purchased the lands that we now call Providence Plantations. There are many things we can teach these savages, but first we must earn their respect, and today the Indians have very little respect for the English."

Samuel frowned. "Do you think it appropriate to call them savages?"

"I believe it to be a technicality. Our English brothers use it as a demeaning method to legitimize killing these Indians. Compared to our English upbringing, they do live as savages, but this does not diminish their value as men. I also believe there are many things they can teach us. In this respect, I think 'savage' is probably not an appropriate term."

"I am fascinated by these people and should very much enjoy the opportunity to learn their language and some of their ways," Samuel responded.

"I should be happy to assist you in that endeavor."

Over the next couple of hours, the two men discussed politics, religion, and life in the colonies. The two had many things in common, though Gorton was sure he could not simply leave a conflict, as Williams had done on several occasions. Williams was a clear-thinking strategist whose method was to avoid conflict and find a harmonious path to accomplishing his goals, while Gorton was a bit of a firebrand, willing to fight to make a point.

"Samuel, you must exercise caution in your life amongst the Pilgrims of Plymouth," Williams told Gorton. "They are not a tolerant group." He trailed off, wanting not to clearly create animosity but instead to provide ample warning to a man with whom he felt he had much in common.

"I shall work to take your advice, my friend. One thing is clear this eve. The two of us are of a similar mind-set, though I tend to take the adversarial firebrand pathway while you take that of the pacifist."

"Perhaps both shall reveal their value with time, Mr. Gorton. I just hope that your pathway does not get you killed or imprisoned."

As the evening came to an end, both men believed this was the beginning of a long friendship and collaboration.

Plymouth Collaborations

Rich gifts wax poor when givers prove unkind.
—Shakespeare

July 1637

Two weeks following Reverend Reynor's chastisement of Mary and Samuel, the militia returned from its short participation in the Pequot War. Gorton was back in Plymouth, resolved to attend church every Sunday in spite of Reynor's presence. Through their attendance, they met and befriended a number of families. The more the Gortons opened up about the oppression of Archbishop Laud and the Church of England that had spilled into the New World and about the way that Reynor had acted in their first meeting, the more their friends shared their own stories.

Sunday, July 12, was normal until around lunchtime. The Gorton family attended church in their usual faithful manner. Upon returning home, Ellen made lunch, and the family ate. Then Samuel sat down with his family and the Bible, and they all discussed the book they were currently working through. This month, they had begun working through Ephesians. Then a knock came at the door.

Samuel stopped in the middle of reading a sentence and glanced up from his spectacles.

"I wonder who that could be," he mumbled, marking the page and then standing up to make his way over to the door.

He opened it to face a man and a woman, both dressed in servants' clothes with cloaks tied around their necks and the hoods up. Perplexed, Samuel's brow furrowed. He said only, "Hello," then waited for an explanation.

In a rough, English-country accent, the woman responded, "With due respect, sir, can we please come in quickly? If our mastah knew we were here, he'd have us hanged before nightfall. An' I know none of us wants that!"

"Please," Samuel said, and he moved aside to allow the strangers into his home. His wife and children gawked, confused.

"I'm sorry, but may I ask who you are and why you are here?" Samuel questioned as politely as he could manage.

"M'name is Joseph Rawlins, sir, and it's a pleasure to make yer acquaintance," the man said, reaching out to shake Samuel's hand and doing so vigorously.

"And I'm his wife, Isabel. We're here because we overheard you whisperin' about religious freedom an' all that, and we wanna stand by yeh. We wanna know more." Isabel paused for a moment and then continued, "Yeh see, I'm—er—pretty outspoken fer a female, if yeh haven't already had the displeasure of noticin', and I'm sick of gettin' smacked, whipped, or hit with a switch every time I voice my opinion around the reverend."

"Isabel?" Ellen emerged from the kitchen.

"Ellen, hello, dear. See, Ellen's the one who told us about yeh. She said you was lookin' to hear stories and mebbe help us," Isabel explained. "I fink that's mighty noble of yeh, sir. Yeh see, we need more—"

Samuel cut Isabel off, feeling that he would never get a word in if he didn't say something now. "Excuse me, Isabel. If I may interrupt you for just a moment. We are just having our family study of the Bible now. I'm flattered by your visit and your kind words, but I won't rob my family of this time with the Lord."

Forefathers & Founding Fathers

"Don't let us get in yer way. If it's OK, we'll join yeh and listen quietly!" Isabel said, and she plopped her round figure down on an open chair, and her husband followed suit.

". . . All right, then. If you don't mind, I'm just going to—umm—have a private word with my wife in the other room. We'll be right back," Samuel said, grabbing Mary's hand and then pulling her into the kitchen.

When they were out of earshot, he spoke to his wife.

"What do you think we should do?" Samuel asked.

"We let them stay," Mary responded calmly.

"Of course, you are right. I was simply startled to see that woman and her husband invite themselves into our home and sit in our chairs like they own them," Samuel responded.

"This is how it starts. This is how we get people to start standing up for themselves. Remember?" Mary assured him. "Besides, I remind you that Anne Hutchinson allowed us to attend services in her home, and that was a good thing."

Samuel stuttered and stumbled over words, searching for excuses, but finally he sighed out a, "Mary, all is not well with Anne and her friends in Boston. Roger Williams has speculated the worst for their conventicles."

"Perhaps, Samuel, but we have come to the New World for religious freedom. You and I can teach, like Anne does, and we can make a difference in these people's lives."

"OK, sweet wife, but please remember this is a jeopardous path we are embarking on."

"I understand, Samuel," she said as she nodded and then kissed his forehead.

As he was walking out of the kitchen and back into the living room, Samuel asked, "Who did you say you work for, Isabel?"

"I did not. But it's Reverend Reynor, sir," Isabel croaked.

Samuel and Mary exchanged a look.

"Reverend Reynor?" Samuel repeated.

"Yessir," Isabel confirmed.

"Well, then. We had best keep this a secret as long as possible. I'd like to avoid physical abuse and hangings." Samuel laughed nervously.

The following Sunday, the Gortons were joined again by Isabel and Joseph. However, no more than fifteen minutes into their study, a rapping came at the door. It was a young couple from the congregation and their two children. The man said they had come to the colonies seeking freedom of religion but had found themselves sorely disappointed. Again, the Sunday following that, the Gorton household was joined by one additional family from the congregation.

Each week, Samuel would begin in prayer and would encourage everyone to feel free to chime in at any time. The first week, only Samuel and his family really prayed or spoke up during the study, but with each passing week, members of the private conventicle got braver and more outspoken. Although the time was mostly a study of the Bible and discussion about true religious freedom, the conversations were not limited only to religious topics.

By early spring of 1638, Gorton's household had become a regular meeting place for colonists who wanted more passion in their religious education and principles of freedom that were lacking in Reverend Reynor's services. At this point, many people in the colony were aware of these meetings, but most ignored them. They did not represent a political threat to the main governance in the colony, and Gorton and his family had brought much to their community.

It was in early April 1638 that a surprising visitor came to the door of the Gorton house during a Sunday service. The group had stopped meeting in the front sitting room in the late fall of 1637, so as to be less blatant. Samuel rose from his seat and made his way to the front door. Upon opening it, he came face to face with Mary Smith, the wife of his landlord, Ralph Smith.

"Mrs. Smith. Is everything OK? To what do I owe the pleasure?" Samuel greeted her, his tone as calm as possible, even though he was concerned that her visit might mean her husband or Reverend Reynor was finally reacting negatively to their meetings.

"Samuel, I've heard about your conventicles," Mrs. Smith said, pausing and just staring down at the ground. "Well, I was wondering if, well . . ." she trailed off.

"Mrs. Smith, I can assure you that—"

"Mr. Gorton," Mrs. Smith interrupted, "I've come to tell you that I have heard good things about your teachings. The things I have heard sound like a perspective in alignment with my own. With your permission, I want to start joining you for your meetings. I need to hear the word of God preached like a saving grace again instead of a weapon. However, you also must know that my husband is very faithful to Reverend Reynor. If he heard of this, I am sure that he would take action. You should know that his house, this house, is still property of the colony. My husband is very careful to maintain a position with the reverend and governor that does not inspire them to take it back."

"But he isn't suspicious yet?" Samuel asked.

"Not yet," Mrs. Smith nodded. Samuel invited her inside.

And so Ralph Smith's wife—the same Ralph Smith who was landlord at the Gorton's home; the same Ralph Smith who had warned Gorton not to participate in any chicanery in Plymouth—joined the meetings at the Gorton household. As 1638 progressed and summer wore into fall, more than half of the church congregation joined the secret meetings. Many of the conventicle members, or *Gortonists*, as they called themselves, stopped attending Reverend Reynor's church congregation altogether, even though Samuel and his family continued to attend and begged the others to continue.

Members of the Gortonist services came to view Samuel Gorton's home as the only "real church" in the town of Plymouth. They did so because his teachings were simple and harmonious. Gorton taught that the Holy Spirit was present in everyone. He also believed that all men were created equal, and this belief transcended gender, color, and ethnicity. Finally, he believed there should be a separation in the powers of the church and those of the state.

In October of 1638, Ralph Smith began to complain of Gorton's visitors to the house each Sunday afternoon. He told his wife, Mary

Smith, that he was concerned that her open advocacy of Samuel and her attendance at the Gorton services could cause serious problems in Plymouth. Even though he begged and threatened her, she continued to attend.

Smith felt it was time to take matters into his own hands. He took his complaint to Nathaniel Morton, who had maintained a friendship with Gorton but was also becoming concerned about the Gortonist movement in his town. In the beginning, Morton believed that his friendship with Gorton would prevail, and he took it upon himself to meet with Samuel.

Gorton stepped into the pub where he had met with his "cousin" Morton on several occasions. The two embraced.

"How are you, cousin?" Gorton asked as they embraced.

"I am well, cousin," Morton said with a broad grin. "Life is busy and consumes far too much of our time. As expected, your crops have been great, and the Gorton clan continues to bring value to the town of Plymouth."

"Thank you, my friend. Thomas and I work hard and have been blessed with good soil and fortune these last two crops."

"Perhaps, but I suspect it is more than that. You two work hard and diligently and resolve problems before they grow out of control. So tell me, how are your wife and the family?"

"We are well. Because of the good year for crops, we have sufficient provisions for the winter. Next year, we should all work to grow our yield."

"That is good. Have you produced enough to sell some to the stores?"

"Yes, Thomas is handling that and will begin carting and selling this week," Samuel answered. "Cousin, as you have said, these are busy times. Why have you invited me into this tavern today?"

"There is a matter of grave concern to the colony," Morton began. "When we first met, you told me you wanted only to contribute to the growth of Plymouth."

"Indeed, and that remains the case," Gorton assured Morton, with his infectious smile.

"You should know that Ralph Smith has been spreading rumors that you are conducting services in your home," Morton said.

"I can confirm that. As you know, it is quite common for individuals to do this, even in these colonies. I have continued to be present with my family at Reverend Reynor's Sunday services. Further, I have prevailed upon everyone to continue Reynor's services."

"Indeed, I have observed you and your family at church. The complaint is not that you are holding these services but that the message you are teaching in your home is subversive and contrary to that of our Plymouth community."

"Mr. Morton, I teach only what I believe in my heart, and nothing in those teachings could be construed as subversive or destructive to our community." Samuel was trying to find a way to reach Morton, a man whom he had come to respect. Morton was a solid, stalwart, knowledgeable, and educated man who loved to write. Gorton had always seen the differences between himself and Morton, but he had hoped for a great and long friendship based on their common interests.

"Smith tells me you are teaching that we have the Holy Spirit in each of us and all should be treated equal. These things are radical, my friend."

"I know from my studies these things are true," Samuel argued.

"What do you mean, the Spirit is inside us? We are all sinners! How could the Spirit be inside us, Gorton?"

"We are all God's creatures. Why would he create us and yet not put the good of his Spirit inside us?"

"You cannot believe that God has put his spirit in the savages that live in this land. You must know they are godless creatures who cannot be saved," Morton contested, still convinced that Samuel was simply jesting.

Samuel thought about his friend's comment, and then he recalled Jonathan slitting the throat of a helpless Pequot. "Cousin, I believe that God has created us all equally. It is the job of those of us who have been taught to read to teach those who have not."

"No!" Nathaniel shouted. He stood and slammed his fist onto the rough wooden table. "If you believe these things and the other things

I have been told, then you are at best a fool, and you most certainly do not belong in this Plymouth Colony."

"Nathaniel, cousin and friend, come to one of my services and open your heart to hear what we have been teaching."

"I will not participate in the teachings of a fool and an idiot. Furthermore, I caution you to never again call me cousin and friend. I could be neither of these to an aberration such as yourself, Samuel Gorton!"

At this point, Gorton had heard enough. In a matter of a few short minutes, Nathaniel had transformed from a man he wanted to cherish as a friend to a close-minded idiot who could see only one perspective. He blazed up as well. "If you will not open your mind to learn what is clearly written and right, then you are the fool and idiot!" Gorton stood, turned on his heels, and left the pub while Nathaniel and all of the others stared in astonished silence.

It was the beginning of a war.

<hr/>

As the New England weather grew progressively colder with the arrival of November, the Gortonist meetings were warming up. Close bonds of friendship had begun to form as turmoil and opposition grew amongst the mainstream powers and religious leaders in the town.

The visits of the conventicle members were no longer limited just to Sundays. The young couple—Nathaniel and Charity Stuart—would bring their children, Kenna and Leo, over to play with the Gorton children. Mrs. Mary Smith came over even more often than the Stuarts, as she lived right next door. She would bring baked goods and hot tea over to share with Mary Gorton. The Gortons had learned that Mrs. Mary Smith had been previously married to a man named Richard Masterson. They had sailed to the New World on the *Mayflower* when they were still very young and had been members of John Robinson's church.

"Your theology reminds me very much of Reverend Robinson's," Mrs. Smith told the Gortons one Sunday after everyone else had left. "Before he left England, Robinson was a Separatist. Some say he came over to the New World simply because England wanted to get rid of him. My husband was already a little old when we boarded the *Mayflower*. He made it to the New World, and we lived here happily for a few years in spite of the intense struggles we experienced. It was the local Indians who saved us and taught our colony how to live in this new land. I wish Governor Winslow would simply remember that we would not be alive if those Indians had not helped. These are not the godless savages that my current husband claims but, instead, men who simply lack the same education and experience as us. It seems they have taught us things, just as we should teach them."

"What became of your husband?" Mary Gorton asked.

"Richard contracted an illness he could not shake and eventually passed away. Those were difficult times in the Plymouth Colony. I miss him every day. When Ralph first came to town, he was in miserable condition, but as a Cambridge graduate, he quickly established himself and soon became our minister. It was in 1634 when he and I were married. I thought him to be a good sort but did not foresee the man he would become simply to protect his position in this community. I am sincerely sorry that Ralph is causing problems for us. I have tried to reason with him, but he has moved well beyond the ability to listen."

"Thank you so much for sharing that," Mary Gorton said, taking Mrs. Smith's hand. "As you know, Samuel is quite hardheaded and can be a real hothead when he believes he is right. I suspect that either his firebrand nature will remedy this problem or we shall end up in great difficulty."

"I just want you, both of you, to know how glad I am to come into a family of believers like this and to have my soul refreshed by the true word of God, just as it was years ago," Mrs. Smith said. "I have heard so many stories of individuals who have stood up only to be prosecuted, punished, or killed."

"I do not think that will happen here," Mary Gortowwn responded with some hesitation.

"Indeed, I pray that you are correct," Smith said before returning home.

One chilly November evening, after all of the children had gone to bed, Mary and Samuel sat together by the fire, discussing how much they had accomplished together since their move to Plymouth. They were snuggled up under a thick patchwork quilt, the only light left in the room coming from the fireplace. The light danced playfully on their skin as they spoke softly, trying hard not to wake the children.

"Adjusting from being of relatively high social class and living in a lavish and comfortable home to rough frontier life—that has been an accomplishment!" Samuel said, laughing.

"A healthy family," Mary added, "and friends who have come to rely on our mentorship."

"We made it across an entire ocean on a boat filled to the brim with people, illness around every corner. None of us came down with an illness. Our children didn't kill each other. We all made it, slow though it may have been. We are in the New World!"

"Being slapped by Reverend Reynor only once!" Mary jested.

"Hah! Do you remember the three shoulder slaps your own father used to give me every time we were together?"

"Yes, I do, Samuel, Samuel, m'boy." She smiled, and the two laughed at the memory while tears came to their eyes.

"I once hated those shoulder slaps, but today I would give much for just one more . . ." Samuel reminisced.

"How I miss him! And Mother," Mary sighed.

"I wonder how Mother Mary is faring in London," Samuel mused.

"Well, I am certain," Mary responded.

Samuel hugged his wife affectionately. "Our Sunday gatherings have become something to be celebrated. Even though we started simply to teach our children, those conventicles have grown into something bigger than the two of us."

"Indeed. We now have a responsibility to continue, though I think we should exercise caution and not alienate ourselves from the community."

"We do have a responsibility to caution," Samuel agreed, "but our teachings will only continue if we do not falter in the darkness of their threats. If we are to be successful, we must stand strong."

"By standing strong, we will most assuredly be punished, expelled from the colony, or killed, Samuel."

"I do not think that will happen. We have been good and contributing members of this community. I think the majority of the Plymouth community likes having our little family here, and they will support us in any challenges we might face."

"Speaking of our little family . . . I've been meaning to tell you: we are going to have another little one!" Mary exclaimed, her hands on her belly.

"Mary! That's wonderful!" Samuel said, lifting her from the couch and spinning her round just as he had on the day they posted banns nearly a decade ago.

When he set her down and gazed upon her lovely face, he reflected upon the past ten years with Mary and how blessed he had been to have fallen for such a strong, beautiful, and intellectually brilliant woman. The years of their marriage had not been easy by any means. At times, their fiery personalities had clashed, and it had felt like the whole world was crumbling down around them. Yet if there was one lesson Samuel had learned over the past ten years and was continuing to learn each day in his efforts to change the course of New England, it was that nothing worthwhile was ever easy.

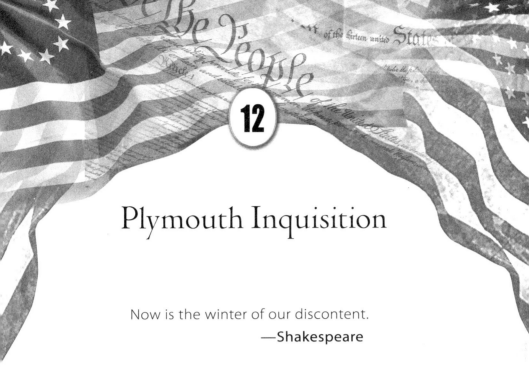

Plymouth Inquisition

Now is the winter of our discontent.
—Shakespeare

November 1638

It was a chilly morning in Plymouth. The leaves had changed color and had mostly fallen. The first frost had hit, which led everyone to believe it would be a cold winter. Reverend Reynor was feeling very pleased with himself. Very pleased, indeed. He had just made a discovery that would explain a lot of the mysterious happenings that had been occurring in his congregation over the past six months. At least five families that had been in regular attendance in his church had stopped coming altogether, and he had been hearing whisperings of who might be behind those departures. He didn't doubt that the rumor was true, but he sent for one of his most trustworthy and favored congregation members, Ralph Smith, to discuss what could be done.

A knock came at his office door, signaling Mr. Smith's arrival.

"Do come in," Reverend Reynor said coolly.

"Reverend Reynor," Smith said in greeting. "Why do I have the great honor of being sent for this morn by one of the greatest men I know?" Smith asked, even though in reality he hated Reynor and resented the fact that he had taken his rightful position as reverend and religious leader of Plymouth.

"Because, Mr. Smith, I have reason to believe there is treason occurring within our church congregation, and I think I might know to whom it's tied," the reverend said, fidgeting with a feather quill.

In spite of his Cambridge education, Smith was not the brightest or quickest to realization. He just nodded his head with a blank expression on his face. "And why am I here? I can assure you that I would not involve myself in treason to our community, Reverend."

"Not you, Ralph. I think it's your tenant, Mr. Gorton," Reverend Reynor said, folding his hands on the desk in front of him and leaning in closer to Mr. Smith as he spoke Gorton's name.

"Really? Agh! I knew his family was trouble!" Smith lied, wanting to give Reynor the idea that this was his own great realization. "I told 'em when they rented from me that they must strictly adhere to the rules of our community," Ralph growled, shaking his head angrily.

"Indeed, but we must have a plan. Here's where you come in," Reynor explained. "I want you to find out who from our congregation attends his . . . conventicles . . . and I want you to scare them. I have a preliminary list of whom I *suspect* must go to his house each week, but I want you to confirm it and then return a complete list to me. I don't know how we end this subversion, but it must end. I know that Samuel and Thomas have brought value to our community, and as much as I hate to admit it, we would definitely feel their loss. Let us give the Gortons a chance to stop their foolishness and avoid punishment. Kill their spirits. Terrify them!" Reverend Reynor spoke intensely.

"Oh, I would be most honored to aid you in this mission, Reverend. You are such a merciful pastor to give them an opportunity to stop what they are doing. I think if I were you, I would have been tempted to just have 'em hanged or burned for their betrayal to their church and their God," Ralph said.

"But we are called to model the forgiveness of Christ, are we not? Besides, I suspect that Gorton has some supporters in this town, some of whom may be high up in our community." Reynor smiled his signature serpentine smile.

"Understood, Reverend. I'll have them scared witless by the week's end!" Ralph promised with a bow, and then he exited the reverend's office.

⟫━◆━⟪

Ralph Smith sat in a rocking chair in his living room, brainstorming a plan as to how he would find out who had been visiting the Gorton's house. *Creak.* Perhaps he could follow people home from church? *Creak.* Too creepy, maybe. *Creak.* Maybe he could peek into their windows. *Creak.* No, that wouldn't work. He knew Gorton was smart enough to draw the curtains. *Creak.* Maybe he could pretend to want to join the conventicle himself. *Creak.* Now, there was an idea.

Ralph's thoughts were stopped by his wife entering the front door. Then something clicked into place in his mind, like an ornery puzzle piece that, at last, had connected with its match.

"Mary. Come here, please," Ralph demanded.

The woman did as he asked and stood expectantly in front of him.

"What is it, husband?" Mary asked, her gentle voice wavering just enough for her husband to notice.

"Where have you been going for the past couple of months? You leave the house so often. Don't you enjoy spending time with your husband?" Ralph stood up and pulled her into a hug.

"Ralph, dear, I tell you where I go each time I leave the house," Mary reminded him, pulling out of the hug.

"And where have you come from just now?" Ralph asked, his suspicions growing.

"I had trading business in town," Mary responded in an instant.

Ralph looked at her, noticing that she had no wares or any other evidence that she had been trading.

"Yet you return empty handed."

Mary started to walk up the stairs, ignoring him, but Ralph caught her hand, forcing her to spin around and face him.

"Just answer me truthfully. Have you been at Gorton's house again today? Have you been attending his unlawful, sinful conventicles again?"

Ralph asked, his voice nearly a whisper.

Mary cast her eyes down at the floor, deliberating silently what to say. Then, finally, "Yes," was her answer.

Ralph, without a second's hesitation, struck his wife once, twice, then a third time until she fell to the ground, and then he stormed out the house. He rushed to the stable, mounted his horse, and rode wildly straight to the rectory of Reverend Reynor. Hearing the horse ride up to his home, the reverend walked outside to greet whoever might be coming at this dinner hour.

"What is it, Smith? I know you haven't already completed the task I assigned you," he said as Ralph Smith dismounted the horse and strode furiously up the reverend's front steps.

"It's my *wife*, Reverend. I had hoped she would see the flaws in his teachings and would cease, but she has not. She's been attending those illegal meetings under that—that *devil*. I want them gone before morning's light, Reverend! I want those Gortons out of Plymouth." Smith appeared as if he were about to cry.

The reverend held up his hand and shushed Smith. He thought silently for a moment.

"Breathe, Smith," said the reverend calmly. "Tell me exactly what happened. How did you figure this out?"

"I knew some time ago and admonished her for attending. I thought she had quit, but I realized when she came in the door after having been gone all day that this has continued. She'll say that she's off to pick up supplies or that she's going to visit a friend. But this time, I asked her for the truth. I asked her if she'd been at Gorton's, and she said yes. So I struck her . . . I feel so awful. I shouldn't have done that." Smith wept.

"Hold on, hold on," Reynor said, holding up his hand again. "Sometimes we must discipline our wives. Otherwise, they would never learn right from wrong. Now, you will give it time. The conventicles mean enough to your wife for her to have disobeyed you and attended them all these months. She will continue to go, I'm sure. Perhaps she will even tell Gorton about your episode.

Maybe she won't have to—maybe a bruise will tell the story for her. If Gorton cares at all for the members of his little group, he will stop subjecting them to rightful punishment before something worse happens. Understand, Smith?"

"Yes."

"I have been collaborating with Governor Prence to find a way to punish Gorton and his family," Reynor explained. "Because Gorton served with him in the war, Prence is suggesting some simple charge to provide Gorton an opportunity to cease these conventicles and continue his status of a valued member of our colony."

"Thank you, Reverend. I would be most obliged if Mary were not publicly charged," Smith responded.

"We will see to it, provided she discontinues her affiliation."

"I will make certain of that." Smith wiped his nose with his sleeve, walked down the rectory steps, mounted his horse, and rode straight back home.

<hr />

Mary and Samuel Gorton sat on either side of Mary Smith as she recounted to them what had happened two nights ago when she had returned home from the Gorton residence. Her left eye was swollen and bruised from her husband's angry fist. When she finished her story, Mary Gorton spoke.

"Mrs. Smith, dear, please forgive me. You cannot stand idly by, *we* cannot stand idly by, as Ralph and Reverend Reynor continue to wander about and control people with their iron fists! You have been wronged!"

"I think my wife is correct, Mrs. Smith. We have got to do something. We cannot stand around idle while women are treated with such disrespect. I think the best thing we can do is continue on as we have been doing. I say we throw a conventicle Christmas party just to spite them and show them we have joy in the midst of their oppression!"

"But Christmas is not illegal, Samuel."

"No, Mrs. Smith, it is not illegal, but if we believe Morton and Reynor, our meetings are. Our Christmas party will be an opportunity to celebrate our blessed Jesus and come together as a community," Samuel answered.

Mrs. Smith gently dabbed away her tears with an embroidered handkerchief and then defiantly said, "I will roast a turkey and make certain that Ralph is invited. I do not wish to create a rift, but I believe in the things I have been learning here in your conventicles. Perhaps there is hope for my husband."

"That's the spirit!" Samuel said, squeezing her shoulder. "And we shall welcome him like a brother."

"I will have Ellen prepare some buns and desserts! I believe Nathaniel Stuart and a few of his siblings play instruments. We could have them provide music for our celebration!" Mary Gorton added cheerfully. "We shall make it a joyful celebration for all who attend!"

"Well, it seems that planning a Christmas celebration will keep the two of you occupied and focused on important issues. May this celebration be in honor of two of the strongest women I know. Two lovely Marys celebrating a merry Christmas!" Samuel laughed.

While still over a month away, they all agreed that Christmas Eve would be the perfect time to have the celebration, and preparations began the following morning in the Gorton household. Samuel visited the Stuart household to ask Nathaniel if he would be interested in playing a few jigs at the party with some of his other musical family members. Nathaniel Stuart agreed, happy to hear there would be a Christmas Eve party.

⟫‧○‧⟪

On November 7, Nathaniel Morton intercepted Samuel while engaged in his daily activities.

"Mr. Gorton, as I have said, your current activities and derelict teachings must cease," Morton explained as he handed Samuel a parchment. "Many in Plymouth still believe you can be rehabilitated from your transgressions. I have reached a point where I do not agree."

Forefathers & Founding Fathers

Samuel unfolded the parchment, which notified him that his house servant, Ellen Aldridge, was being charged with smiling in church. Gorton was to immediately pay a fine of ten pounds and to be prepared to appear before the general court on December 4.

"This charge is ridiculous, Nathaniel. How can you expect me to take this seriously?" Gorton questioned.

"It is meant simply to show you we are serious about upholding the fundamental principles of Puritanism for which this colony was founded. We cannot stand for an uprising like that staged by Hutchinson in Boston."

"You are a peasant's fool!" Gorton proclaimed as he turned to walk away without giving Morton an opportunity to respond.

Samuel immediately returned to his house, collected the money he would need, and began the short walk into town. Once there, he paid the ten pounds at the general court and announced that it would be he standing before the magistrate on December 4, not Ellen Aldridge. With that, the court had accomplished its goal, and so had Samuel.

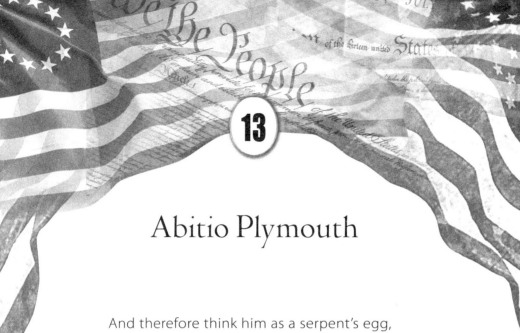

Abitio Plymouth

And therefore think him as a serpent's egg,
Which, hatched, would, as his kind,
grow mischievous,
And kill him in the shell.
—Shakespeare

During the days leading up to Samuel's December 4 court appearance, Ralph Smith fought with his wife Mary to cease her attendance at the Gorton conventicles, but Mary Smith remained defiant, attending each session. Exasperated by his inability to successfully deter his wife, Ralph appealed upon the general court to terminate Gorton's lease, even though he had paid several months in advance with a significant bond. The court agreed to consider such at the hearing.

On December 4, Gorton appeared at the appointed time, as did a large contingent of the residents of Plymouth who had become enthralled in the melodrama.

Reverend Reynor read his charges, followed by Ralph Smith.

When Gorton stood to defend his position, jury foreman Jonathan Brewster immediately instructed him to cease from speaking. "We will not allow you to aggravate this matter more than it deserves, and as such, you shall not be allowed to speak in your defense."

Gorton was astonished and infuriated by this course of events. "This is not an appropriate court hearing under English law," Gorton protested. "I have studied both the law and theology, and I can assure you that every man has a right to speak in his own defense!"

"You will remind yourself to hold your tongue, Gorton, lest the charges, penalties, and fines be increased!" the foreman shouted.

With that, Gorton turned his back on the officials of the court and addressed the amused onlookers. "This proceeding should be an affront to our sense of justice and fair play. Is this how we want our court to collect evidence and administer rulings? This hearing lacks both reasonable charges and a fair sense of procedure or justice. I urge each of you to protest!"

Several onlookers were nodding, and for a moment, it appeared that an uprising would ensue.

Sensing a shift in the balance of power, Plymouth governor Prence then took control of the proceeding by slamming his fist on the pulpit. "Any person who speaks or protests will find themselves fined and possibly imprisoned. This court shall hear this case as it sees fit, and it is our pronouncement that Gorton shall not be allowed to speak!"

The court became quiet. Many would not question the governor's mandate, while others feared reprisal for siding with Gorton.

"The clerics have a ruling," Prence announced, "and that ruling shall be that Gorton must leave Plymouth within a fortnight of the coming Monday. Under no circumstance shall Gorton be allowed to return to Plymouth at any time. Furthermore, Gorton shall be required to pay an additional fifteen pounds for belligerence in this court."

⪼―◦―⪻

When Samuel returned home that afternoon, he, Mary, and his brother Thomas discussed the best strategy for the next two weeks.

"I should like to appeal this ruling with Governor Prence. I have supported him in his recent election and served under him last year in the Pequot War. I believe he will allow us to continue living here with appropriate reparations."

"Do we want to continue living here, Samuel?" Mary asked incredulously. "This place seems to lack a reasonable sense of justice, tricking you into court by charging Ellen for smiling. The charge is foolish and without merit."

"I agree," Thomas nodded.

"Winter has arrived in Plymouth. We do not want to be in the wilderness in search of a new home with such extreme conditions before us. For now, only I have been banished, and if I am forced to leave, Thomas can stay with you and the children until the spring, when it will be safe to travel. In addition, I think if the governor knows you are with child, he will show some lenience. I shall wait a few days and meet with him after tensions have cooled. We have established ourselves here and given much to this community," Samuel argued. "I am certain the governor will overturn this ruling."

"And what of our Christmas celebration?" Mary asked.

"Even a strict Puritan cannot protest a celebration of Christ's birth. Our Christmas party *must* still happen."

Unfortunately for Samuel, Governor Prence and Nathaniel Morton had traveled to Boston two days after the trial to meet with larger leadership of the entire Bay Colony. They were all concerned about uprisings like Hutchinson's and Gorton's and felt these matters required strict and strong responses. Governor Winthrop, who was still enduring the repercussions of the Hutchinson trial, added that men like Gorton should not be allowed to live anywhere within the Massachusetts Bay Colony. It was his argument that Prence should take the same posture in the Plymouth Colony.

<hr />

Upon learning that the governor would not return until December 21, the Gortons notified their friends that the Christmas celebration would be held on December 20, just two days before the court-ordered departure of Samuel. In a lighthearted tone, Samuel suggested it could be both a Christmas celebration and farewell party, though most people in Plymouth did not believe that the governor would actually enforce the ruling of the court. Many argued that Samuel should just ignore the ruling and simply stay. Samuel, Thomas, and Mary had become a familiar and welcome fixture in the town, and most residents enjoyed the constantly lighthearted and well-mannered nature of the Gorton children.

On the morning of December 19, Mary and Ellen gathered the necessary ingredients for the recipes they would make. Samuel gave the children a list of chores to complete before the guests arrived.

On the day of the celebration, Plymouth awoke to a thick blanket of powdery white snow, which was still falling steadily.

"Papa! Mama! Can we go out and play in it?" little Sam begged, tugging at the arm of his father, who was busily helping his wife prepare the house for guests.

"Yes, children! But you must stomp the snow off your boots when you come indoors. You don't want to make a mess of the floors we just cleaned yesterday," Samuel answered, finding joy in the expressions of wonder on his children's faces.

"And you will put on your warm, woolen coats, mittens, scarves, and warmest stockings, children!" Mary called after her little ones as they scurried upstairs.

Mary asked Ellen to ensure the children got layered up appropriately for the bitterly cold New England weather. The Gorton family had never experienced so much snow or cold in England, so the first appearance of the imminent harsh winter filled the parents with some fear and anxiety. Their previous winter in Plymouth and the lessons of the other town inhabitants had taught them to stock up on cured meats and other foods that would keep well throughout the season in the event they got snowed into their home, so they felt somewhat prepared, but they had been warned by their friends of winters when the snow fell, blew, and piled so high that it literally blocked the door and made it close to impossible to get out of the house for days or even weeks at a time.

Samuel and Mary gazed outside for a few moments, watching their children frolic in the foot-deep snow that covered the ground. Little

Sam scooped some up, molded it into a ball, and threw it at a target. He then dropped his body into a pile of powder, giggling, and spread his arms and legs back and forth. Then young Samuel stood up and gazed at what he had made and showed his siblings how it resembled an angel. Even the little toddler, John, went out to play with his brothers and sisters for a short time. He squealed and giggled in delight at the feeling of the fat snowflakes falling on his face, and he then picked up a fistful and put it right in his mouth. Before long, the joy of the snow for John faded—his little ears and cheeks were rosy with the cold wind, and he was screaming, tears rolling down his cheeks.

For Mary, that signaled time for everyone to come inside.

"Time to come inside, little ones!" she hollered out the door. "We can't afford to have anyone catch a chill!"

Sam, Mary, and Maher grumbled and groaned, stomped and dusted the snow off their clothes, and were ordered by their mother to sit by the fireplace with blankets around their shoulders.

The guests were to arrive before sunset. Around midday, the conditions of the weather had improved, but the whole sky was painted a thick, ominous white, threatening a blizzard later that evening. Mary Smith came over, a thick cloak lined with wool draped over her shoulders with the hood up.

"Brrr! It's frigid out there!" she exclaimed. Her servant, Rose, trailed behind.

"I've brought a roasted turkey. Mrs. Smith and I glazed it in spices. It's sure to be delectable!" Rose said, passing the cooked bird along to Ellen, and the two servant girls went to the kitchen together.

The last light of day, barely peeking through the snow clouds, was beginning to fade. Mary Gorton used Mary Smith's arrival as an opportunity to go upstairs and get herself dressed for the evening festivities. She requested Mrs. Smith and Rose watch the children and assure that everything stay clean. Everything was ready to go except for her and Samuel.

Mary excitedly made her way upstairs, followed by Ellen, and from her humble wardrobe pulled out a cream-colored gown with artichoke-colored embroidery. She had not worn anything so ornate since living in London, and she had decided that, just for tonight, she would do away with the gray Puritan-style gown and plain bonnet. Tonight, she would wear something that made her feel lovely, for her heart told her this might be the last occasion for quite some time that she would have the opportunity to do so.

In England, Mary had owned a large wardrobe filled to the brim with dresses of many colors, shapes, and exciting fabrics. She had also had an ornate vanity on which she had kept a few bottles of fragrance, powder, rouge, and eye makeup. Her family's status had allowed her these luxuries. But when Mary and Samuel made the decision to move to the New World, Mary had come to terms with the fact that she would not be able to dress, smell, or decorate her face so elaborately. To her, the cause was worth being rid of these unnecessary luxuries, and she had done so with a joyful heart.

Mary received Ellen's help with the corset, which she asked be kept loose due to her belly having grown with pregnancy. Then she curled her hair and pinned it half up, powdered her face, and gracefully skipped down the stairs. She was greeted by her husband, who kissed her cheek and told her she was lovely before mentioning that the snow was starting to fall again.

"I am nervous our guests will get caught in a blizzard on their way here," he said. "There's talk that the worst storm since the Pilgrims first moved here is upon us."

"I am sure everything will be fine. God is watching over our guests and this household," Mary said, taking Samuel's hands.

The guests began to trickle in early to avoid the storm. The Stuart family found a corner to sit in with their instruments, and they played a few familiar baroque tunes as their children danced with the Gorton children. The guests all clapped merrily on beat while the children danced. By dusk, all of the guests had arrived as planned, and Samuel called everyone to the dining-room table, where the Christmas feast had been laid out. The conventicle members, now as close as a family, joined hands and bowed their heads for a blessing, led by Samuel. The pall of the general court's ruling seemed a distant memory as all merrily celebrated a successful year, great food and friends, and the birth of Christ.

Then everyone was seated, and they began to pass the courses around family-style as they talked and laughed gaily, the spirit of Christmas filling the room. The meal was just as good as the ladies had promised it would be, and everyone's bellies were filled. After the meal, Samuel shared some of his favorite ales with the gentlemen as Nathaniel began to play his violin and his family followed his musical lead. Some of the guests chatted while many others danced to traditional Scottish and English music.

Samuel watched the group of people he had grown quite fond of joyfully celebrating their Savior's birth. They had experienced the harshness of the New World wilderness together, they had grown and challenged each other's faith and beliefs, and they had even learned from each other what it might look like to stand up for one's civil liberties. Now, as he watched these dearest friends, he couldn't ignore the sick feeling in his gut that this might be the last time he would see many of their faces.

With that thought lingering in his mind, he cleared his throat and prepared to speak.

"Excuse me, dear friends!" he yelled above the commotion, raising his glass. "I would like to make a toast. You are some of the most wonderful people I have been blessed to know. We have shared some challenging, meaningful, and intentional discussions in our time spent together, pouring out our mutual education over God's word. We have also broken many rules and barriers. Perhaps my perspective is misguided, but I believe this is only the beginning of a movement that will spread across the New World and define those who live within her borders. I believe if we begin to instill these views in our children, our grandchildren, and our great-grandchildren that we will bring to life this dream we have of freedom from oppressive leaders and freedom to practice our faith as the *Bible* tells us to, rather than the Church of England, or even the current governor of the Plymouth Colony."

The room whooped, hollered, and clapped in agreement. After a few moments, Samuel put his hand up to signal silence, and then he continued.

"Now for the unfortunate news. Try as I might, Governor Prence has either refused or been unable to meet me. I believed he would be amenable to such, but now I am certain that is not the case. It seems this Christmas celebration might amount to our last time together. As I depart from our home in Plymouth, I want to remind each of you that this is a New World with new possibilities. I would encourage you to find opportunities to take a stand for your faith and the civil liberties you deserve. If you are questioned about these meetings, proudly discuss with your friends the great conversations we have shared about God and the New World of which we dream. Tell them about civil liberties and equal rights for all. As I have said, the only way we are going to bring this dream to life is if we start *doing* something. We must not fear those who stand against us because, truly, they fear us. They find comfort in control . . . and when there is a sign that they may be losing that control, they try to get rid of us. Let's not let them this time."

The conventicle members looked around at each other and then back to Gorton. Silently, they all began to hug each other, shake each other's hands, and address each other fondly. Then, as if on cue, there came a heavy pounding on the door. Before answering it, Samuel hurried over to his wife. They spoke quietly as they held each other.

"What's going to happen?" Mary asked, her brow furrowing worriedly.

"I don't know, Mary. If we get separated for whatever reason, I want you to take the children and hide away at the home of friend John Wickes until I send for you." He paused for a moment and looked intensely into his wife's eyes. "If I don't make it . . . you must move on. While I expect you and the children to carry on fighting for your freedoms, I don't want you living under the iron fist of Reverend Reynor. We have heard the rumors that Anne and William Hutchinson have purchased an island, called Aquidneck Island, in the Narragansett Bay. I believe you would be safe with her."

Mary's sky-blue eyes were full of tears, which she spoke through. "Don't talk that way, Samuel Gorton. This family will find a way to prevail. We have to."

Samuel kissed Mary on the forehead and then on her mouth. "I love you, Mary. Get your coat on, and get the children dressed as well."

"Yes, dear. I love you."

Samuel then paced over to the door, which had been pounded on at least two more times in the time it took for him and Mary to discuss a plan. When he opened it, the fierce winter wind roared into the opening and filled his house with a frigid draft. He came face to face, not surprisingly, with Reverend Reynor, Ralph Smith, and two magistrates.

"Think you're so clever and secretive, do you, throwing this huge party? You're a fool, Gorton!" Reverend Reynor shouted over the blowing snow.

"Actually, no," Samuel said back matter-of-factly. "I expected you to find out. I'm just not afraid of you. Furthermore, I take pride in the ability of my family and friends in our celebration of the birth of Christ."

Ralph Smith angrily pushed past Samuel and yelled to all the guests, "I want all of you heretics out of this house, *now!*"

The guests began to collect their belongings and make their way toward the door as commanded until Reverend Reynor, more sensible, held up his hand to signal them to stop.

"Wait," he said. "This storm is fierce. Truly one of the worst I have seen. I believe it would be wise for us all to wait this out. Everyone can and probably should stay at the Gorton home tonight. I do not want the death of any Plymouth residents on my hands."

Reynor looked around the room, and then his eyes fell again on Samuel. His mouth curled up into a serpent-like smile as he added, "Except, of course, the Gorton family. You are hereby exiled from the town of Plymouth, effective immediately. Where you go and whether you survive is no longer of my concern."

"You can't do that!" little Samuel screamed defiantly. "We'll freeze out there!"

Samuel saw Reynor transform from quite pleased with himself to livid in seconds. He watched the look in the reverend's eyes and saw him jolt forward. Samuel knew what was coming before the reverend even made a move. He watched him start to draw his arm back to strike the child, and before Samuel could even process his thoughts, he acted. In one fell swoop, he sidled in front of the reverend, shoved him backward, and wedged the reverend's neck tightly between his forearm and the wall. Samuel could feel his pulse in his temples and heard it ringing in his ears. Through gritted teeth, the hotheaded Samuel said his final words to the man he detested so ardently.

"From the moment my family arrived in this town, you have continuously looked for every possible opportunity to make our lives a living hell. We have tolerated stupidity and boredom in your church and with your preaching. We have dealt with your belief that you may strike anyone you please. That ends now, Reynor. You shall not hit my son, and if you lift another hand against any member of my family, we will respond with ten-score force."

The reverend, terrified, struggled beneath Samuel's firm hold and attempted to peel his arm away with his fingers. Samuel only shoved him back harder.

"You are an idiot and a fool, Samuel Gorton," Reynor hissed. "You believe you can come to our peaceful town with your disorderly and insubordinate ways, but we have quelled your power, and now you will learn to deal with the most severe winter any amongst us has ever seen! God has delivered this storm as punishment to you and your family."

"Listen to me, Reverend," Samuel demanded. "You hit my wife. You put our maid, Ellen, on trial for *smiling*. You come to our celebration of Christmas—our Savior's birth—and have our landlord *throw us out of our home* in a dangerous winter storm. You continuously treat your entire congregation in a similar fashion, and you expect the people of this town to look upon you as a Christian man of faith. What kind of example are you setting? The gates of heaven are not open to men like yourself."

"I need not listen to you," Reynor said, struggling a little. "You have been tried and convicted in our court. If it seems unfortunate that you are being evicted on this dangerously cold night, perhaps you should get down on your knees and ask God why he has delivered this punishment to you and your family. As for my perspective, I believe I am simply delivering you unto God's wrath!"

"You know nothing of God's wrath because you know nothing of God's love, Reynor. You are unworthy of your post." With that, Samuel turned to his wife and nodded at her as a signal to leave, which she and the children did.

The stunned reverend remained very still, terrified that Samuel might grab him again or perhaps do something worse. Samuel walked past him, grabbed his coat and gloves from the wooden stand in the corner, and exited the home as well. When the family was outside the front door of what had been their home for the past eighteen months, they huddled together in the midst of the howling wind, trembling.

"Please remember, Mary, that we don't fail until we quit, and we should never quit anything important."

"I shall never forget that advice, dear husband."

"Good. Then we shall adhere to our plan. Be safe, and know that I love you all." Samuel kissed the foreheads of his wife and each of his children and watched as they disappeared behind the curtain of falling snow. He felt confident they would soon be in the warm safety of their friend's home.

Samuel knew he had little time before he was frostbitten. He could even die from exposure. He began walking in the direction of Aquidneck Island, hoping he might find some manner of shelter. It mattered not whether it was a barn, a wood, or the home of a banished "witch" that might be living in the woods. He struggled to recall some abandoned shelter but could not.

It did not take long for Samuel to understand the intensity of this winter storm. Having never experienced such, there was no way he could have grasped its magnitude until now. Even with his layers of wool and heavy furs, the cold bit through, a deadly challenge he was uncertain he could survive.

Because of the depth of the snow, he was not making good progress in his trek. His fingers and toes were becoming numb in the subzero air. The situation was quickly becoming desperate, and he evaluated his options. He had heard tales of forming a small shelter in the snow that would break the wind and keep temperatures at approximately the freezing temperature of water. Still, for now, he chose to push on.

Samuel . . .

It was like a whisper on the wind—or perhaps a distant shout. He looked around, saw nothing, and shrugged it off.

Samueeeeellll! He heard it come again and thought for a moment that perhaps it was an angel from heaven trying to tell him which way to go. He shook his head and continued to trudge through the knee-deep snow, deciding that his imagination was playing tricks on him.

"SAMUEL!"

That had to have been a voice, he thought. He stopped in his tracks and waited to see if it might call to him again.

"SAMUEL! It is I, John Wickes!"

John Wickes, he thought. *What on earth is he doing out here!*

Samuel turned to face his friend. Walking with him was Samuel's brother, Thomas.

"What *are* you two doing out in this storm!" Samuel shouted above the howling wind.

"Did you really think I was going to let my little brother brave this storm on his own?" Thomas responded. Samuel could see his smile even through the thick, blowing snow. The two brothers embraced. "You have never been as good surviving in the outdoors as me, brother."

"We are coming with you, Samuel!" John added. "Your Mary and children are now safely in my home with my wife. Ellen and Mary Smith also snuck out the back door to stay in our home. My family will join us when we find a new home on Aquidneck."

"Mary Smith is leaving Ralph?" Samuel asked, making idle talk in an attempt to help forget the bitter sting of the cold.

"So it would seem," John answered.

"While I applaud her courage," Samuel said, "I fear her decision might bring further repercussions on us and our friends in Plymouth."

"Another reason why we must quickly find a new home, Samuel."

"When we arrive at Aquidneck Island, I will prevail upon our friend Anne Hutchinson to help us find a place to move our families and to help us become quickly settled in the new environment."

Samuel was cut off by his friend. "You are *friends* with Anne Hutchinson?"

"Yes, of course, but we can discuss it later. For now, we must find shelter, or we shall not make it through the night, much less the three-day journey to Aquidneck."

"I am impressed but also better understand the hatred for you in Plymouth. Most believe Hutchinson is a witch or the devil's own personal servant."

"I fail to understand their reasoning, John. Anne is a good woman, a faithful believer in Jehovah, and a great teacher. No one in their right mind should see her as a witch."

"Samuel, no one ever suggested that the Massachusetts Puritans are in their right mind!" John joked. "Anyway, we have an immediate problem, and I know of a Narragansett village just a few miles from our present location. It may be they represent a lesser threat than the cold, which we most assuredly will not survive."

"Are they peaceful or savages?" Thomas asked. He had not spent as much time engaging with the Indians as Samuel.

"The Narragansett are quite friendly," Samuel responded. "I have made the acquaintance of a few of them in my wanderings in the woods, and Roger Williams has become friendly with their chieftains. I believe they would take us in and offer us shelter until this storm ends."

"Then let us waste no more time! We must get out of this storm!"

So it was that the three men trudged through the growing mounds of snow in what was the worst winter storm the colonists had experienced to that day.

The journey was not a simple hike through the woods but instead a treacherous battle against the elements. Their hands, faces, and toes were burning due to the sharp, biting cold wind from which there was no escape. Their eyes watered, and those tears froze immediately to their faces. Their noses ran, creating mustaches and goatees of ice crystals. Soon, their skin was completely numb, and their entire bodies ached deeply to the bone. John's thick, brown beard was soon white, coated with ice. Within a few hours, the men's pace slowed, and their muscles felt rigid. Thomas was falling behind, feeling sleepy and disoriented.

"Brother," Samuel said, putting his arm around his older sibling. "Are you doing OK? You must find a way to persist."

Shuddering, Thomas looked to his brother. "I f-feel sluggish, as if I am about to f-fall asleep. I d-d-d-don't think . . . I c-can't go on much longer." Thomas's eyes were barely open as he uttered those words. Samuel looked down at the ground, supporting much of his brother with one arm, and saw that Thomas's feet were barely able to move. Samuel had heard that frostbite could lead to the onset of gangrene, and he hoped that his brother was not at that point.

"John!" Samuel shouted ahead. "Can you see anything ahead, friend? My brother is not looking good, and I am not certain I can carry him much farther myself."

"I am seeing signs of the Narragansett tribe and can smell the smoke of their fires," John responded, not stopping. "Just follow my footsteps."

At that moment, Thomas went limp. Samuel caught him before he fell into the knee-deep snow. By now, John had disappeared from their view, but Samuel could make out the trail John had left behind as he half dragged, half carried his brother through the dark, snowy night.

A few minutes later, John appeared, accompanied by three Narragansett men. Two carried Thomas, and the other led Samuel to a thatch hut with a fire pit.

In spite of the language barrier, their Narragansett saviors were successful in cautioning them to warm up slowly rather than getting too close to the fire.

<hr />

Canonicus, sachem—or lead chief—of the Narragansett, had become familiar with the English since they had first settled in Plymouth. He

Forefathers & Founding Fathers

was not fond of them but had become friendly with Roger Williams. When he learned of Gorton's connection to Williams, he agreed to allow the three Englishmen to stay in the village until the storm subsided.

Gorton took advantage of the opportunity to befriend Canonicus and learn a little of their language and customs. During their three days in the Narragansett village, the two men struck up a friendship. Canonicus spoke reasonable English, but more importantly, he was a good and patient teacher of his native Algonquin language. Because of the adverse weather, the two men spent most of three days in Canonicus's home, talking while Samuel took notes on language and culture.

Canonicus was a wealth of information on tribal history and legends. He spoke with great pride of how the Narragansett traded and lived peacefully in the Narragansett Bay area. He also spoke of the long-standing friction between the Narragansett and the Mohegan.

Even in the midst of weather the likes of which he had never seen before, cast out of Plymouth and forced to seek a new home in the dead of winter, the days Samuel spent in Canonicus's village proved a blessing, as two men from very different cultures struck up the beginnings of a strong friendship.

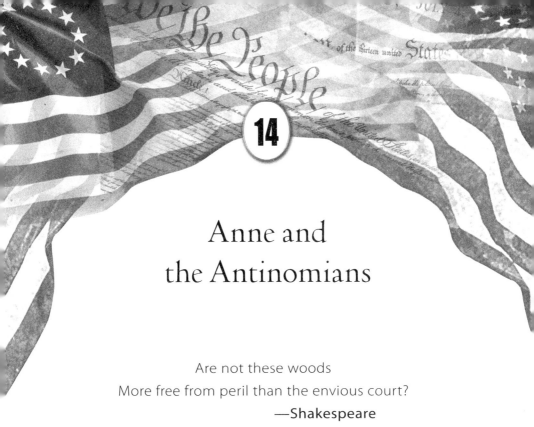

14

Anne and the Antinomians

> Are not these woods
> More free from peril than the envious court?
> —Shakespeare

1636–1638

"It is good that we have a large house, William. If our conventicles continue to grow, we shall need to build our own church," Anne remarked to her husband.

"I would build you a church, Anne, but you should be aware that elders in the colony are fearful of a woman teaching so many. The leadership of Boston does not hold with our values. The more popular you become, the more dangerous your position," Anne's husband told her.

"This is the New World, William. It is fresh soil where we can plant seeds that will forever change the English heart. We must stay the course, and I am certain we will prevail."

"I love your spirit and positive perspective. I think it is that spirit that your followers sense in your weekly teachings."

"I think as long as we have the support of Henry Vane and Reverend Cotton, we shall not have a problem. After all, Governor Vane is not just an advocate but a student in our conventicles."

In December 1636, Winthrop called together the mainstream Puritan leadership to discuss the growing Antinomian Controversy in the Boston colony. After much debate, they decided to accuse Hutchinson and her followers of Antinomianism and familism. There was much discussion about how to handle Cotton, but he was popular, and his services were the most attended in all of New England.

In the spring of 1637, believing they now held a major controlling interest in the colony, Hutchinson's advocates became extremely vocal. They had Governor Vane on their side but virtually all of the mainstream Puritan leadership on their heels, and in April, the tide began to turn.

Anne Hutchinson stood up, red faced, as the general court issued its ruling on her brother-in-law, Reverend Wheelwright: guilty of contempt and sedition. Something inside warned her this was a turning point, but then the court chose not to sentence him.

"Why do you think they chose not to sentence you?" Anne asked Wheelwright later that evening.

"I think they are concerned that Governor Vane would simply overturn any sentencing," Wheelwright speculated.

The former governor, John Winthrop, had been biding his time. In May 1637, Governor Vane was ejected from the governor's seat. Within weeks of being ousted, he sailed back to London. For Vane, the New World experiment had ended. He would not return to the colonies, though after his return to London he would achieve high posts in the English government.

On November 2, with Vane out of the way, Wheelwright's sentencing was issued: banishment from the colony.

Anne Hutchinson would face even greater judgment. Most men in the colonies held an idealized view of women, but this view did not hold for women who acted outside their expected role. Anne Hutchinson was teaching Scripture, a massive step outside the expected role of women in the colonies.

Winthrop, pleased with the results of the last few months, knew the time had come to act against Anne Hutchinson. He expected that, as she was a woman, he would crush her easily.

Later in November, Hutchinson's trial began, with John Winthrop serving as both accuser and judge. At the end of the first day, it became clear something needed to change.

That evening in the Hutchinson home, William made Anne sit so that he could fix her a warm drink. It was an uncommon role for him, even in the home of Anne Hutchinson, but William did not mind supporting Anne whenever she needed it. The world may have seen her as a calculating, hard woman, but to William, she was soft, gentle Anne Marbury—the woman he had loved since childhood.

"You surprised the magistrates and constantly out-fenced Winthrop today, Anne. I think they thought you would be easily overcome, and instead you have dominated them in their own court room."

"I am tired, William. I know that I must not let them see it, but the last year has worn on me. Tomorrow, I would be pleased if I could simply rest for the day."

"I have been in many such battles in my occupation, Anne. When you have wealth, power, or influence, people always want what you have. They will steal and kill to eliminate you or acquire your success. It is unfortunate that this is the way of so many men, but in life I have found it to be so. Winthrop has made it clear that he believes his role is to issue in the second Protestant Reformation, right here in the New World."

"Perhaps a reformation would be good, but Winthrop's is a reformation in the wrong direction," Anne said. "Why can't he see that he is taking us back to the overly powerful church theocracy that existed before the Renaissance?"

"I do not know. What I do know is that you must stay strong. If you need to, fall down or collapse in this house, for here, I can pick you up, but do not show weakness in front of these men."

"I do not see how we can win. The corruption of these men toward their beliefs is so great they care not for the facts, only for how to quash our teachings." Anne sipped her hot tea, clearly in need of rest.

"Your father, Francis Marbury, fought many such battles. What would he advise, were he here today?"

Anne smiled. "Yes, he fought many battles indeed," she remembered. "Father often told me to hold my temper and not give up on my beliefs."

"Then that is the path you should follow, but I think, my dear Anne, you may be correct that we cannot win the court in this town. These harbinger pioneers live under a different mandate than the bishop of London."

"This is true," Anne responded thoughtfully.

"What we can do is plant seeds of doubt in these men so that perhaps, someday, hope and a new light will spring from them. And for those who escape the vice of this court, we can give those followers of our teachings an example they can pursue in their own endeavors: a woman who would not bend under the hammers of corruption."

"And if I am banished or sentenced to death, as Winthrop desires?"

"Edward and I are working on that. Banishment we survive, and death we shall cheat by escape. We have assembled a group of a dozen who are looking for a new home. There is much land in these colonies, and most is outside the grasp of the Massachusetts Bay Colony. I know you are familiar with Roger Williams, who has befriended the Indians and has a haven. We have already begun speaking with him."

<hr />

The days of the trial continued, and Winthrop seized on a plan to blame all of the maladies of the colony on Hutchinson's presence. He said that God was punishing Boston for allowing Satan's very own serpent to live amongst them and preach to their populations.

William Coddington defended Hutchinson, asserting that there were no clear witnesses and that Winthrop was both accuser and judge and no man should be allowed to serve in both roles. Most importantly, he further pointed out there was no law of church or state that Hutchinson had broken. Coddington did not tell the court he was already working with William and Edward Hutchinson to secure an island in the Narragansett Bay where Hutchinson and her followers could move after the inevitable banishment.

In the end of the civil trial, Hutchinson was called a heretic and an instrument of the devil. She was a woman not fit for Boston society, and therefore, she must be banished as soon as events would allow.

With the end of the civil trial, Hutchinson was removed to detention in the home of Joseph Weld in the town of Roxbury. This detention would stay in place until the town elders were ready for the church trial. Many in the town wished to visit her during detention, but Winthrop pronounced that she was a dangerous woman who should not be exposed to any in the town, including her family.

She was frequently visited by members of the clergy, but it was their job to interrogate Hutchinson in preparation for their prosecution in the church trial.

Hutchinson's church trial began in the spring of 1638 at Cotton's church in Boston. Cotton had long been a friend and teacher to Anne. While he wanted to help her, he also wanted to maintain his status in Boston. It was a difficult balancing act, and one that ultimately worked for him, but the situation likely made Hutchinson's case even more desperate.

Near the end of the trial, Cotton secured the permission of the court to have Hutchinson stay in his home. By this time, Hutchinson had taken ill and was quite weak. Unbeknownst to any other than her husband, she was also four months pregnant. As a midwife, she well understood that being pregnant at the age of forty-seven was dangerous enough. Being ill while pregnant compounded that danger.

"I think we can end this entire calamity, Anne, if you would just recant and confess. This court will show mercy," Reverend Cotton told her as the two of them sat at his family dining-room table.

Anne glared at her mentor of over ten years, horrified that he would make such a suggestion. "I cannot do that, John. I simply cannot do that!"

"You must, Anne. The repercussions of what is happening in Boston will be felt not only by you but by dozens, perhaps hundreds, of others in this colony."

Pale and weakened by her sickness, her pregnancy, her long days in court, and house arrest away from her family, Anne stood. "Why, Reverend Cotton? Why would you ask me to recant what I know to be right and just? What you know to be right and just? These things I believe in my heart to be right. I cannot do as you ask. I cannot bow to this Puritan theocracy that smothers Boston and the Massachusetts Bay Colony. I simply cannot."

"I understand why you would take that perspective, Anne. Please sit, rest, and hear me out. Our goal of teaching and transforming must succeed, but it cannot if we are banished. I see a pathway, one that is right and just. In that pathway, I stay in Boston with you and our other followers. We should take small steps, and slowly we shall convert this community. That is how we shall succeed in this goal. As for you, Anne Hutchinson, I have a sense that you are an uncommon, great woman. You are a force that must not be defeated and banished here in Boston only to be forgotten and lost in the wilderness. You can make a difference here if we can only find a way for you to stay."

"Reverend . . ." she started to protest, but Cotton stopped her.

"This is not just about you, Anne. If you are banished, several dozen others will be too. Your pathway impacts them, and I do not believe you want their fates in the wilderness on your conscience."

Cotton stopped and studied Hutchinson, who seemed to be hearing what he said. "We can do this here in Boston in a way that allows you to continue your mission," he concluded.

"Let me sleep on this question, Reverend. I am weak and tired, and that does not allow me to clearly think this through."

The following morning, Anne Hutchinson agreed to Cotton's request. "Let us do this in a way that does not hurt our cause."

"That is a wise decision, Anne."

"Perhaps not. I heard my father tell tales of standing his ground against the bishop of London. How have I honored that here?"

"You honor it by protecting the lives of your followers. Your husband and son have already secured a new home a safe distance from the Massachusetts Bay."

Over the next couple of days, a recantation was developed by Anne and Reverend Cotton with the assistance of Reverend John Davenport. On March 22, 1638, she delivered the speech to the elders and congregation. Anne never felt comfortable with the strategy and immediately regretted having given the speech.

Unfortunately, Anne's reservations proved well founded. The entire plan backfired. Reverend Shepard argued that Hutchinson was a notorious imposter and a liar, adding these charges to her already long scroll. At this point, the tide against Anne turned to an avalanche, which, in a strange turn of events, caused even Cotton to fear for his own safety and terminate his support for her.

The elders delivered their guilty verdict, sentencing Hutchinson to banishment for life and excommunication from the church. Repercussions rippled through Boston as Winthrop and his sheriffs disarmed Hutchinson's followers in Boston and the surrounding towns.

But seventy miles to the south, Anne's eldest son, Edward, had prepared the pathway to their new home. Twenty-three men, including William Coddington, had already signed the Portsmouth Compact and had begun building a new town on Aquidneck Island. With Hutchinson's verdict, that number swelled by several dozen more. Those who still believed in religious freedom hoped the new town would be a safe place to live.

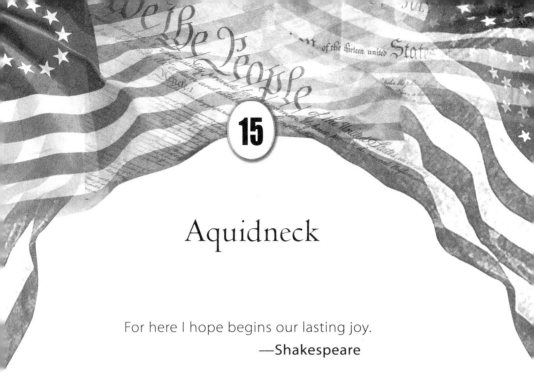

15

Aquidneck

> For here I hope begins our lasting joy.
> —Shakespeare

Christmas 1638–January 1639

Samuel, along with his brother and John Wickes, departed from the Narragansett village on Christmas Day of 1638. Canonicus assigned two of his young braves to escort them safely to their destination. Because of the snow and ice, the trip took them a week.

Upon their arrival in Aquidneck, Samuel, Thomas, and John were warmly greeted by William Hutchinson, who immediately insisted that the three travelers stay in the Hutchinson house until they were settled. Less than a year old, Aquidneck was a very small settlement that did not have an inn or tavern, but it did support a small trading post.

"Welcome to our home, Samuel," Anne said as Samuel came in. Samuel embraced Anne and could not help but observe that she seemed to have aged immensely since their last meeting.

"How are you, Anne? I have heard bits of news of your ordeal with those atrocious Boston Puritans."

"I fear the church in Boston is beyond repair, but I am pleased we have a new home upon which we can build the foundations of our beliefs," she responded.

"Indeed. Please tell me of this new colony," Samuel asked.

"I will, Samuel, but tell me of Mary and your family."

"I left them as the winter storm arrived. They are in hiding in Plymouth and await fairer weather and news of a new home."

"We should send for them soon," Anne told him. "A new home can be built as weather permits and be complete with the beginning of spring. Plymouth is not a good place to hide, and we do not want Governor Prence to discover them and rule badly on their behalf."

"I shall begin work on the home immediately, as I choose not to be long away from my fair Mary. She is with child and should be in safer holdings when the child is delivered."

"I would consider it a great honor to serve as the midwife for her delivery, Samuel."

"Hah! Mary would think you are the Lord's angel. I am certain you are aware by now that she is quite the admirer of you and your work."

"We must educate her otherwise, Samuel," Anne joked.

"You do not know my wife! But about this colony."

"Yes, of course, Samuel. As you know, when Winthrop replaced Vane as governor of Massachusetts Bay Colony, I was constantly taunted and imprisoned. It became clear that we would ultimately be forced to leave Boston. We dispatched William Coddington to meet with Roger Williams with a goal of securing lands on which we could establish a settlement."

"I have always believed that the church should not also be the government. It is too much power concentrated in one place, and it is that which Winthrop now holds," Samuel commented.

"This is true," Anne nodded.

"Why did you not move to Roger's colony in Providence?" Samuel suggested.

"He did prevail upon us to do so. It was a consideration, but as you know, Williams prefers to maintain a peaceful connection with Boston. I do not think that would have been possible if we had moved there. Winthrop now considers me a firebrand enemy, and I did not wish to exact any retribution on our friends in Providence."

"I understand," Samuel responded.

"I imagine you do." Anne smiled. She continued, "Anyway, we secured this piece of land in a rightful purchase from the Narragansett and established a legal Portsmouth Compact. We have elected Coddington as our governor, though we are now regretful of that decision."

"Coddington was one of your supporters, was he not?" Samuel asked.

"Indeed he was, and that was not an easy decision for him to stand by once Vane was replaced. You may be aware that even Cotton has turned against our small group to protect his position in Boston. If you had asked me two years ago, I would have guessed the opposite—that Cotton would support us and Coddington would side with the Puritans. Still, now that he has power, Coddington has become autocratic and is working to convert our colony into his own private feudal domain, like Winthrop's in Massachusetts Bay."

"Alas, we left England to escape these things only to come to Boston and Plymouth, where an even worse plight has been created. Now we move to newer parts and find our friends prefer power over rightful freedom and peaceful living," Samuel remarked. "What would you do, Anne?"

"It is most unfortunate we find ourselves in this situation. Coddington rules as a king rather than an elected governor. I fear we must either move or find a way to replace him."

"You should not leave. This is your rightful home, which you have paid dearly for in gold and in deed. We must stand our ground and challenge the legitimacy of Coddington and his magistrates."

"Samuel, we feel the same, but we are weary from our last fight in Boston. We have chosen to live, at least for now, under his rule."

"You must stand and remove this tyrant. I will organize a way for him to be deposed and for you to take his place. This new colony would have opportunity and liberty under Anne Hutchinson as governor!"

"Ah, Samuel, your witticism is worthy of light frivolity!" Anne laughed.

"I do not speak in jest, Anne," Samuel told her. "These colonies have been ruled by men who seem to know not the historical value of our present appointment. They wish to return us to the theocracy of the church before the Renaissance, and we cannot allow it. There is no one better in this New World to govern than you, Anne Hutchinson."

"Thank you, Samuel, but even this colony is not ready for a woman governor," she argued.

"Perhaps not, Anne, but we shall not know unless we try. I feel certain my Mary would advise me to defend and support you as governor."

Anne was firm. "And Mary, too, would make a fine administrator in that office, but no, Samuel, my election would not be a demonstration of prudence. Were I elected governor, I feel certain that both Boston and Plymouth colonies would dispatch militias to arrest us all and then hang us from the gallows."

Samuel considered her comment. His frequent conversations with Mary had convinced him that in many ways, women would make better superintendents of the governor's office, but he could see Anne Hutchinson was resolute. His eyes scanned the room and stopped on William. What Samuel knew of William was all favorable, but in many ways, he lived in the shadow of his infamous wife. Still, he was a successful businessman as well as a gentle and well-educated individual who would serve the office well.

"I believe, then, that we should support William Hutchinson for governor of Aquidneck," Samuel suggested.

The room was silent as all heads turned to William. "Samuel, might I suggest that you begin calling our colony Portsmouth. It is the suggested name as stated in the compact," was William's simple response.

"Portsmouth it is, then, and I will take that as a yes! Does anyone in this room not support that move?" Samuel asked.

"I am certain my children would," Anne joked.

"And how many is that, Anne?" Samuel half joked.

"Fifteen at last count, but sometimes we must count again!" Anne answered, to which everyone laughed.

"At this rate, my dear friend, you will have a city of your own progeny!"

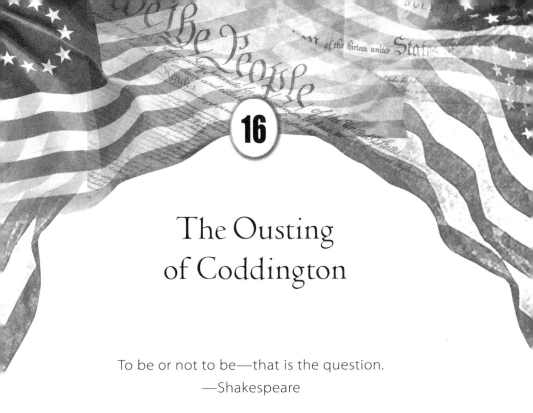

The Ousting of Coddington

> To be or not to be—that is the question.
> —Shakespeare

1639–1640

For the next two months, Samuel and several residents of Portsmouth worked on construction of the new Gorton home, along with homes for Thomas and John Wickes. When the homes were completed in late March, Samuel sent for his wife and children. By the first week of April, Mary Gorton arrived in Portsmouth with the children and six other families.

While the Gorton children and Hutchinson children began forming friendships, the focus for the adults now turned to ousting Coddington. Residents of the colony were prepared to remove control of the governorship from him in favor of handing it to the highly respected husband of Anne Hutchinson.

The lead decision makers and Hutchinson proponents convened at her home to discuss and finalize a strategy. Several of Gorton's supporters had arrived from Plymouth, which shifted the balance of power clearly to Hutchinson's camp.

"I have heard that Coddington and his supporting magistrates will be departing for Boston specifically to discuss how to remove you from this colony," John Wickes explained to Samuel.

"Me? Why me?" Samuel asked in surprise.

"The winds have informed him that you are planning to have him removed. He is desperate to retain power and will do so even if he must collaborate with Boston," Wickes answered.

"I think it would be quite easy to mobilize to oust him while he is gone," William Hutchinson suggested.

"I agree," Anne chimed in.

Samuel scratched his chin and looked around the room. "Well, I am certainly in favor of the passive strategy. Any other thoughts on this?"

Everyone nodded in agreement.

Immediately after Coddington departed, Anne Hutchinson called an assembly of all residents of the colony. An election was held, with Gorton overseeing the votes and with several others providing checks. While Gorton was offered a position in the new government, he refused, saying he only wanted to support Hutchinson and the community. The resulting vote was unanimous, and William Hutchinson was elected. What followed was the formation of the first civil democracy in America.

Upon his return, Coddington tried to protest the outcome but was unable to do so. "Gorton, this election was illegal, and I shall see to it that Hutchinson is deposed," Coddington threatened.

"A just civil government has been established in this colony. Using parliamentary procedures, you may oppose Mr. Hutchinson any time you feel appropriate," Gorton answered simply.

"You are a fool and a scoundrel, Samuel Gorton! I shall see to it that you are appropriately punished when my position is restored!"

"It seems unlikely, knowing how heavily the votes were weighted against you," Gorton answered. "The Hutchinsons have planned, negotiated, and paid for this piece of land, and it is primarily their followers who have joined them here on this island."

"So you say, but Massachusetts has recognized me as rightful governor. In your ignorance, you have replaced me and shall now have to contend with them," Coddington argued.

"We think not. This land was legally purchased from the Narragansett with the approval of Roger Williams. We are subjects not of the Massachusetts Bay Colony but of the crown of England. Enough of you, Coddington; be gone. It is the voting public that has ousted you, not me!" With that, Gorton turned and left the room, with Coddington still trying to make his case.

Coddington did try to achieve a parliamentary reelection but was unable to achieve even a modicum of support. After that, he took his belongings and small number of supporters to the south end of the Island and founded the town of Newport. Once established at Newport, Coddington realized he was still in possession of all the legal paperwork and bill of sale for Aquidneck Island. Even though he had not contributed an ounce of gold to pay for those deeds, he began using those documents to usurp any legal authority held by Hutchinson. Coddington essentially controlled the deeds, thus preventing any land grants to be made by the government in Portsmouth. This chokehold on the progress should have resulted in repercussions for Coddington, but William Hutchinson was unwilling or unable to find a way to overcome this obstacle.

With his newfound illegal chokehold on commerce, in mid-1640, Coddington was able to once again seize control. Interestingly, once in control, he kept the civil government in place, as it was performing far more efficiently than the theocracies of Boston and Plymouth or the somewhat simpler government of the Providence colonies.

After returning to power as governor, Coddington immediately set out to get revenge on the Hutchinsons, Gortons, and several other members of Hutchinson's government. He called in his most trusted advisers and posed the question in diplomatic terms.

"It seems to me we must now remove from our presence and colony those individuals who have been obstacles to our success," Coddington said.

"While you are now in power, you should remember that Gorton and Hutchinson are very popular," William Dyer cautioned. Dyer respected Gorton and Hutchison and wanted to protect his friendship with them. "Furthermore, we have adopted the civil government that they established, and that government has begun producing much success and growth. I would caution against a path of revenge and allow these peaceful settlers to stay amongst us."

"NO!" Coddington shouted. "We will find a way to extricate them. With Anne Hutchinson and Samuel Gorton, this colony will never see harmonious rule from our government."

"They have committed no crime," Dyer said. He understood Coddington's anger and wished to maintain his position in Coddington's government, but he could not appreciate the man's methods of governance or his vengeful intent.

"I think your opinion is twisted by your long-standing friendship with both families," Coddington told him. "If you wish to maintain a position in my government, you will aid me in this endeavor."

"Gorton is a smart man and is content to maintain his household so that he can stay in Portsmouth. I do not think he will commit a crime," Dyer responded.

"I am told that Plymouth had this problem and brought charges against Gorton's servant. I suggest we do the same here. Find a way to bring charges against Gorton, even if it means creating charges against his servant again. Get it done quickly!"

Coddington's advisors were not in favor of his request, but they also knew that failure in this task would create reprisals from Coddington that they did not wish to see. Over the next month, as the autumn of 1640 dwindled into frost, they concocted a plan to have a cow trample crops and property on Gorton's homestead.

Samuel, Mary, and their children were out for the day visiting with the Hutchinsons. William had recently fallen ill, and many in the town were making visits to support Anne and her very large family during his illness. The Hutchinsons were the richest family on Aquidneck, so support came in the form of visits, cooked meals, and time spent with William, Anne, and their children.

Forefathers & Founding Fathers

While Samuel, Mary, and the Gorton children were at the Hutchinson house, Ellen Aldridge heard commotion outside the Gorton home and exited the house to investigate. A cow was trampling what remained of a small patch of corn. Ellen called out for its owner but received no reply. "Git, you miserable bovine! Who has set you free on this property?" She spoke to the cow, not really expecting a reply. The cow seemed somewhat stubborn and content to wander just where Ellen had found it, in the middle of her crops, destroying what would become precious winter resources.

Running back to the house, Ellen grabbed the switch she used on her own family's cattle and then returned and began to prod the oblivious cow out of her cornfields. It was at that moment the owner appeared from the woods.

"What manner of molestation have you perpetrated upon my property!" the clearly angry female owner of the cow demanded.

Ellen stared at the woman, whom she did not recognize. The entire circumstance seemed strange to Ellen. Why would a stranger come so close to the Gorton home with her cow? Ellen and the Gortons knew everyone living in this part of the colony. And there was not much point in herding a solitary cow. "Madam, your animal was trampling my crops. I am quite familiar with livestock and have done no harm to this beast," Ellen answered. "Your cow, on the other hand, has destroyed crops necessary for my family's survival during the winter months."

"How little you know of such things. You have done significant harm to my animal, and I shall take this up with our local government immediately!" With that, the cow's owner wrapped a rope around its neck and led it off the Gorton property.

When Samuel returned home, Ellen explained the situation, and both felt this was not an issue worthy of the local government. Nevertheless, the next day, the magistrate appeared at the Gorton homestead to serve Ellen, demanding she appear at the court immediately on the charges of assaulting a cow and its owner.

As Coddington's advisors had predicted, Samuel would not allow Ellen to appear but instead went to the court himself the following day at the appointed time. He did not realize until his appearance that he had fallen prey to the same trick used in Plymouth a couple years earlier.

Many Gorton supporters had heard about the incident and wished to observe the spectacle. Coddington had anticipated this and barred or arrested anyone who tried to enter the courtroom.

"Mr. Gorton, this court has already determined your servant to be guilty, and since she is your *servant*, she may not speak in this courtroom."

"Ellen is an employee in our household. How can she be guilty of a crime when all she did was lead a trespassing cow off of my crops? It seems the careless owner who allowed her cow to trespass and trample my crops has committed the true crime. Further, how can you have already reached a verdict without hearing evidence or allowing a defense of the supposed crime?"

"The court does not recognize women or servants, Mr. Gorton, and you are therefore responsible for her crimes. Furthermore, this court shall decide how it reviews evidence and issues verdicts, not ordinary citizens and blasphemous liars like yourself."

"There have been no crimes committed here other than a cow trampling my crops!" Gorton shot back, already angered by the incident and proceedings.

"We have determined otherwise."

"And if you have come to such conclusion, you are fools and jackasses!" Gorton said.

With that, the magistrate approached Gorton and forcefully restrained him. The scene immediately escalated, perhaps as Coddington had hoped or planned, and a brawl broke out in the courtroom. The few Gorton supporters that had managed to be present were shouting in the melee, but this time Coddington was prepared and held the upper hand.

With the ensuing ruckus, Coddington took over the proceedings. "Samuel Gorton, you are not the sort that we want in this colony."

"And what sort would that be, William Coddington?" Gorton asked. "The sort that, once put in power by his friends, subjugates them like a king, or the sort who absconds with public records so that

Samuel Gorton in Coddington's Court

he might steal his way back into power against the will of the popular vote? Perhaps the kind of person you want in this colony is one who tricks house servants in order to snare honest citizens like myself into your court for trumped-up false charges?"

"Enough of this blasphemy!" Coddington shouted over what had become a roar of agreement in the court supporting Gorton's assessment.

Coddington began to slam the gavel until the courtroom calmed a bit. "This court and government finds you guilty of fourteen counts of transgressions against our colony. We will not hear your words spoken in defense, as those will be nothing but lies. All you that adhere to the rules of the king should consider taking Gorton from this court and carrying him to prison."

"This court is a perversion of justice, and so are you!" Samuel cried. "When the good people of Portsmouth established this civil government, we intended not for such to happen. Yet you have taken us to the lowest depths of depravity. You have committed the worst crime of all, that of pushing swords into the backs of those who supported you and trusted you as a friend! You say that I should be carried away, but I say instead: all you that adhere to the rules of the king, take Coddington from this court and carry him to prison!"

"You have no case here, Gorton, only platitudes. This court has ruled that you shall not speak, and now we will enforce that ruling along with your sentencing of lashings and banishment from this colony and island." Coddington raised his hand and motioned to the marshal to proceed in what apparently was a predetermined move.

With that, the marshal grabbed Gorton and attempted to escort him out of the courtroom. Gorton and several of his followers protested. Several people tried to bar the door, demanding that Gorton have the opportunity to formally present his case, though none really understood what crime he had committed. Most realized Coddington was using his position of power to take revenge upon Gorton for having orchestrated his overthrow.

Coddington came down from the bench and, along with several other magistrates, assisted the marshal in escorting Gorton to the town square, where he would be publicly whipped prior to his banishment.

Gorton's friend and ally John Wickes was placed in the stocks in the town square, facing the whipping post where Gorton was tied by the wrists.

Obadiah Dunster, whip in hand, proudly claimed to be a fifth-generation executioner. He often bragged that his great-grandfather had lopped off the head of Anne Boleyn, second wife of King Henry VIII. He had come to the colonies in 1634, been kicked out of Boston, ousted from Plymouth, and then lived in the wilderness for a year. He had recently joined Coddington's colony at Newport and looked forward to exercising his talents of delivering appropriate punishments to the sinners of the New World.

As Samuel's wrists were being tied to the post, the fear began to knot up in his stomach. In his lifetime, he had never been exposed to significant pain, and he only came face to face with the fear as the threat of pain was now about to arrive. He glanced at Dunster, who appeared to be a brawny individual well tempered and designed for his trade. Dunster cracked his whip in the air for effect, and Samuel jerked, startled by the sound. Dunster awaited the nod from Coddington so that he could begin.

The nod came, along with a command for fifteen lashes.

Dunster smiled, aimed, and took a full swing. It was his belief that the first stripe was the most painful one, and he liked to take extra efforts to make certain that was so.

Samuel felt the crack of the whip on his back with a searing pain that violently ripped through his body. With that first hit, he did not know how he could possibly survive fourteen more. The second came, nearly as violent as the first, and then the third. By the fifth, he could no longer count, only feel the cumulative, searing pain as warm blood began to trickle down his naked back. His mind simply did not acknowledge the thirteenth, fourteenth, or fifteenth. Some observers thought perhaps he was already dead as he hung limp from his bonded wrists. He returned from consciousness when someone poured water on his bleeding back.

Samuel Gorton sat up, knowing this memory and the scars from those lashes would remain with him for an eternity. He scanned the faces of the onlookers, many whom he knew, all of whom were shocked by the suddenness of the day's events. After another minute, he struggled to stand but was unable to do so. His back burned and felt wet, though he did not know if he felt water or blood. After another minute, he tried again, and this time, he managed to stand and then, slowly, to take a step.

Ignoring the fear that they might be next if they helped him, several onlookers swept in to support the determined Samuel Gorton as he attempted to show he would not be defeated by this event.

Coddington rode up on horseback beside Gorton. The contrast between the two men was startling: Coddington, with perfect posture, sitting upright on his horse with his wig and frilly, bright English attire; and Gorton, sweaty, barely able to stay upright, standing in a pool of blood. The scene created an image that many would recall for a long time.

With a smile of satisfied revenge and a flash of anger in his eye, Coddington glared at Gorton. "Be gone, you miserable, blasphemous son of Satan. Should you ever return to this colony, you will experience double that number of lashes."

Bleeding, shirtless, and now banished from the Portsmouth colony—but with the assistance of many from Portsmouth—Gorton began to hobble toward his house. He and the Hutchinsons had attempted a great experiment, forming the first civil democracy in the New World. They had been defeated by the wiles of a power-hungry man who was intent on creating his own personal fiefdom.

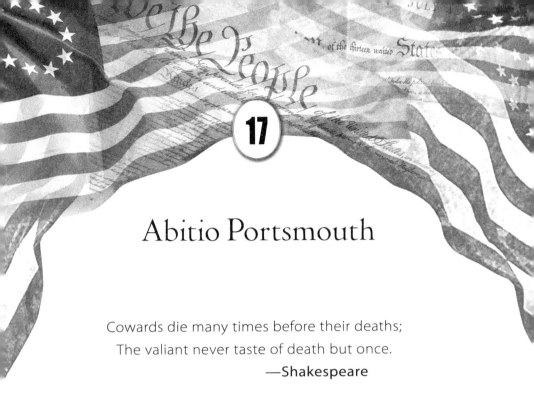

Abitio Portsmouth

Cowards die many times before their deaths;
The valiant never taste of death but once.
—Shakespeare

Bleeding from his lashing and still carrying his shackles, Samuel rambled through town as shocked bystanders stood watching on the side. Most had heard that Coddington was arresting anyone that appeared to be a supporter of Gorton's, and as such, there was fear of similar retributions. On the edge of town, a magistrate removed Gorton's shackles, leaving only the bloody lacerations as a reminder of his punishment. Samuel finally made his way to his home, where Mary and his children greeted him with horror and helped him into the house.

"I am so sorry, Mary. I lost my temper in the courtroom, and Coddington saw that as an opportunity to prevail. The circumstance and their methods anger me. It is unjust that Anne, William, and I have formed this colony, established this civil government, and I allowed my temper to thwart our maintaining it."

"This is not your fault, Samuel. You went to court believing they wished to resolve a dispute about a cow and trampled crops. That was never the case. Everyone in town is quite aware that Coddington intentionally tricked you. He relied on the fact that he knew you would defend Ellen and that he could spark your passion in this situation."

"Yes, I have thought as much, and for a time in the courtroom, I believed the people might rise up. As I remember who was in the court, very few of those who support our position were present. I suspect Coddington anticipated an uprising and arrested several to prevent certain people from being there."

"I am aware that many have been arrested today," Mary offered.

"The entire circumstance is unfortunate," Samuel said bitterly. "We have worked so hard to create civil liberties and religious freedom in this colony, and Coddington has now hoodwinked the population and circumvented the laws to his own end." As he spoke, Mary gently washed the blood from the stripes on his back.

"What will become of us now?" Mary asked.

"We have been banished once again and are forced to fall back on my creed . . ."

"Yes, Samuel: we don't fail until we quit, and we should never quit anything important," Mary quoted.

Samuel smiled in spite of the stinging pain radiating from his back. "I think we shall accept Roger Williams's invitation and move to Providence. Perhaps there, with his pacifist nature and protective veil, we can secure some peace."

"How do you think Coddington will treat Anne and William?" Mary asked.

"We should prevail upon them to join us, though I suspect William is not fit to make the trip," Samuel suggested. "It is good that Coddington has focused on me. Perhaps he will leave the Hutchinsons in peace so that William can recover from his illness."

While Mary was treating Samuel's wounds, a group of colonists had gathered at their door. Samuel pulled down his shirt and went out front to address them.

"Mary and I will comply with our banishment. We would appreciate any assistance in packing our belongings and selling those items that will not make the journey. We will be accepting Roger

Williams's invitation to move to Providence. My family would very much appreciate any help with a boat that can provide us and our belongings passage across the bay."

There was some discussion by many in Portsmouth about joining the Gorton family once they were established in the new location. Many had come to appreciate the civil liberties and peaceful nature of the government established by Gorton and Hutchinson.

—≫•०•≪—

By the next morning, all of the Gorton belongings had been packed on the same flatbed wagon the Gortons had purchased upon their arrival in Boston. One of the villagers provided a boat that would carry them on the half-day trip to Providence. Samuel and his family took the morning to visit with Anne and William Hutchinson.

Anne looked at the lashes on Samuel's back and showed Mary how to properly treat them so they would not become infected. "Samuel, I am distraught that our old friend Coddington would be willing to exact such punishment on you," Anne commented.

"I never imagined anything could be so painful. Needless to say, sleep was quite impossible last night, and I expect it to stay that way for some time."

"I suggest you find some willow trees and boil the bark into a tea. I have found that to be quite good for getting rid of pain," Anne told him.

"I will do that. With regards to our move, you must consider joining us in Providence. If necessary, I will return and help you and the family make the move," Samuel insisted.

"No. We cannot travel with William in this condition, and it would not be wise for you to return to Aquidneck. It is our hope that Coddington and his government will leave us alone now that he has exacted such extreme revenge upon you and some of the others," Anne said flatly.

"I have the same hope for you, but what if Coddington persists with you?"

"We shall not go to Providence, Samuel. My family and I have had our fill of Puritan government theocracies and oppression. If we cannot live peacefully here in Portsmouth, we will move south to one of the Dutch settlements of New Netherland."

This news hit Samuel and Mary hard. They had become good friends with the Hutchinsons. Their children had become friends, and Samuel had come to believe that together their families would pave a way to a world where religious freedom existed in a government that treated all men and women fairly and equally.

"Anne, this is sad news. Our family has become attached to yours. If you move south, we will not likely see you again," Samuel said.

There was silence in the room as the realization struck home for both families.

"Of course, if you stay in Portsmouth, we should plan annual gatherings," Samuel pointed out.

"Let's dispense with this pall!" Mary Gorton cried. "We shall see each other again, and perhaps we shall be blessed with a marriage between two of our children someday."

Susanna Hutchinson, now seven years old, came running up to hug Samuel. "I hope you come visit me, Uncle Samuel. I shall miss your jokes and playtime." She kissed him affectionately on the cheek.

"I promise that I shall come visit, but I will not play tea party with you, though perhaps I can convince young Sam to do so!" Samuel had noticed that his young son seemed to have a childhood interest or attraction to Susanna. Perhaps it was her unusual red hair or some other unexplainable chemistry, but the adult parents had noticed it while the two children denied it.

"Nooooo, he's a boy!" Susanna exclaimed.

Samuel glanced at Sam, who had flushed red at the thought of playing with a girl. "Then I will come to check up on your fiery red locks," Samuel said as he twisted a ringlet of her strawberry blonde hair. He then lifted her up and kissed her on the forehead. "Since you refuse to play with young Sam, run along, and go play with that infinitely large number of siblings you have."

Forefathers & Founding Fathers

"It's not infinite, Uncle Samuel!" Susanna protested, giggling. "Mum has had only fifteen of us!" She ran out of the room.

After a fair amount of tears and hugs, the families said their goodbyes, promising to meet again in the near future.

With that, the Gortons made haste to catch their boat north to Providence.

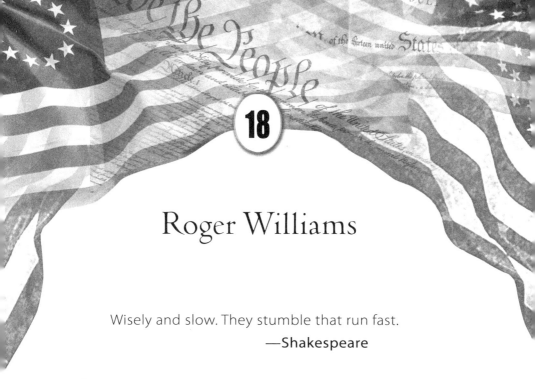

Roger Williams

Wisely and slow. They stumble that run fast.
—Shakespeare

March 1640

Awaiting the arrival of Gorton and his family, Roger Williams and a small group of Providence colonists were at the makeshift dock built earlier that year.

"I know it is not under the best of circumstances, but accept our welcome into the Providence colony," Williams said. "You and your family are welcome in my house over the coming weeks as you plan where you will live and how construction should begin on your house."

The two men embraced, and Samuel introduced Mary and the children to Roger and his associates.

"I do not know if it makes sense for us to stay here in Providence. We said our goodbyes to Anne Hutchinson and her family this morning, and they have made a point of reminding me that we are neither liked nor welcome in the military confederation of colonies, also known as the United Colonies, particularly Plymouth," Samuel answered as they began walking up an embankment toward the small Providence settlement.

"It is true, Samuel, that you and the Hutchinsons have become a gathering point for antagonism by the Massachusetts Bay Colony. I can assure you that amongst the settlers of Providence, that will not be the case, but I cannot promise that Winslow, Winthrop, Coddington, and the others will not seek reason to antagonize you. I should say that I cannot imagine why they might care so much about Samuel Gorton that they will reach into Providence to harass you when they have other problems to resolve."

"I hope what you say is, in fact, true, and we have suffered enough that it would be our preference to quietly go about our business," Samuel answered.

"Let us not speculate negatively on this matter, Mr. Gorton. Boston has left me and this colony to our own means over the past few years, and I expect them to continue doing so unless we do something to stir up that hive," Williams pointed out.

"I will look at securing land south of Providence in an area that isolates my family and those who plan to follow from Portsmouth," replied Samuel. "I believe it is important that we do this in the event the government of the Massachusetts Bay Colony decide to intervene. Perhaps it might be prudent for you to write a letter to Winthrop complaining of me so that he and his magistrates do not take the occasion to orchestrate an annexing of your settlement."

"I should like to consider such a letter. As you know, it is my preference to passively avoid confrontation with our neighboring colonies."

"And I would not savor the prospect of any ill coming your way, Mr. Williams. I would suggest you tell them that I am bewitching the people of Providence or some such."

"Perhaps I shall consider that but ask nothing of them in return. With regards to land, Canonicus has told me that he met you two winters ago," Roger said. "His nephew, Miantonomo, has lands south of Providence that you could purchase. I will see to it that you have the opportunity to meet with him."

"Thank you. Your hospitality and support are very much appreciated." Samuel smiled. "I met Miantonomo several years ago, before he became chief. One very cold night, after I was banished from Plymouth, I wandered into the village where Canonicus was living. At the time, it was clear that Canonicus was going to pass the chief title to Miantonomo."

"I am glad you have had cordial dealings with the Narragansett. We are happy to have men of your vision in our colony. Anyway, enough of this! Tell me how your friends Anne and William are doing! I should imagine having Coddington abscond with the colony's legal documents and using that to retake control is weighing heavily on William."

"Coddington is also now claiming that he is the sole founder of the colony. In truth, it was William Hutchinson and his eldest son who planned, negotiated, and financed the founding of Portsmouth," Gorton added. "It is sad they had a friendship that has fallen to this level."

"I know who truly purchased Aquidneck. I participated in that negotiation with and for the Hutchinsons. Coddington is a scoundrel, mostly out for his own interests. William Hutchinson put up over half of the money for that purchase," Roger observed.

"As you said, Coddington seems mostly out for his own interests. I now wear the sting of Coddington's whip on my back and wish not to take a Christian approach to him, though I suppose in time I shall learn to do that." Samuel lightly touched his back, recalling the pain of the public whipping just three days earlier. "With regards to Anne and William . . . Anne is doing well, though she has not added to that very large family in some time. We hope the days of her bringing new children into the world are now done, but do not be surprised if she makes claims that she'd like another. William, on the other hand, is not well. He is sickly and spends most of his time in bed."

"Do you think this political issue in Portsmouth has worn on him, Mr. Gorton?"

"I believe it has contributed," Samuel conceded, "but William has not been a healthy man for some years. If you must know the truth, when we decided to oust Coddington last year, I prevailed upon them to elect Anne as governor."

"Surely you jest? A woman governor would most assuredly effect the wrath of the surrounding colonies!"

"No, sir, I do not jest on this matter. I think she would have made a fine governor, and perhaps she would have had an equal sum of cleverness to have stopped Coddington from returning to power. We made a grave error not protecting our patents and charter."

"Gorton, you are far more progressive than I. While I agree with your assertion about Mrs. Hutchinson's intellect and wit, I do not believe a woman should govern."

"That is a debate for another time, my friend. For now, let us plan how to grow this colony without enduring the acrimony of Massachusetts Bay."

Roger Williams noticed John Greene walking with his family and motioned for him to come over.

"Mr. Greene! Meet Samuel Gorton. I think you and John have much in common, Mr. Gorton. Mr. Greene, along with myself, was one of the original twelve proprietors of the Providence Plantations deed." The two men shook hands. Williams smiled as he studied the two men. "Each of you is incapable of suffering obtuseness from Massachusetts Bay. Each of you is open in your opposition to those governors who would oppress your beliefs."

"Then it is good to have a brother-in-arms," Samuel said.

Roger Williams frowned, suddenly aware of an aspect to making this introduction he had not yet considered. He felt a weight deep inside his being. "I say to both of you, I appreciate your strength of character, but I entrust that you will not antagonize the harmony of Providence Plantations."

"I will respect your harmony, Mr. Williams," Greene began, "but you cannot expect me to discontinue my opposition to the oppression for which I crossed the ocean to escape."

Samuel felt a need to stay silent, though he immediately felt drawn to the open and staunch nature of John Greene. "Might I suggest we find a tract of land outside the immediate bounds of Providence Plantations?"

Gorton and Greene walked off together to discuss Gorton's new home, conscious of the fact that they had each met a kindred spirit in the quest for religious freedom and individual rights.

Shawomet

> This above all: to thine own self be true,
> And it must follow, as the night the day,
> Thou canst not then be false to any man.
> —Shakespeare

1640–1642

Shortly after his arrival in Providence, with the assistance of John Greene, Samuel purchased a small tract of land from Robert Cole in an area five miles south of Providence. This region of the Narragansett Bay had been settled by several families, including William Arnold, Robert Cole, William Carpenter, and William Arnold.

Almost immediately after Gorton completed construction of his new home, the Arnolds decided they wanted to be annexed by the Massachusetts Bay Colony. Naturally, Roger Williams and Samuel Gorton were horrified by this idea and expressed vehement opposition. The Gortons and several other families likewise opposed worked to prevent the annexation. But the Arnolds had a stronghold, and Roger Williams was in London securing a permanent patent for the Providence colonies. In his absence, the Arnolds took the opportunity to work against Gorton's interests and finalize arrangements with Massachusetts.

The Arnolds took a two-pronged approach to the strategy. First, they accelerated their negotiations with Massachusetts Bay authorities, who were more than happy to comply, and second, they started a campaign to undermine Gorton personally.

With the prodding of Arnold and his associates, Gorton soon learned that Massachusetts was preparing many different charges against him, with the ultimate goal of securing a death penalty. He recalled Anne Hutchinson's reluctance to deal with the Puritans further. She had moved her family to New Netherland, well out of reach of the Puritan colonies.

Gorton was now convinced that Anne had been correct in this decision. He believed it would be best for his family, along with eleven other families who held similar political views, to move once again.

The twelve families pooled their resources and purchased land from Indian chief Miantonomo. Since his move to Providence, Gorton had begun to spend significant time with Miantonomo and the Narragansett. Samuel had come to appreciate the Indian customs, had learned the language, and had become an advocate for fair treatment of the Indians.

The land purchased was thirty miles outside of any current land claims made by the Massachusetts Bay Colony and, at least theoretically, should have provided a buffer of distance and time.

Samuel sat with Mary in the small family room. A fire burning in the fireplace provided warmth against the subzero temperatures of the nighttime New England winter.

"With spring coming soon, we should be able to begin construction of our new home in Shawomet," Mary said as she stared at the flames dancing around and consuming the split logs.

"Yes, another move, my dear. I must admit that I shall not miss this place," Samuel answered. "The tensions and constant attacks from the Arnolds have made our life here more difficult than anyone could have anticipated. It is troubling that this man and his associates, who were taken in by Roger when they were tossed out of Boston, have chosen to turn their backs on the primary objective of Providence Plantations: inspiration of religious freedom."

"I wonder, Samuel, how William Arnold does not see the irony of this? Had Roger Williams and our Providence Plantations been part of Boston when Arnold was exiled from Boston, he would not have been allowed to come here. Yet, now that he is here, Boston is willing to let him return, and he is working to make that happen."

"Well, my dear, it is not the first time we have experienced swords in the back from those we have supported," Samuel observed. "I think, from the Massachusetts Bay perspective, this is an opportunity to grow their territorial reach. They are eager to do so, even if it means partnering with a man they have banished."

Mary sighed. "Well, no one can say that our life is not a great adventure. We could have never predicted these things and this life when we met at the civilized Globe Theatre. We are so far now from Shakespeare and *The Taming of the Shrew*." Mary placed her head on Samuel's shoulder, enjoying the moment.

"I believe I am still learning how to tame the shrew, my dear," Samuel joked.

Mary smiled and kissed Samuel's cheek. "We both know that will never happen."

"This new life is such a far cry from the haberdashery. Still, we asked for the wilderness, and that is exactly what we got. I do not think Shakespeare could have imagined greater."

"I see why Massachusetts wants to expand," Mary mused, "but I still do not understand why William and Benedict Arnold have chosen to be annexed."

"Arnold does not like our perspective and religious beliefs. He has worked to secure the approval of Roger Williams, but to no positive end."

"What do you think will come of his quest to join the Massachusetts colony?" Mary asked.

"I believe William Arnold and his clan have succeeded in their request to join the Massachusetts Bay Colony. Let us just hope that Roger's efforts are successful in London. If he can secure a patent for

Providence, then Massachusetts will not be able to annex this land."

"Will he succeed?"

"Yes, I believe he will. The Arnolds are scoundrels, and I am surprised that even Boston has accepted these renegades with alacrity."

"Samuel, you should not speak such of these gentlemen. You are, after all, a Christian man."

"My dear Mary, these are not good men. They have committed scandalous offences and are known derelicts," Samuel pointed out.

"Alas, my dear, many in this New World might say the same about you."

"Mary, you know this is not true about me. But Robert Cole, who sold us this land and has now reneged on his sale, was censured to wear a *D* on his back during an entire year in Boston for drunkenness on the Sabbath. William Arnold's son Benedict is an even worse sort, having been caught selling gunpowder to Indians during the Pequot War and then lying about the offense. How many good English men and women were killed by that very powder?"

Samuel paused, rubbed his chin to collect his thoughts, and then continued, "Furthermore, how many innocent Indians were killed in the Pequot War's extension with the firepower provided by the lying Benedict Arnold? But his father is the worst of the lot. First, for assembling this band of derelicts, and second, for the unjust way he has treated the Indians and Roger Williams. Mr. Williams invited William Arnold into Providence when no one else would accept him, and what has Arnold done in return? He has committed the worst offense of all by handing our colony to Massachusetts. Further, he has done this while Mr. Williams is in London."

Heaving a heavy sigh, he said resolutely, "This is an event that shall negatively impact Providence for a long time to come. And this man, who has claimed to his associates in Boston that *we* treat our Indian friends unjustly, has lied, cheated, and stolen from them on many occasions. Our friends Miantonomo and Canonicus have both told me they do not like or trust the Arnolds. I have always held for equality amongst Englishmen and Indians. Indeed, we have many friends amongst the Indians. It truly bothers me when English trade with them and constantly look for ways to cheat these people."

"It almost seems that you are making a case of civil law against the Arnolds," Mary remarked.

"Alas, my legal training does show itself from time to time. You must be frustrated as I am with the events in this New World. This should be a place where we can learn from our mistakes of the past and build anew."

"Samuel, why do we not consider Collins's offer of removing ourselves to New Netherland?" Mary suggested. "It seems the Quakers have begun to adopt some of the religious values we have advocated. Perhaps it would be a sanctuary more amenable to our values and a better place to raise our children."

"To go there would mean we no longer are subjects of the King of England. Can you imagine yourself a subject of the Netherlands? Now that your brother, John Maplett, has joined King Charles as his private physician, I suspect we may have some leverage in our English home. And of course, now that our friend Anne Hutchinson is in New Netherland, she will carry the torch of our similar beliefs."

"I hope the Dutch colonists are ready for Anne Hutchinson. She will surely bring in the winds of change to her new home." Mary smiled. "I wonder if she will marry again now that William has passed?"

"Anne Hutchinson will have a hard time finding a man that can keep up with her views and large flock of children. Still, it is my hope that she finds peace and happiness in her new home. We should fulfill our promise of paying her a visit once we are established in Shawomet and she is established in New Netherland," Samuel said.

"Samuel, in spite of all our troubles, you continue to dream of a time when things are settled and we have the opportunity to travel with the sole purpose of visiting our friends."

"One day, all of our labor will pay off, and we shall have a home built on the principles of religious and gender equality, as well as freedom for all English and Indian inhabitants of this region. I simply hope we can achieve these things for our children."

"You have been a good father and a stalwart example," Mary responded, then added, "Do you know how many we now have?"

"You test me on that often, and I always pass, do I not?"

"Perhaps, husband, but what is the answer?"

"I believe it is still a smaller number than Anne Hutchinson," Samuel joked.

"That is true, but it is not the answer to my question," Mary prodded.

"Well, Samuel, Mary, and Mahershallalhashbaz were born in London, and John, Benjamin, and infant Sarah were born here in the New World. I suppose my math would suggest six."

Spring 1643

Construction of the settlement in Shawomet began in March of 1643, during the same time that Roger Williams was negotiating with Sir Henry Vane in London to seek a legal patent for the Providence Plantations colonies. Williams knew that success in obtaining the patent would legally separate his settlements from the Massachusetts Bay Colony.

But before their homes were even built, Gorton received a summons from Boston informing him that his land purchase from Miantonomo had been outlawed by the Massachusetts Bay Colony. His immediate reaction was to ignore the proclamation, but he decided instead to respond in writing. The one thing he absolutely did not want to do was travel to Boston and contest the ruling, as that was the den of the lion. He had fallen prey to that tactic in the past and would not do so again.

Massachusetts's argument was that Miantonomo did not have the authority to sell the land. The Arnolds had claimed the land was really owned by chiefs Socononocco and Punham. It probably seemed like a viable argument to Boston, but Punham and Socononocco were minor village chiefs, while Miantonomo was head chief of the entire Narragansett. Under Indian custom, this issue would have been easily resolved: if Miantonomo made a proclamation, it was law.

Portsmouth Compact

Understanding tribal hierarchy, Gorton ignored the Massachusetts claim. Unfortunately, he failed to recognize the fact that the colonial governments would not ultimately follow the protocol established by the Narragansett.

Samuel and the other eleven families chose to focus on the construction of their new homes. Those efforts were hastened as the English settlers were assisted by several members of the Narragansett tribe, assigned by Miantonomo.

Gorton worked closely on the construction project with Randall Holden, who had been a signer in the Portsmouth Compact but had chosen to leave Portsmouth and join Samuel when he was banished from Aquidneck Island. Holden also liked the idea of accepting help from the Indians. Not only did the Indians provide essential labor for accelerating the task, but working with them was an excellent opportunity for the colonists to teach their new friends construction techniques. For Gorton, having the Narragansett around also provided an avenue to advance his understanding of their language and culture.

Once construction began, Miantonomo came regularly to inspect the progress and discussed with Gorton the possibility of building similar structures for the Narragansett. On one of the days when he was observing construction, William Arnold appeared with a group of soldiers and a sheriff from the Boston colony.

"Miantonomo, chief sachem of the Narragansett," the sheriff accompanying Arnold read, "I hereby summon you to the general court in Boston to face charges of illegally selling land already owned by the Arnold family and registered in the Pawtuxet."

"I am not subject to English law. I am chief of the Narragansett and will not come to Boston with you."

Arnold stepped up. "We thought you might feel that way, but we are willing to take you by force.

Gorton and two other Shawomet settlers, observing the group surrounding Miantonomo, came over to find out what was going on.

"You have no right to restrain this man," Gorton said. "He is a member of an independent nation and does not adhere to the laws that your thieving machinations in Boston have contrived."

Almost as if on cue, Gorton and the two other settlers were surrounded by musket-bearing soldiers and tied to a tree. Meanwhile, to the horror of the Narragansett helpers in Shawomet, Miantonomo was bound in chains. Tension escalated as those Indians approached, intent on halting the incarceration of their chief.

John Greene and Randall Holden intervened just as tension was about to boil over. "Let us fight this legally in Boston," Holden argued, "rather than with bloodshed in front of our wives and children here in Shawomet."

With that, Miantonomo was restrained and dragged out of Shawomet. During their slow trek to Boston, Miantonomo was humiliated, chastised, and tortured on Arnold's orders. He had no hope of being treated with decency and propriety in Boston.

20

Miantonomo

> Set honor in one eye and death i' th' other
> And I will look on both indifferently;
> For let the gods so speed me as I love
> The name of honor more than I fear death.
>
> —Shakespeare

For as long as Miantonomo and his Narragansett fathers before him could remember, the Pequot had been the most powerful Indian tribe in this region. Five years ago, that had changed when the Pequot and English settlers fought each other in the Pequot War. The Narragansett under Canonicus and Miantonomo had aided the English, and the Pequot were decimated. Massacre had not been Miantonomo's intent, but Uncas, chief of the Mohegan, also an ally of the English, fully supported and participated in the annihilation of the Pequot.

John Winthrop, who had once relied upon the Narragansett, stared into the eyes of Miantonomo. Today, in the general court, he wore a full chieftain headdress that accentuated his chiseled features. Winthrop had dealt with Miantonomo before and found him to be bright, reasonable, and strong willed. This was a proud man who looked out for the best interests of his people. It was not surprising that the great Canonicus had selected Miantonomo over one of his own sons to become sachem of the entire Narragansett people. He was the epitome of a chieftain, and he always put the interests of the Narragansett above his own.

Unfortunately for Miantonomo, the interests of the Narragansett were no longer in alignment with those of the Massachusetts Bay Colony. Winthrop was a master of the chessboard that contained the New England sector of the American continent. Today, he had set a trap for Miantonomo that could only go one way.

"This court accuses you of selling lands in Shawomet to Samuel Gorton and others. That land belongs, in fact, to two other chiefs who had already sold the land to Massachusetts Bay settlers."

"I am chief of all the Narragansett," Miantonomo declared. "No chief may sell land without my permission, and that land has belonged to my tribe for longer than the trees have grown there. We sold what was ours to those willing to pay for it."

"You are a liar, Miantonomo. I have sworn testimonies from Socononocco and Punham, Narragansett chiefs who have converted to Christianity, that you had no rights over that land."

"This is two ways wrong. First, those two are minor chieftains of villages, and these villages do not even control the Shawomet region. Second, in our Narragansett hierarchy, I am chief over all tribal villages. Only the great Canonicus may overrule my mandates."

"As I have already said, you are a liar. You are a savage testifying against the word of good Christian Indians."

"Those Christian chiefs have disgraced themselves and will be replaced by Canonicus," Miantonomo explained, not fully understanding that Winthrop had no interest in the facts, only the chess pieces as he had set them on the board. "How short is the memory of my Boston neighbor?" Miantonomo asked. "Just five years ago, I brought my braves together to help you in a war against the Pequot. It is a war you would have lost without the support of Canonicus and me. There was no Socononocco or Punham making decisions then."

"Those days are not important in this case. What is important is that you have sold land to outlaws of the Massachusetts Bay Colony. Land that was not yours to sell."

With this, Miantonomo began to understand that Winthrop, who had sat in negotiations during the Pequot War, could not really believe that Soconocco and Punham were true tribal chiefs. He finally began to understand this was about something perhaps not even related.

"This court has heard enough from the savage. The land sales from Miantonomo to the settlers in Shawomet are hereby absolved, and those from Soconococco and Punham to William Arnold shall replace those. That land is now under jurisdiction of the Massachusetts Bay Colony."

Miantonomo stared blankly into Winthrop's cold eyes. Perhaps Winthrop did not understand the fact that he, Miantonomo, remained chief, and Soconococco and Punham would soon be punished for placing him in this situation. Clearly, the Englishman did not understand Narragansett hierarchy, while he, Miantonomo, did not understand the English courts.

"There is one further issue, Miantonomo. A treaty has been signed between the Narragansett and Mohegan. We understand there has been conflict, and for our part, we will call this an Indian matter for you to resolve with each other."

"The English will not interfere with us handling this in our own way?" Miantonomo clarified with a furrowed brow.

"We will not," Winthrop answered in a blatant lie. In fact, Winthrop had resolved to expand the Massachusetts Bay Colony into the Narragansett Bay, and Miantonomo's friendship with Roger Williams and Samuel Gorton stood as a clear impediment to that objective. A war between the Narragansett and Mohegan tribes, with the English supporting the Mohegan, would clear that path. But of course, Miantonomo, who had supported the English in the Pequot War and who held the superior numbers against the Mohegan, did not know this.

<hr/>

Uncas, chief of the Mohegans, knew that Miantonomo had superior numbers in this conflict. He also knew, because of Massachusetts's interest in annexing Providence, that he had the support of the English.

To make matters worse, Uncas knew he could take advantage of the fact that Miantonomo mistakenly believed the English would stay clear of any conflict between the two tribes.

The trap was set.

Miantonomo returned to his tribe in a time of escalating tensions between his own Narragansett and the Mohegans.

Both tribes, prepared for war, stood in an open meadow with less than one hundred meters separating them. On either side of the meadow was a thick tree line.

Uncas sent an emissary to Miantonomo suggesting a friendly parley between the two chiefs. As Miantonomo listened to the emissary, he wished he had Canonicus with him to advise. On one hand, he wanted his braves to experience the victory, and on the other, he preferred to negotiate rather than begin a battle that would result in many deaths. He did not trust Uncas, but he decided to meet with him.

Uncas, fast on his feet and strong, yet a fox among the northeastern Indians, greeted Miantonomo. In the distance, he could see Miantonomo's braves waiting for the result of the parlay. Some were standing, watching, while others were relaxing, preserving energy in anticipation of the inevitable battle.

"Miantonomo, great chief of the Narragansett, I suggest a treaty that allows our tribes to live in peace," Uncas lied. He had no intention of signing a treaty and knew Miantonomo would refuse. Mohegan braves were already spreading out through the woods, preparing for a surprise attack.

"Why would I do this, Uncas? Mohegan attacks on villages have killed many of our women and children. Like your name, you are a fox who cannot be trusted."

"You could do this because I ask. You could do this because we have a treaty with the English that prevents us from starting a war."

"You have no power to ask, Uncas. You are not a great chief but a drunkard who slinks around in the woods seeking opportunity you have not earned. As for the English, the great Governor Winthrop has told me this is an Indian matter, which I should handle."

"You are the fool, Miantonomo, and in truth there will be no parlay, nor will you have English support! It is I who have the support of the English." With that, Uncas dropped to the ground, a signal his braves had been awaiting.

Five hundred arrows were loosed at the unsuspecting Narragansett braves in a shower of death. A second round of arrows was loosed before the Narragansett could react. What should have been a battle easily won by the Narragansett quickly became a mortifying and bloody rout.

As the storm of arrows rained down on the unprepared Narragansett, Uncas and his five strongest braves ran down and captured Miantonomo, who was trying to return to his braves. Seeing their sachem Miantonomo ensnared by the Mohegan and realizing the tide would not turn in their favor on this day, the surviving Narragansett turned and ran. This treachery would be dealt with, but not today.

———◦———

Randall Holden delivered the news to Samuel, who was in the final stages of building his home. "Along with the ill treatment of our friend Miantonomo, I have just gotten news that he asked the Massachusetts general court to enforce a treaty they had demanded between the Mohegan and the Narragansett. The court told Miantonomo to handle this on his own."

"This is no less than Puritan tyranny," Samuel interrupted. "Do the magistrates in Boston not recall that it was Miantonomo who supported the English for years? Do they not know that Miantonomo helped us win the Pequot War?"

"Perhaps they have more interest in annexing new land and disrupting the tenets of freedom and civil liberty brought to reality by yourself and Roger Williams."

"In retrospect, it appears that it was folly for Mr. Williams and me to leverage our friendship with the Indians to help *all* English." Samuel felt ashamed that his fellow Englishmen in Boston had perpetrated such a crime against the trusting Indians. "It seems that Boston has no appreciation for our relationship with the Narragansett. Worse, they set it back!"

Holden nodded gravely. "Indeed."

"What has become of our friend Miantonomo?" Samuel asked.

"I understand he was released by the magistrates in Boston and has been captured by the Mohegan chief Uncas."

"I know this sachem Uncas, and believe I have some leverage. Let us immediately dispatch to negotiate a release, and let us do so in the name of Providence and Shawomet, not Boston."

<hr>

Within three days, Gorton had delivered a letter to Uncas, but he chose to release Miantonomo to the Massachusetts Bay authorities, not to Providence and Shawomet. Miantonomo's case was brought to the Federation of Colonies, a recently created legal body formed less than a year earlier. This political group chose to remand him to the church elders, who decided that while Miantonomo lived, Uncas was in jeopardy. Miantonomo needed to be killed, but he needed to be killed by Uncas and the Mohegans, not the English.

In August 1643, the English authorities remanded Miantonomo to Uncas with appropriate instructions to dispatch with him on Mohegan-owned soil, not on English land.

Uncas and his brother Wawequa were waiting when the marshal and two deputies delivered Miantonomo back into their custody. Uncas had seen the English topple the great Pequot tribe. Now the Narragansett were the most powerful. With English help, his Mohegan would topple the Narragansett. Today would be a proud moment for Uncas, sachem of the Mohegan. Today would be the beginning of Mohegan dominance amongst the tribes of the northeast.

"I would rather die from an English rope than be delivered to you, Uncas," Miantonomo spat. "Your attack on my people was trickery, not noble war that would make your ancestors proud."

"The Narragansett may not speak of Mohegan ancestors," Uncas answered.

"You are a deceptive fox and not a true man."

"It is true, I am a fox, and my strategy has raised the stature of the Mohegan to the most powerful tribe."

"You are a fool, Uncas, and I fear your foolishness shall be fatal for all of our peoples."

"You will not live to see our great people rise. I will savor this moment as the greatest of my life. My braves have defeated the great Miantonomo in battle, and now I will send you to the spirit world."

"You have won a single battle through trickery. The Narragansett are not defeated. My great tribe will exact our revenge on you and your people, Uncas. If I am living, I shall lead that charge, and if I am not, my people will."

"I think you may not know that the English now support the Mohegan, and like the Pequot, the Narragansett will now fall like tree leaves in autumn. My Mohegan tribe, now supported by the English militia and muskets, will prevail."

Uncas and Miantonoma

"This cannot be true. We have supported the English, and they are our allies!" Miantonomo cried

"It is true, Miantonomo. The day of the Narragansett is now over."

Miantonomo bowed his head and thought as they walked. If it were true the English now supported Uncas, it would be bad tidings for his people. He must find a way to warn the Narragansett of this treachery.

Uncas and Wawequa led Miantonomo for several hours until they were in Mohegan country. Then, on Uncas's signal, Wawequa shrieked and buried his tomahawk in the back of Miantonomo's head.

Before Miantonomo was dead, Uncas carved a piece of raw flesh from Miantonomo's shoulder and ate it before his adversary's dying eyes.

"This is the greatest piece of flesh I have ever eaten! Eating it shall make my heart strong," Uncas whooped as Miantonomo died.

21

The Raid on Shawomet

> Some are born great, some achieve greatness,
> and some have greatness thrust upon 'em.
> —Shakespeare

September–October 1643

Samuel was working in the fields with fellow Shawomet settler John Greene when he learned of Miantonomo's fate. He sat down in shock and tried to comprehend the chain of events that had led up to the death of an Indian chief he had admired and come to call friend.

"Will we see no end to the abominable transgressions of the colonial governments? Surely this is the most egregious deed our English brethren have ever perpetrated upon our Indian neighbors and hosts in this New World."

"What I have been told," began Greene, "is that, fearing repercussions from the Narragansett, William Arnold has used the prospect of further land expansion to poison the minds of the Massachusetts leadership."

"Perhaps, but how could they justify this murder of one of the greatest friends and allies the English settlers have in this New World?" Samuel asked.

"I think," Greene said, "they have conveniently forgotten the value of this friendship with the Narragansett."

"Have they forgotten that were it not for the Narragansett, the Plymouth settlers would have surely perished in their first year?" Samuel interrupted. "Have they forgotten that the Pequot and Mohegan have always held the belief that English settlers should be removed before we become too strong and that the Narragansett have parlayed to keep them at bay? Have they forgotten that Miantonomo himself fought alongside the English in the Pequot War?"

"They may indeed remember these things, my friend, but they also know that the Narragansett stand in the way of their expansion into our Providence settlements. They also know the Narragansett are friendly with Roger Williams and Samuel Gorton, two men who have managed to escape their controlling doctrines."

"These things they have demonstrated to be true," Samuel answered.

"I wonder if our non-Puritan beliefs are not the biggest factor in their actions," Greene mused. "They have come to this New World, advocating they believe in religious freedom, and have created a new form of oppression that eclipses all else in the Old World. We are a threat to this power."

Samuel shook his head. "I fear this murder of Miantonomo will create terrible repercussions for us and Providence as Boston stretches its ugly arm south to our Shawomet colony. Now that Miantonomo is out of the way, their biggest obstacle is gone."

"We must prepare for this," Greene suggested.

"Yes, but for now, we should meet with our Narragansett friends and arrange to participate in an appropriate memorial."

⊱ ⋅ ⊰

Within days, Gorton learned that Boston had dispatched a posse consisting of forty armed soldiers accompanied by another twenty Mohegan braves. While Gorton had requested an arbitration, the word was there would be no negotiation and that Gorton should be taken in dead or alive. Friends of the Shawomet settlers in Providence sent a note to the Massachusetts magistrates requesting they be allowed to mediate, but that request was summarily dismissed.

Fearing that Boston's ultimate goal was to murder Gorton and his followers like Miantonomo, panic set in on the Shawomet families.

Hearing that the soldiers would arrive within the hour, Samuel instructed Mary Gorton and their children, along with the other families, to quickly collect important belongings from their homes and pack them on boats for a quick escape.

"Mommy, is Daddy coming with us on the boat to Providence?" Maher asked.

"No, sweetie. Daddy and the other men need to stay behind and protect our homes. Now, you and Sam need to hurry along and make sure your siblings are ready to go right away."

The settlement had grown to sixteen families, and all were running back and forth, carrying their personal belongings to the boats. As the soldiers entered town, a couple of muskets were fired, turning the quick pace into a frantic one.

"Sam, help your sisters carry their things, and hurry. The soldiers are here!" Mary Gorton barked at her son, now in his midteens.

They had arrived. All around her, Mary saw the Boston soldiers knocking women down and shoving children out of the way, deploying

Shawomet women and children escaping on boats

excessive force. In the frenzied moment, two women were killed, and two pregnant women miscarried. Mary was also pregnant but managed to stay calm and not create a situation that would result in the loss of her child.

The soldiers were ransacking homes, and Mary saw that most of them were not looking to kill or capture. Instead, they were mere thieves, searching for spoils they could acquire from the fleeing families.

The Shawomet men, knowing that they were the focus of the attack, barricaded themselves in a well-protected house. Most were concerned when they heard musket blasts coming from the settlement, but those quickly ended.

When the soldiers finished despoiling the Shawomet homes, they focused on their mission of extracting Gorton, dead or alive.

Captain George Cooke studied the barricaded home where the Shawomet men were entrenched. He quickly realized that if they were appropriately provisioned, they could remain for weeks. That was not an outcome that he saw as favorable. Alternatively, he could set the building afire, but that result would not be acceptable. It was likely that all inside would be killed.

"Samuel Gorton!" Cooke shouted. "I am here with an official summons to arrest you and the men of Shawomet and return you to Boston."

"We do not recognize your authority in this settlement and will not go with you to Boston!" Gorton shouted back from inside the fortified house. He knew that to go to Boston would likely result in a death sentence for himself and several other Shawomet men.

"We do not care what you and your fellow blasphemers believe is our authority. We are here to take you to Boston and will do so whether you be alive or dead."

"We are subjects of King Charles and have rightful ownership of these lands, which are under the domain of England, not Boston." Samuel had hung the English flag in hope that the soldiers would not fire on their own countrymen. He would soon learn that he was wrong.

Once the shouting match ended, Cooke consulted with his lieutenants, who all believed they should entrench and then mount a full attack. Nighttime had fallen, so the attack was to begin the next day.

As Saturday ended, Gorton gathered the men together to discuss strategy.

"I do not think they will attack us until Monday morning. As tomorrow is the Sabbath, we should eat well, pray, and worship, as is our custom," Greene suggested.

"That seems a reasonable assumption. How does everyone else stand on this?" Gorton tucked his right index finger behind his ear, the other three fingers rubbing his cheek, as he studied the men in the room.

All agreed but Thomas Gorton, who said, "I have seen too many aberrations in behavior in these Massachusetts settlers to believe them capable of any consistency on our sacred day. You may enjoy your meal, and I shall stand watch."

The men all nodded agreement that they would prepare a meal, spend the day in prayer, and study the word while Thomas would maintain vigil.

On Sunday morning, with the first light of dawn, Captain Cooke mounted his attack. Thomas did not need to report as the steady and continuous fire of muskets began.

"Should we fire back on them?" Thomas Gorton asked.

Samuel listened to the musket shots that were hitting but not penetrating the walls of the house. The work they had done reinforcing the house had been effective. "No. We should enjoy our breakfast and then begin our prayer session in accordance with our plan. Thomas will maintain watch and inform us if they change strategy."

After breakfast and a formal church session within the besieged walls of the house, Samuel shouted out to Captain Cooke, "Thank you, Captain, for the entertainment during as good a Sabbath-day breakfast and prayer session as any we have ever experienced!"

In the continuous musket blasts, Cooke had not noticed that the barricaded men had not fired back a single shot. Frustrated with their lack of progress after having discharged over four hundred rounds at the house, Cooke called together his lieutenants.

"I say we burn the house to the ground. Gorton and his men are evil, and any end that might come to them in an inferno of flames would be right and justified," one of the lieutenants recommended.

"What say the rest of you?" Cooke said,

The men all looked from face to face. There was not a unanimous agreement, but each was afraid to dissent, so they all voted in favor. Cooke himself would rather have captured Gorton, but he recognized that an extended engagement upon a house full of farmers would not look good in his report back in Boston. It was better to finish this deed quickly than to have the embarrassment of failure.

"So be it," Cooke resolved. "Samuel Gorton and the Gortonists shall meet Satan today with eternal conflagration."

As the men were preparing torched arrows, the sky filled with rain. Though they shot volley after volley of torched arrows, the flames were immediately extinguished, and this attempt, too, seemed foreordained to failure.

Cooke again ordered a barrage of musket balls upon the fortification, but after a few hundred rounds, even that became difficult in the rain.

"It seems the wheels are falling off your chariot of war, Captain Cooke!" Gorton taunted them from inside the warm and dry house.

⟫·◦·⟪

The following day, the rain continued, and Cooke, observing smoke from the chimney and smelling the scent of a meal being cooked, asked for a truce.

"Samuel Gorton!" he shouted. "Let us meet and talk so that my lieutenants might get out of this rain and we might find a peaceful resolution to this conflict."

Boston militia attack on Gorton home

"A peaceful resolution has always been my objective, Captain Cooke," Gorton answered. "In light of a truce and possible arbitration, we shall open the doors to you and your lieutenants."

As Gorton opened the doors for Cooke to enter, the captain and his men rushed the perimeter and seized Gorton and several of the other men, along with their arms.

"So despite our goodwill, you demonstrate deception to the last!" Gorton protested.

"We made no sacred oath or faithful promise worth keeping to you, followers of the king of hell," Cooke answered, defending his action.

Shackled and chained, Samuel Gorton and nine others began the four-day march to Boston. In spite of the conflicting nature of their coalition, during the four day walk back to Boston, Gorton spent a great deal of his time chatting and joking with his captors. While his lighthearted and humorous personality never won Cooke over, he did manage to do so with several of the other lieutenants. Most had expected him to be Beelzebub incarnate. Instead, they learned that he was a very spiritual man who believed passionately in freedom and civil liberties.

On the third day, Gorton learned the militia held in tow eighty head of cattle, several dozen sheep, and all of the ripened crops from Shawomet. All of these things were the rightful possessions of the Shawomet settlers and would be critical supplies for surviving the winter.

"What will you do with all of our crops and livestock?" Gorton asked Cooke.

"They are the spoils of war, to be divided amongst my men," answered Cooke, who by now was angered that Gorton had spent so much time fraternizing with his soldiers.

"How can they be the spoils of war when we, like you, are loyal subjects of King Charles? And what of our women and children, who worked to maintain those items? That which you have stolen represents their survival for the winter."

"We care less for the well-being of those who fled your camp than a simple fish in the ocean. I will assure you that some are already dead. Others will find their end, like you, soon enough," Cooke answered, detached from their fate as if they were meaningless objects.

Samuel and the other men were shocked by the apathetic and heartless response from Cooke. They began immediately planning the escape of three men so the women and children could be taken care of. Several women, including Mary Gorton, were pregnant and due to give birth within the next few months, and Gorton, like the rest of the men, wanted to make sure all were OK.

The Shawomet men wanted Samuel to be the one to escape. They argued that Massachusetts Bay authorities would most assuredly give him a death sentence.

"If I escape, they will exert all efforts to come after me. Therefore, it must not be me. Our real goal should be to have some men return to the village and make certain the women and children are OK." The men nodded in agreement to Samuel's suggestion.

That night, John Greene, Nicholas Power, and Richard Waterman silently sneaked into the woods and escaped. Once they returned to Shawomet village, they found the women and children had returned and were already rebuilding and collecting items that would help them survive the winter months. Several members of the Narragansett were also helping and had delivered portions of corn and other stock that would be necessary for survival.

Greene was distraught to learn that his wife had been killed in the attack, along with another woman and two children. All of the men had survived. Of the fourteen families, though, only the three men that had escaped were now working with the women to restore the village.

Samuel and the remaining twelve men who had been captured were now in Boston beginning a trial that none of the Shawomet residents dared to attend.

From the perspective of the Shawomet settlers, they had intentionally moved thirty miles outside of the borders of the Boston colony specifically to stay out of the reach and jurisdiction of the Boston magistrates. In their lifetimes, none of them would ever fathom reasonableness in the actions of their general court or Governor Winthrop.

22

Abitio Hutchinson

> Now boast thee, Death, in thy possession lies
> A lass unparalleled.
> —Shakespeare

Portsmouth, June 1641

Anne Hutchinson sat by her husband William's bedside, firmly holding his hand. Much as she had prayed for recovery, his health had continued to deteriorate. The bright, warm summer, which he had so loved in New England, did little to change his health or demeanor. As she studied the face of the man she had loved for over thirty years, she knew the end was near.

William opened his eyes and smiled at the sight of Anne sitting next to him. "You are here every time I awaken. It gives me great peace, wife."

"It would give me peace if you would find a way to get on your feet. The children have been handling all of your chores," Anne tried to joke.

William chuckled lightly at her comment but then became serious. "I am afraid, sweet Anne, that I shall be seeking a permanent reprieve from those chores."

"Don't say that, William!" Anne retorted, squeezing his hand more tightly. "You need to be strong. This family needs you to recover."

"From the first moment I saw you, I have loved you. You are such a beautiful and soft woman, with the imperial nature of a king. In our lifetime together, you have accomplished things as a woman that no man could have ever hoped for, and my life has been better for it."

"Thank you, dear." Anne had known William long enough to understand that now was the time for silence and listening. She had lived her life as a strong woman, but William had also been a strong and successful man. Now was his time to talk, and she understood that well.

"Once I am gone, you need to leave Portsmouth. Coddington will not let you rest as long as you remain on this island. We have acquired significant wealth during our time together, so you may go wherever you wish and live comfortably. I would urge you to follow Samuel, where you can live in Roger Williams's Providence Plantations."

"I think peace can be made with Coddington . . ." she trailed off, knowing now was not the time to debate this and also recognizing that her husband was likely correct.

"Well, I will not press this issue, but it is my last hope that you can find a home where you will be allowed to believe as you wish and continue to teach, as you must. Samuel's children and our own are very close, and I suspect having them near might bond our families further with a marriage or two." He closed his eyes and tried to summon a bit more strength, but almost nothing remained. After a few minutes, he opened his eyes to see Anne dabbing the tears from her eyes.

"I know you will find the best path for yourself and our children." He closed his eyes again. He did not want that to be the last thing he said, and he struggled for one last ounce of strength. William Hutchinson began to fade, but then he felt his wife's vice grip on his hand. He opened his eyes one last time and thought perhaps she was an angel, greeting him as he came into the ether of heaven. "I love you . . . angel . . . Anne."

As Anne felt the life depart from her husband's body, she put her head on his chest and began to sob. Seven mourning children, waiting outside the room, rushed in to join their mother.

As the Hutchinson family endured the remainder of 1641, Coddington did, in fact, continue to exert irrational pressure on them. It was clear he would never be able to maintain peaceful control of Aquidneck while Anne Hutchinson and her family lived there. Meanwhile, the Massachusetts Bay Colony began its efforts to annex the entire Narragansett Bay. Anne would have liked to move to Providence, but she had had enough of the Puritans. Her friend John Throckmorton had moved to New Netherland to live amongst the Dutch Quakers. Throckmorton's reports were positive. He painted a picture of a colony more tolerant than those under the thumb of Massachusetts Bay.

In the summer of 1642, the Hutchinsons, with Throckmorton's assistance, loaded their belongings on a small barge and said goodbye to Aquidneck for the last time. The family arrived in New Netherland a few days later.

Anne Hutchinson studied her friend John Throckmorton. He was a kind and decent man who was well known for having a strong work ethic. "Our primary goal is to make a decision on where we will purchase land. You may be aware that Captain James Sands, who is my nephew, has offered to build the house."

"I would imagine, if your construction plan is anything like the houses you built in Boston and Portsmouth, it will be a substantial project." Throckmorton smiled, remembering the very large Hutchinson house practically in the center of Boston.

"We have been lucky to have the resources to afford nicer accommodations. I expect to live and teach in this house for the remainder of my life and will, therefore, build accordingly," Anne responded.

"Indeed. You have now visited several tracts. Which do you like?"

"I like the one up by the Split Rock," Anne answered, knowing how Throckmorton would respond.

"You would be better living closer to the main settlement, Anne," Throckmorton argued.

"That land has good, fertile soil, is close to fresh water, and has ample trees for building materials. The woods will supply game for hunting until we can get our livestock established. I like this place and shall not be convinced otherwise, Mr. Throckmorton."

"Well, I know that you are not a woman with whom to argue when you have stated your intentions. Instead, we shall endeavor to accommodate your wishes and welcome you to the settlement."

"I do appreciate that," she said with a smile.

"In the meantime, I should like to find a location where my rather large family can stay until construction of our *castle* is complete."

"Ha! Ha! Ha! Yes, Anne, until your castle is built, we must find temporary living for your large family of fifteen children. You should know that your family size is well known and broadly anticipated in these parts!"

"I do indeed have fifteen children, but several of them have chosen to stay behind in the Narragansett Bay. Coddington was focused on me and does not seem to hold the same animosity for my children, some of whom are now adults and prefer to make their own way in the Puritan parts of the colonies. Still, we have a significant number whose sum adds up to sixteen, with seven children and various other members of the household."

"I would not recommend the inn for that troop!" Throckmorton offered, "I am aware of an abandoned home that might serve your interim goals well."

Summer 1643

Construction on the Hutchinson home began with the first warmth of spring and continued through the early part of summer. By July, the house, while not complete, was ready for the family to move in. During the spring, the family had spent every day working with Captain Sands, doing construction projects or working the land, planting crops, and preparing fencing for livestock.

One day in late July, when the Hutchinsons were tending to matters in town, a group of local Indians visited the construction site. Because the Indians did not speak English and Sand and his workers did not speak Algonquin, communication was sparse. The Indians were relatively friendly, but they gathered all of the tools and set them in a pile. They then handed Sands his broad axe and motioned for him to go away.

"We have never had a problem with these Indians," Anne Hutchinson responded after hearing from Sands about the visit. "We have legal title to the land, and I believe we can learn to live peacefully side by side with our Indian neighbors."

"You would have us finish the construction, then?" Sands clarified.

"Yes, James, finish the construction. I shall deal with these Indians and do so in a way that works to their benefit and ours. These things have a way of working out in the end."

"I want you to know, Aunt Anne, that they were friendly, but this is a risk, maybe even a considerable risk. You may know the Narragansett, but these are not the same tribe, and they do not have the same mind-set. Furthermore, Governor Kieft has not treated these people with the same respect you seem to hold for them."

"Well, then we shall just let them know there is a difference between us and the Dutch governor!" she clarified.

"They believe that Kieft has stolen their land, and the story is that an entire village of Siwanoy men, women, and children was massacred at Kieft's hand. They are none too happy with the Dutch right now."

"The Dutch, James, not us. I assure you there is nothing to worry about. We shall be fine!"

—◆—

In early August 1643, Wampage, chief of the Siwanoy tribe, sent a warning to all the settlers advising them to leave. They marched through the settlement, burning vacant homes and shops. When they arrived at the Hutchinson house, they were surprised to find men, women, children, and livestock.

Hutchinson Massacre

Anne Hutchinson came out to greet them, but none of the braves spoke English. She regretted not having spent time learning at least some basics of the Algonquin language, but she only knew a few words, none of which would be helpful here. As more braves arrived, the situation escalated, and the Hutchinson pet and work dogs started barking and snapping at the Indians. Wampage arrived just as the dogs were getting out of control. He barked in Algonquin for the Hutchinsons to restrain their dogs, and then again in broken Dutch. His shouting drove the dogs into a frenzy, and this was the tipping point. Wampage and his braves drew their tomahawks and did not put their weapons away until every member of the Hutchinson family and their servants on the farm that day were dead. The bodies were dragged into the house, which was torched and burned to the ground. Thus, the colonies saw a brutal and unfortunate ending to one of America's first great women.

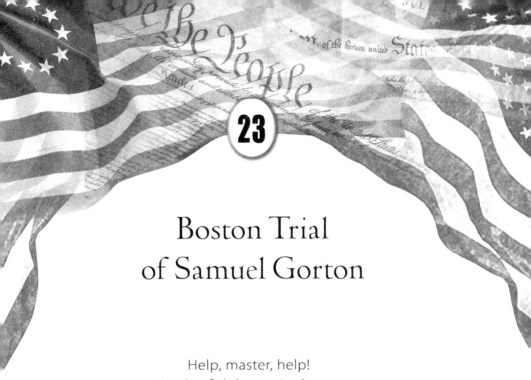

Boston Trial of Samuel Gorton

> Help, master, help!
> Here's a fish hangs in the net
> like a poor man's right in the law.
> **—Shakespeare**

In Samuel Gorton's mind, the land issue was straightforward and could only be ruled in their favor. Failure to respond to summons by the Boston legal authorities required that Boston have jurisdiction, which they clearly did not. Ransacking the Shawomet settlement and being responsible for four deaths, along with stealing supplies and personal belongings, was the real problem, and Gorton could not see a way that Boston authorities could defend that position.

Gorton had formal legal training and was ready, or so he thought. The waiting time between being delivered to Boston and beginning trial was less than a week. During the final day prior to the trial, Gorton was told he had a visitor.

Samuel was brought in chains to an open area where Edward Hutchinson was waiting. Samuel immediately recognized the son of his good friend, Anne Hutchinson. "Edward!" The two men embraced as well as possible with Samuel's chains. The atmosphere immediately changed.

"Samuel, I bring tragic tidings," Edward said. "Mother and seven of my siblings were killed in a massacre in New Netherland sometime last month."

Samuel crumpled onto a nearby wooden bench, eyes filled with tears. No other person in the New World was closer to him in her beliefs, and Samuel had planned on maintaining contact with Anne and her children as they helped to usher in a free and moral New England. After a few minutes, he wiped the tears from his face and focused again on Edward, who was also red eyed. "How could this— how did this happen?"

"We do not know, Samuel. We only know that the Dutch angered the local Indians, and an entire village was burned to the ground. Many of the settlers were massacred. I learned that none from my family survived. I have been petitioning the magistrates to tell you as soon as I learned of your detainment here, but only today was I allowed to meet with you."

Samuel felt a pain deep inside like no other. He tried to recall the faces and names of each of the Hutchinson children: William, Katherine, Zuniel, Mary, and, of course, the always energetic Susanna. "Edward, this is tragic news."

"I do not think I have fully come to grips with it as yet," Edward responded, looking away so Samuel would not notice his eyes filling with tears.

"I am so sorry . . ." Samuel trailed off and then tried to get back on focus. "What are you doing in this settlement again? How is it that you are allowed to live in Boston?"

"As you know, Mother was always the target. After Coddington took Portsmouth, I found it impossible to stay under his rule. Reverend Cotton offered to sponsor me in a petition to return to Boston as a freeman. While I hold a fair amount of animosity toward these people for what they did to my family, I find Boston to be the best place to live in the colonies. Unlike Mother, I could not see moving into Dutch territory. My family has moved back and now lives in the same family house where you and I met several years ago."

"Edward, the news of your father's death reached us only after we began to settle in Providence. His death was a great loss. This further tragic news of your mother and siblings brings such weight to my heart. My wife, our children, and I felt such friendship and admiration for them."

"Yes, Mother and Father had similar feelings for you and held great hopes for you achieving your goals in the New World. Your fight is not an easy one, as is exemplified by this trial."

"Worry not, Edward. We have a good case. Providing the magistrates are willing to listen to facts, we shall be released in no time."

"You presuppose the government is willing to listen to facts, Mr. Gorton. You believe you have been brought here on charges dealing with the rightful ownership of land, but that is not how you will be charged and tried. Massachusetts believes they have rightful ownership of the land and will not even hear that question."

"But it is the question on which we have been debating in our correspondence," Samuel argued.

"Indeed, it is, but the magistrates know they cannot win on that question, so they shall not allow you to speak on that matter. You are to be tried on charges of blasphemy and lack of adherence to Puritan ethics. They know they can prevail on these charges, and in doing so, you will be out of their way. Once you are removed, their plans to annex Rhode Island will progress without your opposition."

Samuel considered what Edward was telling him. "How do you know these things, Edward?"

"I have taken a position in the Boston militia. In my current post, I hear things."

"I do not understand how you have come to live in this colony."

"While I share much of what Mother taught, I am not a target, and I suspect Cotton has given me leave because of the long-standing connection between our families. I know things are bad here. The Puritans control the church and the government, but I have still come to enjoy life as my wife, Katherine, and I begin to grow our family."

"Tell me, how are Katherine and the children, Edward?"

The jail master motioned that Edward's time was up. "They are well, Mr. Gorton. We have four children now. I shan't catch up to Mother and her brood of fifteen, but for now, we will continue to grow this Hutchinson clan. I am sorry we do not have more time . . ."

"It is OK. We shall find a way to prevail. It has always been the way of the Gortons to find the positive in the negative things that happen."

"Indeed, I have observed that to be true. Katherine, the children, and I will pray for you, Mr. Gorton. You have been a good friend to my family, and I shall always remember that."

The two men embraced again, and Samuel was escorted back to his cell.

***

Gorton and his nine cohorts were brought to the general court, which was well attended by curious onlookers who had followed the melodrama or were familiar with the way Gorton's beliefs were similar to Anne Hutchinson's. Most Bostonians knew that Anne Hutchinson and Samuel Gorton had been friends, and by now, everyone in Boston knew about the massacre of the Hutchinson family in New Netherland. Having just learned about it on the previous night, the impact weighed heavily on Gorton as the trial began.

As predicted by Edward Hutchinson, the trial began with theological issues and no mention of Shawomet land or Massachusetts's interest in annexing Rhode Island. The elders in attendance gave each man the opportunity for release and freedom to live in Massachusetts-controlled Shawomet.

The elder read aloud to the men in the courtroom, "Each of you may be released today to go live peacefully as residents of the Massachusetts Bay Colony in your settlement of Shawomet. To secure such release, you need only denounce the religious teachings of Samuel Gorton and adhere to the correct precepts of the Puritan faith."

One by one, each man refused to do so. Some simply stated *no*, and others stated that they came to the New World in hopes of escaping the religious tyranny of Archbishop Laud and the Church of England.

"Then you shall all be charged with being blasphemous enemies of the true religion and, likewise, of this Boston government."

With that, the elders gave Samuel a pen and parchment with a demand that he write a response to several religious questions. Samuel worked diligently on his responses, which consumed the remainder of that Friday and all of Saturday. As was his custom, he took the Sabbath off. On Monday, he was brought back before the court with a dozen magistrates and forty deputies, all led by Governor Winthrop.

Each of the elders spent considerable time scrutinizing the answers scribed by Samuel Gorton. They then spent several days interrogating him.

Finally, after a full week of questioning, the court was ready to deliver its final charge.

"Upon much examination and serious consideration of your writing and your answers, we do charge you to be a blasphemous enemy of the true religion of our Lord Jesus Christ and his Holy Ordinances and also of all civil authority among the people of God and particularly in this jurisdiction," they proclaimed.

"What manner of Spanish Inquisition is this court of Boston?" Gorton demanded.

"You shall ultimately come to the same fate as your friend Anne Hutchinson," Reverend Thomas Weld began. "The Indians in New Netherland have never committed a massacre, but they have now, and that massacre killed only the Hutchinson family. It is God's hand that has delivered this punishment to that woeful woman."

"Reverend Weld, I feel sorry for a man such as you who might convince himself that God would slaughter a family such as the Hutchinsons. Your impression of God and his worldly deeds is truly distorted," Samuel spat, angry that anyone would suggest such a heinous act could be pinned on God.

"You of similar faith shall come to a similar end, Samuel Gorton," Governor Winthrop added. "I think it pleases the Lord to discover this great imposter, Anne Hutchinson, an instrument of Satan, is now in hell with her master, where she belongs."

Samuel had had enough of their taunting. "In spite of your transgressions, I do not think hell is where even you belong, but most assuredly a God-fearing woman such as Anne Hutchinson and her beautiful children have found their home at God's side in heaven."

"Blasphemy!" several shouted in concert.

"You, Samuel Gorton, may soon find out," Winthrop responded in a cold voice. "You have been charged under the laws of the general court of Boston. Our verdict is guilty, and our sentence, by a vote of nine to three, is death by hanging."

Gorton and several others in the courtroom were stunned by the verdict and sentence. Most in attendance agreed that, theologically, Gorton's beliefs had nuanced differences but, in many ways, were similar to those of the Boston elders. Many wondered if the underlying objective of the governor had little to do with blasphemy and more to do with the expansion of the boundaries of the colony, but no one dared speak such doubts aloud.

The sentence of death required ratification by deputies from all of the towns in the Massachusetts Bay Colony. Fortunately, they flatly refused to ratify the sentence. The neighboring towns' lack of support began to concern Governor Winthrop. Support was weakening for his oppression of Samuel Gorton, Roger Williams, and the Providence Plantations. With the failure to ratify death by hanging, the burden fell upon the governor to provide a sentence. While he knew that he could choose to enforce the sentence, he chose instead to sentence Gorton and his followers to a life of hard labor.

For several months, Gorton did labor in chains on various development projects in the Massachusetts Bay Colony. As news of the Gorton story spread amongst the settlements, sympathy began to grow amongst the populace. Members of the clergy continued to speak out about those that called themselves Gortonists, but with each day, their support dwindled. Most settlers viewed Gorton as an ordinary individual who had only wanted to settle in this New World. Instead, Boston had seized his family's land, stolen their belongings, and even murdered women and children in his settlement. In a surprising turn of events, the towns of Salem, Roxbury, and Charlestown all let the governor know they felt Gorton had been wronged in both trial and verdict.

On March 7, 1644, Samuel Gorton and all of the others sentenced with him were released. On March 8, they returned to Boston, where they were warmly greeted by the citizens who had stood up to their government against the former prisoners' unfair treatment. Upon hearing of this, Governor Winthrop issued an order permanently banning Gortonists from the Massachusetts Bay Colony and informing them that a return would earn an immediate death sentence.

"We will grant you one month to leave our territories," Governor Winthrop told Samuel once he and his small group had returned to Boston.

"Does this include our lands in Shawomet?" Gorton asked.

"It includes Shawomet, which is part of the Massachusetts Bay annexation. This order applies to you and all current settlers of Shawomet," Winthrop answered.

"And what of our homes? What of the cattle and other livestock you have taken from us?"

"Those things, those cattle, livestock, and personal items already taken, will not sufficiently cover the costs of court and incarceration. We shall also take the deeds and houses on that land. This banishment shall apply to all Gorton followers," Winthrop decreed. "Because under this banishment you are no longer Englishmen living under the protectorate of Massachusetts, you shall not be entitled to protection from the savages." Understanding the struggle between the Narragansett and the Mohegan, Winthrop made this decree in the hopes that the people he still viewed as savages would see this as an opportunity to execute what his courts had been unable to and kill the Gortonists.

Learning of Gorton's release, and hearing that Winthrop had declared that the Gortonists were not Englishmen and not protected by the Massachusetts Bay Colony, Canonicus, chief sachem of the Narragansett, invited Gorton to come visit.

Samuel's trip back to Shawomet took him and the other men through several settlements, where they were greeted warmly. Upon their arrival at Shawomet, young Samuel ran out to greet the returning party.

"Father, Mother is in labor!"

Samuel Senior gazed upon his fourteen-year-old son, who now seemed a young man. He smiled and embraced his strapping son, and together, they ran the final half mile to the Gorton home.

The midwife delivered the healthy baby girl just as the Samuels, father and son, arrived at the house.

Samuel went to his wife. "Mary, you have given us another beautiful baby girl. What shall we name her?"

Tears of pain and joy ran down Mary's cheeks as she greeted her husband. "We have all worried so about you, darling husband."

"And I have thought about you every day, but knowing your strength, I knew you would be well," Samuel answered.

"We have survived the winter, thanks in part to Canonicus and the Narragansett," Mary answered.

"Enough of those things, my lovely shrew. What shall we name this baby?" Samuel persisted.

"I have been so distraught these last weeks that I have not considered it much," Mary answered.

"Well then, we should get past these concerns and remember that Gortons never quit," Samuel responded as he kissed Mary on the cheek. "So, what name, then?"

"Maybe Ann, after our lost friend."

"That is a good choice, Mary. Let us christen her Ann Gorton."

Mary smiled as she looked into the eyes of her husband, whom she had thought she had lost.

"Ann Gorton it is, then," Samuel said as he lifted the baby in the air. "For now, sweet Mary, I shall take my leave, as you must get some rest." Samuel handed the baby to the midwife and joined the other men, who were surveying the town.

Samuel called together all of the adult men and women so they could collectively decide their future. It was quickly determined that in order to properly evaluate their situation, Samuel should first visit with Canonicus and the Narragansett to determine if there would be other lands where they could safely take haven. Because the men had been away from their families for nearly half a year, and because Ann Gorton had just been born, they agreed to wait two weeks before departure.

<hr>

The following two weeks, Samuel spent time with Mary and their seven children, including the infant Ann. During that period, he and Mary decided that young Sam should join his father in his visit to the Narragansett village to meet Canonicus. They caught up and made plans for how they would move again under their adverse conditions.

Samuel told Mary the details of his trial, imprisonment, and time of hard labor. Samuel described how, in chains, he and several other prisoners had cut trees to clear land and worked on several structures in the Bay Colony.

Samuel stopped to appreciate the strength and beauty of his wife and the beginnings of the community they had built at Shawomet. "Here we are again, Mary. I wonder, had you known how much trouble I would create in this New World, would you have willingly married me sixteen years ago?"

"My father forced me to marry you, Samuel. I had no choice on the matter," Mary joked. She laughed. "Samuel, I would marry you again today even if you told me we would endure this all over again. We have asked for a life of adventure and have been granted one. I never believed a life of adventure would be easy. Certainly, it is not. I daresay Shakespeare or Cervantes could not pen a better tale."

"Yes, Cervantes . . ." Samuel said. "I remember it was your favorite. How I should like to study it again!"

"With the lack of libraries here in the colony, along with our tribulations, it may be difficult for us ever to do so."

"Alas, that is true, my love. We traded our libraries, culture, and theaters in London for this life of adventure."

"And I miss them," Mary replied. "But not the gross restrictions, the oppressive Anglican church, and the predictability. I do not regret our life."

The route to Canonicus's village included a half-day boat trip across the Narragansett Bay, followed by a full-day hike on rough trails through the woods. The last time Samuel had been here, the sachem had been living in a traditional Narragansett hut. Because of his friendship with Gorton and Williams, many of the Narragansett had been instructed in English building techniques. One of the results of this was that Canonicus was now living in a four-room house. While simple on the inside, it provided significantly more shelter and convenience than the hut he had been living in before.

Young Sam had been learning simple phrases in the Algonquin language of the Narragansett, which he eagerly practiced when being introduced to members of the tribe. Because of this, he was warmly received by the tribe.

"Your son is becoming a man, Samuel. It seems that you and Mary have raised him well," Canonicus remarked as they began discussions in his house.

"He has taken a deep interest in Narragansett language and culture. Perhaps we should talk about Sam spending time here and expanding that education?"

"Let young Sam Gorton come live for a time with the Narragansett. I can promise you that he will be treated as a brother among my people."

"My thanks. On to more important matters," said Samuel, changing the subject. "What does the tribe think of the expansion of Massachusetts?"

With that, several other sachems entered the room.

"Samuel, I do not know if you have met Pessicus. He is the brother of Miantonomo and is now chief sachem of all Narragansett tribes." Canonicus said.

Samuel stood and greeted the new sachem. "Your brother was a good friend and a great man, Pessicus. My family, village, and I mourn his loss as we would a brother and as a friend."

"He spoke well of you, Samuel Gorton. The trials through which you have prevailed add credence and speak well in support of my brother's opinions."

"When we learned of your capture, we assumed you would be killed, as my nephew Miantonomo was," Canonicus said. "Rumors spread through our villages that your death sentence had been decreed and was near. Then we learned that you had escaped this sentence and would be forced into a lifetime of slavery. After this, we learned you had been released."

"It was not slavery, but a sentence to perform work for the colony as a prisoner of the court," Gorton corrected.

"You English always confuse simplicity. To work in chains with no freedom and no payment for that work is slavery," Canonicus responded.

Gorton smiled bitterly at the succinct and accurate analysis. "Yes, when you put it that way, I suppose you are correct."

"I have been told the English believe the Narragansett or the Mohegan will take your release as an opportunity to kill you and your people," Canonicus continued. "Pessicus and I believe your ability to overcome these English settlers makes you the more powerful leader."

With that, Samuel broke into laughter, joined by his English companions and then followed by the tribal leaders.

When the laughter ended, Canonicus continued, "As with the followers of Samuel Gorton, the Narragansett wish not to be subjects of the Massachusetts Bay Colony. How can we align with you, Samuel, and make this happen?"

"It is our thinking that the only way for us to stay in Narragansett country is to secure a separate patent from the king. To accomplish this, I will need to travel to London and meet with people who would be willing to help us," Gorton explained.

"And will they help us?" Canonicus asked.

Samuel thought about that in silence for a minute. "I believe they will, my friend."

"In good faith, the Narragansett have helped the men of Plymouth, Boston, and other colonies. We have fought beside them in their war with the Pequot, and still they chose not to respect my nephew and our chief, Miantonomo. With his death, our hearts have grown sore, and we do not trust the men of Massachusetts Bay Colony, but we do trust Roger Williams and Samuel Gorton."

"The way your people have been treated is shameful, and I regret that my English brothers in Boston have done these things."

"I ask again, Samuel, how shall we prevent this in the days to come?"

"Come with us to London," Samuel suggested.

"I cannot do that, Samuel. I would consider sending one of the village sachems, but to what end? Would the king even hear what the Narragansett have to say?"

Samuel thought about the probability of the king hearing their petition against the Massachusetts Bay Colony. It seemed unlikely. "I do not think the king would weigh the interests of a Narragansett sachem over those of Winthrop and the Massachusetts Bay Colony," he admitted.

Canonicus was unsurprised. "We have discussed this, and we have a solution for you, Samuel Gorton. Socononocco and Punham have earned friendship in Boston by pledging to become part of their annexation. The Narragansett will agree to become subjects of the King of England."

Samuel stood up from his chair, startled by the proposal. "I think that would be a terrible idea. I consider myself a loyal subject of the king, but I recognize the authority and laws of England. You do not."

"We have discussed this. The long arm of the king seems much safer than the short, malicious hand of Massachusetts Bay."

"You have suggested sending a village sachem to London with me, but I would urge you or Pessicus to be that emissary. Having someone on that level would increase our chances of securing the ear of King Charles."

Canonicus frowned. "It would not be possible for either of us. We have problems in the conflict with the Mohegan and would not be able to leave our home for two years." Samuel waited as the great sachem considered the issue. After a few minutes, he spoke. "How would the king respond to the son of Miantonomo?"

Samuel smiled. "You are a wise man, Canonicus. Miantonomo's family and the Narragansett have been gravely injured by the policies of the Bay Colony. I believe this would help your cause."

After much discussion, Canonicus and Samuel refined their strategy and agreed it was the best path for the Narragansett. Samuel then helped the sachems draft a deed of submission whereby the Narragansett would become subjects of King Charles. This deed would be presented in London by Samuel and one of the village sachems of the Narragansett. Samuel also helped to draft a letter notifying Winthrop and the Massachusetts Bay Colony that they had dispatched a sachem to present the deed in London and that the Narragansett would now become "fellow subjects of the king."

24

Return to London

> I'll make a journey twice as far t'enjoy
> A second night of such sweet shortness which
> Was mine in Britain, for the ring is won.
> —Shakespeare

In July 1644, Samuel Gorton and his family—accompanied by Thomas Gorton, John Greene, Randall Holden, and young Nanuntonoo, son of Miantonomo—embarked for London. Because of their banishment from Boston, they were not able to sail from Boston Harbor directly to London. As such, their route took them to New Netherland and from the port in Amsterdam on to London. In spite of the roundabout path, their journey was relaxing and comfortable. The great migration of Pilgrims from England to the colonies had begun to slow down a few years earlier. While ships were still carrying people across the Atlantic, the numbers had decreased. Ships were still arriving, but they were more often filled with trade items than families.

During the voyage, Samuel began writing his first book, entitled *Simplicity's Defence Against Seven-Headed Policy*, which he planned to use as a tool for making his case against the egregious behavior of the Massachusetts authorities.

In September 1644, Samuel Gorton and his family arrived at the dock in London. Thomas took leave and made plans to return to

Manchester, while Samuel and Mary hired a coach to take them to the home of Mary's mother, who had no prior warning of their arrival.

As their carriage rolled through the familiar sights and smells of London, they told their children stories of the many events that had occurred on these streets. They circled onto Milk Street toward St. Lawrence Jewry and the row of homes where Mary had grown up.

Mary Maplett opened the door in shock to find Samuel and Mary Gorton, along with their children Mary, Maher, John, Benjamin, and baby Ann. "Oh, my beautiful grandchildren, my daughter!" said Mary Maplett, and she was in tears as she hugged and kissed her daughter, curtsied to her son-in-law, hugged her grandchildren, and then hugged her daughter again. "I thought I would not see you again in this world."

"Nor we you, Mother," Mary answered, her face wet with tears of joy.

"It is so wonderful to see you and my grandchildren again! Have you returned to London to live again?" she asked hopefully.

"No, Mother," Mary answered. "We are here to secure a patent for a new colony we have formed in the New World."

"A patent? With whom shall you meet to secure this patent?" Maplett asked.

"I plan to visit with the Earl of Warwick," Samuel replied. "He is friendly to our cause, familiar with the colonies, and I believe he is in a position to help us with this matter, Mary."

"I see. Well, you know your brother John is now the private physician to King Charles. I would daresay he can also be of help, should you need it."

"Yes, Mother, we had heard that great news about brother John. I should very much love to see him, along with all of my siblings, on this trip."

"And I would love to visit with him about the best strategy toward persuading the king and Parliament to support our initiatives in the New World," Samuel added.

"What has become of my lovely grandson Samuel?" Maplett asked, hoping to not hear sad news.

"Sam is a young man now and has been invited by Canonicus, a chief of the Narragansett Indians, to live with them for a year," Mary Gorton answered.

"Is that safe, Mary?" Mother Maplett asked.

"Yes, of course it is, Mother. Canonicus is our friend. Your grandson has become engrossed in the Indian language and culture. Not many English settlers truly understand the Indians, so we are quite happy that Sam has this enthusiasm and focus. Samuel's friendship with the Indians has paid off on many occasions, and I suspect it will bode well for him in the future."

"Well, so much has changed since you departed. I just hope these savages are a prudent choice for entrusting my grandson."

"Mother, we prefer not to call the Narragansett 'savages.' They are our friends and have been better neighbors than many of our fellow English settlers. Most importantly, they are *not* savages."

"Yes, Mother Mary," Samuel added. "These Indians have given so much to us and to all English settlers in the New World. They have taught us new farming techniques and have their own unique foods, dance, and spiritual insight. I would not be alive were it not for the grace of my friend Chief Canonicus."

"I see," Mary Maplett responded. "I do apologize and did not intend to insult these Narragansett. Most people in London refer to the *sav* . . . I mean, Indians, that way."

"Well, you will get to meet one of these Narragansett. We have brought the son of one of the chiefs over with us. He is with one of our travel companions for now, but I hope he can spend some time here with us so you have the opportunity to get to know him. Nanuntonoo is his name," Samuel said.

⇒►◦◄⇐

Three weeks after their arrival, Samuel was able to get an appointment with his old friend Robert Rich, Earl of Warwick.

"Gorton, it is excellent to see you again!" Rich stood up from his desk and came around to embrace Samuel. "I daresay the wilderness is far different from the streets of London, and I have missed our chats at the haberdashery. The new chap running Maplett's is quite boring."

"Hah, well, I do hope that he has not run the shop into the ground. More importantly, thank you for seeing me, my lord," Samuel said.

"I have been keeping up with your doings in the colonies. You have managed to create quite a stir over there. Besides Roger Williams, you have few friends and some very powerful and influential enemies."

"The colonies have become an even more oppressive environment than that created by Bishop Laud here in England," Samuel reported. "I think they have forgotten their history and decided to turn the colonies into a rebirth of the Church before reformation."

"Your assessment is an accurate one, Samuel. Meanwhile, with the civil war raging here, things are even more difficult," Rich answered.

"What will become of this civil war, my lord?"

"I do not think it will go well for the king. The years of King Charles's rule have not been good ones for his British subjects. I would not establish any special affiliation with him, as that could turn out poorly."

"My brother is now personal physician to King Charles. Do you think that a blessing or a curse?"

"Your brother is safe. As a physician, he has achieved that honor because of his skills and medical knowledge. Regardless of what happens with the king, John Maplett will do well."

"With whom should I establish affiliations?"

"Oliver Cromwell will usher in a new era, I should think."

"Do you know Lord Cromwell?" Samuel asked.

"I do indeed. While most of us are guarded in our respect and support for him, we mostly wake up in the mornings with hope that he will prevail."

"Well, I shall plan on getting up to date on the politics of Lord Cromwell and King Charles while here, but my primary objective is that of securing a clear patent for Shawomet in the colonies and for registering a deed from the Narragansett to become subjects of the king . . . er, subjects of England, perhaps."

"How extraordinary! How did you manage to convince Canonicus to become a subject of the crown?"

"It was Canonicus's idea," Samuel responded.

"As I said, that is extraordinary, and, in my opinion, most welcome news. This other request will be complicated. I support what you are requesting, but we have just granted a patent to Roger Williams, and it took some convincing on his part to secure approval from the Committee for Foreign Plantations. In Williams's case, he leveraged a relationship with Henry Vane, who ultimately granted the patent. Yours will be more problematic because we will require that you present to the committee."

"Do you know any of the members of this committee?" Samuel asked hopefully.

"I suppose I should, as I am the head of that committee," Rich responded with a broad smile. "Of course, while I will aid you in your efforts, the task of convincing the others shall be all yours. I will not allow our friendship to secure special favors here, and I can assure you that you do not want me to. If you build a good case, it will endure any storm. My guess is that if you prevail, the Massachusetts Bay authorities will be none too happy."

"Well, congratulations for being selected to serve in that post," Samuel answered.

"I was the obvious choice. Many of the members of Parliament have not been to the New World, while I have been half a dozen times. In any case, my two primary roles in government consume so much of my time that I have little remaining these days for my hobbies in the colonies."

"I heard you have been named lord high admiral of the fleet. That is truly an accomplishment."

"Only if you like spending your time with all these pompous aristocrats, which I believe you know, Samuel, that I do not. I imagine, as with my position on the committee, they selected me because of the extreme amount of time I have spent at sea."

"Well, it seems the high posts and times have not changed you for the worse, my lord. I have great appreciation for that." Samuel pulled out the stack of parchments he had been writing over the past few months. "This book is intended to document the actions of the Massachusetts Bay Colony authorities. I have written it for publishing, but I believe it is a good starting point for you to become familiar with our plight."

"And when will you have it printed and published?"

"It is already in progress."

"I shall read it as soon as it is available." Rich stood up as Samuel was preparing to depart. "You should know that Roger Williams was very guarded in his praise of you when he came before our committee. I was not clear on whether he is your friend, ally, both, or neither."

"We certainly have similar viewpoints, but our approach is quite different. I suspect Williams is intentionally guarded, though I would call him both ally and friend."

"Well then, next time we meet should be in the pub, where we can enjoy an ale," Rich offered, indicating their meeting should come to an end.

"You still find ways to frequent the pubs, with all your high posts and titles?" Samuel asked incredulously.

"I would not give up the pleasure of evenings in an English pub, and shall not! I have learned to dress the part in disguises that blend in. When I do not, I am constantly accosted by aspirants and patrons."

Being back in London was comfortable for the Gorton family, though they missed young Samuel, the wilderness, and the challenges of the colonies. Still, Samuel and Mary found time to see plays at a few underground theaters in London. Several religious factions had closed the Globe, ostensibly because of the plague but really because their extreme religious viewpoints were counter to the literature expressed in the theater. Samuel also spent time in the library rereading Cervantes's well-known work *Don Quixote*. He became transfixed by the book and found himself making notes he thought would carry himself through the coming years. In some ways, he saw a parallel between his fight with Massachusetts and that imagined by Quixote.

"Mary, I have become enchanted by your quixotic manuscript."

"It is yet another example of how well I know you and how much I love you. I always saw the man from La Mancha in you, my dear. Miguel Cervantes penned a story that I believe will live for eternity."

"I have made a note that I'd like to read you. I think I shall carry this with me as we prepare our case: 'Destiny guides our fortunes more favorably than we could have expected. Look there, Sancho Panza, my friend, and see those thirty or so wild giants, with whom I intend to do battle and kill each and all of them, so with their stolen booty we can begin to enrich ourselves. This is noble, righteous warfare, for it is wonderfully useful to God to have such an evil race wiped from the face of the earth.'"

"Destiny has perhaps guided our fortune, Samuel, but your persistence in efforts to prevail will ultimately decide *our* future. Few men in the colonies or here in England have endured so much for their cause."

"What a charming thing to say, Mary."

"It is true. I have watched you pursue the path of righteousness though you have been beaten, banished, and imprisoned. Many would have given up, but you have persisted. Surely somehow, some day, we shall find our reward for your efforts."

Over the next four months, Gorton, Holden, and Greene worked diligently on their petition to the Committee for Foreign Plantations. The Earl of Warwick did play a role in tweaking the proposal, but he promised to not intervene should Samuel's efforts be rejected by the committee. The final petition was submitted on January 14, 1645. The document was one of the largest ever reviewed by the committee and detailed wrongs committed against the Shawomet settlers by the Massachusetts Bay Colony. Amongst those were titles and papers demonstrating a legal purchase of land from Miantonomo and how that chief had been subsequently murdered with the approval and endorsement of the Bay authorities.

The document detailed the Shawomet colonists' religious beliefs and how the Massachusetts government was working to quell those beliefs. Gorton wrote of how Boston had sent out a militia of forty soldiers and several dozen Indian braves to ransack Shawomet, whereupon two women were killed along with two infants. In that raid, Boston militia had stolen crops and livestock along with other personal belongings. Even with a lack of evidence, Boston elders had sentenced Gorton to death, a sentence that was opposed by the other towns, but still Gorton had been sentenced to a life of hard labor. When the citizenry had risen up in protest, Governor Winthrop had been forced to overturn the verdict. With that, Winthrop still banished Gorton from lands that he rightfully owned and that Boston could only claim jurisdiction over through murder and deception.

The case was so complicated that the committee called Gorton and his two associates in on three separate occasions for further details and cross-examination. Nanuntonoo, who had become a celebrity in London and who, along with the Narragansett tribe, had been granted full rights as an English subject, was also brought in and cross-examined on the subject of the true ownership of the Shawomet land. Finally, on May 15, 1646, the committee called the three Shawomet settlers in for a final hearing.

"Are you nervous about the decision today?" Greene asked generally of Gorton and Holden as they awaited their hearing.

"We have provided a vivid delineation of the Massachusetts government," Samuel said. "We have brought in Nanuntonoo, who has testified about the lack of legitimacy of the Punham/Socononocco deeds to the Arnolds. The Boston authorities have no jurisdiction, and I believe we have clearly made this case to the committee. Still, we have on many occasions in the past stood justly in front of a court of magistrates and been found guilty. I do not believe that will happen today."

Forefathers & Founding Fathers

"That is refreshing to hear from the infamous Samuel Gorton, who has been pronounced guilty 100 percent of the times he has been tried!" Holden joked.

"We may lose today, but at least we are all in a light and cheerful mood," Samuel responded. "Perhaps we can prevail upon Lord Warwick to drown our troubles at the local pub after our hearing."

They all were laughing when the clerk instructed them to come in.

The gavel was struck three times. "Lord Warwick, chairman of the Committee for Foreign Plantations, has reached a decision in the request for a patent for the Shawomet settlement."

Robert Rich, the Earl of Warwick, lord chair of the Foreign Plantations, and lord high admiral stood and cleared his throat. "This committee praises the Massachusetts Bay Colony and the Boston settlement authorities for conducting their affairs under long-standing principles of justice, prudence, and zeal to God. We hold that Governor Winthrop should maintain the principles upon which he has governed said colony," he said. He paused for a minute to allow the pronouncement to be fully comprehended by the audience and plaintiffs.

Samuel's stomach turned upside down as he listened to Warwick's pronouncement, which he was clearly reading from a parchment. He glanced at Greene and Holden, who were both standing in pale-faced shock. All of this work in developing a very clear-cut case, only to come to this. With this, it would be nearly impossible to return to the New World, which once seemed a challenging yet perfect home of adventure and so much opportunity and which was now a New World of oppression and unjust fiefdoms.

The noise level in the room began to rise as Warwick stood motionless, observing the room full of onlookers. As the noise reached a crescendo, Warwick motioned to the clerk, who again slammed the gavel three times. The background noise dropped like an ocean-side cliff.

"Our pronouncement should be further clarified. While we approve of the Massachusetts Bay authorities for conducting affairs within their colony, we do not approve of their methods of annexation through deception, murder, and trickery. This committee, by unanimous concert, therefore grants in accordance with the wishes of Samuel Gorton a patent to establish a separate charter in Shawomet. That charter may, if Gorton and his delegates so wish, join the patent recently granted to Roger Williams and the Providence Plantations. This mandate, which shall be delivered to Governor Winthrop, orders Massachusetts Bay authorities to allow Shawomet families to live, raise livestock, and plant peacefully in their settlement. Massachusetts may not interfere with the religious or government practices of that Shawomet colony. Further, Gorton and his companions shall be allowed to pass peacefully without arrest though the port of Boston and into the Massachusetts Colony, as is necessary for trade and commerce."

Samuel, Greene, and Holden could hardly believe what they were hearing. After years of oppression and struggle, the English crown was now supporting their mission to build a colony based on civil liberty and freedom of religion, one free from slavery and open to any who held similar beliefs. A greater victory could not have been received.

The three men, who over the many years of struggle had become such solid friends, stood in the courtroom, tears running down their faces. Few battles in their lives had been harder fought, and none were more deserving of victory. From this courtroom, there was only one place to go next, and that would be to the pub.

"On the first ship back to Boston, we shall be with patent in hand!" Greene toasted with a pint of ale.

"To the Earl of Warwick, lads!" added Holden.

"Indeed, to the Earl of Warwick, who had us aghast with his pronouncement, only to provide haven and sanctuary," Greene chimed in.

"Yes, Robert Rich, the Earl of Warwick, who worked with us to develop our presentation, who scared and crushed us, and then granted that which will allow us to live and grow in peace in the New World, now emerges as our proponent."

"Hear, hear!" they all chimed together.

"I know you feel there is work yet to be done here in London, Samuel, so I must know, will you be joining us on the boat home?" Greene asked.

"I will not," Samuel answered. "There are two pressing issues here in London that will keep me for another year, I should think. First, Mary's mother has taken ill and is in need of our care. Second, Thomas Lamb has asked that I spend some time teaching his flock in the London Bell Alley church."

"Samuel, I think it a bad idea for you to affiliate with the Puritan underground," Greene protested. "These people do not hold the support of the powers here in England, and as Puritans, they hold similar theocratic beliefs to our current adversaries in the Bay Colonies."

"Yes, John, dangerous it is, but I think it necessary. It should be noted that these Puritans are very different from Winthrop's. The *underground* Puritan movement here understands and supports religious freedom and diversity."

"Perhaps," Greene mused.

"In any case," Samuel continued, "Cromwell is introducing ideas that could change everything here in London. I have good insight that he would support greater freedoms as King Charles's reign falters. Those freedoms need a seed, and with the help of Thomas Lamb, I am planting those seeds."

"Let us not do things here in London that cause us to lose the goodwill of Warwick and his committee," Holden warned.

"But Lord Warwick also supports these causes," Gorton pointed out. "The winds of change are in the air, and those winds blow not only in the New World but in England as well."

Winslow in London

> Send danger from the east unto the west,
> So honor cross it from the north to south,
> And let them grapple. O, the blood more stirs
> To rouse a lion than to start a hare!
> —Shakespeare

Over the next six months, Samuel worked diligently with Thomas Lamb to establish a Puritan underground in London that would ultimately reform the Anglican Church. Samuel became quite popular as an educator and teacher, speaking passionately as he wove tales of the New World into spiritual and philosophical lectures. Oliver Cromwell's concept of a Commonwealth of England was beginning to grow amongst the masses and was very popular on the streets of London. King Charles's reign had been a financial and political disaster for the country, and people seemed ready for a bit more normalization. An underground version of the theater was thriving in spite of attempts by the church to prevent it. The theater became a regular evening out for Mary and Samuel.

Mary Maplett encouraged Mary and Samuel's adventures. "Children, my health may be failing, but that shall never rob me of precious time with my grandchildren," she said. "You should enjoy what you can of London culture before you return to that godforsaken wilderness."

"Mother, our home in the New World is anything but godforsaken," Mary Gorton reminded her mum as she kissed her on the forehead.

While she was enjoying the time in London, particularly the precious time with her mother and siblings, she was looking forward to returning to their home in Shawomet.

"What play will you see this evening?" Mother Mary asked.

"*Hamlet*, finally *Hamlet*!" Mary Gorton exclaimed happily.

After getting in the carriage, the driver began the twenty-minute ride across the Thames to the theater.

"Which has been your favorite thus far, Samuel?" Mary asked.

"I think the comedy of *A Midsummer Night's Dream*. 'The course of true love never did run smooth,'" he quoted.

"Except, of course, with ours."

"Indeed. And your favorite, my dear?"

"Oh, that would definitely be *Taming of the Shrew*," she answered without a second of cogitation.

"It has been many years, Mary, but I found the *Taming* to be somewhat confusing and not as clever as some of the others we have seen this past year. What part of it makes that particular play your favorite?"

"Oh, it was not what was happening on the stage that night, my dear Samuel. It is my favorite play because that is the night we met," Mary said, and she kissed Samuel affectionately.

"You have tricked me in that question then, Mary. If your analysis must include the impact of our meeting, then I should agree there has been no better night, no play by Shakespeare or any other, that is better than *Taming of the Shrew*."

Three days later, Samuel received notice that Lord Warwick wanted to see him.

⟶•◦•⟵

"How is Mother Maplett doing, Gorton?" Warwick asked as Samuel sat.

"Brother John tells us she will continue to deteriorate, my friend. But she is a tough woman who stays happy, and I would not be surprised if she outlives us all."

Forefathers & Founding Fathers

"Of course, such is our wish, but no parent wants to bury their children."

"True, and should these be our last days with her, I am glad these circumstances of the Massachusetts Bay Colony brought us back to London for this time so we could be with her. I suppose we can find good in all difficulties. My children shall cherish the opportunity to get to know this town and their grandmother."

"Well, it is the Massachusetts Bay Colony that has caused me to call you here today. It seems they are not happy with the decision of the Foreign Plantations Committee. They have dispatched Governor Winslow, a most impressive man, to appeal and overturn the decision."

"Winslow?" Samuel thought about the impact. Of all the authorities in the colonies, Winslow, former governor of Plymouth, was probably the best known and best respected. "It seems they have sent their finest advocate. They must truly want our Shawomet patent overturned."

"This may be the case, Samuel, but in my opinion, he has given us no cause to support his claim, delivered nothing more than acerbic, vengeful, and personal attacks on you. I have not yet conferred with the committee, but I would guess they have made the same observation," Warwick responded.

"And what happens now?"

"Now you must prepare a defense. In preparation, you must remember that Governor Winslow is perhaps the most recognized and respected member of the colony governments. His reputation will carry significant weight in our decision-making process. I believe his thoughtless and angry attacks will diminish his reputation and may work in your favor."

"Are you allowed to tell me specifically what his claims are?" Samuel asked.

"Their statement is that they have not gone outside their jurisdiction in arresting you. They claim you are living in lands actually controlled by two Indian chiefs named Punham and Soconococco and that these chiefs have become 'praying Indians' and have joined the Massachusetts Bay Colony. They claim Miantonomo had no right to sell you land in that area. They also assert that your charges were false and scandalous toward them. And finally, Winslow has further asserted that your preaching is unorthodox, which ultimately leads the individual to an inconceivable political liberty."

"Yes, of course, all of these claims are predictable and claims for which we have an impermeable defense. Do they know yet of the testimony of Nanuntonoo and the Narragansett becoming English citizens?"

"I do not believe Winslow has heard this news. But with regard to your preaching, I have received comments about it here in England. Is it correct that you have been preaching in many churches around the country and that some bishops have even been in attendance?"

Samuel hesitated, concerned about the repercussions of these activities and remembering that he had been duly warned by Greene and Holden before they departed. "I have, on invitation, spoken at some churches."

"Mr. Gorton, the committee and I are aware of all of your activities around the country. I suggest you clearly articulate what you have done, where, and why," Warwick scolded.

Chastened, Samuel bowed his head. He did not want to hurt his cause with his strongest source of support. "Yes, my lord. I will provide a full accounting."

Warwick's tone softened somewhat. "I continue to support your efforts to establish religious freedom, Gorton, but you may make enemies by continuing. Right now, you do not need enemies, as they are always more vocal than friends. Some bishops have been praising your teaching. This is a good thing, but many bishops tend to be capricious and will not defend you if charges are leveled."

Samuel continued to listen as Warwick provided advice on how to handle his coming accuser.

<hr />

Over the next six months, the committee held five hearings with Gorton and Winslow. In his days living in the colony, Gorton had earned a reputation as a hotheaded firebrand. Winslow, Reynor, Coddington, and Winthrop had all experienced this, and Winslow worked hard to spark Gorton into a diatribe. Gorton anticipated this and prepared, and Winslow's endeavors failed. In spite of direct attacks and attempts at sparking his hotheaded nature, Gorton always maintained a respectful manner in the committee presentations. On March 18, 1647, the committee ruled once again on the case, again in Gorton's favor. This time, Gorton was in no mood to celebrate, as his mother-in-law, Mary Maplett, was on her deathbed. She died two days later on March 20, 1647. Over the next few months, Samuel and John Maplett III worked to clean up her estate and prepare her home for sale.

While Samuel was focused on family matters, Winslow was working on a second appeal and looking to discredit Samuel. While Winslow did approach several bishops, none were willing to testify against Gorton, as Samuel's preaching was very popular among the clergy and congregation. He did manage to dig up an old debt Gorton had taken out from a John Duckingfield in 1634. Duckingfield, now deceased, had a rather unscrupulous executor named George Walker who was willing to lay charges against Gorton. Samuel was working in Lamb's church when the sheriff arrived to arrest him.

"Samuel Gorton, you have a debt in the amount of two hundred pounds owed to the estate of John Duckingfield, whose executor, George Walker, has filed complaint." The sheriff had arrived with Walker in tow.

"I have no such debt. That amount was paid thirteen years ago."

"Our records show otherwise, and we now demand payment before you escape again to the New World," Walker added.

And so, on April 19, 1647, with no notice to family, Samuel was incarcerated in the London city jail, less than five blocks from the old Globe Theatre. The following day, Winslow added this charge to his amended claim against Gorton. It took nearly a week for Mary Gorton to find out what had become of her husband. The same day, she returned to the jail with the fully executed legal receipt from Duckingfield for full payment, dated 1634. Samuel was immediately released, and the charges against him were dropped. Winslow still tried to use the fact that the charges had existed as an instrument to prove his case in the final hearing, but based on the evidence presented, the committee rejected his allegations against Samuel Gorton's character.

In July 1647, the Committee for Foreign Plantations issued the third and final report, signed by Warwick and all twelve other members of the committee, once again reaffirming the previous demands but this time also proclaiming that the United Colonies protect the Shawomet settlers in all fit ways.

This time, Samuel Gorton and his family could finally celebrate, and so they did. With the estate of Mary Maplett now completely resolved, Samuel and Mary packed all final belongings along with a few new family heirlooms and scheduled transit on the next ship west. Before they left, they managed to see one more play at the London theater. It would be their last time to visit this theater. The play was *Hamlet*.

"I think that play teaches us an important lesson in our life, Samuel," Mary suggested as they left the play.

"What lesson is that, my dear?"

"In Hamlet's famous soliloquy, he says,

'To be or not to be—that is the question:

Whether 'tis nobler in the mind to suffer

The slings and arrows of outrageous fortune,

Or to take arms against a sea of troubles.'"

"Indeed, dear wife. I do see what you are saying, for we have surely suffered slings and arrows in our quest *to be*."

Mary grinned broadly and kissed Samuel on the cheek. "Correct, dear husband. You are correct."

"And yet, through all of those trials, we have stuck to our beliefs," Samuel said.

"And that, Samuel, is what I have come to love about you. Our life has not been easy. Oh, it has been a wonderful adventure, but the slings and arrows have never ceased, and they have never stopped us from continuing our quest."

Samuel, Mary, and their family looked forward to their return to the New World, but as the time came for them to depart once again, Samuel's brother, Thomas, made the choice to stay behind and permanently return to his childhood home in Manchester. The two brothers had lived through many adventures in the New World, but for Thomas, those had finally come to an end.

Return to Shawomet

> Now is the winter of our discontent
> Made glorious summer by this son of Warwick.
> —Shakespeare (modified)

September 1647

With help from their friend the Earl of Warwick, chairman of the Committee for Foreign Plantations and lord high admiral of the fleet, the Gorton family was able to sail back to Boston in comfort on a fast boat. Where their first trip had taken nearly three months, this one lasted less than a month, and rather than being cramped with dozens of other settlers, they shared a small quarters in the officers' deck of the ship.

All was well until they landed at the port of Boston. Within an hour of arriving in port, as they were collecting their belongings from the hold, a posse met Gorton to arrest the entire family. The sheriff refused to look at the documents provided by the earl.

The ship's captain, who observed the arrest from the deck, immediately collected two lieutenants and followed the posse to the magistrate's office to demand release of Gorton and his family. Within hours, that was accomplished, with a note from the governor stating that Gorton had two weeks to remove himself from Massachusetts's jurisdiction. This all occurred in spite of the clear fact that Gorton held papers allowing him to travel in Massachusetts any time.

Gorton didn't care that Boston was not interested in the details of the papers Lord Warwick had given him. He had little interest in staying within the borders of the Bay Colony. Within three days, Samuel and his family were back in Shawomet.

As the Gorton family rolled into Shawomet, everyone was there to greet them. Young Samuel, now seventeen, had grown into a man, strong and tall. His knowledge of the Algonquin language and customs now surpassed that of his father and Roger Williams. Along with him was Pessicus, still chief of all Narragansett, and Nanuntonoo, who had traveled back from London with Greene and Holden.

Randall Holden was a reserved man who seldom showed emotion, but he was clearly happy about the Gortons' return and bear-hugged Samuel at the first opportunity. "We have a festival planned to celebrate the return of you and your family. Our neighbors, the Narragansett, will join us!"

"Give us a day to settle and unpack from our journey, and let us meet on official matters of the town before our festival," Gorton suggested.

Samuel put his arm around young Sam. "You must tell me of your stay with the Narragansett. The things that you have learned should be preserved and used to help our two peoples work together into the future."

"Yes, Father. These people, while not yet Christian, have so many good attributes."

"What has happened with the Narragansett during my stay in London?"

"We, I should say, they have defeated Uncas of the Mohegan tribe. But after our victory, the United Colonies intervened. For now, a payment of significant wampum has been exacted from the Narragansett. I think Pessicus is mostly ignoring the authority of the Colonies and will not make payment."

"This is a most complex and troubling development in the list of poor treatment by the colonies," Samuel observed.

"It is indeed, Father."

Samuel stopped and looked into the eyes of his son. "We missed you in London and often wished you could have joined us. Still, I think what you have gained far exceeds that which you would have experienced in London."

———⟫•⟨———

Two days later, Gorton, Greene, Holden, and two other men met in the small structure they had designated for such public meetings.

"You heard they sent Winslow to contest our patent?" Gorton asked.

"We did hear that, and we were thankful you were still in London. What we learned was that Winthrop thought we would all be on the boat home together and Winslow would have an uncontested hearing," Holden responded.

"Can we assume we should once again be thankful to the Earl of Warwick?" Greene asked.

"Indeed, yes! We should be thankful to Lord Warwick, which is why I would like to propose that we change the name of our settlement from Shawomet to Warwick," Samuel suggested.

"We thought perhaps the town's name should be Gorton," Greene suggested, "recognizing, of course, that such a name might cause our friends in Boston to descend upon us with musket and cannon!" They all laughed.

"I would never agree to such a name," Samuel asserted once the laughter died down. "But Warwick is a good name for this settlement and a just reward to our benefactor in London, who has provided the patent that will keep the Puritans at bay."

"In which case, I agree that it should be Warwick," Greene voted.

"Aye. He was not only our benefactor but a member of nobility with whom we could share an ale in the local pub. I shall remember our times with Sir Robert Rich fondly," Holden added.

Samuel looked at the other men attending this meeting, all of whom were nodding consent. He wondered for a brief second what his Narragansett neighbors thought, but he chose not to slow the decision and ask.

Rhode Island during 1636-1650s

"And so, let us have our festival in a few days and, in that time, christen our colony with her new name: Warwick!" Samuel announced.

"We have dispensed with issues specifically related to Massachusetts and their jurisdiction, but they have not completely relinquished their attempts at control. Our old *friend* Coddington has informed us that he holds a higher patent and wants us now under his jurisdiction." Greene stopped abruptly when he noticed Gorton shudder. "What is wrong, Samuel?"

"My apologies," Gorton responded in a shaky tone. "That name still creates anxiety deep in my bones. I continue to have nightmares of the lashings delivered at Coddington's word, the scars that remain for this lifetime on my back, and the loss of things we dreamed and built in Portsmouth."

"Should we not say the name in your presence?"

Forefathers & Founding Fathers

"We should say *Coddington* whenever necessary. It is my burden, and I shall carry it. I promise also to forgive but, similarly, to constantly maintain disbelief should Coddington ever again side with our perspective," Gorton answered.

Greene placed his hand on Samuel's back. "None of us know the sting of those lashes, Samuel, but we all remember them well."

"I remember the sting of those lashes, and I can touch the scars they left, but those things can fade with time. The offense that far eclipses my corporeal punishment is the ultimate end for the Hutchinson family. Had Coddington just allowed them to live in peace, our friends would still be alive." Samuel bowed his head as he felt the real sting of the loss of a good friend who had died before her time.

After a moment of silence, Gorton stood. "Let us forget the pains of the past for now and plan a festival to rename our settlement! We shall deal with Coddington as we have with all other issues, with due attention to the demands of reason and righteousness."

"Hear! Hear!" they all chimed in.

Fire Flower

How far that little candle throws her beams!
—Shakespeare (modified)

Summer 1648

Samuel was in a conventicle when Edward Hutchinson arrived in Warwick.

After quick greetings, Samuel sat down and asked, "What brings you to Warwick, Edward?"

"I have learned the Algonquin just west of New Netherland are raising an English girl who is about sixteen years of age. That girl has red hair."

Samuel felt a chill over his entire body. "Susanna? Could this be Susanna?"

"I do not know for certain, Mr. Gorton, but when I heard the story two weeks ago, I could not shake it from my bones. I have woken each day thinking about that possibility and have become obsessed with finding out for certain."

"Yes, Edward, you must go there, determine if it is indeed Susanna."

"Mr. Gorton, I want . . . I *need* you to help me."

"Me? I love young Susanna, but I am not a soldier like you. Much as I'd like to, I can do little to secure the release of that lovely child."

"Few know the ways of the Narragansett better than you. Few have as many friends amongst them, and among those few, only you have a personal stake."

Samuel considered what Edward was proposing. If Susanna were truly alive, this could be a worthy expedition to secure her release, as well as a tribute to the memory of his friend Anne Hutchinson.

"OK, Edward. The Algonquin are cousins to the Narragansett, but they speak a very similar version of the same language. I will help, but you must let me formulate a plan that does indeed center on negotiations and not on force."

"That is why I have come to you. Your friendship with my mother and father is first and foremost, but your familiarity with the Indians and your ability in negotiations is why you will not fail," Edward asserted.

"My ability with negotiations?" Samuel asked, grinning incredulously.

Edward smiled. "It is no secret in the many towns of the Massachusetts Bay Colony that you are among the most despised individuals in the New World. Winslow, Winthrop, and Coddington have thrown everything they have at you, and yet you prevail. Winslow himself faced you in London courts, where again you prevailed. You have never lifted a finger as a weapon in your defense but have nearly always triumphed."

"I think it a tragic mistake on your part to assume I have always prevailed, when, in fact, I have almost always failed. What I have done is never quit, and by following this path, you have concluded I cannot fail."

"No, I have, on so many occasions, seen the attacks upon you, and yet here you stand, free of Massachusetts government and living in a town that they annexed."

"I still feel the lashes on my back and the dread that I would be hanged and not see my precious children, but this is no magic skill. I have simply stood on the side of what is right. This is a worthy venture, so I suggest we begin planning this emancipation."

"Thank you, Mr. Gorton. With your assistance, I know we shall be successful."

That day, Samuel sent messengers to Roger Williams of Providence and to Pessicus, chief of the Narragansett, soliciting their support or advice. Williams sent back a note apologizing that he could not join them, but he did send one of his lieutenants who knew the Narragansett. Pessicus came in person, along with Nanuntonoo.

When he arrived, Pessicus was in full tribal clothing with feathers and shawl. "Because of the friendship we have long held with you, and in memory of our deceased brothers Miantonomo and Canonicus, we shall accompany you and help secure the release of Susanna Hutchinson."

"We are grateful to you, Pessicus. As with Miantonomo, we mourn the death of Canonicus, who was one of the great chiefs," Samuel answered.

"The Narragansett mourn the passing of Canonicus's spirit. He lived long and shared much with us during his lifetime."

"He was a good friend to me. I think I would not be alive were it not for the friendship of Canonicus," Samuel replied.

Moving on to business, Edward asked Pessicus, "What do you know of the tribes in New Netherland?"

"I have discussed this with some of my other chieftains. Wampage is the Siwanoy chief of this tribe that holds young Susanna. He is a warrior at heart, and we do not believe a white man would be able to secure the release of this young girl. Wampage also claims to have taken the lives of your family, Edward Hutchinson. It is a deed in which he takes great pride. When we are with him, you must not rebuke that act, or we will fail."

"How do we know it is Wampage?" Edward asked.

"He claims this victory amongst his tribe. It is their custom to adopt the name of the most notable person they have killed. Amongst Wampage's names is *Annhook*, an Algonquin pronunciation of your mother's name," Pessicus explained.

"I will accompany this expedition to New Netherland, but perhaps I should remain in one of the Quaker settlements nearby while you negotiate her release," Edward responded.

"I think that wise," Pessicus noted. "And you, Samuel? Can you join this negotiation knowing that Wampage has killed your friend and her family?"

"Yes, Pessicus. For the salvation of young Susanna and the result of her rejoining her family, I can do this."

"I also request your son Sam join as well. No white man has better knowledge of the Algonquin language and cultures. His presence and interpretation skills will bode well for our cause and will carry much weight with Wampage and the Siwanoy."

The small expedition consisting of Samuel, Nanuntonoo, Pessicus, Sam, Edward, and Roger Williams's lieutenant, John Smythe, set out on a small boat. Their route took them south through the Narragansett Bay to the inner part of New Netherland, or what would later be called Long Island.

Once back on the ground, they hiked a few hours inland to the Siwanoy village where Susanna was rumored to be held. Pessicus and Nanuntonoo both donned their feathers so that members of the tribe, who would clearly be monitoring their hike, would recognize in advance the significance of the travelers.

Wampage himself greeted Pessicus as they walked into the Siwanoy village. "Welcome to my village, brother of the Narragansett," he said in the common Algonquin language.

"Greetings, great chief of the Siwanoy," Pessicus responded with his open hand raised.

Wampage glanced at the others traveling with Pessicus.

"Who are these others that travel with you?"

Pessicus introduced his travel companions. Both Samuel and Sam responded with greetings in Algonquin.

"Are these Dutch men that speak our language and know our culture?" Wampage responded with surprise.

"They are English, and they are longtime friends of our people. Samuel was a brother to Miantonomo and Canonicus," Pessicus explained. "Young Sam has lived amongst our people and is considered a brother in our Narragansett tribe."

Wampage studied Samuel and Sam. "Canonicus and Miantonomo are great spirits. If you travel with them, then you travel well. Please come to my home, where we can discuss the reason for your journey to the Siwanoy."

Once the group was settled in Wampage's hut, Pessicus explained that Sam had lived with his tribe for three years and that he would be best to tell the story. In reality, Pessicus understood that Sam's understanding of the language and culture of the tribes would carry great weight in Wampage's decision to become an advocate of their cause.

"Great Chief Wampage," Sam began. "We have heard many tales of your victories. We have learned of the war with Kieft, in which you and the Lenape people fought the Dutch. My father is the uncle of the children of Anne Hutchinson, who died with her family during that war."

"I know Annhook," Wampage interrupted. "I have taken her name as my own. I have named my daughter Ann in respect for her great spirit."

Both Sam and Samuel recognized the custom of taking the name of notable kills but were surprised that Wampage would name his daughter after Anne.

"I came to learn much about Anne Hutchinson after her death. I did kill her, but had I known her during life, I would not have taken that earthly spirit from her," Wampage explained. "My daughter will now carry her spirit into the future."

"We have learned that amongst your people lives a young girl with red hair. That girl is the daughter of Anne Hutchinson."

"Yes. Because of her red hair, some in my tribe call her Autumn Leaves, but I prefer Fire Flower. She is a spirited girl who has become part of our people, a member of our family."

"We have come to ask you to allow us to return her to her family. Her brother who lives in Boston would very much like her to come home."

"Fire Flower *is* home. I cannot allow you to *take* her from us."

Samuel's heart sank into his stomach at hearing this from Wampage. He knew that it would be impossible to argue with the chief on this matter.

"Might we see her?" Samuel requested.

Wampage considered this. "Yes. You have traveled a great distance and should visit with the young woman who is your kin," he agreed.

Samuel wondered if Wampage would have agreed if he had known Susanna was not really a blood relation.

Wampage motioned for one of his braves to take Nanuntonoo to the hut of Susanna's surrogate family, and then all of them stepped outside into the bright afternoon. After about ten minutes, he spotted Susanna Hutchinson walking with Nanuntonoo and several other Siwanoy.

No one had told her why she was being brought to the chief's hut, so she looked down and did not observe her surroundings. Once standing in front of Wampage, she paid close attention.

"Fire Flower," he explained in the Algonquin tongue, "some visitors have come to see you. They want to take you away from your home, but we will not allow this."

Susanna looked up to study the strangers and locked on Samuel, who was smiling broadly with tears running down his face.

"Uncle Samuel!" she shouted in a language she had hardly used in the last three years. She ran and flung her arms around him in an emotional catharsis. "Uncle Samuel, Uncle Samuel, Uncle Samuel," she kept repeating.

Samuel held Susanna's embrace for a long time before she released him. He studied the girl. Now nearly grown, she bore a great resemblance to her mother. "Hello, Susanna. I have come to tell you that, even though I swore not to have a tea party with you, if on this day you wish to have a tea party, I shall join you!"

Susanna hugged Samuel again. "It is so good to see you. I have forgotten many things over the years, but I have never forgotten your promise to come visit. I knew, I just knew, in my heart, that someday you would come."

She then looked at Sam. "Sam, is that you? You're so tall!"

"Hi, Susanna," was all Sam could think of to say to the girl. He had admired her as a child. Now she was a woman, strikingly beautiful, and she carried herself like an Indian woman. Sam was transfixed and breathless.

Wampage observed the scene, which touched his heart. He knew that if Fire Flower chose to leave, he must allow it. Both Fire Flower and Anne Hutchinson's spirit had been with the Siwanoy for over three years, and even though they had changed his tribe, perhaps it was now time for her to return to her own people.

"Fire Flower," Wampage said in Algonquin, "Samuel and the great Chief Pessicus of the Narragansett have come here asking to return you to your family, the white people up north. I had told them this would not be allowed, but after observing you and Uncle Samuel, I will allow you to decide."

Susanna Hutchinson had lived amongst the Siwanoy for nearly four years. They had been formative years, and she had come to love them as family. Still, deep inside her was a little girl who had always longed to return home.

"Great Chief Wampage," she said in Algonquin, "I love my Siwanoy family, but I want to return home with Samuel."

"Then you shall return, but know that the Siwanoy will always welcome the return of Fire Flower to our village. Go now, and gather your belongings. We shall prepare for your departure."

Susanna took Sam with her back to the hut where she had been living. She gathered up a few items of clothing, stuffing them into a deerskin pack, which she handed to Sam.

"Have you spent much time with Indians?" she asked.

"Yes," he responded in Algonquin. "I lived nearly three years with the Narragansett. I have come to love their culture, food, and language. I have many friends amongst them."

"You do speak the language of my adopted family, but you do so with such a peculiar accent." Sam just stared at Susanna. She smiled at him. "It seems we have something in common and plenty to discuss," she said. She tugged his arm and pulled him from her hut. "Quit staring at me, and let's go, Sam!"

Susanna stopped and took one last look at the village she had come to know and love. After appropriate goodbyes, the troop set out to pick up Edward and head north.

Edward was happy to see his baby sister, alive beyond hope, but when Susanna occasionally wept, missing the tribe she had lived with for four years and overwhelmed by the expectations of the now-unfamiliar culture she was expected to return to as a young Englishwoman, Edward could not understand her love for the chief and the tribe who had murdered their family. Because of this, it was Sam who spent the most time with Susanna on the return trip. He had a strong understanding of the differences and similarities between their Indian and English cultures and had himself lived among the tribes for much of the past few years. In addition, Sam and Susanna were about the same age and had known each other fairly well back in the Portsmouth years.

"How much time have you lived with the Narragansett, Sam?"

"Mom and Dad went back to England and stayed for over three years. I spent that entire time living in several Indian villages. The oldest and wisest man I have ever known was Canonicus, who mentored me and helped me to learn the ways of the Narragansett," Sam explained.

"That is almost as long as I have lived with the Siwanoy. How did they treat you?" she asked.

"Pretty well, for the most part," Sam replied. "In the beginning, there were tribal members who hated the English and treated me poorly, but ultimately, I think they appreciated my interest in them, their lifestyles, languages, hunting, and customs. They came to see me as an Englishman who had adopted their customs. I think it was compelling. How about you?"

"In the beginning, I was a prisoner. It was terrible. I cried for my mother and family and wanted to go home. None of them spoke English, and I did not speak Algonquin. It took several months before we could communicate much beyond simple concepts. I knew they were trying to tell me that all my family was dead, but I refused to believe it. They told me I had no home to go to."

"I assume they did that by drawing pictures in the dirt?" Sam said.

"Exactly." Susanna smiled. "I think, in the first six months, nearly everything I learned was from pictures in the dirt or snow. Anyway, after a while, I began to get a grasp of the language. Once I did, I learned the details of the massacre. It was not easy for me to live among the very tribe that was responsible for the death of my entire family."

"How did you come to grips with that? It seems like you were living happily and peacefully amongst the tribe," Sam observed.

Susanna spread her arms helplessly. "I can't explain it. They treated me well. As they came to know me, and as they heard things about my mum, they came to respect me. I made friends and came to look upon them as family. I think when Wampage added my mother's name to his own and named his daughter Ann, I began to relax and accept my situation. It has felt like a long time. A lifetime, really."

Sam was fascinated by Susanna. The hardship she had endured was beyond his comprehension, yet her outlook seemed so positive. "How did you survive the massacre?"

"I was not at the house when it happened. That morning, I had asked Mother if I could go pick blueberries. At first, one of my brothers was going to join me, but he changed his mind. When I filled my basket and had eaten all I could, I headed back to the house. By then, it was over. I saw the Indians, got scared, and hid behind a giant rock, which we called Split Rock, near our house. Next thing I knew, they found me."

"But after killing your entire family, why didn't they kill you?" Sam asked.

"It was a long time before I knew the answer to that. Wampage is the one who discovered me, and he was fascinated by my red hair."

"I can understand that. I am too." Sam grinned.

"Excuse me?" Susanna frowned and glared at Sam.

"I'm, I'm sorry . . ." Sam's face turned beet red as he stuttered in embarrassment.

"Sam, I'm kidding with you. I have grown quite accustomed to the fascination with my red hair."

"I really am sorry, though. I guess I don't remember being fascinated by your hair back at Portsmouth."

"Then you were a boy. Now you are a man with different interests."

Sam studied Susanna as the impact of her comment settled inside. "Yes, I was a boy . . ." He wanted to say more but did not.

<hr/>

Two days later, Pessicus and Nanuntonoo headed northeast overland to their home. Samuel would have likely crossed the channel to Warwick, but everyone had noticed the chemistry between Sam and Susanna, so instead, Samuel added another day so that he and Sam could escort Edward and Susanna to Providence.

As Edward and Susanna were preparing to continue their journey back to Boston, Sam was at a loss for words. He was choked up inside, and his heart hurt.

"Once I get established in Boston, you should come visit, Sam," Susanna suggested.

"I, well, I am not allowed in Boston. Our entire family has been banned from the Massachusetts Bay Colony," he answered. "Do you think you could come to Warwick?"

"Of course, Sam. Yes, I will come to Warwick."

Once Edward and Susanna were headed north overland, Samuel and Sam turned south over the water back to Warwick. While they traveled, Sam was completely quiet.

"You were really taken by her, weren't you, son?" Samuel asked his son.

"I've never met anyone like her, Father."

"Well, let's give her a little time to get accustomed to living back in the English settlements, and then we shall find a way for you to get to know her."

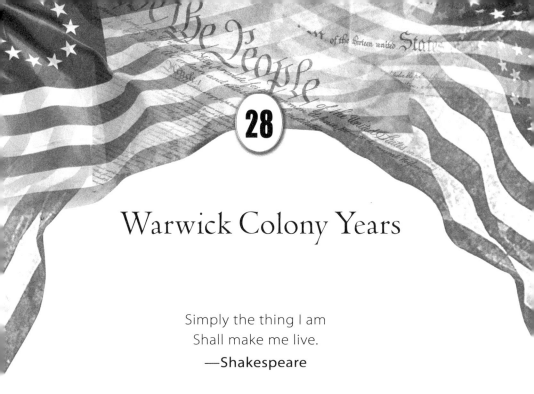

28

Warwick Colony Years

Simply the thing I am
Shall make me live.

—Shakespeare

1648–1654

The fireplace in the Gorton home was blazing, providing warmth against the Warwick winter. Upstairs, the children were asleep in a large room, also with a blazing fire.

"I think that 1648 has brought us peace at last, Samuel," Mary Gorton commented, mesmerized by the dancing flames.

"Yes, but Boston has not given up on their endless tirade. On the surface, they have claimed to leave us alone, but they still claim Warwick as being in their jurisdiction."

"In spite of Lord Warwick's patent?" Mary asked, almost incredulously.

"Yes, in spite of his proclamation."

"It does not seem to adversely affect your mood, my dear," she commented.

"We have certainly seen worse, Mary. I think they will bluster, plot, and scheme, but they will leave us alone."

"I do have good news . . ." Mary smiled and waited for Samuel to fully focus on her.

"Good news?"

"We are with child, Samuel." She smiled broadly.

"Is this possible? Mary, I am now fifty-five and you forty-one."

"I am with child, husband. There is no doubt."

"That is splendid. Let me see, is that number thirteen or fourteen? Shall we catch Anne Hutchinson in numbers?" Samuel asked.

"It is not fourteen, and if you do not stand and recite the names of our children right now, I shall banish you to the barn frozen this evening!" Mary playfully threatened him.

"I have been banished to far worse places than our barn, my dear, but very well. Let's see; from top down, we have Samuel, Mary, Maher, John, Ben, Sarah, Anne, Lizzy, and now this new and unnamed gift from heaven. I count eight, with one on the way. Does that satisfy you, or am I banished anyway?"

"Sit down, husband. You have passed my test, and I shall not be as harsh as the good Governor Winthrop," she joked.

"Yes, the *good* John Winthrop . . ." Samuel reiterated. He then sat down next to his wife and kissed her affectionately. "And do you have names prepared for this child?"

"I guess you have found me predictable," she answered, almost a question.

"And I will support you in any name as long as the spelling is shorter than Mahershallalhashbaz Gorton."

"Maher is a beautiful child," Mary sniffed. "She has provided much joy to this family, not to mention the spelling lessons we have been able to give the other children in learning the spelling of *her* name!"

"But for *this* child?" Samuel persisted.

"I think, Samuel, if she be a girl, we should name her Susanna."

"I do like that. Perhaps she will also have red hair. In any case, Susanna Hutchinson will be a good role model for this next child."

"And, God willing, this will be the last child. I shall be forty-two when this baby is born. I should think we have found our stopping point."

"Of course, God willing," Samuel responded. "The name if it is a boy?"

"Perhaps Robert or Warwick would be appropriate," Mary answered. "It seems only appropriate that we should use that name, given the support from Lord Robert Rich, Earl of Warwick."

"I also approve. So be it. Susanna or Robert!"

Five months later, in the spring of 1649, Susanna Gorton was born in Warwick Colony. She would be the ninth and final child of Samuel and Mary Gorton.

England in 1648 and 1649 was in complete turbulence. King Charles had essentially been removed from power by the Parliament, which he had tried to suppress. Oliver Cromwell had assembled momentum and an army, which ultimately took control of England. Under Cromwell, the monarchy ended and was replaced by the Commonwealth of England. King Charles was beheaded on January 30, 1649, at the palace of Whitehall.

This was important to the New World colonists for several reasons. Most significantly, it gave Massachusetts Bay reason to believe it could continue pressing for annexation of lands that included Warwick, Providence, and Aquidneck. While King Charles had been beheaded, those responsible did not anticipate that he would come to be seen as a martyr for the people. The end result was that, ultimately, Charles's son would retake the throne in 1660.

It is perhaps important to note that the Earl of Warwick had befriended and sided with Cromwell's forces and, as such, maintained significant power during the period of the Commonwealth of England. Rich's grandson and heir married Cromwell's daughter. Warwick's relationships with Gorton and several others in the New World would continue to impact events and decisions as they pertained to England until his death in 1658.

Young Sam Gorton found that his relationship with the Narragansett and understanding of English law combined to give him credentials that were much in demand. He spent much time working with magistrates to resolve issues, along with developing deeds and grants. He wrote several letters to Boston authorities requesting the ability to work in Massachusetts Bay territories and specifically in Boston. His argument was that he could bring value as a negotiator with Indian issues. His goal may have been to be able to travel freely and see Susanna Hutchinson. Unfortunately for Sam, the Gorton name held such a stigma amongst the magistrates and officials that his request was never granted.

Sam learned of Susanna Hutchinson's engagement to John Cole in 1651. In his lifetime, he would never completely recover from his attraction to and love for her. In fact, Sam Gorton would not get married for another thirty-four years. Once married, he would name his first daughter Susanna.

***

Emboldened by the turbulence in London, Massachusetts Bay and Plymouth passed "ownership claims" back and forth on the Warwick Colony in their continued efforts to annex various parts of Rhode Island. In 1651, Coddington announced that the colonies of Portsmouth and Newport would be joining the Massachusetts Bay. Promptly, and without proper authority, Massachusetts Bay *gave* Coddington the title of "governor for life." Because of this, Roger Williams and Samuel Gorton's position was greatly weakened, which also provided a platform from which annexation of the remainder of Rhode Island became highly probable. In response, the towns of Warwick and Providence raised a total of two hundred pounds so that Roger Williams and William Dyer could make a second trip to England and protest.

In October of 1652, William Dyer returned from England to report the results of their endeavor. Samuel Gorton had first become acquainted with the man and his wife, Mary Dyer, in Boston during the Antinomian

Forefathers & Founding Fathers

Controversy. The two had later been instrumental in establishing the Aquidneck Colony. Their wives held similar beliefs and had each formed great friendships with each other as well as with Anne Hutchinson.

"William, welcome back to the colonies!" Samuel exclaimed when Dyer came to his door.

"I came here first, Samuel. No one has suffered more at the hands of Coddington and the Massachusetts Bay Colony."

"So, let's have it. What tidings do you bring from our efforts abroad?"

"Simply put, Coddington's commission has been revoked! Our charter has been fully restored." Dyer smiled broadly with the news.

"That is excellent news, my friend! Coddington's scheme to become permanent governor of our colony has finally ended. Why has the trip taken so long, and where is Mary Dyer? I should think that my wife, Mary, would enjoy seeing her."

"England is still spiraling in a fair amount of turbulence after the execution of King Charles. Lord Warwick and Lord Cromwell have remained informed and helpful to our cause, but securing a hearing took some time. As for my Mary, she has become involved in the Quaker movement in London. In any case, Mary has decided to stay and continue her studies in London for another year."

"Quaker? William, I think the Massachusetts Bay Colony may despise only one thing more than me, and that is the Quakers," Samuel joked.

"That is not true, Samuel," Dyer objected in a matter-of-fact tone. "Boston most assuredly hates you more than they do the Quakers."

"Indeed, that may be true, but I fear for the Quakers in the United Colonies," Samuel said gravely. "You must make certain your Mary does not fall victim to their courts."

"If you know my Mary, and I think you do, she has no fear," William replied. "It is my fear that she might challenge them."

"Yes, I have observed that on many occasions," Samuel answered. "Both of our Marys have that courage in common."

"And thus, the friendship," Dyer agreed.

"So, it is not just their common love of Shakespeare!" Samuel laughed. "When will Roger and Mary return from London, William?"

"Roger will be on the next ship. I expect him in November, or otherwise in the spring. As for Mary, I shall await word, but I do not expect her until sometime next year."

"We have much planning and work to do now that we have a charter that the United Colonies may not contest."

During the time period beginning in 1649, Gorton served as magistrate of Warwick, a post he did not want to serve. In fact, both he and John Smith, president of Rhode Island, were fined for refusing to take posts in the government. After some convincing from members of the town and Mary, Samuel and John Smith decided to serve their terms. In 1651, while Coddington was in London working to solidify his title as governor for life, Samuel was elected president of Providence and Warwick. He stepped down after one year and resumed his position as magistrate.

It was in the fall of 1651 that Samuel Gorton became concerned about the growth of slavery in the New World. In his opinion, slavery was an institution that stood against his religious beliefs and should not be allowed in his colony. As a result, he penned what would become the first antislavery ordinance in the New World. As written, the law was designed to prevent the involuntary servitude of both white men and Negroes. Whosoever would hold any man against this law would be subject to pay a penalty of forty pounds.

Because of his influence as founder of Warwick, former president, and magistrate, he managed to get this piece of legislature approved by Roger Williams and passed in the Rhode Island Colony in early 1653.

In 1654, the four main towns of Providence, Warwick, Newport, and Portsmouth were permanently reunited in an independent colony that would ultimately become the state of Rhode Island.

Mary Dyer and Quaker Persecutions

My words fly up, my thoughts remain below;
Words without thoughts never to heaven go.
—Shakespeare

In 1656, Mary Dyer returned to live with her family in Rhode Island. At the same time, the problems between the Quakers and Boston heated up. William Dyer came immediately to Samuel with the news.

"The ship *Speedwell* landed at Boston Harbor. Among her passengers were eight Quakers and Captain Robert Lock," William Dyer said.

"I know Captain Lock. He was captain of the same ship when I returned from London. What news does Captain Lock bring?"

"Lock is in jail, along with the Quakers he brought to the colony," Dyer explained.

"In jail?" Gorton asked incredulously.

"As with most else, Boston has taken a hard stance on the Quakers," Dyer answered.

"This picture becomes ugly, I would guess. Can I assume that Lock has delivered his passengers to Boston and defended them with the magistrates?"

"Correct," William answered flatly.

"I can attest to the fact that a Boston jail cell is not a good place to rest after a long sea voyage," Samuel remarked. "Let us immediately dispatch a messenger to these Quakers in their Boston jail cells and offer them refuge here in Warwick."

"If you are educated on these matters, Samuel, please help me understand the Puritan hatred for Quakers."

"It is quite simple, my friend," Samuel began. "Puritans by their nature believe the Quakers to be heretics. They believe this about Quakers because of a subtle but important difference: the Quakers do not believe in a hierarchy. The Puritans believe Roger Williams and myself to be heretics for exactly the same reason, and you know firsthand how we have been treated. Still, the Quakers have been more blatant. In Boston, they have marched into churches and protested on the streets. They have set themselves out as an affront to peace in Boston."

"Yes, we know well how Boston treats those who do not adhere to their mandates."

"I would tell you and your wife that the best course of action is to stay away from Boston. There is sufficient land to be had in this New World. There is no need to cause inflammation where you can only be crushed."

<hr />

Captain Lock was fined five hundred pounds, an exorbitant fee that would be refunded only if he returned his passengers to England. The captain could not afford such fines, and as such, he had no choice but to return them to England. Less than a year later, two of them returned again to Boston on a different ship. The Boston authorities immediately cut their ears off and banished them again.

One evening in 1659 when the Dyers and Gortons were together, Mary Dyer asked Samuel his opinion on the Quaker controversy.

"I have seen enough of Puritan theocracy for one lifetime, Mrs. Dyer," Samuel answered gravely. "The Boston authorities see things only one way. Speaking out for other perspectives is punished with imprisonment, banishment, and death. I would not want to test their laws."

"I believe I should go there and test the resolve of this Boston theocracy," said Mary Dyer, standing in determination with hands on her hips.

"Mary, I strongly advise you to stay away from Boston. Quakers are welcome in Warwick, and I fail to see why so many are traveling to a place where they will be persecuted."

"The Quakers that go there believe they can inspire change," she answered flatly. "It is our creed to do so."

Samuel took a deep breath and exhaled slowly. "I was once like that. Now, at my age, I would advise caution."

"I have often heard you say that we don't fail until we quit, and we should never quit anything *important*. Two of my friends have been jailed in Boston for their religious beliefs. I believe that falls in the category of *important*, and I must go visit them," Mary Dyer announced. "You must understand that Quakers do not believe in being meek. Quite the opposite—we believe we should stand up and fight for that which we believe."

The room was dead silent in reaction to Mary's announcement. Samuel and Mary Gorton knew this would not end well.

Mary Gorton stood up and put her hands on Dyer's shoulders. "Do not go!" she said emphatically. "Boston still remembers the Antinomian Controversy. Even after her unfortunate death, they still hate and condemn Anne Hutchinson. Boston authorities have pronounced her death as God's punishment for being a *woman* teacher. Furthermore, the United Colonies continue to look for every opportunity to cause problems for Samuel and me, and because of our open friendship, you are also at risk."

"I know, my dear Mrs. Gorton, but I feel I have no choice and must go," Mary Dyer responded.

"They know your connection to Anne and to us. They know you are a Quaker. You must reconsider this decision! Do not go!" Mary Gorton implored. "You have too many things working against you, and you have a family here in Rhode Island that needs you!"

In spite of the advice from friends and family, in October 1659, Mary traveled to Boston to visit her friends William Robinson and Marmaduke Stephenson. Mary and her two friends were jailed and summarily sentenced to death.

On October 27, the three were led to the gallows where they were to be hanged. First Stephenson was led to the gallows. A rope was tied around his neck, and, without a word, he was hanged.

An elder arrived just as Stephenson was being hanged. He watched as the next man's neck was placed in the rope. The elder then looked at the executioner and nodded, whereupon Robinson was hanged. Then, when the noose was placed around Mary Dyer's neck, he shook his head *no*, as if to instruct the executioner to wait.

"Mary Dyer, we have decided to allow you a reprieve on the promise that you leave Boston for good," the elder pronounced.

Mary, pale but mentally prepared for her hanging, crumpled to her knees and began to sob. "You have killed my friends; you have killed my friends."

The executioner untied Mary's hands and feet and prepared to escort her from the gallows, but she refused to leave.

"I shall not leave this place of execution until you change the law banning Quakers in this town," she finally managed to say.

"Go now, and pray to Lord Jehovah for your salvation," the elder commanded.

"No!" By now, Mary was regaining a bit of her strength. "I will not leave unless you change the law. Hang me, or change the law."

The elder analyzed the predicament. He did not want the situation to get out of control, which was quickly happening. He was well aware that many in Boston did not approve of the strict rules and harsh punishments regarding Quakers, but he also felt certain that none had the courage to stand up. Still, he did not want to test that here and today in front of the crowd that had gathered at Boston Common for the public hanging.

"Executioner, bind this woman, and escort her to the Rhode Island Colony to join her husband," he barked. With that, he turned and left so there would be no more discussion.

Upon Mary's return to Rhode Island, Mary and Samuel Gorton, along William Dyer and many others, prevailed on Mary to find another path to spreading the Quaker word.

"I was prepared to die with my martyr friends that day," she explained.

"We should have you talk to Roger Williams. He has always found a peaceful pathway to achieve his objectives. Please drop the insanity of this decision. Your death will mean nothing to the authorities in Boston, and your life means so much to your friends and family," Samuel argued.

"They must be taught tolerance, and perhaps after they kill enough Quakers or Gortons, they will be forced to see how they have been wrong," Mary Dyer said. "There is no sense quibbling over this issue, for which I know in my heart that I must stand strong."

<hr />

Inspired by Mary Dyer's plight, Samuel wrote a letter to Oliver Cromwell complaining about Massachusetts's treatment of Quakers in hopes that Cromwell would issue a mandate instructing Boston to stop imprisoning and hanging Quakers. In the letter, Gorton stated he had tried to intervene by offering refuge to Quakers arriving in the New World but indicated that this was not enough to halt the atrocities being committed by the Massachusetts Bay Puritans. Cromwell died of malaria and would never respond to the letter, but things were changing in London as King Charles II took the throne. Unfortunately for Mary Dyer, they were not changing fast enough.

In late May of 1660, Mary Dyer announced to William and her family that she would again return to Boston. William adamantly tried to stop her, but Mary would not be blocked.

Upon arrival in Boston, she was summarily jailed and then brought to court. Governor Endicott presided over her trial.

Endicott studied Mary Dyer standing before him. "Are you the same Mary Dyer that was here before?"

"I am the same Mary Dyer that was here with my friends Robinson and Stephenson," she responded.

"You will own yourself a Quaker, will you not?" Endicott questioned.

"I am," she answered.

"Sentence was passed upon you in the last general court; and now, likewise, you must return to the prison and there remain till tomorrow at nine o'clock. Then you must go to the gallows and there be hanged till you are dead."

"This is no more than what you said before," Mary answered, without any noticeable change of expression on her face.

"But now it is to be executed." Endicott was startled that she showed so little emotion in this sentencing. "Therefore, prepare yourself tomorrow at nine o'clock."

"I came in obedience to the will of God to the last general court, desiring you to repeal your unrighteous laws of banishment on pain of death. That same is my work now and my earnest request. If you refuse

Mary Dyer

to repeal these laws, the Lord will send others of his servants to witness against them."

"Mistress Dyer, do you think yourself a prophetess?" Endicott asked, hoping she would give him and the court reason to become outraged and offended.

"I am but a woman who hears and speaks the word of God."

The following morning, at the gallows on Boston Common, many still hoped Mary Dyer would renounce her beliefs, giving the court a reason to set her free, but Mary would not yield.

As the rope was tightened around her neck, Mary Dyer spoke her last words: "I came to keep you from blood guilt, in hopes you would repeal the unrighteous and unjust law made against the innocent servants of the Lord. I will not now repent of that."

<hr />

When Samuel learned of Mary Dyer's execution, he immediately set out to spend time with his friend William and the Dyer children.

"The death of Mary Dyer has begun to resonate through the colonies," Samuel told Mary's widower. "It is yet another reminder of the weakness of Puritan theocracy. When one man holds the keys to the church and the keys to the government, these things happen. I only wish our Puritan brothers would remember the historical lessons that led to the reformation of the Catholic Church."

"I did prevail upon Endicott to show lenience and release her, but he never responded," Dyer answered.

"It is unfortunate that Mary was bent on this being her only path. The passage of the martyr is one I little understand but greatly appreciate," Samuel observed.

Mary Gorton put her arm around William Dyer. "In one of our first conversations, my husband reminded me of the story of Joan of Arc. It seems of little consequence right now as we grieve Mary's passing, but I should think history will remember Mary Dyer, and because of this, she did not die in vain."

Samuel Gorton—
Later Years

> To be or not to be—that is the question:
> Whether 'tis nobler in the mind to suffer
> The slings and arrows of outrageous fortune,
> Or to take arms against a sea of troubles
> And, by opposing, end them. To die, to sleep—
> No more.
>
> **—Shakespeare**

Gorton would continue to actively serve the people of Rhode Island and work with his friend Roger Williams. Interestingly, after the death of his nemesis, Governor Winthrop, in 1649, Samuel would become friends with Winthrop's son, a physician who had risen to the rank of governor in the Connecticut colony. The two met on several occasions and corresponded frequently until Samuel's death.

Samuel Gorton retired from politics in 1671 at the age of seventy-eight. He and Mary lived peacefully in his Warwick home.

One evening, as he wrote by the light of the fireplace, Mary came in to read what he was writing. By now, seven of their children had married and left home with their new families. Their firstborn, Samuel Junior, was still not married, but he continued to be actively involved with translation and negotiation work with the various Indian tribes. Friction between the colonists and the Indians was escalating on a daily basis, and much as Samuel Junior worked to intervene, war now seemed inevitable. As Samuel and Mary were discussing the possibility, Samuel Junior, who had come home two days earlier concerned about friction between the English and the various Indian tribes, joined them in the main room of the house.

"Might I join this conversation?" Samuel Junior asked.

"Of course." Mary studied her son. "Sam, sometimes you remind me of my father."

"So you have said on many occasions, Mother," Sam acknowledged.

"I wonder what old John Maplett would think about this New World?" Gorton asked rhetorically.

"Mom, Dad," Sam interrupted their all-too-common reminiscing. "I am really concerned about what Chief Metacomet will do next. So many crimes have been committed against the Indians. I think they will truly go to war this time."

"I think Metacomet, or King Phillip, as our people call him, knows there are more English soldiers than he can possibly fight," Samuel suggested. "As Roger Williams has told them, it is fruitless to fight the English, because their soldiers will be replaced on boats faster than they can be killed."

"I do not think it matters now. He has been pushed too far. First, he was forced to sign the peace treaty, and then his guns were taken away. Then, when Plymouth hanged three of his warriors . . ."

"But son, those warriors were justly convicted of murder," Samuel interrupted.

"No," Sam answered flatly. "I believe this should have been handled by Indians. The murderers and the murdered were all Indians."

"Yes, yes, perhaps you are right, Sam. I can see this."

"Metacomet has had enough. The bad thing is that most of the other tribes will likely join him," Sam explained.

"Can you educate me, Sam?" Mary interjected. "How is it that Metacomet came to be known as King Phillip?"

"Metacomet is the son of Massasoit, chief of the Wampanoag tribe, Mother. I think you may recall that Massasoit was friendly and helpful in the first years of the Plymouth Colony. Most people believe that Plymouth would not have survived without the assistance of Massasoit."

"Yes, I do remember that. Everyone in Plymouth was starving after that first winter. Massasoit brought them food and helped those settlers learn how to survive in the New World," Mary recalled.

"Correct," Sam smiled. "Metacomet is the younger son of Massasoit. Because of our close alliance, the English have given Metacomet, chief of the Wampanoag Indians, the name King Phillip. It has stuck because he likes the reference, which he believes gives him similar powers to our King Charles II of England."

Samuel looked at his son. "You were saying that perhaps the other tribes might join any potential conflict?

"Yes, Father."

"That would be a most terrible situation and a bloody war. Are you still friendly with Metacomet?" Samuel asked.

"Yes, though I may be one of the few remaining English he does trust. Listen, this is a tough situation. You are friends with the Narragansett, but when the situation escalates, I fear even they may join, and it will not be safe here in Warwick."

"Sam, I am an old man. I do not travel well, and where could I go? I daresay many in Boston would not recognize me, but the prohibition still stands against me going there. Providence is no safer than Warwick, and if the Indians want revenge on anyone in Rhode Island, I would think it would be Coddington."

"I think perhaps one of the Narragansett villages might take you and Mother in," Sam suggested.

"And if the militias decide to massacre another village, I would not be safe there either." With that, Samuel got a glint in his eye, smiled at Mary, and slapped his son three times affectionately on the back. "Samuel, m'boy, your mother and I will be fine right here in our Warwick House."

"This is not a joke, Father. Metacomet is not to be trifled with, and he is set on vengeance. I am worried about you!"

"We will be fine, son."

"Sam, your father and I have been through countless challenges in our life. Many were more difficult than this one. With each, your father and I found a way to prevail. We will do so again this time."

"Mother, you are the most amazing woman I have ever known, but this is different. I do not want you to have the same fate as Anne Hutchinson," Sam argued.

<hr />

King Phillip's war began in 1675 and would ultimately become one of the most tragic and bloody conflicts in the early American colonies. Both Roger Williams and Gorton opposed the war, and yet the Rhode Island area was one of the most significantly impacted during the hostilities.

At one point during the war, an invading Indian party entered Warwick, intent on burning the entire town to the ground. Samuel and Mary, refusing to leave their home, were saved when a group of Narragansett braves sneaked them to a boat and took them across the bay until the siege ended. Samuel and the other families who had fled Warwick returned in 1677 to a town completely obliterated. Virtually every family and shopkeeper was forced to tear down the charred remains of their homes and shops to rebuild.

At the end of the war, Samuel was eighty-four years old. He began to rebuild his home. He would finish it as his health was beginning to fail in the summer of 1677.

"Mary, I must pen one last letter to John Winthrop Junior."

"Samuel, I have never understood your friendship with that man. His father set calamities in motion that have caused suffering to our family and many others for thirty years after his death. I understand the Christian need to forgive, but your capacity to befriend him bewilders me."

"I would imagine that in his household, perhaps there is a wife wondering why John Winthrop Junior would befriend the mortal enemy of his celebrated father. Still, the son is his own man, and a most extraordinary

Samuel Gordon's home.

one at that, who has become a good physician and a dependable governor of Connecticut. These are things that I respect and admire."

"And what is it that you would say to this esteemed physician and governor?" Mary asked.

"At eighty-four, I think I should like to recollect the significance of this great adventure to this New World, delivered by God's hand and will. In the early years, many thought this adventure to be much more insanity, and perhaps insanity is exactly what it was. Still, we persevered with courage not diminished to this day. We have multiplied beyond what we thought possible in our hearts and have found great success."

"Those are bold words, Samuel. You said that we have persevered with undiminished courage, but I wonder if you would apply those words to Winthrop Senior, or Winslow, or Coddington?"

Samuel placed his right index finger behind his ear and rubbed his cheek with the other three fingers as he considered her question. For many years, he had remembered the sting of the lashes on his back delivered at Coddington's order. It had been at least ten years since he had last been limber enough to touch those scars with his hands, as he often had during his younger years. Winthrop Senior had once sentenced him to death. Were these acts of courage? Samuel had pondered that question many times.

"I think, my dear, that I would indeed include those men in that application. We may have opposed the way they ran their colony. We may have been disgusted by the Boston authorities' response to the massacre of Anne Hutchinson and her children, but even that was slanted by their passionate Puritan perspective. Those men had great courage to travel to this wilderness, cutting almost all ties to England's comfortable living with merchants and markets. I do not agree with their theocracies, but I must admit, in their lives they have exhibited great courage."

"I am surprised you would say that, Samuel, but I am pleased to hear it."

Samuel smiled and enjoyed the moment. "There is one that I would not give the title of courageous, and that is Reverend Reynor. He was an angry man who could not preach. He had no redeeming quality that could make up for his striking of women and children. He was a pitiful man, and Plymouth was a lesser place because of him."

Samuel looked back at his letter, added another paragraph, finished writing, and looked up at Mary. What he saw was that same beautiful young girl he had first met at the Globe Theatre fifty years earlier. That memory caused his eyes to fill up with tears.

"What is wrong, my dear?" Mary asked, gently placing her hand on Samuel's wrinkled face.

"I was just remembering the *Taming of the Shrew*, dear Mary. I was transfixed at first sight, as I often still am when I look upon you. In the first minutes of our meeting on that night, I wanted to say something, to begin a conversation, but I could only think of silly things like the weather or the happenings in Parliament."

"Though it was fifty years ago, I remember. Do you recall what you said?"

"Uh, I think it went something like this: *What play is it we are seeing, Miss?*"

"*The Taming of the Shrew*, Mr. Gorton," she replied curtly.

"And uneducated as I was, I asked, 'Who wrote it?'" Samuel laughed.

Mary joined her husband's laughter as both of them remembered that night. Sam Junior, now forty-seven years old and still unmarried, came into the room to see what the noise was. "Are you two reminiscing again?"

"We are old and have little else we can do, son," Mary beamed.

Sam knew that smile. "I know, Mother, I look just like your father." Seizing the opportunity, young Sam slapped his father three times on

Forefathers & Founding Fathers

the back. "Samuel, m'boy, in spite of the fact that you have dragged young Mary to this Godforsaken wilderness, I see that you have taken good care of me daughter. For that, I am most appreciative."

The three laughed.

On December 9, 1677, the cold Rhode Island winter was in full force. Inside their newly rebuilt home, Samuel was sick in bed. Fearing the worst, his wife, Mary, and his eldest son, Sam, remained in constant vigil by his bedside.

Samuel opened his eyes and smiled at his wife as she entered the room bearing a mug of hot willow-bark tea. "My darling shrew, now tamed and serving tea in bed."

"Only for you, my Samuel," answered Mary, forcing a smile.

"I have dragged you across the ocean and into the wilderness, and you love me still." Samuel smiled and sipped his tea. "I wish I had more to give you than a memory of adventure, a lifetime struggle, and an unfulfilled promise of freedom in the New World."

"I would not trade it, my dear." Mary kissed his forehead. "What you have given me is far more than any of my best childhood dreams."

"I have often asked myself how I could be worthy of a woman such as yourself. What more could I do to accomplish what we set out to achieve?"

"Samuel, you must not suggest such things! We have brought our children into a world where the opportunities are boundless. Someday, the battles you have fought will become permanent victories in this wilderness."

Samuel started to respond, but Mary put her finger on his lips. "Together, we have planted the seeds. With time, those seeds will sprout and bear fruit to our children's children."

"I am sorry that I lay here in bed, reflective, but I question the path of our lives, Mary."

"You must never do that! One of the great philosophies of your life, to which your children now adhere, is that we don't fail until we quit, and we should never quit anything important. Though the odds were against us, we never quit, Samuel. And now we can rest with the knowledge that the seeds you have planted will sprout through your children and those who have observed your life."

"Thank you, my pearl." Samuel smiled and closed his eyes, making an effort to relax.

"Rest now, my dear husband."

———⟫•◦•⟪———

Samuel Gorton died on December 10, 1677. Within a month of his death, Mary Elizabeth Maplett Gorton would follow him. The history books have written much about Samuel but, in a sad way, have neglected the influence of his extraordinary wife during a time period when such women were extraordinarily uncommon.

Much of the historical writings about Samuel thus far have been done by Winthrop, Morton, and others who abhorred his beliefs in freedom of religion, civil democracy, and equal rights for all races and genders. During his lifetime, Samuel learned to cope with and ignore their opposition. As is often the case, the victors wrote the history, and as such, most of what has been written about Gorton is negative. Those written words became the slings and arrows that Gorton was forced to suffer during his lifetime.

Samuel was buried in a small, unmarked grave on his property in Warwick. His last wish was that he be buried with the one artifact he worked hardest to achieve: the patent for Rhode Island.

From Gorton's perspective, this patent, won during his battle in England granting freedom from Massachusetts Bay, was the crowning accomplishment of his life. It was a simple piece of paper, but it kept the Puritans at bay. It is unfortunate that he never personally saw the transformation over the next hundred years whereby the assault on Rhode Island from the neighboring colonies would subside and the tides would turn the other direction. Once that happened, the ideals born in Warwick would spread across the continent and become the seeds of our American Revolution.

Forefathers and Founding Fathers

> There is a tide in the affairs of men
> Which, taken at the flood,
> leads on to fortune;
> Omitted, all the voyage of their life
> Is bound in shallows and in miseries.
> On such a full sea are we now afloat,
> And we must take the current when it serves
> Or lose our ventures.
>
> —Shakespeare

Nathanael Greene took a sip of the wine and looked at Thomas Jefferson, who had listened intently to the tale. "That is the entire story as I know it, Thomas."

Thomas Jefferson sat back in his chair and slowly clapped three times. "Bravo, General Greene! I am in total agreement that Samuel Gorton was a haberdasher, but he was certainly no haberdasher!"

"Thank you, Mr. Jefferson." Nathanael Greene smiled broadly. "As you can tell, it is clearly a story I love to tell."

"Yes, and what an excellent story it is! Your tale reminds me of something Thomas Paine said five years ago. Excuse my slight changes as I paraphrase . . . Those times in the early colonies were the ones that tried men's souls. Summer soldiers, sunshine patriots, shrank from the pursuit of true religious and personal freedoms in service to we who came afterward. Men like Samuel Gorton deserve the love and thanks of the patriots of *our* time for their persistence, in spite of relentless hardship. Indeed, tyranny, like hell, is not easily conquered, yet through their deeds, Samuel and Mary Gorton, Roger Williams, Mary Dyer, and Anne Hutchinson planted the seeds that would ultimately conquer tyranny. We should remember them with the glory they rightfully deserve."

"Thank you, Mr. Jefferson," answered Nathanael as he studied Catharine, who had long since fallen asleep. "It is a story that has been passed down through my forefathers, and one in which I take much pride."

"Certainly, one of the highest duties of the citizen is a scrupulous obedience to the laws of the nation. But I think our forefathers have shown that it is not the highest duty. Samuel and Mary Dyer stood against the bad laws and, through their efforts, ultimately changed them."

"Indeed, Boston is not the theocracy it was when my forefathers landed on these shores one hundred forty years ago. Clearly their efforts have paid off, and as Mary Gorton has said, the seeds they planted have borne fruit to us, their children's children."

"They have indeed, General Greene. And we should remember how far Boston has come. It is amazing that the first sparks of the revolution started in Boston with their tea party. It seems our wisdom, to this point, has grown with our power."

"And may it continue to do so as *our* grandchildren take the reins of this great country," Nathanael said as he stood. He had no idea how late it was, but he knew he and Thomas Jefferson had spent most of the night exploring their forefathers' tale.

Thomas Jefferson also stood, gathered his coat, and turned to Nathanael. "Nothing can stop the man with the right mental attitude from achieving his goal. Samuel Gorton proved as much. You have done so as well, General Greene. It is too bad Samuel cannot be here to see what we have accomplished over the past twenty years. I should think he would be proud!"

AFTERWORD

Samuel Gorton had many followers and admirers who were saddened by his death in December of 1677. On the other side of the coin, men like Nathaniel Morton continued to pen negative articles about Samuel and the Warwick settlement right up until and after the date of his death. While it would be difficult to defend much of what the Puritans did in the United Colonies, those colonies ultimately evolved into what Samuel and Mary Gorton, Roger Williams, Anne Hutchinson, and Mary Dyer had dreamed of when they first set foot on the new continent in the 1630s.

Unfortunately, it was Boston and the United Colonies that wrote much of the history during that founding time period. One has to carefully read the lines of all the acerbic attacks on Samuel Gorton to realize they were attacking him for beliefs that we all adhere to in these modern times. The first civil government in America, along with the principles of freedom of religion, separation of church and state, abolishment of slavery, and equal rights for women were ideals that Samuel Gorton fought for in the 1630s. They were firm convictions for which he would be beaten, banished, and humiliated over and over again.

While the United Colonies were setting the tone and writing the history, little Rhode Island was planting the seeds of democracy. The Puritans did everything in their power to uproot them, but ultimately, the seeds did grow, and the concepts spread to all of the colonies. One hundred years after Gorton's death, the founding fathers of the United States would introduce to the new nation the concepts of civil government, freedom of religion, and separation of church and state, all of which Samuel had introduced in Rhode Island. Ninety years after the American Revolution, Lincoln would abolish slavery in this country in a piece of legislation similar to the one penned by Samuel in the 1650s. Unfortunately, it wasn't until shortly after World War I that women would finally be given the right to vote.

Boston authorities banished Anne Hutchinson because of her views on women's rights. When she and her children were brutally massacred, those same authorities applauded her death, saying it was the hand of God warning others not to follow her path. Now, a statue of Hutchinson stands prominently in front of the Massachusetts State House—an interesting and appropriate twist.

Mary Dyer has a similar story. Mary Dyer willingly became a martyr for religious freedom. Her hanging on Boston Common shocked many in the colony, and that shock may have been the beginning of the spark of real change. Like Hutchinson, a bronze statue of Dyer sitting on a bench can be found outside the Massachusetts State House.

Thomas Jefferson and John Adams were perhaps two of the most significant political visionaries of all time. In this country, we are lucky to call them our founding fathers. Their experiment has become one of the most successful political infrastructures in the history of the world. But Jefferson's and Adam's ideals had their roots in the ideals set forth by Samuel Gorton, Anne Hutchinson, Roger Williams, and Mary Dyer. These are the true forefathers whose works and struggles influenced the founding fathers of our great nation.

It is not a stretch to see Samuel Gorton's influence in Amendments 1, 13, and 19 of the Constitution. It can be seen in the Emancipation Proclamation and the Civil Rights Act as well.

The nine Gorton children would all marry and have children, whose lineage continued to impact the course of events in this country. Even Sam Junior would finally marry Susanna Burton in 1684. The eldest

Samuel Gorton

of his three children would go on to become this author's forefather. Nathanael Greene and Benjamin Gorton, cousins and great-great-grandsons of Samuel, would both serve admirably in the American Revolution. Nathanael would become George Washington's most trusted general. History credits Greene with saving the south from Lord General Cornwallis and setting up the victory in Yorktown that would win the war. Captain Benjamin Gorton served on the naval side of that war, but he also fought in the French and Indian War of 1758. When Greene was pushing Cornwallis to the final blow at Yorktown, his cousin Ben Gorton was captain of a ship in the Yorktown harbor that blocked Cornwallis's escape.

To my knowledge, no one has ever done a thorough search for famous and notable descendants of Samuel Gorton. I hope that the popularization of this historical novel will inspire many such searches. Beyond Nathanael Greene and Captain Benjamin Gorton, among the notables I have found is Slade Gorton, founder of the Gorton Fish Company of Gloucester, Massachusetts, home to the iconic memorial known as the Gloucester Fisherman's Memorial. The rugged fisherman who represents the spirit of America is well represented as the logo of the Gorton Fish Company.

Other well-known descendants are Julia Ward Howe, author of "Battle Hymn of the Republic"; Lucille Ball, comedienne and actress known for *I Love Lucy*; and Thomas Gorton, former US senator from Washington State.

One could easily imagine that Mary Gorton was smiling down from heaven as Julia Ward Howe penned the indelible lyrics that speak to our souls and span the times, beginning with the founding of America to the present. I would think Samuel would have appreciated part of the fifth verse, "Let us live to make men free," and no doubt Mary would have loved the third verse most of all. Here are the lyrics for the first three verses of Howe's famous poem:

Mine eyes have seen the glory of the coming of the Lord;
He is trampling out the vintage
where the grapes of wrath are stored;
He hath loosed the fateful lightning of His terrible swift sword:
His truth is marching on.
Glory, glory, hallelujah!

I have seen Him in the watch-fires of a hundred circling camps,
They have builded Him an altar in the evening dews and damps;
I can read His righteous sentence in the dim and flaring lamps:
His day is marching on.
Glory, glory hallelujah!

I have read a fiery gospel writ in burnished rows of steel:
"As ye deal with my contemnors, so with you my grace shall deal;
Let the Hero, born of woman, crush the serpent with his heel,
Since God is marching on."

LINEAGE

JULIA WARD HOWE
LUCILLE BALL

LINEAGE

JULIA WARD HOWE
"Battle Hymn of the Republic"

Samuel Gorton   Mary Maplett

Benjamin Gorton   Sarah Carder

Mary Gorton   Samuel Greene

William Greene   Catharine Greene

William Greene   Catharine Ray

Phebe Greene   Samuel Ward

Samuel Ward   Julia Rush Cutler

Julie (Ward) Howe
American Poet

Family relationship charts from FamousKin.com.

LINEAGE

LUCILLE BALL
I Love Lucy

Samuel Gorton   Mary Maplett

Anna Gorton   John Warner

Priscilla Warner   Jeremiah Crandall

Experience Crandall   David Sprague

David Sprague   Amey Sweet

Bridget Sprague   Stephen S. Hunt

Elvin Hunt   Sylvia Lee

Reuben Hunt   Eveline Grances Bailey

Frederic Charles Hunt   Flora Belle Orcutt

Desiree Evelyn Hunt   Henry Durrell Ball

Lucille Ball
TV Actress – *I Love Lucy*

TIME PERIOD NOTES: HISTORICAL CONTEXT

During the time period of this book, the world was going through a great transition.

The **Gutenberg press** was 170 years old at the start of this book. Prior to Gutenberg, books were hand copied and very costly. As a result, book ownership was rare. Now, even the middle class could own books, and a new industry was created. Education also became much more widespread.

The first **King James Bible** was published in 1611.

Right before the beginning of the 1600s, **analytic trigonometry** had been invented by François Viète.

Queen Elizabeth died in 1603.

London during that time period was an overcrowded city that had outgrown its medieval infrastructure. There was constant disease in this city of somewhere between three hundred fifty thousand and four hundred thousand. As rough as life in **the New World** was, in many ways, it may have been an improvement over the typical European city.

René Descartes published his famous book *Geometry*.

William Shakespeare died in 1616.

Samuel and Mary were sailing to the New World.

During the seventeenth century, **one in three children** did not make it past the age of one.

Galileo had just used the first telescope to study the moons of Jupiter, which gave him an understanding of the laws of gravity. In 1633, the Roman Inquisition forced Galileo to recant his theories.

To be or not to be—that is the question:
Whether 'tis nobler in the mind to suffer
The slings and arrows of outrageous fortune,
Or to take arms against a sea of troubles
And, by opposing, end them. To die, to sleep—
No more.

—Shakespeare

HISTORICAL NOTES:

Canonicus, sachem (chief) of the Narragansett, supported the Pilgrims at Plymouth after their first devastating year. He was uncle of Miantonomo, to whom he passed the reins during the period when Gorton and Roger Williams's land purchase was challenged by the Boston colony. The unfortunate murder of Miantonomo is one of the early factors that may have led to King Phillip's War. That murder also sparked retaliation from the Narragansett, which erupted into a war. The Narragansett were joined by many other tribes and would have won except that the English supported the Mohegan. Ultimately, a peace treaty was signed, ending the war. Canonicus died shortly after the peace treaty, presumably of old age.

John Winthrop. Before I began researching this book, John Winthrop was one of my favorite historical characters from the colonial period. His inspiring vision of a shining city on a hill is one that compels hope for a bright future. Even Presidents Kennedy and Reagan reiterated that phrase, which Winthrop borrowed from the Bible. Most certainly, the founding of the Massachusetts Bay Colony and success in the early colonies can be attributed to Winthrop. Still, the authoritarian theocracy he created was not an example that would make a modern, freedom-loving American smile. Winthrop was opposed to democracy, abhorred equal rights for women, and approved of slavery, and his treatment of the Indians was manipulative and destructive. He created a government that would weather the early years of colonial America but that would need to be remade in order for this country to become the America it is today.

William Arnold, who caused much trouble for Roger Williams and Samuel Gorton in the 1640s, was the great-grandfather of infamous Revolutionary War general and traitor Benedict Arnold. A fair amount of work has been done on the genealogy of the Arnolds, as, at one point, a claim was made showing a lineage to ancient Welsh kings. This lineage turned out to be incorrect.

William Coddington retired from politics when his commission was revoked during William Dyer and Roger Williams's trip to London. Williams remained at odds with him for the remainder of his life. Samuel Gorton was not known to have communicated with him again. According to the history written by G. J. Gadman, Coddington dishonestly claimed to have discovered and solely purchased the island so that he could acquire a patent for Aquidneck in his sole name. In fact, the compact was initiated by Hutchinson and her husband and signed by twenty-two other joint purchasers, the largest stakeholders being William and Edward Hutchinson. Ultimately, history has looked upon Coddington as an important part of the founding of Rhode Island. His Newport settlement became one of the most successful of all the colonies, and his pioneering spirit helped pave the way for a successful Rhode Island colony and state.

Had Coddington not put so much pressure on Anne Hutchinson, she likely would have remained on Aquidneck Island and not ultimately been a victim of the massacre in New Netherland. In a strange turn of historical events, Edward Hutchinson's daughter, the granddaughter of Anne Hutchinson, would marry the grandson of Coddington in what must have been considered a Romeo and Juliet scenario! The children of that marriage would ultimately become the forefathers of both Franklin D. Roosevelt and George Bush.

Susanna Hutchinson moved back to Boston to live with her brother Edward, where she slowly learned how to integrate back into the Boston lifestyle. Unlike Edward, she was never able to completely forgive Boston for the treatment of her mother during the Antinomian crisis and the response upon hearing of the massacre of her family.

The specific historical records of her are scarce, but one can imagine that, as a girl who was raised in part by Anne Hutchinson, in part by the Siwanoy, and in part by her brother Edward, she must have been a fascinating young woman.

Unfortunately for young Sam Gorton, the tidal wave of events after her return did not work in his favor. In the first two years after

Forefathers & Founding Fathers

her return, she met and fell in love with John Cole, the son of Boston innkeeper Samuel Cole. During the 1630s, while living in Boston, Anne Hutchinson had become friends with the Cole family, and Edward had continued that friendship during his years living in Boston. It was because of that connection that Susanna and John met.

Susanna and John Cole were married in 1651, just over two years after her return from living amongst the Siwanoy. The couple remained in Boston for a number of years, but when the opportunity arose, she and John moved to Rhode Island, very close to Warwick. Susanna and the Gortons remained friends for the rest of their lives. While Susanna did not match her mother's fifteen children, she and John Cole did have eleven. To one of those children she gave the name Samuel.

The City of Boston ultimately made peace with their mistakes in the Antinomian crisis. A bronze statue now stands in front of the Massachusetts State House depicting young Susanna and her mother, Anne Hutchinson. Susanna and John Cole's children would become the forefathers of Stephen Arnold Douglas, Henry Bull, and Mitt Romney. In 1998, Katherine Kirkpatrick published a book about Susanna's life titled *Trouble's Daughter*.

Nathanael Greene, along with George Washington and Henry Knox, were the only generals to serve the entire eight years of the war. After the surrender by Cornwallis at Yorktown, Greene was awarded huge land grants from the states of Georgia, North Carolina, and South Carolina. Much of that land was sold, along with his family home in Rhode Island, so that Greene could pay some of the debt he had acquired fighting and personally funding the war effort.

He remained friends with George Washington until his death. Washington offered him the position of secretary of war on more than one occasion, but Greene refused each time.

The Georgia government gave Greene a plantation outside of Savannah named Mulberry Grove. Greene and his family moved to that plantation in 1785, but at the age of forty-three, he died of heatstroke just a year after his relocation to the south. Shortly after Greene died,

Eli Whitney came to Savannah and began working for Greene's wife, Catharine. It was during his time at Mulberry Grove that Whitney invented the cotton gin, a machine that would ultimately revolutionize the production of cotton.

Several towns are named after Greene, including Greensboro, North Carolina; Greenville, South Carolina; Greeneville, Tennessee; and Greensburg, Pennsylvania. Statues or monuments to Greene can be found in each of these locations, along with the recently commissioned work in Valley Forge.

Greene was descended from Samuel Gorton through his father, Nathaniel Greene, the son of Mary Barton Greene, the daughter of Samuel Gorton's daughter Susanna Gorton Barton.

ACKNOWLEDGMENTS

To my daughter Alaina, a very special young woman to whom God bestowed many special gifts: beauty, intelligence, and creativity. Some of the creativity and important aspects of this book came from her. As the project began, she and I worked together on character development and writing style. May this book inspire her as much as it inspired me!

To my wife, Shelley Laine-Gorton, who read the story over and over, making sure all the pieces connected as they should.

To my boys, I hope that along with your love of science, computers, and mathematics, you will come to appreciate the value of understanding your family history and roots.

To my mom, who just left us and will hopefully get to read the version printed in heaven. To my dad, who sparked the beginnings of this book many, many years ago during a family trip to Rhode Island.

To Jill Vermeulen, for reading the very first, rough draft and providing creative input. Your suggestions were sheer genius!

To Laura Carabello, a great friend, excellent and successful author, and a tireless reader/editor.

To Aimee Brown whose relentless creativity created a national market for this book.

Finally, I want to acknowledge Milli Brown and the team at Brown Books Publishing Group. You have taken in a personal project and turned it into a real book with impact.

This book would not have been possible without all your efforts – Thanks!

BIBLIOGRAPHY

Adams, Charles Francis. *Antinomianism in the Colony of Massachusetts Bay, 1636–1638*. Boston: Prince Society, 1894.

Anderson, Robert Charles. *The Great Migration: Immigrants to New England 1634–1635*. Vol. 3, G-H. Boston: New England Historic Genealogical Society, 2003.

Arnold, Samuel Greene. *History of the State of Rhode Island and Providence Plantations*. Vol. 1. New York: D. Appleton & Company, 1859.

Gorton, Adelos. *The Life and Times of Samuel Gorton*. Philadelphia: George S. Ferguson Co., 1907.

Gorton, Thomas A. *Samuel Gorton of Rhode Island and His Descendants*. Baltimore: Gateway Press, Inc., 1985.

Humpherey, Grace. *Women in American History*. Freeport, New York: Bobbs-Merrill, 1919.

Janes, Lewis G. *Samuell Gorton: A Forgotten Founder of Our Liberties*. Providence: Preston and Rounds, 1896.

Moriarity, G. Andrews. "Additions and Corrections to Austin's Genealogical Dictionary of Rhode Island." *American Genealogist* 20 (April 1944): 186.

Porter, Kenneth W. "Samuel Gorton: New England Firebrand." *New England Quarterly* 7 (1934): 405–444. doi:10.2307/359672.

Staloff, Darren. *The Making of an American Thinking Class: Intellectuals and Intelligentsia in Puritan Massachusetts*. New York: Oxford University Press, 1997.

Virtualology. "Samuel Gorton." Virtual American Biographies. Last modified 2001. Based on "'A Strenuous Beneficent Force': The Case for Revision of the Career of Samuel Gorton, Rhode Island Radical," by G. J. Gadman, master's thesis, Manchester Metropolitan University, 2004. Accessed January 15, 2016. http://www.famousamericans.net/samuelgorton.

Of course, the modern research tool of the internet played a huge part in this research. It is amazing how easily Web searches can uncover facts, images, and resources. Both Wikipedia and Ancestry.com were utilized for cross-referencing data and facts.

ABOUT THE AUTHOR

Award-winning author Michael Gorton is the eleventh-generation descendant of Samuel Gorton, one of the founders of Rhode Island. He holds degrees in physics, engineering, and law. Raised in an air force family, he is the first of his family to earn a college degree. Gorton is a serial entrepreneur who has founded eleven companies, including Dallas-based Teladoc Inc., the nation's oldest and largest telemedicine company.

Forefathers & Founding Fathers is Gorton's fifth novel. A prolific writer, Gorton at first intended just to give this book to friends and family, but while researching, he realized this was an important and unknown story that needed to be told.

Michael is a runner who has completed eighteen marathons; a black belt in kenpo karate; and a mountain climber. Gorton and his family set their sights high as well, with their goal of climbing the highest point of elevation in all fifty states. They have only eleven states left to conquer.

INDEX

Samuel Gorton is referred to as SG and Massachusetts Bay Company is referred to as MBC in subheadings. Illustrations and maps are denoted by page numbers in *italics*.

A

Abbot, George, 41
Adams, John, 286
Aldridge, Ellen, 77, 128–129, 163
Algonquin Indians, 251–260
Alymer (Bishop), 56
Anglican Church. *See* Church of
England
Annhook. *See* Wampage
antinominanism and Antinomian
Controversy
defined, 60–61
Hutchinson as Antinomian,
85–86, 147–153
unwanted in Boston, 103, 269
Williams on, 106–107
antislavery ordinance passed, 266
Aquidneck Island, 138–139, 143,
155–158
See also Portsmouth
Arnold, Benedict, 4
Arnold, William, 179–182, 186, 293

B

Bacon, Francis, 63–64, 84
Ball, Lucille, 288, 291
banns of marriage celebration for
Samuel and Mary, 45–50
"Battle Hymn of the Republic"
(Howe), 288

battles
Fort Mystic battle, 103–105, 108
Guilford Court House battle,
13–15
Kings Mountain battle, 10
Miantonomo and Uncas, 192–
193
Yorktown Battle, 17
Beowulf, 39
Boston, Massachusetts
amenities and institutions, 72–73
Boston to Plymouth travel, *90*
changes through history, 284
oppressive doctrines of, 80
See also Massachusetts Bay Colony
Boston trial of Gorton, 211–223
birth of daughter, 218–219
Canonicus' help to SG's
family and Gortonists,
218–222
court demands renouncement of
Gortonism, 214–215
failure of death by hanging
sentence, 216
SG banned from MBC, 217
SG charged with blasphemy,
215–216
SG learns of Hutchinson family
massacre, 211–214
SG sentenced to hard labor, 216

SG to London to petition for
Narragansetts, 223
Bradford, William, 100
Brewster, Jonathan, 131
Burton, Susanna, 286–287

C

Canonicus (Narragansett chief)
death of, 253
described, xv
desire for Narragansetts to be
English subjects, 221–223,
228–229
friendship with SG, 145
help English against Pequots, 188
help to Gortonists, 218–222
historical notes, 293
mistrust of Arnold, 182–183
shelter for SG, Thomas, and
Wickes, 143–144
Carpenter, William, 179
Cervantes, Miguel, 230–231
Charles, King of England
Maplett III as personal physician,
66–67, 183, 226, 228
Narragansett petition to become
English subjects, 222–223,
228–229
removal from power and
beheading, 263
unsuccessful reign of, 228, 237
Winthrop's land patent from, 47
Charles II, King of England, 271
Charlestown, settlers' support for
SG, 217
Christmas party, 127–128, 133–
134, 136

Church of England
corruption and oppression of, 56,
82–83, 111
customs for saying grace, 37
escaping oppression of in New
World, 42, 52, 83
limited perspective of, 56
Puritan underground in London,
237
Puritanism as separate from, 91,
98
SG raised as, 37
civil government, 160–162, 169,
285–286
Civil Rights Act, 286
civil war in England, 228
clock-watches, 25–26, 28
Coddington, William
arrests of SG's supporters, 170
autocratic behavior of, 157–158
cow in corn trial, 164–166
described, xvii
discussed by Williams and SG,
177
"governor for life" commission
revoked, 264–265
historical notes, 294
as Hutchinson defender, 150
opinions on SG, 241
ousted and reinstated as governor
of Portsmouth, 159–162
pressure on Hutchinson, 207
SG's memories of, 248–249
Cole, John, 264
Cole, Robert, 179, 182
Committee for Foreign Plantations,
229, 231, 233–234, 242

305

Commonwealth of England created, 263

Constitutional amendments, 286

Continental Army, *11*
 Cornwallis's surrender, 16
 defeats and difficulties faced, 3–4
 funding shortages, 6
 victories over Cornwallis, 13–16
 Washington as commander, 3–4

Continental Congress, 4–7, *5*

conventicles, 59–60, 112–115, 127–128, 133–134

Cooke, George, 198–202

Cornwallis (Lord)
 Dan River race, 12–13
 march to sea, 13–15
 strategies against, 9–12, 287
 strength on southern front, 9
 surrender at Yorktown, 16, *19*
 victories over Continental Army, 9

Cotton, John, *40*, 58–59, 70, 151–153

court hearing against SG, 131–132

cow in corn plot, 163

Cromwell, Oliver, 228, 235, 263, 271

D

Dan River race, 12–13

Declaration of Independence, 21

divide and conquer strategies, 9–12

Don Quixote (Cervantes), 39, 230–231

Duckingfield, John, 65–72, 241

Dunster, Obadiah, 166–167

Dyer, Mary
 death sentence and reprieval in

Boston, 270
 described, xvi
 dreams for New World fulfilled, 285–286
 Gortons meet, 81
 Jefferson on, 284
 martyrdom of, 271–273, *272*
 in Quaker movement, 265, 267–273
 statue at Massachusetts State House, 286

Dyer, William, 81, 161–162, 264–265

E

Elizabeth I (Queen of England), 40

Emancipation Proclamation, 286

Endicott (governor of Boston), 271–272

equality of men, SG's teachings on, 117

F

Federation of Colonies, 192

Fire Flower, 251–260

Forefathers and Founding Fathers, 283–284

Fort Mystic, 101, 105

Founding Fathers, 17–21

G

Gates, Horatio, 9

Globe Theatre, 29–32, 230

Gorton, Benjamin, 287

Gorton, Mahershallalhashbaz (Maher), 73–74

Gorton, Mary Elizabeth Maplett

advice of, 43

alliance with Hutchinson and Wheelwright, 88

birth of daughter, 218–219

children, 184

death, 282

described, xv

on discussing politics, 36, 39

discussion of future with SG, 182–183

dreams for New World fulfilled, 285–286

early days of marriage, 63

on education of women, 31–32, 40

fled Shawomet to Providence, 197–198

as Hutchinson admirer, 80–82, 84

Jefferson on, 284

library and reading habits of, 38–39

meeting Samuel, 29–32

move to Plymouth Colony, 88–91

New World journey and arrival, 77–88

ninth pregnancy, 261–263

Reynor attack, 95–98

on SG's persistence, 231

third pregnancy, 121

wardrobe of, 136

wedding, 51–53

work for freedoms, 20–21

Gorton, Samuel, *20*

arrest on return from London, 245

described, xv

dreams for New World fulfilled, 285–286

Jefferson on, 284

lineage, 290–291

as represented in history, 285

Simplicity's Defence Against Seven-Headed Policy, 225, 230

statue, *287*

Gorton, Samuel – in London

advice of, 43

arrest for Duckingfield debt, 241–242

children, 73

courtship of Mary, 37–43

dreams of New World, 52–53, 69–70

early days of marriage, 63

education, 32

life advice on adventure, 75

at Maplett Haberdashery, 25–28

at Maplett residence, 33–43

marriage advice from Rich, 47–48

meeting Mary, 29–32

purchase of haberdashery, 64–69

reading habits of, 39

return to London for Shawomet patent, 225–235

training of new haberdashery owner, 73

wedding, 51–53

work on Foreign Plantations petition, 231–233

Gorton, Samuel – in Plymouth Colony

alliance with Hutchinson and Wheelwright, 88

antinomianism discussion with

Williams, 106–107
on church and state roles, 83–84
fighting Pequods, 101
introduction to Reynor, 95
killing of injured indian, 104–105
making acquaintances in
    Plymouth, 99–101
move to Plymouth Colony,
    88–91
New World journey and arrival,
    77–88
ousted from Plymouth Colony,
    138–139
prayers in Plymouth Colony, 93
private conventicle growth,
    112–115
Winslow's opinion of, 102
in winter storm, 141–144
Gorton, Samuel – in Portsmouth
cow in corn trial, 164–166
public whipping in Portsmouth,
    166–168, 171
Gorton, Samuel – in Providence
as advocate for Narragansetts,
    180
Anne Hutchinson's death,
    211–213
Boston trial, 211–223
capture by Cooke and transport
    to Boston, 201
children, 184
discussion of future with Mary,
    182–183
land purchase from Cole, 179
life threatened by MBC, 196–199
meeting with Shawomet leaders,
    247

Miantonomo's death, 195–196
return to Shawomet, 246
Gorton, Samuel – in Warwick
communication with Cromwell
    on Quakers, 271
on courage, 279–280
death, 282
home, *279*
in King Phillip's war, 278
later years, 275–282
opposition to slavery, 266
on Puritans and Quakers,
    268–269
retirement from politics, 275
on Reynor, 280
on separation of church and state,
    273
as Warwick Colony founder,
    20–21
in Warwick government, 266
Gorton, Samuel, Jr.
attraction for Susanna, 172,
    256–260
on Indian unrest, 275–278
knowledge of law and
    Narragansett Indians,
    263–264
marriage, 286–287
with Narragansett Indians, 220,
    227
on Narragansett Indians, 246
support for finding Susanna,
    253–254
Gorton, Slade, 287
Gorton, Susanna, 263
Gorton, Thomas
advice to SG, 81

in attack by MBC, 199
New World journey and arrival,
    77–88
Pequot attack, 103–104
permanent return to Manchester,
    243
return to London, 225–226
in winter storm with SG, 143–
    144
Gortonists, 112–116, 118, 216–217
Greene, Catherine, 18–21, 284
Greene, John
    as author's ancestor, 20
    death of wife in militia attack,
        203
    escape from MBC militia,
        202–203
    Foreign Plantations petition, 231
    introduction to SG, 178
    meeting with Shawomet leaders,
        247
    Miantonomo's arrest, 186
    Miantonomo's death, 195–196
    return to London for Shawomet
        patent, 225
    Shawomet charter granted, 234
Greene, Nathanael
    in American Revolution, 287
    Dan River race, 12–13
    described, xvii
    divide and conquer strategies,
        9–12
    Guilford Court House battle,
        13–14
    as GW's general, 4–6
    historical notes, 295–296
    with Jefferson, 18–21, 283

southern command, 9–16
victories over Cornwallis, 13–16
Gregorian Calendar, xiv
Griffin (ship), 55
Groom, Samuel, 80
Guilford Court House battle, 13–14

H

Hamlet (Shakespeare), 242
Hancock, John, 6–7
Harvard, John, 72
heresy charges against Francis
    Marbury, 56–57
Holden, Randall
    housing construction and, 185
    meeting with Shawomet leaders,
        247
    Miantonomo's arrest, 186
    on Narragansett-Mohegan
        conflict, 191
    Shawomet charter granted, 234
    Shawomet patent, 225, 231
    welcome for SG and family, 246
Holmes, William, 101
Holy Spirit, SG's teachings on,
    115–117
Hopton, Owen, 56
Howe, Julia Ward, 288, 290
Howe, Robert, 9
Huger, Isaac, 10–11, 13, 18
Hutchinson, Anne Marbury
    on Aquidneck Island, 138
    in Boston, 59–60
    church trial, 151
    civil trial, 149–151
    described, xv
    discussed by Williams and SG,

106–107, 177–178
dreams for New World fulfilled, 285–286
educating women, 41
emigration to New World, 55, *55*, 59
future plans after Portsmouth, 172–173
Gortons make acquaintance of, 81–86
government threatened by, 84
Jefferson on, 284
massacre of family by Siwanoys, 205–210, *210*
in New Netherland, 183, 207–208
in New World, 70
preaching to men and women, 59–60
pregnancy, 151
Prence's view of, 102–103
recantation plan, 153
on religion in New World, 147
Siwanoy obstruction of house construction, 208–209
statue at Massachusetts State House, 286
as true founder of Portsmouth, 177
welcomed SG, Thomas, and Wickes in Aquidneck, 155–156
Hutchinson, Edward
on Aquidneck Island, 153
journey to New World, 55, 59
praise for SG, 252
search for Susanna, 251

support for SG during trial, 211–214
Hutchinson, Susanna, 251–260, 264, 294–295
Hutchinson, William
in Boston, 59–60
death, 183, 205–206
emigration to New World, 59
as governor of Portsmouth, 158, 160
as haberdashery customer, 84
marriage to Anne Marbury, 57–58

J

Jefferson, Thomas
on Greene, 4–7
with Greene, 18–21, 283–284
on inalienable rights, 17
as visionary, 286
Joan of Arc, 41
Julian Calendar, xiv
Junia, 40

K

Kieft (New Netherland governor), 209
King, William, 65, 67
King Phillip's war, 278
Kings Mountain battle, 10

L

Lamb, Thomas, 235, 237
Laud, William, 41, 59, 69–70, 82–83
leap years, xiv
Lewis (Archdeacon), 56

Lincoln, Benjamin, 9
Littlefield, William, 74–75
Lock, Robert, 267
London, return to, 225–235
London Bell Alley church, 235
Long Island. *See* New Netherland

M

Manchester news, 45–50
Maplett, John III (Mary's brother),
    64, 66, 183, 226, 228
Maplett, John (Mary's father),
    26–30, 33–36, 45–50, 66–67
Maplett, John, Sr. (Mary's
    grandfather), 63–64
Maplett, Mary Elizabeth. *See*
    Gorton, Mary Elizabeth Maplett
Maplett, Mary (mother of Mary
    Gorton)
    breakfast at Maplett residence,
        35–38
    death of, 241
    Gortons' return, 226
    illness of, 235, 237–239
Maplett Haberdashery
    offered to Gorton, 34–35
    purchase by Gortons, 65–69
    sale of, 71–72
    SG as employee, 25–28
    SG's last visit to, 74–75
    status in London, 67
    transition to new ownership, 73
Maplett residence, 33–43
Marbury, Anne, 55–61
Marbury, Francis, 56–57
Marshalsea Prison, 56, 57
Massachusetts Bay Colony (MBC)

antagonism to Gortons and
    Hutchinsons, 175–176
attack on Shawomet, 197–200,
    201
denied SG's land purchase from
    Miantonomo, 184–185
discussed by Williams and SG,
    177–178
in Foreign Plantation petition,
    231–232
growth and transition, 80
Miantonomo trial, 187–189
Narragansett Bay expansion
    plans, 189, 207
ownership claims to Warwick
    Colony, 264
SG banned from, 217
SG's land annexed to by Arnolds,
    179–182
Shawomet charter granted,
    233–234
Shawomet livestock and crops
    taken, 202
Massasoit (Wanpanoag chief),
    276–277
Masterson, Richard, 118–119
mealtime grace at Maplett residence,
    37
Metacomet (King Phillip), 276–278
Miantonomo (Narragansett chief)
    arrest and transport to Boston,
        186
    Boston trial, 187–194
    death by Uncas' hand, 192–194,
        194
    deceived and captured by Uncas,
        189–192

described, xv
as head chief, 184
land purchase from, 176, 180
mistrust of Arnold, 182–183
released to MBC, 192
militias, 101, 105–106
Mohegan Indians' treaty with Narragansetts, 189
Montaigne, George, 51
Morgan, Daniel, 11, 18
Morton, Nathaniel, 99–100, 116–118, 128–129, 282, 285
Mosquito Coast, 46

N

Nanuntonoo (son of Miantonomo), 225, 227, 232, 246
Narragansett Indians
distrust of MBC, 221–222
helped Shawomet settlers build, 185–186
London petition to be subjects of king, 222–223
SG on friendship with, 227
sheltered SG, Thomas, and Wickes, 143–144
support of colonists, 101, 195–196
treaty with Mohegans, 189
with Williams, 87
Narragansett-Mohegan conflict, 189–191
New Netherland
Gortons consider move to, 183
Hutchinson in, 207–208
search for Susanna Hutchinson, 252–254

New World, journey to
Gortons emigrate to, 69–70, 77–88
SG dreams of, 52–53
ship and voyage conditions, 77–79
Newport, Coddington reinstated as governor from, 161

P

Paine, Thomas, 283–284
Paul on women as church and civic leaders, 40–42
Pennsylvania troops mutiny, 4
Pequot Indians
Arnold sold gunpowder to, 182
attack on colonists, 103–104
discussed by Williams and SG, 107–109
fear of during travel, 90
growing tensions with, 100–101
killing of injured indian, 104–105
Pequot War, 99–109, 187
Pessicus (Narragansett chief), 221, 246, 252–253
Pilgrims, 42, 98, 109, 225
Plymouth Colony
court hearing against SG, 131–132
Gorton prayers in, 93
Gortons leaving Plymouth, 131–145
Gortons move to, 88–98
map, 80
Plymouth inquisition, 123–129
religious abuse and oppression in, 42, 95–98

religious freedom in, 91

SG ousted from, 138–139

SG's banishment, 169–173

Portsmouth

Coddington's ousting and return
to power, 159–168

Gortons leave, 169–173

Portsmouth Compact, 157, 177,
185

renamed from Aquidneck, 158

SG's punishment and banishment
from, 164–168

See also Aquidneck Island

Power, Nicholas, 202–203

Prence, Thomas, 100–103, 127,
131–133

Providence Plantations

described, 105

founded by Williams, 87

Gortons' arrival in, 175–178

legal patent sought by Williams,
179, 182, 184

militia training at, 101

Punham (village chief), 184,
187–188, 222

Puritans/Puritanism

abandonment of Miantonomo,
191–192

charges against SG, 213–214

hatred for Quakers, 268

Hutchinson's teachings against,
60–61, 85, 148

Laud's views of, 69

opposition to, 21

opposition to Rhode Island
democracy, 285

Plymouth Colony founded by, 91

religious oppression of, xiii

Reynor's views of, 95–96

theocracy of, 84, 107, 152, 172,
180, 273

underground Puritan movement,
London, 235, 237

Vane's views of, 86

Williams' opposition to, 88, 102

Winthrop as supporter, 86

See also Antinomian Controversy

Q

Quaker movement

Lock and passengers jailed,
267–268

Mary Dyer as, xvi, 265, 268–272

Mary Gorton considers, 183

in New Netherland, 207

Puritans' opposition to, xiii, 265

SG's letter to Cromwell on, 271

R

Rawlins, Isabel, 112–114

Rawlins, Joseph, 112–114

religious abuse in Plymouth, 95–98

Revolutionary War

Cornwallis' surrender, 16, 17

Greene and southern command,
9–16

Greene as southern commander, *9*

southern activity map, *15*

Washington on Greene, 4–7

Reynor, John

attack on Mary, 95–96

complaints against Gortons,
116–117

conspiracy with Smith against

Gortons, 123–127
Gortons ousted from Plymouth
  Colony, 139–141
Gorton's view of, 102, 280
opinions on SG, 241
warning about, 92
Rhode Island Colony
annexation plans by MBC, 213,
  264
patent buried with SG, 282
1636-1650s, *248*
Rhode Island (state), 266
Rich, Robert (Earl of Warwick)
as Cromwell ally, 263
described, xvi
government positions, 229
help Gortons to New World, 70,
  71–72
SG consults on Shawomet patent
  application, 226–229
as SG's friend, 26–27, *26*
Shawomet charter granted,
  233–234
as Somers Isles Company
  controller, 46–47, *46*
on Winslow's appeal, 239–240
Robinson, John, 118–119
Robinson, William, 270
Roxbury, settlers' support for SG, 217

S

Saint Mary Magdalene Church,
  51–53, *51*
Salem, settlers' support for SG, 217
Sands, James, 207–208
separation of church and state, 83,
  273

Shakespeare, William
Gortons' favorite plays, 238
Hamlet, 242
The Taming of the Shrew, 30–31,
  280
The Tempest, 39
Shawomet, 179–186
attack by MBC, 197–200
charter granted, 233–234
livestock and crops taken by
  MBC, 202
name change to Warwick,
  247–248
raid on, 195–203
return to, 245–249
SG banned from, 217
women and children's escape
  from, *197*
See also Warwick Colony
*Simplicity's Defence Against Seven-
  Headed Policy* (Gorton), 225,
  230
Siwanoy Indians, 208–210, 253–
  259
slavery
defined by Canonicus, 221
Lincon and, 286
SG's antislavery ordinance in
  Rhode Island, 266, 285
Shawomet as free from, 234
Winthrop's support of, 293
Smith, John, 266
Smith, Mary, 114–115, 118, 119,
  124–125
Smith, Ralph, 91–92, 116–117,
  119, 123–127, 139
Smythe, John, 254

Soconononocco (village chief), 184, 187–188, 222
Somers Isles Company, 46
southern command, 9–16
Stephenson, Marmaduke, 270
Stuart, Charity, 118
Stuart, Nathaniel, 118, 128
Symmes (Reverend), 60

T

The Taming of the Shrew (Shakespeare), 30–31, 280
The Tempest (Shakespeare), 39
Throckmorton, John, 207–208
timeline, 298–299
Treaty of Paris, 17

U

Uncas (Mohegan chief), 189–194, *194*
underground Puritan movement, London, 235, 237
United Colonies
  as military confederation of colonies, 175
  Narragansett Indians and, 246
  protection for Shawomet settlers, 242, 265
  Quakers in danger in, 265, 269

V

Vane, Henry, 60–61, 85–86, 88, 147–148

W

Walker, George, 241
Wampage (Siwanoy chief), 209–

210, 253–257
Warwick Colony, 20, 247–249, 261–266, 278
  See also Shawomet
Washington, George, 3–7, *3*
Waterman, Richard, 202–203
Wawequa (Uncas' brother), 192–194
Weld, Joseph, 151
Weld, Thomas, 215
Wheelwright, John, *40*, 59, 70, 81–87, 148
Wickes, John, 138, 142, 155–156
Williams, Roger
  antinomianism discussion with SG, 106–107
  antislavery ordinance passed, 266
  described, xvi
  dreams for New World fulfilled, 285–286
  Gortons' arrival in Providence, 175–178
  Jefferson on, 284
  London trip to protest annexation, 264–265
  meeting with SG, Prence, and Holmes, 105
  militia training, 101
  with Narragansett Indians, *88*
  opinions on SG, 230
  portrait, *20*
  Prence's view of, 101
  religious beliefs, 87–88
  religious freedom efforts of, 21
  support for finding Susanna, 252
Winslow, Edward, xvii, 88, 99, 241
winter preparations, 134

Winthrop, John
   Antinomian Controversy, 86–87, 148
   colonial land patent from King Charles, 47, *47*
   described, xvi
   historical notes, 293
   on Hutchinson, 60–61
   Hutchinson civil trial, 149–151
   Miantonomo trial, 187–189
   Narragansett Bay expansion plans, 189
   part in Foreign Plantation petition, 232
   reinstated as governor, 88
   sentenced and banned SG from MBC, 216
   on SG, 241, 282
   Shawomet charter granted, 234
Winthrop, John, Jr., 278–279
Winthrop fleet, *78*
women's rights
   Hutchinson as preacher, 59–60, 81–84, 149, 286
   Mary Gorton on, 31–32, 40–42
   in New World, 83–84, 126–127
   recognition in courts, 164
   Reynor's attacks on women, 96, 280
   SG's support of, 83, 158, 285–286

Yorktown, Virginia, Revolutionary War victory, 15–16